DARKSIDERS
THE ABOMINATION VAULT

DEL REY BOOKS BY ARI MARMELL

DARKSIDERS
THE ABOMINATION VAULT

ARI MARMELL

BALLANTINE BOOKS / NEW YORK

A Del Rey Trade Paperback Original

Copyright © 2012 by THQ, Inc.

All rights reserved

Published in the United States by Del Rey, an imprint of the Random House Publishing Group, a division of Random House, Inc., New York.

DEL REY is a registered trademark and the Del Rey colophon is a trademark of Random House, Inc.

RANDOM HOUSE WORLDS and House colophon are trademarks of Random House, Inc.

Darksiders and the Darksiders logo are registered trademarks of THQ, Inc.

ISBN 978-0-345-53402-6
eBook ISBN 978-0-345-53586-3

www.delreybooks.com

Book design by Susan Turner

146122990

To the two Cs—Colin and Cargill—without whose
friendship and support
I could never have gotten this far

HISTORICAL/MYTHOLOGICAL NOTE

The Abomination Vault takes place eons prior to the Apocalyptic events portrayed in the games Darksiders and Darksiders II. The Horsemen's abilities, weapons, magics, physical features—and, just perhaps, their true motivations—have changed and evolved, sometimes dramatically, during this time.

DARKSIDERS
THE ABOMINATION VAULT

CREATION IS NOT WHAT YOU BELIEVE IT TO BE. One world or one universe at the core of reality, crafted exclusively for humanity, presided over by a kind and benevolent Almighty? An eternal afterlife of reward or punishment? Angels swooping above, loyal to a Father whose every purpose they understand and exalt?

Hopeful misunderstanding at best; at worst, a deliberate lie.

Oh, there was a Creator, certainly, but what He intended, or even where He has gone, are mysteries to even the wisest of living minds. An afterlife? Hardly. No reward, no punishment. Only a purifying of the spirit, a purging of all memory, all *self*, before it passes through the Well of Souls to rejoin the flow of energy through Creation, to form new souls for new generations.

Angels? A hidebound, nearly stagnant people—and not remotely the eldest race of the cosmos—fighting in defense of a Creation they only *think* they understand, slaves to the ancient traditions and laws of Heaven.

Yes, there is a Heaven.

And there is a Hell.

And oh, so many worlds above, below, and beyond. Worlds that the angels of Heaven and the demons of Hell would kill—and *have* killed, millions of times over—to master.

Only the Charred Council—not angel, not demon, not Old One, but something *other*—holds the warring factions at bay. Only the Charred Council, and their fearsome servants, stand at the pivot point of all Creation, protecting the Balance from all who would see it shattered.

Barely.

Creation is far, far more than you believe it to be. And it is far, far older . . .

PROLOGUE

THE LIGHT WAS BY FAR THE WORST OF IT.

Here, beyond the farthest outskirts of what could only laughingly be called the "civilized" reaches of Hell, any visitor—of which there were precious few—should certainly have expected horrors. Nor would they have been disappointed. The cramped passageways of this particular sanctum were flesh scraped raw; a wet, glistening, infected pink. Perspiration and other fluids, both fouler and more intimate, seeped from the ever-undulating surface. Each corridor flexed and trembled, an orifice trying to clamp itself shut, held open only by a thin latticework of what might or might not have been age-browned gristle.

Every footstep was treacherously slick. Every inhalation carried the acrid, choking stench of old sweat. Every hint of a breeze brought the echoes of unheard moans that might have been ecstasy, agony, or some unholy combination of the two.

And still the light was worse.

It flickered and danced, as firelight should, but its rhythms were subtly off, unnatural. The ambient hue was a jaundiced yellow, painful to view, somehow hot and sticky on the skin. It brought a sheen of perspiration to everyone it touched, as though the illumination itself were diseased.

Scattered at seemingly random intervals, in alcoves throughout the hallways and around the perimeter of a central chamber, glowed the sources of that awful light. Thick, ugly candles, from two or three to almost ten paces in height, arose from oily puddles. Only a close study of those waxen pillars revealed the figures encased within: mostly demonic, some few representing an array of Old Ones and even the occasional angel. Each blurred at the edges, flesh melding seamlessly into the surrounding wax; and each melted slowly, so slowly, body and life and soul providing fuel for the flame.

Flames that danced and flickered, not at random, but in time to the still-beating hearts within.

At one end of the vast hollow, nestled at the intersection of those passageways, sanity regained some semblance of a foothold. An array of gossamer curtains added a peculiarly stylish touch of color to the chamber. A raised dais, standing proudly against the wall of flesh, was constructed of mundane granite—although the interlaced web of gristle holding some of those stone blocks together spoiled the effect a bit. Atop that platform, a heap of demons writhed around a throne, carved of marble, cushioned in supple skin and locks of hair. Pressed tightly together, they moved almost as a single mass. Most were humanoid, but beyond that they had little in common. Some were beautiful, some hideous; some winged and some earthbound; some male, some female, some both, and a few neither. They squirmed and thrashed, moaned and gasped, as every so often their mistress would reach down from her throne and stroke their exposed flesh with hands as soft as burial shrouds.

Her skin was the deep purple of a nighttime storm, her dark hair wreathed in horns that only accentuated her unearthly allure. Emerald eyes that could coax an angel to sin—and had, on more than one occasion; a face to make a dead man ache; a figure to make a golem sweat. She was desire made flesh on a nearly divine scale. A palpable lust exuded from her, like an animal musk, with every gesture. Few indeed, in Heaven, Hell, or between, could stand resolute before her. Most would have gladly allowed her to skin them alive, if only they might gaze upon and worship her as she carved.

Lilith. Queen of Demons, Mother of Monsters, lover and betrayer, temptress and traitor. Creation's most exquisite lie.

The chamber hummed, faintly but consistently, with the crackling of the candle flames, the sighs of Lilith's current favorites, the susurrus of her diaphanous silks. Lilith herself remained largely silent, however, her attention centered on the bulky figure standing at the foot of the dais, the source of the room's only *meaningful* sounds. Visitors and petitioners were rare here in Hell's outer reaches, in the domain of those demons currently out of favor. And this visitor, at least, had promised interesting things to say.

He was cloaked and hooded in a tattered robe of gray, his features swathed in shadow—as though such a simple effort could possibly have kept his name from Lilith in her own home. Still, she'd allowed him his charade, and considered his words as he told her of his plans, and of what he'd hoped the Demon Queen might contribute to his efforts.

He kept his gaze lowered as he spoke—perhaps a sign of deference, more likely a feeble effort to protect himself from the overwhelming strength of her presence. She found the attempt amusing.

"Why?" When she finally spoke, interrupting the last of the stranger's presentation, her voice was thick, sultry, somehow enticing and repulsive at once. Addiction, given speech. "Why come to me with this?"

"I thought I'd made that clear." The stranger's words, in contrast, were gruff with only a hint of melody, like a troubadour who had long since lost his voice. "We all know that you dealt heavily with the Nephilim before their extinction, for all that you've kept the details of your relations hidden. You're said to know more of them than anyone, save perhaps the Charred Council. Who else has a better chance of unlocking the legacy they left be—"

"Yes, yes, yes." Lilith ceased caressing the demons at her feet long enough to wave her fingers in dismissal. Even that brief cessation was enough to draw a despairing cry from her pets. "I understand *that,* idiot boy. I mean why waste the time? It was courageous of you to come here—some might say foolish—but to what end? What could possibly have made you think I'd *want* to involve myself in your scheme?"

The shabby hood twitched back, blatantly startled. "I . . . I assumed that you would see the value in the power we might unlock together. You've no reason to love Heaven *or* Hell. You could lay waste to everyone responsible for your current status, perhaps even force the great factions and the Charred Council to restore what was taken from you! You—"

"What was taken from me," Lilith hissed, leaning sharply forward, "is of less importance than you seem to believe. Certainly not enough for me to set myself against all the forces of Creation! I have my own projects, far more subtle than the wars you hope to ignite. You offer enormous power, yes, but power shared. Power focused toward your own agenda. And I've no intention of abandoning plans already in motion. I will regain all that is mine, and more—but in *my* time, *my* way!

"You will, I'm afraid, simply have to unearth your precious secrets elsewhere."

"I see." The supplicant below her nodded. "Then we have nothing further to discuss, I think. I should—"

"Oh, I wouldn't go *that* far." Lilith stretched languidly in her throne, arching her back and pressing her breasts against the flimsy silks with blatant intent. "I wouldn't want you to leave here unhappy."

"You wouldn't want me to leave here as a potential *enemy,*" the other said. "Just in case I *do* succeed."

He was good, this one. He *almost* hid the tremor in his voice, the quiver of longing in his body.

"I won't deny that." Lilith's lips, darker than wine, parted as she slowly ran her tongue across teeth that should have gleamed white had the ambient light not cast them as an almost lightning yellow. "But surely you wouldn't want *me* as an enemy, either. Not when we can part on better terms, when even an informal alliance could be *so* much more—pleasant."

She knew the effect she was having on him, the effect she had on just about everyone. It wasn't even seduction, not really; seduction implied a *choice,* and Lilith's very nature stripped that choice from most sentient minds. She could practically see her influence crashing down on him in a deluge of need. He took a shuddering step, placing one foot upon the stairs of the dais, a hand reaching upward . . .

And just as swiftly he straightened, pulling away. "No. I'm not leaving as your enemy, Lilith, you can content yourself with that. But neither will I leave as your plaything."

Lilith recoiled hard enough to rock the granite throne. For a long moment, her features twisted between astonishment and rage, slowly settling into a wary respect.

"She must have been truly special to you," she said.

It was his turn to recoil, clearly stunned and more than a little alarmed at his host's clear knowledge, not only of his identity, but his history and motivations as well.

"Go," Lilith continued before he could draw breath to speak, "before I decide to take offense. Go and find your toys. I'll be fascinated to see whom you invite to play once you have them."

He was gone without another word. Lilith stared at the far wall long afterward, ignoring the plaintive cries of her pets, her fingers drumming thoughtfully on the arms of her throne.

FROWNING WITHIN THE SHADOWS of his hood, the visitor marched stiff-legged through the fleshy corridors. Every curse in Creation hovered about his lips, but he refused to give them voice—not, at least, until he was certain he was beyond the range of Lilith's hearing. He truly couldn't afford to make unnecessary enemies.

Not yet.

Throughout his trek, he passed not one single room or passage leading off the main hallway. He had no doubt they existed; presumably the flesh had some means of opening whenever an orifice was required.

Beneath his robe, his own flesh crawled.

Viscous fluids squelched beneath his tread or dripped on him from above as the corridor quivered. At one point he stepped on a particularly soft and pliable spot, sinking nearly to his knee before the substance ceased to stretch, and was rewarded with an obscene sigh from somewhere far behind.

It was actually a relief when he finally reached the door—or the hideous folds of leathery skin that passed for a door—and found himself outside Lilith's "palace," on the blasted plains of Hell proper. Blackened rock crumbled with every step, and he could feel his face cooking in the heat, for all that the great pits and pillars of flame were many leagues distant. Impossible spires, the homes and towers of potent demons, reached crookedly up from the horizon like threads on the frayed borders of reality.

For all the distance between him and the infernal societies, however, he found that he was not alone.

She was waiting for him, crouched idly on the cracked

earth. She was, upon first glance, everything Lilith was not. Her features were broad and vaguely flat; not ugly, really, so much as *shallow*, as though carved by a sculptor who'd ultimately thrown down his tools and decided "Close enough." Hair the color of cooling magma fell across shoulders clad in harsh, blocky armor. Her entire aspect was squat, even as she stood to greet him, and it took the hooded visitor a moment to realize that, in fact, he barely reached her chin.

She was accompanied, one to each side, by a pair of only vaguely humanoid shapes, half her size, hewn of rough stone and covered in glowing sigils. Even without her artificial cohort, the visitor would have known her for a Maker—one of the greatest of the progenitor races called, collectively, the Old Ones.

"I could have told you it wouldn't interest her much." The woman spoke with the voice of a particularly gruff and surly avalanche.

"I . . . I'm sorry, what?"

"Lilith. Your plan. I have free run of the complex, heard the whole thing. I could have told you it wouldn't interest her." A massive shrug made her armor shift slightly across her torso. "She was desperate, once, to regain the knowledge and power that were stolen from her, but that was long ago. She's moved on to other goals, and they don't require the sort of brute force you're offering."

"And you're certain of this because . . . ?"

"Because I've spent centuries trying to convince her otherwise. I cast my lot with hers, abandoned my realm and my people, because I was fascinated at the thought of the wonders she might perform, might *create*. I've devoted far more time and effort than you, to no greater effect."

The gray-robed figure reached up, scratched briefly at his hidden chin. "I see. And who are you, exactly?"

"Belisatra."

Another shallow nod. "I've heard of you. Lilith's pet Maker."

Belisatra scowled, and the two figures at her sides shifted idly, stone scraping deafeningly against stone. "You might devote *some* effort toward not being offensive," she told him. "Considering that I'm offering to help you."

"You? Why?"

"Because if we succeed, *I* can make the Charred Council restore Lilith's power. I can stand at her side as she changes Creation. And because, Lilith aside, the legacy you seek is almost as fascinating to me as the greatest of her creations."

He had doubts and suspicions, of course; would have been a fool not to. And she'd have been as great a fool not to *expect* him to have doubts and suspicions.

But in the end, where else had he to turn?

"All right, if you think you—"

"But I want to see it first."

The hooded man offered up a sigh that seemed to come from the depths of his soul. "Why does everyone here insist on interrupting me?" Then, before Belisatra could answer, "You want to see *what?*"

The Maker laughed, low and gravelly. "Don't ever take me for a fool. You'd never have come to Lilith with this if you weren't absolutely certain they still existed; if you hadn't already found at *least* one of them. Besides, I can practically *smell* the emanations. I may lack Lilith's experience and expertise with the Nephilim, but I recognize their scent well enough."

The robes shifted and shuffled, the hood twisting about as though checking for spies. Then, with a simple flick of the wrist, it sat in the shrouded traveler's hand.

Not particularly impressive in any way, it was just a pistol, clunky and thick. The Forge Makers had been crafting sleeker weapons for centuries, if not longer. A complex array of multiple polygonal cylinders sat heavily at the weapon's center, rotating and revolving with ungainly clicks, feeding ammunition to the weapon's triple barrels.

Belisatra frowned. "I was expecting something more . . ."

She started to look away, and found for the barest instant that she couldn't. The weapon seemed more solid, more weighty, more *real* than the man holding it or the badlands plain on which they stood. It tugged at her gaze like a petulant child, refusing to relinquish its grip.

She saw the inner workings, the mechanisms, though she couldn't possibly have seen. The gun didn't open, the pieces didn't slide apart; she simply saw inside the horrid thing, as well as out. She saw, and she knew that the metal of the frame had been melted down from treasured heirlooms and ancient works of art. Saw the tendons that wound through the jagged gears; the shriveled eye, crammed between the barrels, to assist the wielder's aim; the old blood, still impossibly fresh, pumping through the iron itself; the hammers of bone, and the seemingly infinite supply of teeth, drawn through the dimensions to serve as projectiles.

In its own way, it was far more disturbing even than the organic passageways that wound through Lilith's home. Those had been grown, but this? This had been *taken,* forged from the hopes and organs, synapses and souls, of the living.

On some primal level she could sense but not quite hear, it still screamed.

"This," the traveler said, his own voice hushed and almost reverent, "is Black Mercy."

"What . . ." Belisatra took a step back, finally tore her gaze from the deadweight in his hand. "What does it . . . ?"

"Now? Now it simply kills. Now it's just a particularly potent gun with a rather distasteful shot. But at its height? When the Nephilim rode between worlds, trampling whole races as they passed? A soldier armed with Black Mercy could slaughter armies. This isn't a pistol, Belisatra. Black Mercy is a hand-held massacre, a herald of genocide. You and I, we're going to wake it up—and we're going to find the others. *If,*" he added intently, challengingly, "you're still game, of course."

"Yes . . ." Again her gaze had locked on the weapon, but now their bond was one of fascinated avarice, not startled revulsion. "Oh, you couldn't keep me away."

Within the hood, teeth glinted in a crooked smile. "Well, then, my companion . . ." A second flick of the wrist, and Black Mercy disappeared up a voluminous sleeve. "You get to suggest a starting point."

"I think I can do that. I . . ." Her head cocked to one side. "We'll need to gather my little helpers." She idly reached out, brushed her knuckles across the nearer of the stone figures. "They'll try to stop us, you know."

"Let them. I know the ways of Heaven and Hell too well for them to—"

"And the Horsemen?"

Again he stopped mid-sentence. "The Charred Council's attack dogs? What of them?"

Belisatra smiled without an iota of mirth. "You've heard of the Horsemen, clearly. And just as clearly, you've heard nothing *about* them."

"Deadly, obscenely powerful, without mercy, and all that, yes, yes . . ."

"I mean *who* they are. The Four Horsemen are the Council's enforcers, yes. They're *also* the last of the Nephilim."

The other sucked in a breath. "The Nephilim are dead!"

"As a race, yes. But to the very last? Not quite. And should they learn of your efforts—*our* efforts—I can't imagine they'll respond kindly."

A few calming breaths, and then, "I don't much care *how*

they respond, really. My quarrel is with the generals of the White City and the Dukes of Hell, not the Horsemen. But after all they've done? I'm quite certain that not a single tear will be shed, anywhere in Creation, when the Nephilim have gone well and truly extinct."

CHAPTER ONE

THE ASHES SEEMED TO GO ON FOREVER.

A thin layer at first, very much like a gentle coating of gray, clinging snow. Deep enough, if only just, to retain the imprints of passing feet—or would have, had there been any.

After barely a few finger widths, however, the fine particles began to compress, suddenly and swiftly. A light dusting became a shifting grit, then a sucking mire. And below even that, the ash had lain so deep, for so long, it had condensed into a layer as unyielding as any earthen crust. If this world even *had* a surface beyond the omnipresent dust and cinders, it was buried so utterly that it would never again appear to the living.

It filled the air as well, that ash, casting a constant veil across the face of the horizon. It diffused the light into perpetual dusk, blotting out the lingering embers of what had once been a sun. For those rare few unfortunate enough to pass through, it smelled of burnt oils and singed meats; clung to the nostrils and throat in an oily film. The wind was perpetual across the barren land, unimpeded by mountain or forest or wall, refusing to ever let the choking soot settle.

Equally constant, audible over the roaring winds only if

one made the effort to listen, came the tolling of an impossible, and impossibly distant, bell. It could not exist, *did* not exist, anywhere in this blasted realm. Only a lingering echo of what once was, it sounded not so much in the ears as in the memory.

Not merely a dead world, this, but a *murdered* one. What wide and varied life had once thrived here was long since stripped away, leaving nothing behind but death.

And, more recently, Death.

He stood at the edge of a colorless dune, before a squat, rounded structure, little more than a blister in the ashes, browned and pitted with age. Even the windswept soot seemed unwilling to touch him, rushing around him in short, sharp flurries. The soles of his age-worn boots remained atop even the flimsiest layer of packed ash, as though he were weightless— or perhaps, again, it was merely that the ash wanted nothing to do with him.

Hair as black as a demon's shadow hung to his shoulders in matted, greasy locks. Below them, torn and stained streamers of bruise-violet fabric whipped and trailed from the back of his belt; perhaps the only remnants of what had once been a tunic or cloak, perhaps something more. The dark leathers and piecemeal armor he wore from the waist down, and the fraying strips that wrapped his palms and forearms, were equally grimy and unkempt. The skin of his exposed torso, shrunk tight over a wiry frame, was the dull gray of a corpse even without the filth in the air.

Only the deeply scored mask hiding his face from all Creation still retained some semblance of cleanliness, of its original bone white. The gaping sockets—through which eyes of burning orange gleamed, unblinking—and the mask's general shape were enough to evoke a skull in any viewer's imagination. The lack of mouth, or most other features, somehow made it even worse.

No sentient being remained anywhere in this world to gaze upon him, and the ash-choked air would have made him almost impossible to see even if there were. And still he did not remove the mask; had not, in fact, even given thought to the possibility. It was a part of him now, an immutable barrier between who he was and who he once had been.

Death stood, his hands raised before him, his mask shuddering slightly as his mouth formed constant, silent chants. The magics of the oldest Horseman swept through the winds, delving deep into the ash, and where nothing lived, the ancient dead responded.

Bones, petrified by time and stained by soot, worked and wiggled like snakes on their way to the surface. They punched through to open air, rearing into a veritable thicket and slowly pressing themselves tightly together. They danced, however briefly, to an orchestra that only Death could hear.

Long since dried to flecks of powder, the blood of a thousand corpses transformed once more to liquid, sluicing and bubbling from the depths. Where the bones did not fit perfectly together, that blood surged into the gap, mixing with ambient ash to form a thick, viscous mortar. And where the macabre construction required more meticulous handling than the raw materials could manage, there appeared Death's helpers. Ghouls—the desiccated corpses of beings never native to this world—materialized from the ether, reanimated and drawn through the walls between realms by the Horseman's will. With mindless obedience but impossible precision, they arranged the jagged bones just so.

With surprising rapidity, guided by Death's magic and servants both, a low building began to form over and around the smaller structure. Every so often, faces appeared briefly in the ash to study him as he worked his necromancies—phantoms, perhaps, of the world before, or maybe just tricks of the light.

He sensed the sudden surge of life, a creature appearing nearby where there had been none, at the same moment he heard a warning squawk from above. Wings beating rapidly against the wind, shedding mangy feathers, a hefty crow circled twice and settled on his shoulder.

"Yes, Dust." Death's voice was low, sonorous, a stale draft from a yawning sepulcher. "I feel it, too."

He raised a hand, and the weapon he'd casually laid aside heaved itself into his waiting grip. The scythe was enormous, taller than its wielder. Its blade was a hideous thing, jagged and crafted like the wing of some great beast, longer than Death's outstretched arms fingertip-to-fingertip. The ghouls ceased their labors and turned in unison, ready to march at the slightest thought.

Dust emitted a second piercing call and took to the air once more—partly to scout for enemies, yes, but also in part to remove himself from possible danger.

"Coward," Death said, though his tone was not unkind.

He squinted, peering into the soot-thickened wind, and made a swift decision. As quickly as he could think it, his scythe flowed, fluid for less than the blink of an eye. Death was now holding two weapons where there had only been one: two crescent blades, thick and heavy, shaped like knives but larger than most swords. Blades that would be easier to swing and thrust through the violent gusts than the longer, broader scythe.

"I didn't know you could do that."

Death had never heard that voice, high and sneering, before. But between the sound and the silhouette appearing through the cloud, he recognized his visitor all the same.

"I am Death," he said simply, without pomp or vanity, "and Harvester is bound to me. Whatever tools I require to serve my function, it can emulate. Hello, Panoptos."

"You've heard of me! I'm flattered."

The dusky figure that finally materialized was peculiar even by the Horseman's standards. Gaunt, almost spindly, humanoid from the waist up, tapering off into semi-solid vapors below. Its arms and fingers were stretched and distended, its wings serrated and broad. Its oblong face, like Death's mask, lacked anything resembling a mouth, though this didn't stop it from speaking. Instead, it boasted an array of emerald eyes, shifting and flowing across a vaguely gelatinous surface. Nine of them, usually; though between the constant motion, and the fact that one or two would occasionally disappear, only to sprout anew, the number varied moment by moment.

"Don't be. The Charred Council told me about you," Death said. "My brothers told me *more* about you. Care to guess who I'm most likely to believe?"

"Aww . . ." The creature sniggered softly. "Surely you know better than to listen to rumor and gossip!"

"Depends who's spreading the rumors." Death allowed Harvester to return to its innate form, that of the single great scythe, and leaned it against the partial wall of bone. At his silent command, the ghouls resumed their labors.

"So," Panoptos said, flitting this way and that, untouched by the wailing winds. "Welcome back. Such a lovely home you've chosen. Very . . . you." Already concealed beneath the newer walls of bone, the older, inner structure had apparently escaped his notice.

It wasn't an oversight Death felt compelled to correct. "I enjoy the view."

"Heh. Strife *said* you were a sarcastic bastard."

"What do you want, Panoptos?"

Clearly, the creature had no interest in answering Death's question, at least not yet. "Where have you been these past centuries, anyway?"

"I wouldn't tell the Charred Council when they asked. What makes you think I'll tell you?"

Again that irritating little laugh. "Why, as a gesture of friendship! I *so* want us to be friends."

"It's good to have goals. Keeps us motivated," Death told him. "But I wouldn't wager anything you can't do without, were I you."

"How unkind! We've only just met!"

"And I already despise you. Imagine how much greater my loathing will become when I *have* gotten to know you."

Panoptos might have had a retort for that, or not, but Dust chose that moment to decide the newcomer was safe after all. He dropped from above to settle comfortably on Death's shoulder, puffing out his feathers and shaking off the worst of the soot.

Every one of Panoptos's eyes blinked in unison. "Where did the bird come from?" he screeched.

"His name is Dust," the Horseman said.

"That is *not* what I asked!"

"And yet, it's the answer you got. The universe works in mysterious ways."

"Hmph!" Panoptos darted upward, apparently for no other reason than so he could look down on Death. "Does the Crowfather know you've absconded with one of his creatures?" he asked petulantly.

The Council's errand boy doesn't care for surprises. Could be a useful thing to know. "What do you *want*, Panoptos?" he repeated. "I have work to do."

"Indeed you do. I'm here on behalf of the Council."

Death just looked at him.

"Ah, well . . . Yes, I suppose you guessed as much. Listen well, then. A phalanx of the White City's finest soldiers was ambushed recently, by an unknown enemy. The Charred Council wishes you to learn who and why, and to—"

"No."

Four or five of the creature's eyes threatened to pop from his face. "What do you mean, *no*?"

"I wasn't aware the word had multiple meanings," Death said.

"When you returned," Panoptos growled, "after *half a millennium*, you told the Council you were finally ready to assume your duties!"

"And I am, when necessary. But I'm not required for this. Angels under attack? That's hardly the Council's affair at all, unless it represents a violation of the treaties with Hell. Assign one of the others; War and Fury are always eager to—"

"The Council sent for *you*," Panoptos said. His voice had gone so cold, frost practically formed along the edges of the words.

"I'm busy trying to make a home for myself." Death began to turn back to his endeavors.

"You'll want to look into this yourself, Death."

"Oddly, I don't."

"Oh. Did I neglect to mention that this happened at the borders of Eden?"

Death spun back quickly enough to dislodge Dust from his shoulder. The crow offered an offended caw and fluttered over to perch, sulking, on the half-built structure.

Even without a mouth, Panoptos gave the impression of a sly grin. "I suppose I probably ought to have mentioned that first thing, shouldn't I?"

The Horseman's fist were clenched around the haft of Harvester; he didn't even remember summoning it back to him. Had Panoptos been nearer, it might well have been his throat in the weapon's place.

"What were the angels doing *there*? Did anyone breach the garden? Did the assailants get in?"

"I don't know." Perhaps realizing he'd pushed a bit further

than was safe, Panoptos rose even higher, and his tone softened a touch. "Honestly, I don't. The Council's only now hearing first reports of the engagement."

"Anything else you've *neglected* to mention?" Death rasped up at him.

"Only that the Council wants your report the instant you have an idea of what's happening. They need to know if this is just another random skirmish at the edges of the treaty, or if something larger is underway."

Without another word, Death began striding across the desert of ash, leaving the ghouls to finish the work on his home-to-be. A whistle pierced the air, shrill and painful, one as much spiritual as physical.

And something both spiritual and physical answered the call.

If the reek of decay and the crushing weight of hopelessness took physical form, they would have been the same putrid green as the mist that billowed out of nothing a dozen paces distant. A growing staccato beating resolved itself into the sound of hooves.

Other than the grubby mane and tail, the horse that finally appeared was hairless. Its skin was nearly the same corpse gray as Death's, and hung open in ragged tears, displaying bone and rotting muscle. From those wounds, from its nostrils and between its broken teeth, and from cracks in its hooves, that mist seeped in constant clouds. The saddle was black leather, worn and tattered; the bridle, a rusted chain.

Death hauled himself into that saddle with a single smooth motion. Harvester, despite its length, never once impeded him. Scarcely had he settled when Dust landed once more on his shoulder. Death nodded once to the crow, a second time to his mount. The horse broke into a gallop that should have been impossible on the soft and shifting surface.

For the first time in five hundred years, the eldest of the Horsemen rode out into Creation to do the bidding of the Charred Council.

BEFORE THEM, the walls of reality parted, as ephemeral as cobweb and just as readily swept aside. The barren world on which Death had made his home fell away, less palpable than a forgotten dream, and they were elsewhere.

Or, more accurately, nowhere.

Above and all around them were swirling currents of white. Not white mist, or cloud, or haze; just *white*. Calling it "nothing" lacked accuracy, as this was no absence, but a *presence*. It just happened to be the presence of emptiness made manifest.

The only real substance wound below them, a snaking trail of reality on which the beast's hooves trod without sound. Held steady and solid by the power of the Horseman's will alone, it was quite literally a path between worlds. The rolling whiteness around them muffled sound, offered little sensation of motion—but here, distance had no meaning anyway. The journey from one reality to the next would take as long as it took, and not even Death truly knew why.

The tedium afforded him the opportunity to think on what had happened. It wasn't necessarily an advantage.

Eden. He could have gladly gone until the end of time without ever again hearing the name Eden.

A garden realm of wonder and beauty, peace and plenty. Set aside ages ago for the sole use of a people not yet born—by the express command of the Creator Himself, in an earlier age when He still occasionally deigned to speak with His creations—Eden was quite possibly the nearest thing in any reality to a true paradise.

Perhaps it should have been no surprise to anyone, then,

that the Nephilim—caught forever between demon and angel while belonging to neither; a lost and vicious race—had attempted to annex it for their own. It was the last world they ever invaded, the end of their reality-spanning rampage. Many of their corpses still rotted beneath the surface, feeding all manner of ancient power into the soil.

It was a past that Death would have been quite content to leave buried, and gradually forgotten. Apparently, someone out there didn't feel the same.

The horse abruptly tossed its rotting head, uttering a spectral call somewhere between a whinny and a moan.

"Yes, Despair." Death flicked the reins idly. "I *am* paying attention, and I know precisely where we are. I'm not about to get us lost."

The creature—Despair—whickered with blatant skepticism.

"If we're not there shortly," the Horseman offered, "I promise I'll let *you* take the lead."

A final ghostly snort, then silence once more.

Briefly. It was only a few moments later that the billowing pallor surrounding them began to waft away, thinning to reveal the first signs of an actual realm. Despair's hooves began, once more, to make muted *thumps* in the dirt.

Dull patterns of shape and color, very much like blots of dyes and paints not yet dried, slowly resolved themselves into towering trees and heavy brushwood. The light forest stretched from its bed of gently waving grasses toward an azure sky so bright, it was almost painful. The gentle gusts of wind were practically unnoticeable, at least as compared with the world he'd just left, and high, piping birdsong filled the air.

Only for a heartbeat or two, of course. The wildlife fell unnaturally silent at the approach of the Horseman and his half-dead mount—presumably because they were busy scrambling to fit themselves into the tiniest of hiding spots.

Beautiful and bucolic, but certainly *not* Eden. Nor had Death expected it to be. The garden was isolated from the boundaries of Creation as defined by the Tree of Life. Not even the Horsemen could simply enter at will. No, like any other traveler, Death had to wend his way through ancient forests on unclaimed worlds near the heart of reality, until he located the single trail that allowed ingress to that most precious domain.

The first signs of unrest, when he finally came across them, were not difficult to spot.

Entire swaths of trees had fallen, cut down by potent magics and brutal weaponry. Splintered wood and tattered leaves, churned soil and scorched earth, stretched as far as Death could see. He could smell the blood, still wet and seeping into the dirt, but he didn't need to; he *felt* the deaths imprinted on the landscape, sensed the newly freed souls slowly fading from the air.

"Dust."

The crow squawked an acknowledgment and took wing, spiraling high and far, watching for any hint as to what had occurred—or for any imminent danger. Death dropped lightly to his feet, leaving Harvester lashed to the saddle in the full knowledge that it would answer his call should he need it. He crouched, studying the soil, but all he could tell was that a fearsome struggle had taken place.

That much, I knew already.

He pressed his fingers into the rich loam, then raised them to his mask. The blood was angelic, as he'd anticipated. What he *hadn't* expected was to find *only* angel blood. Whoever their opponents might have been, either they did not bleed, or the soldiers of the White City had not managed to injure a single one.

The first prospect was far less disturbing than the second.

Too many signs, too much death and blood in a confined

area; the Horseman couldn't hope to follow any one trail back to its source. If so many had been slaughtered here, though, where were the corpses? Why did only spilled blood remain?

Death straightened and carefully studied the wounded forest. No sign of any other observer, enemy or ally, but *something* was off. It was nigh impossible for anything living to hide from him, yet had someone lain concealed at that precise moment, he wouldn't have been at all surprised. He couldn't see anyone, couldn't hear, couldn't sense; but he did not *feel* alone.

A shrill cry from Dust interrupted Death's musings. The crow was circling deliberately over a spot of woodland some few hundred paces away.

"All right, I see you." Death didn't bother shouting; he knew Dust would hear, regardless. He opened his hand, calling for Harvester to settle comfortingly into his grip, and turned back toward his mount. "Looks tight in there," he said of the thickening trees. "Follow if you can. If not, I'll call when I need you."

Despair whickered once in reply, a distant, uninterested sound.

With an impossible grace the Horseman slipped over, under, or between the obstacles in his way, leaving the ravaged swaths of churned earth and shattered boles behind. The protruding boughs might as well have been hinged doors, the overgrowth a rich carpet. On the very rare occasion when the trail was too thickly occluded even for him, Harvester carved a path with no effort at all.

He sensed Dust's discovery long before he could see it. The growing miasma of blood and early rot, the almost corporeal tang of the soul's recent passing, all served as heralds of what lay ahead.

The angel had fallen in a thicket of brambles and dead leaves as brittle as old parchment. A small gap in the canopy allowed a single finger of sunlight to prod tentatively at the body, as though it were afraid something in the foliage might leap out and bite. Without his personal attunement to the scents and sensations of death—and without Dust having spotted the angel from above—the Horseman would never have located the remains.

No wonder, then, that whoever had recovered the other bodies had also missed him.

Death pushed through the thistles and thorns without pause or even a second glance. The sharpest tore at the pallid flesh on his arms and bare torso, leaving shallow gouges that failed to bleed. If he felt the trifling pains at all, it showed neither in his gait nor in his gleaming eyes.

Oddly wide and jagged gashes formed abstract patterns across the angel's broken body. A carpeting of bloody feathers surrounded him in a disturbingly neat circle, having been knocked and torn from his battered wings. The intricate angelic script on his gleaming breastplate was marred beyond recognition, and the blade of his glaive was badly notched. It had struck something, repeatedly, yet no blood marred the edge.

A moment, to plant Harvester a few inches deep in the soil, where it stood like some petrified pennant, and then Death knelt beside the fallen soldier. He held his left hand, palm-down, above the corpse's heart; the right, with fingers curled toward the sky. His mask quivered as he incanted syllables that no humanoid mouth should ever have been able to produce.

A fragment, the tiniest sliver, of the angel's departed soul split away, swept back through the worlds by the Horseman's necromancy. And though the blood did not flow, nor the lungs draw breath, the eyelids fluttered open as the angel awoke.

CHAPTER TWO

I DO NOT ... WHERE ...

Who are you?

Oh, Creator, that voice! Everywhere, everywhere ...

Who are you?

I do not understand. I saw the most wondrous colors, heard the most beautiful songs. I was at peace ...

And you will return shortly. Who are you?

My name ... I am ... I was Sarasael.

You know who I am?

I do. I know not *how* I know, but I knew you the moment you called me back, before I knew even myself.

You died here.

Yes.

You were murdered here. Cut down by your enemies. I would know who. I would know what happened.

And then I might return to my rest?

I promise it.

Then listen well ...

I WAS A SOLDIER of the White City, and served well for centuries uncounted. My place was, and likely would ever be, with the Faneguard. We were a brigade of steadfast, battle-hardened warriors. Our commander was Malahidael, personally chosen and elevated to the rank of general by our Lord Abaddon himself!

We were a rarity among the legions of the White City: a division tasked with the defense and protection of vital or sacred places, rather than more direct action against the enemies of Heaven. A position of smaller glories, perhaps, less likely to raise us high in the esteem of our brethren, but an urgent and necessary undertaking for all that. We did our duty, followed where Malahidael ordered, and never once resented our lot.

In our day, we guarded military outposts and ancient temples and repositories of knowledge that would make even the archivists of the Charred Council weep with envy. And then, at the dawn of the current age, we were assigned to patrol the borders of Eden.

I can sense your surprise. You had no notion that the angels had taken it upon ourselves to defend the garden. But is it truly so startling? We know the Creator's mind; we know His plans for that place, and for the race yet to be born.

We certainly could not trust the Charred Council to look after Eden. Even if they thought it fell under their purview—and we still do not comprehend their thoughts or motivations well enough to guess whether they would have—who could they send to defend it? One of you? A Horseman? The last of the Nephilim, whose bloody transgressions are the very reason Eden requires protecting at all? No. Unacceptable.

So the Faneguard came here, to this empty little world to which Eden is bound. Our long-term presence might technically violate our pact with Hell and the Charred Council, but we've never interfered with the world itself, nor left the isolated area we were meant to guard. A defensive force only, ready to rebuff any effort by any creature or faction to breach the sanctity of the garden, until the coming of the race-to-be.

Our task was simple, and our battles few. Mostly we engaged the occasional scavenger, a Maker or one of the other Old Ones curious to explore the promised land, or to study its nature, or perhaps to forage the remains of your slaughtered brethren. We drove most away with ease, and killed those who proved too intractable for their own good. Again, perhaps not the most exhilarating of assignments, but we understood its importance.

I do not *believe* we grew complacent. I believe that the forces that came upon us so recently—I cannot say precisely when, having lain here dead for some time—simply overmatched us. But I do not suppose we can know for certain; perhaps we were, indeed, unwary. Careless.

They burst from the trees, making for the gateway to Eden, and we almost failed even to spot them! They had come to this world some distance away, taken their time, crept slowly and silently through the underbrush until they'd drawn near enough to make their charge. They were, too, astonishingly small. Six-limbed, with an almost canine body and a humanoid trunk, but even had they stood upon their hind legs, they'd scarcely have reached my shoulders. Headless. Featureless, save for a smattering of unfamiliar runes scarred into their substance.

Stone, these creatures, not flesh. Constructs, clearly intended either to labor or to do battle as the occasion might warrant. Their fingers were long, far too long in proportion. They twisted and writhed, flexing in ways no natural stone should flex, sometimes blending fluidly together before solidifying once more. They could, it appeared, form only the simplest of tools or the simplest of weapons, but their edges were sharp and their blows heavy.

You know, better than most, how effectively the simplest weapons can kill.

We needed no orders from Malahidael. The Faneguard trained and drilled extensively for any contingency—including a sudden influx of earthbound adversaries from the depths of the trees. We each had our assigned positions, and we took them without hesitation.

I heard the cannons engage from behind, saw bursts of raw force and blessed flechettes erupt across the forest. Miniature volcanoes, they were, or the Creator's lightning! Whole swaths of forest were blasted apart, everything within shredded or incinerated. No simple stone, even mystically vivified as these constructs were, could stand against such a bombardment. The creatures died by the scores!

Yet they appeared by the *hundreds*. Someone prepared heavily for this attempted incursion; by the time I and my brethren had closed to do battle, necessitating the silencing of the cannons, there must have been well over a thousand of them scuttling toward the gate.

I dropped through the trees, wings spread only enough to slow my descent. A blizzard of leaves and broken branches swirled out around me, torn from the boughs at the touch of my armor. Barely a moment's thought was sufficient to call the power inherent in my weapon; lightning and fire flickered across the blade in intertwined arcs.

The earth shook beneath the impact of an entire phalanx of the White City's soldiers. The first of the constructs was directly below, and I cleaved it with the glaive even as I landed. It burst apart, unable to stand against the sacred steel, let alone the powerful energies that danced over it. Several bits of stone shrapnel ricocheted from my armor, and I recall a brief flash of pain as one drew blood across my scalp, but it was a trifling wound, easily ignored.

And just as well, as I had no attention to spare.

A dozen and more of the constructs came at me from all

sides, their hands oozing into blades of rock. At first, they could not so much as touch me. I swept between them in a dance of feet and wings, sometimes stepping, sometimes turning, sometimes rising high above. Every swing or lunge they made cut only empty air, or gouged the tree trunks, while almost every sweep of my glaive obliterated another foe. I could not take the time to look about me, and even if I could, the forest blocked my view—yet it seemed, from the splintering sounds and battle cries, that my brethren were doing as well as I.

But there were so many, so many . . . And they were more cunning than we credited.

Our flight ceased to be an advantage as they started coming at us from the treetops! Apparently their legs were just as malleable as their hands, making climbing as simple for them as walking. They brought several of us down in those first moments, diving upon us from above, crushing with their great weight or stabbing with their jagged limbs.

Whether by skill or fortune, I was not among the first to fall. I heard the rustling of the branches, saw movement just before the creature leapt. I kicked out with both legs, and though it felt as though my feet might break, I succeeded in knocking it back. It struck the tree from which it had just emerged and began to fall, but I had already dived below, glaive upraised. It tumbled past me in two distinct halves, crumbling to smaller pieces well before it struck the earth. I was even able to nudge one such piece aside so that it landed on one of its fellow constructs, distracting it sufficiently for me to finish it off.

We were destroying them, but not swiftly enough. A small mass of them came at me from behind, and I turned my glaive, not on them, but on a nearby bole. The great tree tumbled, crushing many of the enemy, and granting me a moment to recover. And still there were more.

The Faneguard would be overrun.

Or so I feared, for a moment, before salvation appeared above, silhouetted against the burning sun.

I told you before that each of us had our assigned duties for almost any contingency. What I had not known—what *most* of us had not known—was that, should an enemy of overwhelming numbers appear, one of us had been assigned to return instantly to the White City in search of aid.

I understand why we were not told. Some would have found it demoralizing to contemplate. Some would have thought it a slight to our pride. When had the Faneguard *ever* required outside assistance?

Yet now I see the wisdom.

From above, a second phalanx plummeted into the fray. And at their head was not just any captain, any general, but great Abaddon himself!

Have you ever looked upon Abaddon? Have you ever seen him in battle? He is a force beyond reckoning, beyond comprehension. His wings are iron as much as muscle and sinew and feather. His impossible sword, longer than he is tall, he wields as though it were a toy. Taller and broader of shoulder than any of us, his golden armor and ivory-white tabard gleaming more brightly than the sun behind him, he waded into the foe. It appeared that his blade, which he swung so rapidly it seemed to form a solid arch, needed only get *near* one of the constructs to blast the creature to dust. He refused even to acknowledge the presence of the trees, but swung his sword as he needed. If it encountered a trunk on its way to the target, well, it simply swept through without slowing. And somehow, no matter what the direction from which he struck, those trees always fell to hinder the constructs, never even a single angel.

Between Abaddon's ferocity and our newly inflated numbers, we rapidly turned the tide. Only a handful more angels fell to the constructs, while we destroyed them by the hundreds. The woods were filled with the crash of shattering stone, punctuated by sporadic bursts as the cannoneers found an open target.

But even as the seemingly endless horde finally began to taper off, something else appeared in their place. The enemy had reinforcements as well.

These, too, were constructs, but entirely unlike the initial wave. The stone that made up their narrow bodies was all but hidden beneath angled plates and long limbs of brass; they looked rather the way Heaven's champions might be depicted in the stained-glass windows of the White City's grandest chapels. Sharp, angular, jointed in abnormal places. They did not walk at all, but rather sat upon a narrow brass spindle that spun rapidly from the waist downward without ever jostling their upper halves. They boasted four long arms; like their stone forerunners, they had no heads, and their hands seemed capable of forming whatever implements they might require.

Do I even need to tell you that most of them had chosen to form massive, razor-edged blades?

They were horrifically fast, these new constructs, and the whine of their spinning shafts was the only warning of their approach. You would think that the underbrush would impede them, but they sped along without any obvious difficulty. And they could *leap*, as many of us learned in our final moments, high enough to bring down even a soaring angel. We soaked in a monsoon of blood and feathers; limbs both flesh and metal crashed to the dirt.

Still, we outnumbered them, they were not *much* faster than we—and most important, we still had Abaddon. Even with their astounding speed, few could lay a blade on him, and those that did invariably failed to penetrate his armor. His massive sword rose and fell, almost without effort, and the animated warriors died. Through upraised blades and their brass shells, he cut them down, each with a single blow.

We were rallying behind Abaddon when one particular construct appeared, subtly different from the others. Not in build, not in attitude, but in armament. Rather than form its own hands into blades, it carried a peculiar sword, the likes of which I'd never before seen. Something about the weapon disturbed even warriors such as ourselves, and I recall falling back a step as it advanced on our commander.

Abaddon raised his own sword, moving to meet this new threat—

CHAPTER THREE

G ET AWAY FROM HIM, DAMN YOU!"
Death's head snapped around, hunting the
source of that voice where no voice should sound.
Sarasael's spirit, unshackled by the abrupt lapse in the Horseman's concentration, slipped away. The body fell limp once
more, and Death could hear the faintest of relieved sighs fading away in an unreal direction he knew but could not name.

When a new angel appeared from between two trees,
where before there had been nothing but empty space, Death
was already moving. Hanging in the angel's two-handed grip,
a massive cannon of bronze tubing and iron slabs fired burst
after burst. Fearsome energies ran wild, crackling and spitting,
reducing whole trees to ash. Fragments of blessed metals embedded themselves in the earth, punched holes entirely through
the thickest trunks, and the forest trembled with the sound of
thunder.

And none of it touched the Horseman.

He was simply never there when the projectiles soared
past, never in the radius when they ignited. He moved with a
grace the lithest angel couldn't have matched, guided by an
insight that bordered on the precognitive. He swayed from,

rolled under, or tumbled over anything that came near, seemed almost to walk up the side of trees and even change direction mid-leap.

The rage that marred the angel's face twisted his features further still. His body shook with such anger that it began to affect the cannon's aim, and the weapon spat as swiftly as he could physically pull the trigger.

Still he missed, every time. And he'd have been infinitely *more* frustrated had he known that his unyielding barrage didn't even warrant Death's full attention.

Where in the name of Oblivion had he come *from?*

Almost *nobody* should have been able to sneak so close without Death sensing their presence. Certainly not an angel in heavy, clanking armor, lugging heavy artillery!

It was right about the time the *second* angel appeared, opening fire from high above—this one armed with a rune-encrusted halberd that spat volleys of force so fearsome, the blade itself seemed little more than an afterthought—that the Horseman pinpointed what *else* was wrong with his surroundings.

The dead Sarasael had described a vast barrage of devastating energies and explosions, tearing down entire thickets. *So where was all the damage?* Why were the only obvious gaps in the foliage and fallen trees the results of the firepower he currently dodged?

Death twisted aside, letting the hail of bullets sweep past him, but avoiding two separate attackers was proving far more difficult than one alone. "I don't suppose we can discuss this?" he asked without much hope.

In response, a third angel, wielding a halberd much like the soldier above, stepped from inside a tree trunk—or so it appeared, anyway—and took aim.

"On your heads be it, then."

Death dropped into an impossibly low crouch, right knee bent, left leg extended out beside him, bent so sharply forward at the waist that his dangling hair brushed the soil. And in that instant, when every one of the angels' shots arced overhead, before they could even think to adjust their aim, Harvester ripped itself loose from the soil.

The Horseman leapt. Impossibly high, as swiftly as if he himself boasted a pair of the angels' feathered wings. The scythe met him at the apex of his flight.

And then he was falling, twisting in the air beneath and around the soldiers' constant fire. He spread his arms, and held not one single weapon any longer, but a *pair* of scythes—neither nearly as long of haft as Harvester's unified form, but each with a blade nearly as massive.

He hit the earth, feet embedding themselves in the soil, and both scythes spun. Behind his back, one of them deflected a burst of cannon-fire, slinging it high into the canopy above; he hadn't even turned to look.

Before him, the other scythe made three complete revolutions. The first sliced the angel's halberd in half. The second removed both arms at the elbows. And the third cleaved him cleanly from right hip to left shoulder.

Death had come around to face the remaining pair before the top half of the body slid completely free of the lower.

An angel shrieked—Death couldn't tell, and didn't care, which one—and both took to the air. They soared straight up, parallel to the trunks, wings snapping branches and showering the Horseman with leaves and twigs. The barrels of both weapons turned inexorably downward, ready to add far deadlier precipitation to the deluge.

Death hurled the scythe from his left hand. It spun, up and out, severing the branches in its path. The cannoneer easily swooped aside, dodging the swift but apparently clumsy attack. He snickered, tightened his grip on the trigger—

And fell, grunting in pain, as a particularly thick branch—Death's true target—plummeted from above and slammed him back to earth. The scythe followed, retracing its arc and returning to its master.

The half instant in which the other angel was distracted by his brother's fall was more than long enough for Death to dart aside and duck low, vanishing into the thicket of brambles.

He watched, peering between the thorns, as the angel's eyes and weapon tracked this way and that, seeking a target. Then, when he found no obvious sign of the foe, the soldier dropped to check on his injured companion.

Just as the angel's boots touched down, Death lunged from the thorns. When he began the thrust, it was with one of the twin scythes. By the time the blade struck home, he held only one weapon; Harvester had become a long-hafted, broad-bladed spear.

The angel coughed once, and died by the time the sound had faded.

Death yanked back on the spear—only it was no longer a spear, but a scythe once more. The crescent edge sliced through the upper curve of the last angel's wing, just as he was heaving the branch off his back. He cried out, dropping to his knees. Not a lethal wound, by any means, but he wouldn't be flying anytime soon.

"*Now* can we discuss this?" Death asked politely.

"You bastard!" The epithet squeezed through gritted teeth, carried on a spray of enraged spittle. "You just killed two of my brothers!"

"You did attack me first, remember?" Then, "I wouldn't recommend it. You're not *nearly* fast enough."

The angel jerked back, tearing his eyes away from the cannon lying just out of reach. He huddled down on his knees, fists clenched, his wounded wing drooping. "You were defiling Sarasael's body! I couldn't allow that!"

"Defiling? I was only asking him a few questions!"

"Necromancy!" The angel spat. "Defilement enough! And how am I to know you aren't responsible for the attack on us in the first place?"

Death actually blinked. "If I were responsible, why in Creation would I be questioning the dead about what happened?"

"It could be a trick," the angel muttered, his tone obstinate beneath the overt pain.

"A trick. To fool observing angels that I couldn't even see were *here*? Apparently, you think me so cunning that I even outsmarted logic and sense."

"Maybe—"

"Is there someone in command I can speak to? Someone *with* a brain, if that's not asking too much?"

"No. I'm alone."

Death shook his head. "Stupid *and* a bad liar. Your cannon was actually the thinker in the partnership, wasn't it?" Then, before the angel could retort, Death turned his face to the canopy and raised his voice.

"I know you're out there! I know you've hidden yourself! I know what I see isn't real!"

That was, after all, the only possible explanation for how the angels had mysteriously appeared, and why the woods showed so little sign of damage. The Horseman was actually impressed; the illusion had to be a potent magic indeed to have worked on *him*.

For long moments, nothing happened, no one answered. And then the entire forest . . . *rippled*.

Enormous gaps appeared in the trees, swaths of devastation where the soil was melted into solid rock and no living things remained. Twisting helixes of smoke wrestled their way upward, each struggling to be the first to reach the lowering clouds. Flurries of cinders still hovered above the empty places, and Death was suddenly struck by the thick aroma of burnt wood and seared flesh.

A *very* powerful magic, then.

More of the White City's soldiers appeared as the phantasmal image retracted, some standing, some hovering on slowly flapping wings. Most bore deep scores in their armor and dried blood on their flesh. All carried weapons of lethal design. And none looked anything less than enraged.

"Don't be foolish," Death told them. "I'm not the enemy here. Not *yet* . . ."

"And how many of us would you have killed if you *were* the enemy?"

Death glanced up at the one who spoke. The angel descending to land before him was unlike the others. The same pale hair, yes, the same white eyes. He wore no armor, however, and carried no obvious weapon. His ornate robe, an emerald green with trim and all manner of avian designs in gold, was so long it dragged in the dirt while its wearer yet drifted a spear length above. A semicircle of gold, also engraved and sculpted into winged patterns, formed an arch over his head.

Death bowed his own head in respect—a shallow gesture, to be sure, but one he would have offered to few others in Creation.

"Azrael," he said in greeting. *If Abaddon managed to drag him away from his libraries and the Well of Souls, this must be even worse than the Council suspected . . .*

"Death," the angel replied.

"Your soldiers attacked me, Azrael, not the other way around. And in answer to your question . . . All of you."

"I suppose you might have tried, at that." The angel touched down a few paces from the Horseman. His robes, despite their previous length, now hung only to the ankles of his supple boots. "Fortunate for you we were some distance away when this little skirmish began. Had we reached you while you were still in battle, I doubt I could have prevented my friends here from attacking you instantly."

"*Someone* was fortunate, anyway," Death retorted. "You're welcome to believe it was me if that makes you feel better." He gestured vaguely in the direction from which the soldiers of the White City had appeared. "Your work?"

"Of course. The sorceries I've mastered in my millennia would surprise even the Charred Council's vaunted Riders. *If* such a time should come, Creator forbid, that I should have *need* to surprise you."

"I've never heard of angels hiding behind figments and phantasms before."

The glowers of the soldiers grew even fiercer. Some, the wounded angel included, looked as though they wanted to cast their weapons aside and have at Death with teeth and nails.

More like demons than angels, he couldn't help but think. But even he was not so uncouth, or so foolish, as to voice such an observation.

Azrael, however, only shrugged. "We have many wounded, Death. Our strength is not what it should be, and we have no means of determining if the enemy plans to return. It made sense to seize whatever tactical advantage we could, and protect our brethren in every way possible."

"No need to be defensive. I applaud the initiative." He cast his burning gaze across each angel, slowly, calmly. "If we've concluded our efforts to slaughter each other, Azrael, we ought to discuss what comes next."

One snowy eyebrow rose at that. "But you've yet to answer *our* question, Horseman."

"Your . . ." Death thought back a moment. "Azrael, you don't honestly believe the attack was *my* doing!"

"It could have been," the angel said patiently. "The motives of the Council are inscrutable at best."

"Had I sought your blood, I'd have attacked you myself. Perhaps I might have had one or more of my brothers at my side. But I do *not* make use of . . . minions."

"Your masters might, though, yes?"

"As I'm here at their behest, if they're responsible for this, I'll be as surprised as you are. And substantially more confused."

Azrael's lip twitched. "All right. Come, Death. We'll consult with Abaddon and decide our next move."

"Ah. Yes, I assumed he'd survived, if anyone had. He . . ." The abrupt stiffness in Azrael's face gave him pause. "Something I should know?"

"Abaddon survived, but not unscathed. Come. Perhaps you'll know something of his affliction our healers do not."

"Hmm. Show me."

Surrounded by twin columns of angels, they marched from the copses of trees through blasted clearings, smoldering wounds in the primeval woodland, then deeper into the forest once more. None of the angels seemed remotely as comfortable with Death's presence as Azrael did; Death, for his part, would have had to actually be sleeping to care any less *how* they felt.

A soft flutter overhead heralded Dust's reappearance, settling to perch on the dull outer curve of Harvester's blade.

"Interesting," Azrael observed.

"Not really. Crows are very poor conversationalists."

"A good thing you've never had any interest in conversation, then."

Death glanced sidelong at Azrael's expression, but it remained impassive. He honestly couldn't tell if the angel had meant that in jest or not.

A few moments more of leaves and sticks crunching under the warriors' heavy tread, a constant popping as though the forest itself were an arthritic grandparent, and the procession came across the first of the shattered stone soldiers.

They could have stopped to allow a closer examination, but a glance told Death enough for now. He could not quite agree with Sarasael's description. It seemed, to him, less like a canine with a humanoid torso, and more like a blocky insect, rearing up so that its front legs might rend and grab. Everything else was as the departed soul had portrayed: the graven runes, the carapace of rock, and the utter lack of any unnecessary features—such as, for instance, a head.

"Solid stone, all the way through," Azrael said without looking around.

"And the others? The stone-and-brass soldiers?"

"Largely hollow, save for some rods providing the outer surface with extra structural support. Part of why they could move so swiftly, I suppose."

"Hmm." Death allowed himself a few paces to reflect. Then, "I'm not familiar with either design," he admitted. "If I've ever seen them before, I don't recall it."

"Nor were any of us," Azrael told him. "Which means we have no idea who attacked us. Constructs *usually* mean a Maker, but . . ."

"But plenty of others have hired, purchased, or even usurped mastery of constructs before," Death concluded. "Meaning that, for all your deliberations and all the soldiers you lost, you have nothing of any substance."

"Your tact, as always, is overwhelmingly appreciated."

Death chose to let that lie. The next length of their journey passed without conversation, save for the occasional resentful murmur of angels who would much rather be soaring back to their camp than trudging over the dirt like "lesser beings."

Any spiteful satisfaction Death might have gained from their discomfort vanished utterly, however, beneath a tide of agony that flowed from up ahead.

It wasn't *his* pain; he wasn't suffering in any way. But he was *aware* of the torment of others, the anguish of creatures unaccustomed to such things. It was rather like the tang of rain in the air, or that first gust of wind announcing the coming of winter, sensed by the spirit rather than the body.

And he felt, too, the recent passing of so very many souls.

"Our camp," Azrael announced, with just a hint of bitterness.

"How primitive," Death said blandly.

The so-called camp boasted a surrounding rampart of ivory-white stone, some twenty paces in height and easily three times that, lengthwise, on each side. A portcullis of gleaming silver, its bars serrated into thousands of barbed fangs, provided the only means of entry for earthbound creatures. At each of the four corners, a spindly tower loomed nearly as high above the battlements as the battlements rose above the soil— and atop each tower, a double-barreled siege cannon some four times the size of the portable weapons Death had so recently faced.

"Imagine," the Horseman continued, "what you could have accomplished with actual time and resources."

Azrael nodded grimly, apparently oblivious—or perhaps simply naturally immune—to Death's sarcasm. "Sadly lacking, I know. Still, the best we could manage, given the circumstances."

The twin columns of angels, along with their guest, approached the lustrous gate at a casual pace. The nearest cannons tracked their every move, swiveling at seemingly impossible angles to maintain a line of fire even as they stood by the wall itself. The portcullis didn't rise to allow ingress;

rather it faded almost completely from sight, leaving only a wavering mirage in its place. As best Death could describe the sensation of passing through those phantom bars, it felt like stepping through a waterfall, without the getting-wet part.

Only when they'd passed through the battlements did the cannons return their aim toward the surrounding woods and the horizons beyond.

Within the fortifications, a perfectly geometrical array of smaller structures glinted orange in the sunlight. Each was constructed of an amber-hued glass, just opaque enough to allow privacy to anyone within. Death knew, without the need for close examination, that the substance would be as strong as stone or steel despite its crystalline appearance—not due to any special senses on his part, but simply because he knew that angels in the field would accept nothing weaker.

In neat rows between the buildings, bloodied soldiers lay on stiff cots, recovering from their injuries. More angels dashed around them, tending the wounded with medicinal balms both alchemical and mystical. They did their best—their faces had gone slack with exhaustion and effort—but they were so few, and their patients many. Blotches of blood and scattered feathers were more abundant on the grass than fallen leaves.

The accompanying angels peeled off to return to their own cots, or to seek treatment for their injuries, many glaring at Death as they departed. Azrael alone remained to lead the Horseman to the one structure that stood in the perfect center of the encampment.

Of course.

No doors marred the perfect crystal surface. As with the portcullis, a section of the wall simply phased away, allowing the angel and the Rider to enter.

"What is *that* doing here?" The voice was gruff, powerful, clearly accustomed to instant and unquestioning obedience—but it also quavered, ever so slightly, with repressed agony.

"A pleasure, Lord Abaddon," Death replied.

The greatest warrior the White City had ever produced sat upon a chair of ivory-hued hardwood, gripping it so tightly that the armrests had cracked. Shoulders and chest seemingly large enough to uproot a small mountain were encased in gold-trimmed armor so heavy that most angels couldn't have lifted it, let alone worn it. The square jaw, framed by an unkempt mass of the angels' traditional platinum hair, was distended in a furious scowl that seemed quite capable of *chewing* through the defensive walls.

A pair of angels stood, one to either side of the great general, tending his injuries. With balm-soaked cloths and foul-smelling unguents, they prodded—ever careful, ever gentle—at their commander's face.

And it was, indeed, that face that drew Death's attention. Vicious gouges marred the flesh from forehead to cheek on both sides, and a crimson-soaked bandage completely hid the angel's right eye.

Or, to judge by the concave flex of the blood-stiffened fabric, the empty socket that had once housed the eye.

That Abaddon was conscious, let alone functional and rational, was enough to impress even the impassive Horseman.

Azrael stepped between them, speaking softly but swiftly. A few emphatic gestures, a few barked questions, and Abaddon grudgingly nodded.

"All right, Horseman. Azrael's convinced me we're on the same side of this—for now."

"How magnanimous of you."

The general grumbled, low in his throat. "Tell me what you know."

"Less than you do," Death said. "I know of the attack, up to the appearance of the brass warriors. Beyond that . . ." He shrugged.

"There's little to tell beyond that," Abaddon said. "They

gave us some trouble, and I lost some good soldiers, but we rebuffed them."

"Did you?" Death asked him. "Are you certain?"

Abaddon's glower returned, stiffer even than before.

"We did," Azrael said, stepping in. "I know what you're asking, Death, and I can assure you, the garden was not breached."

"Hmm. I'll need to see for myself. Once I've returned, we can—"

"No," Abaddon growled.

While, at the same time, Azrael said, "The way is barred."

"Then unbar it."

"I'm sorry," Azrael told him, and it sounded as though he genuinely meant that. "I understand how important this is to you—"

"You cannot *possibly*—"

"—but we cannot risk it. The enemy may still be watching. To lower the defenses, even for a moment, might grant them the opportunity they require. I won't do so, not even for you."

"I know my way to the gate," Death said, his voice dangerously calm. Only the blazing fire in his eyes, stoked brighter than Azrael had ever seen it, suggested the growing fury within. "Do you believe your wards can keep me out indefinitely if I choose to break them?"

"Not indefinitely," the scholarly angel said softly. "But long. Long enough for our common enemy, whoever he may be, to move to whatever the next stage of whatever plan he's following."

"And you'd be fending off the forces of the White City at every moment," Abaddon said. "*After* having had to kill every one of us present just to begin."

"Myself included," Azrael added.

Death's mask couldn't hide his scowl. "You? You've never been a warrior, Azrael."

"Neither am I remotely helpless on the battlefield, as you well know. Would you really pit yourself against all of Heaven merely to confirm with your own eyes what I swear to you is true? When I've no reason to deceive you?"

The general's two attendants fell back, seemingly pushed away by an almost palpable clash of wills. Three of the most potent beings in Creation watched one another, each considering what the other might say next, *do* next. Azrael looked almost to be holding his breath; Abaddon, with his remaining eye, measuring the distance to the impossibly gargantuan sword standing upright in the corner.

And Death . . . finally shook his head. Azrael had too much control to sigh in relief, but everyone sensed it all the same.

"Know this, though," the Horseman said. "If I find you were wrong, if I find that Eden was breached and the remains of my brethren have been disturbed in any way, not all the blades in Heaven will keep me from you."

"Understood."

Death turned away, staring at the amber wall as he struggled to swim against the rushing tide of anger. Only when he was certain that he'd regained all control did he look back at the angels.

"So what now?"

"We need to decide that," Abaddon said. The Horseman chose to ignore the fact that the general's gaze continued to flicker between Death himself and that sword. "Can you . . ." Clearly he had no desire to say what he was about to say. "Can you ask one of *them* who sent them?"

"No. Some constructs have souls, like any other creature; lesser automatons have life, but no true soul. These are the latter. There's nothing for me to call back and question."

"Then," Abaddon said, "until we can determine who attacked us, I don't see much we *can* do." His lips twisted in a rictus grin: bitter, self-mocking, and utterly without humor. "But then, I'm not seeing as well as I used to, am I?"

"All the miracles of angelic medicine I've heard about aren't enough?" Death asked. "Surely regrowing a lost eye isn't beyond your healers' skills."

"Normally, no," Azrael said. He glanced briefly at Abaddon, who nodded once, reluctantly. "But in this instance, it's not to be. Something about the weapon that struck Lord Abaddon was . . . horribly unnatural. The wounds it dealt turned instantly necrotic. Our healers, and the general's own strength, kept the rot and poison from spreading, but I fear the wounds themselves are beyond even our . . . Death? What is it?"

The Horseman's body had gone rigid as any tombstone. The skin on his knuckles threatened to tear.

"This weapon," he whispered, barely more than a breath. The others had to lean in to make out the words. "Was this the sword that one of the brass-armored constructs carried?" Then, at Abaddon's grunt and Azrael's nod, "Do you have it?"

"No," the general told him sourly. "The construct that carried it was one of those that retreated when it became clear they could not win past us."

"A narrow-bladed sword? Nearly as long as I am tall, but scarcely three fingers wide at the base? Serpentine filigree running up the center of the blade?"

Both angels stared openly now. "What do you know?" Abaddon demanded.

Again Death turned away, apparently scrutinizing some unseen image—or some half-faded memory—hovering between him and the wall. Finally, just as Abaddon was drawing breath to speak again, he said, "We are allies in this? I can trust you to keep me apprised of anything you discover?"

"Assuming you are equally forthcoming with us, of course,"

Azrael said. The general glowered at him, shifting uncomfortably in his creaking chair, but made no overt protest.

"Affliction." Still Death kept his back turned, as though concerned, despite the mask, that they might read something untoward in his visage. "The name of the sword is Affliction."

"Descriptive enough," Abaddon said flatly. "But how do you know of it?"

"Because it's a Nephilim weapon." Finally, the Horseman turned toward them, raising his scythe for emphasis. "Taken from the Makers and imbued with our power at roughly the same time as Harvester."

"I see." Abaddon's sneer had deepened, his single eye narrowed sharply enough to cut, and Azrael didn't seem much happier. "And who wields it now, Horseman? One of you?"

"No. No, Abaddon, that's the problem. Affliction was lost ages ago, on the fields of Kothysos."

"Kothysos? I don't believe I know of that one."

Once it became clear that Death wasn't planning to elaborate, Azrael spoke up. "There's little written of it, even in the Library of the Argent Spire. We know it occurred during the height of the Nephilim rampage across the many realms. Several races of the Old Ones, concerned that they could not defend themselves if the horde turned their way, hired an enormous army of mercenary demons to crush the Nephilim. They met on the fields of Kothysos.

"Death's people won that engagement, but at a high cost. If I'm not mistaken, Kothysos represents the largest single loss of Nephilim life before Eden."

"The corpses were stacked in mountains," Death said, his mind clearly elsewhere. "The world itself was poisoned by all that had happened. The Nephilim—this is *after* the other Horsemen and I turned from them, just in case either of you plan to waste time accusing me—scoured the battlefield, recovering the dead and what weapons they could. But much was lost, either destroyed or buried so deep in the carnage and churned earth that it was thought gone forever."

"Obviously not," Abaddon snapped.

"Yes. Obviously . . ."

"So someone found a Nephilim artifact on Kothysos," Azrael said. "Troublesome, but is it truly so disastrous? It's just a sword, albeit a potent one."

"Affliction," Death said, his voice grimmer even than usual, "was not the only thing lost in that battle." He whistled, a high sound that the others in the room could only barely hear. From outside, a small commotion erupted among the angels as Despair materialized in a sickly cloud, having stepped through the void so that he might appear once more at his master's side. "I have to go. I have to *see*."

"Wait!" Abaddon rose shakily to his feet as the Horseman strode toward the phantom spot in the wall. "You agreed to share what you knew!"

Death looked back over his shoulder. "I *don't* know. I *suspect*. If I'm wrong, my suspicions don't matter. If I'm right, I'll inform you then." He passed through the wall and hauled himself into the ragged saddle.

"Pray to your Creator for the former."

The green mist billowed once more, and the Horseman was gone.

CHAPTER FOUR

To the dominion of the Charred Council, sullenly obeying an abrupt and unwelcome call, came the Horseman War.

He appeared through the clouded borders of the realm, as though birthed anew by the heavy, choking smoke. His long white hair and gleaming eyes could have falsely marked him, from a distance, as an angel—yet even the martial inhabitants of the White City had rarely produced a face so stern and unforgiving, or a frame of such immense and blatant strength.

Thick, angular plates of riveted iron, edged in copper, formed an armor that might well have crushed a weaker wearer. Baroque faces, glowering demons and shrieking skulls, protruded from the shoulders and knees, embossed into the unyielding metal. Atop it all, across shoulders so broad they might just have supported one of Creation's many worlds on their own, were draped the folds of a cloak as red as the wrath in a soldier's heart. The deep hood might, in other circumstances, have concealed the wearer's face in shadow—but here, where the light, though dim, was ubiquitous, no such concealment was possible.

Across his back, held fast by no visible straps or means of

support, was a sword as infamous as the Horseman himself. The leather-wrapped hilt protruded from behind one shoulder, as though trying to see past War's girth; yet it was the blade itself that boasted an array of screaming faces. Portraits, perhaps, of the damned. The barbed and jagged blade, at its widest, was nearly as broad as its wielder's chest, and had it stood point-down upon the earth, it would have proved taller than he, as well. It should have been utterly impossible to wield—but *should* and *impossible* were concepts for lesser beings than War.

And lesser weapons than Chaoseater.

Rock and cinders crunched beneath his heavy tread, while the hazy air swirled at his passing. War squinted against the stinging fumes and blistering heat, so intense it would have proved a tangible barrier for most beings, and once more studied the domain of his so-called lords and masters.

It was always the air that hit him first. The searing, sulfur stench of things burning that should never have been able to burn; of gritty soot; of toxins that partook of an almost sentient joy in the ravages they caused, and were best avoided by any sane creature.

Blackened rock spread before him, to every horizon and beyond. Through that stone, like blood from open wounds, ran endless meandering rivers of magma. They poured from cracks in the stone, from the tops of mountains, even occasionally from beyond the ceiling of smoke that obscured whatever might wait above. The lava gathered in pools, or cascaded into gorges so broad and so deep that they might as well have marked the edges of Creation. Spindly crags stood throughout, scattered with no regard for any laws of nature or geography. Some boasted gaping holes running straight through, or protruding ledges that could not possibly support their own weight. A few such peaks narrowed as they neared the thickest layer of haze, then broadened once more before vanishing from sight—as though they were not mountains at all, but great stalagmites that joined halfway with their stalactite brethren. As though the entire realm boasted no sky at all, but sat instead within a cavern of unimaginable dimensions.

Columns of flame erupted with an even more haphazard disregard for any conceivable pattern, casting their hellish illumination over the broken landscape. They blazed despite an utter lack of fuel, as though the rocks themselves were burning.

It seemed that nothing should be able to live in such a fearsome environment, but every so often a scuttling shadow suggested the presence of some tiny entity, struggling to survive on the blasted plain.

And just as often, something else lashed out from within the magma, or the columns of flame, or just an empty crevice, to feast upon the hapless smaller beasts.

None made any move to attack War, or even appear within his reach. They wouldn't dare.

For wearying leagues, the Horseman trudged. Eventually, a faint sheen of sweat broke out across his normally impassive brow. He cursed the Charred Council silently, internally, but would not offer the satisfaction even of wiping the perspiration from his forehead. The arrogant bastards could easily have permitted him to appear directly before them when he stepped across the barriers between realms—had done so before, in fact, in certain emergencies. But normally, they kept their wards impenetrable, save at the very edges of their dominion, even when expecting visitors.

War was quite convinced that it was entirely an effort to remind him of his place, to make him walk and work his way to them as some lowly petitioner. A brief snarl, a twitch where his hand longed for the feel of Chaoseater's hilt, and then he took the only action he conceivably *could* have taken.

He kept walking.

Finally, just like that, he was there.

His destination hadn't appeared on the horizon and drawn slowly near, as it should. One step, and War saw nothing but more of the same burning landscape. A second step and the stairway was before him, leading up toward the top of a short, thick column of rock. The Horseman didn't slow at that impossible arrival, didn't pause, but merely set his feet upon the stair.

Thus did War, not for the first time, enter the court of the Charred Council.

The top of that pillar—broad enough to have been dubbed a hill, had it been less of a perfect cylinder—formed a relatively flat stage, perhaps a few dozen paces wide. It was, in a way, a microcosm of the entire domain. Jagged protrusions of rock around the edges mimicked the great mountains, and from a raised pool, directly across from the stairs, lava bubbled and fires burned. A molten stream, thin and easily crossed, dribbled eternally from that pool to split the platform into uneven halves.

And there, looming over it all from beyond that peculiar font, the Charred Council itself.

Or, at the very least, their façade.

They were a trio of enormous faces, formed of the living rock. Mouths, literally cavernous, gaped open to show the roaring of eternal flames—and, occasionally visible in the flickering of that inferno, what *might* have been a rough and precarious cave leading into depths unknown. Those same fires burned in the unblinking sockets above, pouring yet more smoke into the already thickened air. The visages were subtly different—this one had the curved horns of a ram; that one was slightly more slender than the others—but while the details might differ, the overall effect was the same from each to each. They appeared as though some mad god had begun to sculpt the skulls of demons from the stuff of the mountain, then given up halfway through.

Were the idols themselves living, or were they the masks of more horrific entities in the caves beyond? Was the Charred Council truly three, or merely a single being with multiple faces? Not even the Council's own Riders could do more than guess.

"**War . . .**" It came from the center effigy, booming enough that even the Horseman almost staggered. The shifting of tectonic plates, given throat and tongue to declare its deepest fury, might have come near to producing such a sound.

He bowed his head within the crimson hood, sufficient to show respect, but never could it be mistaken for submission. "You sent for me?" His own voice was hard, that of a man used to the shouts and calls of battle.

"**We find ourselves presented with a rare opportunity. We have chosen you to exploit it.**"

"I'm listening."

"**Your eldest brother currently walks the realms at our behest.**" This time, it was the head on the right that spoke, in a voice almost indistinguishable from the first. "**He looks into a matter that may or may not prove a trifle.**"

War nodded. "What is it that he—?"

"**Irrelevant!**" That from the center head once again. "**Death's precise purpose has no bearing on you! What matters is this . . .**"

Now the leftmost took its turn. "**Our informants have alerted us that, in the midst of the event that we sent Death to investigate, the angel Abaddon was grievously injured. His recovery progresses slowly, and it may be some time before he returns to the White City—or to his fullest strength.**"

Those rugged features now curled in a fearsome scowl. "If you are about to ask me to slaughter an injured foe—"

"**We do not ask, Horseman! We never *ask*. You would be wise to remember that.**"

"**However**"—now the rightmost head—"**as it happens,**

you misunderstand our purpose. It is not Abaddon's weakness, but his absence from the White City, of which you will take advantage.

"The pacts and treaties that we have enforced between Heaven and Hell are young still. Factions on both sides probe at their limits, seeing how far they can test us. A war between Above and Below is never far from igniting—a war in which we would have to intervene, and which would obliterate worlds and threaten the Balance before its end."

I wonder, sometimes, if Creation is worthy of our efforts to save it. But War was wise enough not to speak such thoughts aloud before the Council. What he said, instead, was, "Yes, I understand."

"Many on both sides hold that such a war is inevitable, even desirable, and take steps to prepare. Abaddon is such a one. He has constructed a weapon of terrific power, an explosive device that harms *only* demons! It emits hallowed energies, and even its fragments and shrapnel are specially blessed.

"A 'sacrament bomb,' if you will."

War was nodding. "And you worry that Abaddon will use this bomb to start a war."

"His emissaries have offered endless assurances that the weapon is to be a deterrent only. Yet we cannot trust the angels' word, not when the device would prove utterly devastating against an unprepared foe."

Yet again the heads traded off; the one on the left now spoke. "Too, there is the likelihood that, should Hell become aware of the sacrament bomb, they would launch a strike of their own, in an effort to capture or eliminate the weapon before it could be turned against them."

"You want it destroyed."

"Yes. Given time, we can work magics through the ethers

of Creation to prevent Abaddon from re-creating the device, but the one he has already built would still pose a threat."

War drew himself up, arms crossed over his massive chest. "Stealth and sabotage?" he spat. "Surely any one of my brethren would be more appropriate for that than I. Even if Death is occupied, Fury or—"

"Again you misunderstand us! There is to be no stealth. We desire to send a message, one that neither Heaven nor Hell can possibly misconstrue. The lords and generals of both armies must know that further research in these directions is unacceptable, and will be met with the most dire consequences!

"Do not sneak, Horseman. Do not hide. Your mandate is to travel directly and openly to the stronghold in which Abaddon has hidden the sacrament bomb; our spies have provided its location.

"And you are to go through anything and anyone that stands in your way!"

For the first time since he'd arrived in the Charred Council's domain—indeed, for the first time in years—War felt himself smile.

CHAPTER FIVE

S TUPID. UNBELIEVABLY STUPID."

Though her words were accusatory, even petulant, Belisatra's tone was flat and cold as a frozen lake. Only the fingers of her left hand, drumming a chiming beat on her armored thigh, gave any further indication of her exasperation.

They left smears of semi-congealed blood, those fingertips—the only remaining trace of recent, distasteful experimentations.

Her companion sat by the worktable, slumped bonelessly in a rickety chair that was clearly not long for this world, and old enough that it probably looked forward to going. In his lap, Black Mercy lay like a sodden lump of flesh—too grotesque to keep, too morbidly fascinating to throw away.

The triple cylinders turned constantly beneath his restless fingers. *Click. Click.*

Click.

"It was worth the risk," he said finally.

Belisatra glared at his hunched shoulders, as he seemed determined not to turn and face her directly.

"Worth the risk?" The ice in her voice was now sharp enough to draw blood. "You compromised our entire effort! The White City knows of our interest in Eden, now. They've seen some of our best soldiers in action, and for what? My pets came nowhere near to reaching the gate, let alone breaking—"

He had trouble hearing her, absorbing the meaning of her words only several long breaths after she spoke them. For centuries, he'd had so little room in his soul for anything beyond bitter regret and simmering fury, at what had been done to him and to . . . to others. He was accustomed to that; perhaps even found some comfort in it. But now, something was stoking those fires, something new. His memories felt smothered in a stifling caul, the world around him tinged a venomous purple by the putrid hatred bubbling up through the cracks between his thoughts.

Only the deadweight of the pistol felt real, only Black Mercy looked stable in the center of his wavering vision.

Click. Click.

"I saw an opening, and I took it," he said slowly, cutting the Maker off in midstream. "The knowledge we might have gained, to say nothing of more tangible prizes, made it worth the gamble.

"Yes, we lost, but consider what we've learned. Your drones are of little use against angels, save in great numbers, but your myrmidons are far more effective. We know now what sorts of tactics the White City is likely to employ in its defensive bastions. And we know that the Charred Council has, as yet, no notion of what we're after."

"And just how do you figure that?" Belisatra asked.

"Because Eden was guarded *only* by angels, not by any of the Horsemen."

"Hmm. Fair, but we can't count on that lasting. And Heaven will certainly have reinforced the garden's defenders at this point. We've lost our shot."

"Our shot at Eden, yes. But only temporarily. And besides, Eden was never our only option."

"True, but—"

The fever was actually squeezing him, reaching out with great tendrils so it might crush his mind to its breast and feel his thoughts burning. He'd begun to sweat across his forehead, his neck . . .

But not his hands. His hands were steady, cool, comfortable on Black Mercy's grip.

"Enough for now!" He refrained from shouting, not out of any desire to remain diplomatic with his ally but simply because he lacked the energy to both remember the meaning of the words *and* spit them with any real vehemence. "I believe you have some constructs to replace before our next attempt, don't you?"

Belisatra grumbled something unintelligible and swept from the room, the heavy steel of her armor adding its own metallic voice as she vanished down the corridor. Behind her, her ally remained beside the table and its scattered tools, sagging in his chair, fixated wholly on the only thing remaining in his sight, in his mind, perhaps even in his soul.

Click.

THE SNOW WAS THE BROWN-GREEN OF MARSH WATER, rather than traditional white or even slushy gray. It even *smelled* vaguely stagnant, not that there were many creatures around to notice. It fell in thick flurries, some of which seemed to ride their own individual winds that spun in utter disregard for the weather patterns mere paces away. Everywhere it fell it froze almost instantly into ice, painting abstract patterns of dull hue across the landscape.

And it fell so swiftly that Death, who had crouched in this particular spot for only a few moments, was already half buried and otherwise coming to resemble just another small geological feature of the terrain.

He lurked low on the slope of a mountain so astoundingly massive that it was impossible, from any distance, to view both the base and the summit at once. Several protrusions of stone jutted from the slopes, a few of them large enough to qualify as mountains in their own right. And this was but one of an entire range, forming a wall in the world—and creating steep valleys and gorges where so many Nephilim and so many demons had fallen, long and long ago.

Jagged rock, eternal winter, and a surface of ice some hundreds or even thousands of hands in depth. This was all that the ancient battle had left of the fields of Kothysos.

Within those valleys, swarming across floors of ice and snowy slopes, were those six-limbed beasts of stone of which the departed angel had told him. Hordes upon hordes of them, transforming all Kothysos into one enormous anthill of industry. That they were, indeed, scavenging the ancient battlefield, Death could have no doubt. Their forelimbs were transformed into digging tools, shovels and picks for the most part, save when they hauled something from the ice. These, whether the tiniest object or an entire demonic corpse, long preserved by the cold, they then carried off to some central assembly point the Horseman had not yet discovered.

He had *not* yet seen any trace of the stone-and-brass warriors, nor any sign of a living mind directing the lesser automatons. The things seemed relatively unobservant as well as unintelligent; so long as he remained on the slopes high above, and let the snow do most of the work, remaining concealed ought to be simple enough.

"Ready?" he asked, his voice almost lost to the falling snow and cracking ice.

Dust, who was currently little more than a puffy ball of disheveled black feathers huddled beneath the Horseman's chest, replied with an ugly look and single resigned squawk.

"A little cold won't hurt you." And then, "Fascinating. I didn't know a beak could scowl like that."

It was a slow and frustrating, if not particularly difficult, journey. The snow was thick enough, and Death silent enough, that none of the constructs below came close to spotting him. The treacherous terrain impeded his progress only slightly, and this far down the slopes, the rocky protrusions were usually near enough for the Horseman to leap successfully from mountainside to mountainside.

No, the difficulty arose when moving among those mountains that *didn't* stand near enough to one another to allow for an easy crossing. Death did, despite his supernatural strength and agility, have limits to how far he could jump. In these instances, when the only option was climbing to ground level and crossing through the small valleys, the Horseman was forced to scuttle around to the far side of the slopes and work his way behind the laboring constructs.

Not even a sizable group of the things would pose him much of a danger, but battling a few meant risking the attention of all. And that would prove, at the very least, inconvenient.

Until, after arduous hours of painstaking progress trailing the encumbered drones back to their central repository, stealth finally ceased to be an option.

Tucked into a smaller valley that formed a tributary off the main chasm, a perfect circle—roughly thrice Death's height in diameter—had been melted into the permafrost. Whatever had occurred here had happened some time ago, and much of the hollow had already filled in with fresh ice and snow, but the outline remained clearly visible. Death would have guessed, even without his extraordinary senses, that he was looking at the remains of a gate between realms. The fact that he could *feel* the weakness in the walls of reality, a fresh scab over a wound in the world, merely confirmed that assessment.

Beside the remnants of the gate, a hill of snow bulged like a blister from the ice. It, too, was clearly fresh. Death watched one of the stone constructs approach with a lump of *something*—he could not, from here, make out what it might be—and place it on the hillside, where it was swiftly covered up.

As he'd suspected, then. This was where the diggers were storing whatever it was they chipped from the permafrost.

The stockpile was only lightly guarded—suspiciously so, in fact. While new drones appeared every few minutes, in order to deliver their payloads, they departed just as swiftly. Only a contingent of five remained nearby at all times, winding in a complex patrol around and around the "hill."

Death considered the situation for some time, again allowing the snow to blanket him. Were the enemy—whoever they might be—truly so overconfident, so *foolish*, as to assume the operation here would never be troubled? Had they overextended themselves, stretching their resources too thin?

Or . . .

Given the depth to which they'd already delved into the ice, the relatively small prizes they delivered to the stockpile, the length of time between discoveries, perhaps the operation was almost *complete*. He'd known they must have been here for some while before the invasion of Eden—otherwise, they'd not have had time to unearth Affliction, not when the Nephilim themselves had been unable to locate the sword—but he hadn't realized *how* long.

The stockpile wasn't guarded well because the enemy had already retrieved whatever prizes they expected to find, and moved the bulk of their efforts elsewhere. The remainder was just meticulousness, in case they'd missed something.

So he was far too late to stop them from accomplishing their goals, at least here on the fields of Kothysos. But Death would be damned to the depths of the Abyss if he'd leave without finding out what the enemy were after.

And still he hoped—would, perhaps, have prayed, had he any remnants of faith left to him—that he was wrong.

All of which meant that he *had* to get a look at whatever it was that lay hidden beneath the snowy mound below.

Death had no way of telling how long it would be before the next constructs arrived. They appeared, not at set intervals, but whenever they had unearthed something of worth to deliver. Still, a few moments, at least, usually passed between arrivals; all he could do was to time the patrol of the five who lingered, and hope.

Two drones appeared, made their deliveries, wandered off once more; three of the patrolling constructs were positioned near enough to one another . . . And it was time.

From a jutting outcrop of frost-slick stone, Harvester spinning in lazy circles, Death leapt.

He landed hard on the middle of the three guards, crushing it deep into the snow and ice. The impact alone might have been sufficient to shatter the magics that animated it, but Death was never to know. He'd landed in a crouch, not merely on his feet, but on his left hand—a hand that clutched half of Harvester, now formed into an impossibly thick and long-bladed knife that punched through the rock as easily as flesh. The runes scribed across the drone's body flared brightly and died.

Even as he landed, Death leaned to the right and thrust with his second weapon, currently in the form of a long, narrow spear. It, too, blasted through the carapace, this time of the construct to the right. The wound itself was narrow, not sufficient to kill instantly.

The thickening of the haft, and the blade punching through the construct from within as Death allowed the two weapons to meld back into a single scythe, *were* sufficient.

The last of the three, to Death's other side, had only just

turned to face him when the Horseman swung Harvester overhead, right to left, the dead drone still impaled upon the blade. It crashed into its target, slicing stone, and both bodies cracked into scores of lifeless chunks.

Three down, and the snow kicked up at Death's landing hadn't yet settled back to earth.

The last pair of drones, the two that had not been standing just beside the others, instantly split off in opposite directions. One moved toward the intruder at a rapid charge, while the other scurried off behind the nearest stone outcropping— whether to work its way around and attack from behind or to fetch reinforcements, Death couldn't know.

A quick mental call, and then Death's left fist shot out- ward. Again Harvester had split, as swiftly as its wielder could think it, now forming the familiar pair of smaller scythes. One spun from the Horseman's hand, whistling as it flew, and two of the charging drone's legs fell from its body at the blade's kiss. It tumbled hard, sending up a puff of snow. It shuddered, struggling to drag itself forward with its arms and its one re- maining pair of legs . . .

The scythe flew from beneath its bulk to merge once more with its other half, meeting Death in midair as his second leap carried him from the carapace of one drone to the side of an- other. Harvester was now a square-headed maul, a hammer so oversized it was almost—*almost*—comical.

Although the wounded creature crushed beneath its bulk, shattered into granules and tiny chunks that were swiftly bur- ied by the swirling snows, probably wouldn't have thought so.

A sepulchral wail arose from nearby, and only Death rec- ognized the sound for what it was. The fifth and final construct hurtled back into view, trailing tiny slivers of stone. It landed on its back, legs thrashing, exposing a pair of hoof-shaped im- pressions gouged into its chest. It might easily have flipped itself over with its arms, had Death not casually brought the maul down once more, pulverizing the thing.

Harvester was a scythe once more before the dust settled.

"Thank you," Death said.

Despair snorted, trotting from around the outcropping, churning snow and drifting mists clouding its hooves.

"Dust!"

Dust stuck his head out from where he'd buried himself in Despair's stringy mane. Death hadn't the first idea when the crow had sheltered there, and wasn't about to give the wretched little beast the satisfaction of showing his surprise.

"Make yourself useful, bird. Keep an eye out for anyone coming our way." Then, after a brief but vitriolic tirade of screeches, "Yes, it's cold and windy and you won't be able to see very far. Do it anyway."

Death waited until the angry squawking had faded, directed Despair to stand guard at the largest entry to the off-shoot valley, and once more planted Harvester shaft-first in the snow. At a languid pace that might, in anyone else, have signified reluctance, he approached the hill of snow.

He raised his arms, hands outstretched as though to rip the clouds from the sky. Sounds that were scarcely syllables, let alone words, rolled dully from behind the faceless mask.

A trio of ghouls, very much like those he'd left working on his home, burst from the snow as though they'd been buried here, rather than worlds away. Instantly they fell to, chucking snow between their legs with both hands very much like digging dogs. A second chant, and skeletal arms slithered up from below, also working to scoop away the thick, freezing skin of the hill.

And finally, Death lowered his left arm, reaching out with his right. The air blurred and darkened, rather like clear water filling slowly with ink. The blackness spread, bulging and growing, until it formed a ghostly hand many times the size of Death's own. Darkness dripped from its hazy borders; tendrils of shadow linked it to the Horseman's own fingers. With slow but steady strokes, the massive appendage made swift work of the mound's slope.

In a surprisingly short time, the guts of the artificial hillock were exposed to the open air. Death snapped his fist shut, dispersing the hand of shadow and dispatching the skeletal limbs back whence they came. The ghouls he chose to maintain a while longer, sending them to aid Despair in guarding against unwanted company.

The bulk of the stockpile consisted of demonic corpses, frozen and preserved since the days of the Nephilim rampage. A few of them, disturbed by the digging, tumbled off the heap to sprawl near Death's feet. Most were imps, the lowest of the demonic castes: flamecallers, duskwings, the occasional shadowcaster. These he ignored. A rare few were of greater power—primarily the Knights of Perdition and their Hell-spawned mounts, twisted shadows of the Horsemen themselves—and these he carved apart with Harvester, just in case a spark of life might linger even after all the gruesome wounds and all the centuries.

Why the enemy would want the bodies of the demons gathered, the Rider wasn't certain. Study? Examination of their fangs and claws, or the wounds that had killed them? A search, perhaps, for weapons or parts of weapons that might have been lost *inside* their victims?

Or simply a means of clearing them out of the way for a more arduous, meticulous search?

He dug deeper, ignoring the acrid stench of dead demon, clear through the freezing ice and the thick, oozing sludge that had once been half a dozen varieties of unnatural blood. And at first, he was relieved. Blades and cannons, pistols and shields, and all manner of far more peculiar devices—these he found, mostly in bits and broken slivers, only occasionally whole. Yes, they might have located Affliction this way, and perhaps a few other usable weapons, but nothing nearly so catastrophic as he'd feared.

Hope was not a feeling to which Death was accustomed. He rarely had any *reason* to hope for anything, and even more rarely was he sufficiently optimistic to do so. But he began to hope now, to believe that, just maybe, he'd grown alarmed over nothing.

It was a pleasant feeling, for the precious few moments it lasted. Until he reached the innermost layers of the constructs' stockpile.

They were almost invisible among the demon corpses: a few strips of leathery flesh, molded into handles and grips; mechanical components of bone and steel, the one blending seamlessly into the other; and even smaller bits, unrecognizable save for the quivers of wrath and loathing Death felt beneath his touch.

Pieces, but no traces of the whole.

So . . . The enemy had found at least one of them. Still, they might not know what they had, might think it just another peculiar artifact of that long-ago war. And they almost certainly couldn't know how to use it. How to wake it up.

Almost certainly.

For some time, Death stood and stared, unseeing, at the pile of refuse that was swiftly being reclaimed by the falling snow. Stared, and deliberated.

He could search for leaders among the constructs, living beings who directed their operations, but such a plan didn't offer great odds of success. If there *were* any such commanders present, they'd almost certainly have been here, at the center of it all. No, more likely—now that the drones were clearly in the final stages of their endeavors here—they'd simply been left with instructions, while the true enemy moved on to the next stage in their schemes.

Try to follow them? He and Despair could certainly step through the walls of the world, but even Death's powers and senses couldn't tell him where the gate had led.

Wait for it to become active once more, and either ambush those who appeared or follow them back to their point of origin? Workable, except that the Horseman had no way of knowing how long that might be. He could find himself sitting around, accomplishing nothing, for quite some time—and again, all that while the enemy's own strategies would be advancing apace.

No, he'd have to act *now*. He was just contemplating a journey to the realm of the Charred Council itself, where he might beg their assistance in tracking the absent gate's destination—much as he hated being reliant on them, or anyone else, really—when the decision was taken abruptly out of his hands.

Still circling above, fighting the drafts with wings dusted in filthy snow, Dust went berserk. Piercing cries rent the air and the ears, high and angry, sharp as Harvester itself. The black-feathered shape plummeted, falling as much as diving, pulling up at only the last instant before he would have plowed painfully into the mountainside. He circled Death over and over, wings flapping with unnecessary fury, squawking so frantically he must surely bring the rest of the construct army down on their heads.

That, and quite possibly an avalanche of prodigious proportions.

"What? *What?*" This was no mere alarm, no warning of a few approaching enemies; of that, Death was certain. As the crow refused to calm, the Horseman watched, timing his flight—and then snatched him from the air with an impossibly swift hand.

And very nearly let the bird go again. Death staggered back with an involuntary cry as a barrage of images crashed through his mind.

Blood. Pain. Flashing blades. Jagged paths and winding stairs. Stone columns taller than any mountain, precarious ledges over-looking a drop so high that clouds drifted below as they passed. Unnatural lights of violet hues and flocks so thick they choked the sky.

A great hall, impossibly vast. A broad floor, slick with ice, and a god-like dais. Everywhere, everywhere, the fluttering of black feathers and the endless screech of an avian chorus a thousand strong.

And at the center of it all, a face of impossible age, lined and leathered as a well-worn saddle, bushy of beard though bald of pate.

A face Death knew well.

The waking dream faded, the world of ice and snow coming once more into focus. Death peered down at the crow, now huddled—shaking but no longer frantically flapping—in his open palm.

"I was not aware," he said darkly, "that you and he still shared any sort of link. Funny how he didn't bother to mention that when he bound you to *me*."

Dust cawed miserably.

"I should leave him to his own fate," the Horseman muttered. But even as he spoke, he knew he wouldn't. Not because he felt any particular affinity, but because the Old One— perhaps the *oldest* of the Old Ones—could prove useful.

And even more, because the blades appearing in the series of images, though seen only briefly, looked very much to him like brass. Like the malleable limbs of the four-armed gilded soldiers Sarasael's spirit had described.

The ghouls Death had summoned collapsed back into the

snow, and out of Kothysos entirely. Despair appeared an instant later in response to the Horseman's silent call.

"Very well, Dust," Death said. "Let's see what dares to trouble your Father in his own home. And maybe, depending on what he decides to tell me, I'll be able to decide whether I should assist him or kill him myself."

CHAPTER SIX

I T HAD BEEN DIFFICULT, AT FIRST, TO TELL THAT HE'D crossed between worlds at all.

The biting, predatory chill; the gusts so cold they nearly congealed into a solid mass; the flurries of swirling snow . . . All were as much a part of where he had gone as where he'd been.

But where the snows of Kothysos were thick, sludgy, discolored by waste and corruption, these were pure, as white as angels' wings. Here was not the sapping cold of the blizzard, but the raw sharpness of the highest peaks.

Death and Despair had emerged from the emptiness between worlds at the very edges of the Crowfather's domain. The ancient hermit's eldritch defenses would allow nobody, not even the Horsemen, to materialize any nearer. From there, under clouded skies as gray as any headstone, Rider and mount had traveled the meandering canyons of jagged rock that ran beside the mountains' roots. For long hours, Despair had galloped tirelessly, carving hoofprints into the cracked, icy surface. Slowly, a thickening of the grim overcast began to suggest the fall of twilight—except, Death realized almost instantly, what he saw wasn't twilight at all.

The heavens ahead were not darkened, but obscured.

Spreading in all directions like an oily stain came a roiling mass blacker and heavier than any storm. Crows. Uncountable, perhaps infinite, crows.

And not merely these, the Crowfather's chosen, but multiple pillars of twisting smoke choked the skies as well. Even from such a distance, the occasional sharp crash or ringing clatter of battle wafted over the open ground. Flashes of searing light silhouetted the swooping flocks, or the occasional gleaming figure both down in the canyon and up atop the towering ridgeline.

The Horseman ordered Dust into the air, though he knew that the snow and the sheer population of those skies might prevent his companion from observing much of use. He and Despair had then charged headlong for the base of the nearest cliff.

It was clear immediately that the mount could go no farther. Continuing along the canyon floor would have been *asking* to be spotted by the dozens of constructs atop the mountain ledges. Death would have to proceed on higher ground; yet the looping switchbacks, narrow shelves, and perilous climbs could not possibly provide purchase for hooves, no matter how dexterous or unnatural. Harvester strapped to his back by a leather baldric that hadn't been present only moments before, Death had slid from the saddle and begun his ascent.

Although the peaks and ledges were crawling with the metal soldiers, their spinning supports providing uncanny balance, Death had faced little opposition during his ascent. He came across several fallen constructs wedged into crannies in the rock, their brass-and-stone carapaces marred by scores of scratches, small yet deep. The crows descended upon the invaders, and the power of the Crowfather bestowed their talons and beaks with more than enough strength to wound the unliving invaders.

The birds themselves, despite their numbers, could never

have defended the domain alone—but they were *far* from their master's only defenses. Seemingly mild breezes abruptly froze attackers solid, or gusted violently enough to hurl them over nearby precipices. The air sizzled and cracked as bolts of lightning gouged the cloudless skies, somehow missing the massed crows, to obliterate throngs of constructs. Rock faces that had stood unyielding for millennia crumbled at the worst possible time, burying invaders by the dozens; fire erupted from the deepest caves.

The Crowfather's mastery of his domain was nigh absolute, and for a time it appeared that Death's presence would prove superfluous. As he progressed across the cliffs, however, the quantity of brass soldiers didn't seem substantially reduced. The Horseman began to wonder just how *anyone* could have assembled such an enormous host of construct soldiers. It should have taken centuries, and surely the Charred Council would have become aware at some point!

Slowly but steadily, Death had neared the Crowfather's abode, ducking low in the mountain passes and sheltering behind outcroppings to avoid numerous battles he could almost certainly have won, but which would have caused unnecessary delay. Unfortunately, he'd finally come across a band of the enemy that he could not easily avoid.

Death found himself clinging like an oversized spider to the underside of a jagged stone spur—a slanted outcropping on which half a dozen of the automatons perched—hanging above a drop deep enough to have been the gullet of the world itself. Below were only drifting clouds and a cracked canyon floor so far away it was all but invisible unless the light and the overcast collaborated *just* so. Fingers and the toes of his boots jammed into any available crevice, clutching with a tireless strength, Death chose to stop peering down at a drop that might just kill even him, should he fumble but once.

Atop that thick protrusion, several of the four-armed constructs circled in perfect military formation, brass hands formed into long blades and heavy bludgeons. The spindles on which they balanced whirred, cutting thin paths into the snow and layers of guano that coated the rock. Although they, like their stone brethren, were headless, the slow back-and-forth rotation of their torsos suggested a methodical patrol.

The Horseman had hoped to sidle along the cliff face and pass beneath them, continuing on unnoticed, but the contours of the terrain now thwarted his plans. Up ahead, the canyon opened further, providing a clear line of sight to distant ledges occupied by yet more of the stone-and-metal men. They would spot him easily enough once he emerged from the shadow of the overhang, and while Death didn't believe they had pistols or cannons, he didn't know what means they had of communicating with one another. If they were to alert their compatriots on the spur overhead, they might have some means of attacking over the edge from above—and Death could find himself too busy hugging the stone to fight them off.

Better, then, to abandon stealth and take them before they could pose a threat.

He tried to listen to the creatures moving above, but the gusting winds, the deafening cries of a thousand avian throats, and the thickness of the stone itself made a mockery of his efforts. That the enemy was watching, he had no doubt—but precisely where, or in what number, he just couldn't say.

So be it. Death had a very simple doctrine for just such a circumstance: When in doubt, strike first and kill *everyone*.

Scuttling sideways until he reached the edge of the protruding stone, the Horseman reached his left arm upward. He felt about until his questing fingers found a crevice on the spur's side that would hold his weight, sank his fingers as deep as they would go, and let go with his other hand and both feet.

For an instant he dangled, his fingertip grip all that kept him from a dreadful plummet. Then, with a single flex, he hauled himself up until he could reach the fingers of his *right* hand up and over the stone. With one last exertion, he brought his left hand up again, so that he hung from the top of the outcropping, and lifted until he could just see over the edge.

He found himself staring at a veritable *thicket* of brass spindles.

One of the automatons was almost directly before him, and it was a stroke of fortune that its attentions were currently directed elsewhere. Numerous others, well over half a dozen, stood at intervals in both directions. Even if Death could hold them off, with their sheer numbers and the limited breadth of the ledge, they could easily bottle him up for a good while.

All the more reason to deal with them swiftly, then.

Again Death let go with his right hand, hanging solely by the left. Harvester tugged itself from his back, the strap vanishing, and flew to his waiting fist. At the whim of its wielder, the potent weapon altered itself once more—not any dramatic change of shape, this time, but simply a dulling of the blade, transforming itself into more of a heavy hook than a scythe. The Horseman hauled himself up to the edge on his left arm, swung Harvester in a high arc, and yanked with all his strength.

The blade sank into the torso of the nearest construct, screeching like the newly damned as metal grated on metal. Rather than slicing through, Harvester instead jerked the brass-coated soldier over backward. For a split second it only wobbled—that spinning base provided an unnatural degree of balance—and then it toppled. The headless shoulders struck with a deafening clang, bouncing once or twice off the unyielding stone.

In that same sharp tug, Death sent himself sailing up and over the edge of the outcropping. He didn't fly high, propelled as he was with only the strength of one arm, but he didn't *need* much height. He tucked his legs under him as he rose, and then thrust down hard in a full-bodied leap.

His boots struck the torso of the construct he'd just brought down, hard enough to dent the carapace. The Horseman shot overhead, well beyond the reach of the enemy's longest weapons, somersaulting forward as he soared. Harvester's edge sharpened instantly, and the weapon sprouted a *second* blade on the opposite end of the haft—becoming, in effect, an elongated *S* with a perfectly straight centerline.

The force of the impact was also more than sufficient to send the fallen construct flipping end over end off the edge and down, down, until it was lost from sight, but Death had already forgotten about it.

He was spinning as he landed, knees bent to absorb the shock, Harvester whirling around him, blades circling in a deadly orbit. Again metal shrieked and shredded, and the five nearest constructs, only just turning to the attack, collapsed to the stone in a scattered collection of parts.

Only two of the squad remained; two that should hardly have been a problem, where the prior six were not. But for all his acumen, Death had never seen these things in battle, had only their clumsier six-limbed compatriots by which to judge.

And he badly underestimated just how quickly they could move.

By the time Death had come out of his spin, Harvester raised, the remaining pair were already upon him. The bits and scraps of their fallen allies proved no impediment at all. The whirring spindles dodged past the bulk of them without the slightest hesitation, and even launched the constructs in surprising leaps *over* the worst of the detritus. It was a peculiar hopping motion, almost silly looking, but startlingly effective.

They advanced together, synchronized as though guided

by a single mind, each swinging all four of its hand-blades in one violent flurry. They rushed in, *leaned* in to the attack.

Death was more than swift enough to parry the array of blades with the haft of Harvester, but there was nothing he could do to mitigate the sheer *momentum* of the attack. The impact lifted him off his feet and drove him up and out . . .

Clear of the ledge, suspended for an eternal instant over the shattering drop—and then gravity began hauling at him with avaricious hands.

Before his knees had fallen below the level of the rocky surface, the extra head on Harvester flipped itself around, so that both blades now pointed in the same direction.

As the topmost blade passed the pitted sides of the thick spur, Death sank it deep into the stone, far deeper than any natural blade could have pierced.

He loosened his grip, allowing his own fall to continue even as Harvester stuck fast, until his hands had almost reached the second blade. Then he clamped down and simultaneously kicked his legs out in front of him. The blade slid through its niche in the stone, serving as a pivot, and Death was swinging forward *beneath* the jutting finger of rock.

A fearsome yank both dislodged the first blade and sank the second one into the *opposite* side of the overhang. Kicking out once more and curling his arms, he knifed his body upward at an angle that none but the most agile of angels could have duplicated. He released his grip on Harvester, which remained dangling from the rock, tucked into a backward roll, and landed in a crouch back on the outcropping, *behind* his attackers.

Again they rotated to face him with blinding speed, but this time he was ready for them. Rather than try to block the brass swords that swung his way—he couldn't even if he'd wanted to, as his weapon was still lodged tight and dangling from the pitted rock—he fell backward, bending at the waist.

The blades hissed over his head in less than the blink of an eye—two of them, four, six . . .

Death reached up, balanced at a backward angle that even he could not hold for long, and snagged the fourth wrist on each of the two constructs as they passed. He gave each a solid tug, crossing his arms over his chest . . .

And sank each blade into the torso of the opposite construct.

They both froze, the animating magics trying to cope with the sudden damage. While those wounds alone might not, perhaps, have proved sufficient to destroy the creatures, the crossed arms provided enough leverage for Death to haul himself upright once more. Then, using only two fingers on each hand, he shoved both the metal soldiers at the shoulder and sent them plummeting over the edge as they had done to him. They twisted and spun as they fell, still locked in each other's death wounds, until he could see no further trace of them.

"Hmm," he grunted, watching for a long moment after they were gone. Then, as the cliff was clear at least in the immediate vicinity, he called Harvester up from where it hung and continued on his way.

THE FARTHER HE PENETRATED into the Crowfather's realm, the more numerous the enemy became—but so, too, did the domain's defenses grow more potent. The crows seemed more plentiful than the stars in the night sky, and while most were of a normal build, an occasional deafening cry or the flap of a wall-thick wing suggested avian defenders of truly prodigious size. Winds froze everything in their wake; lightning spiked and stabbed, a veritable forest of blinding bolts; and the mountains themselves had begun to shake with the crash of falling avalanches and slamming gorges.

So yes, the constructs were many, but Death himself was

forced to deal with few indeed, and most of those were sufficiently distracted that he had little difficulty in taking them unawares. The Horseman ran, crept, climbed; Harvester rose and fell, sometimes a single great scythe, sometimes two, occasionally some other weapon entirely; and enemy after enemy dropped.

Now, not too terribly long after the clash on the protruding spur, Death neared the heart of the matter.

Just ahead, almost undetectable against the natural jagged lines and projections of the canyon walls, a great tower of worked stone jutted from the depths. It rose overhead, impossibly, unreasonably straight and sheer, so that any glance up into the blackened sky felt like a vertiginous drop into infinite depths. Seemingly natural bulges and niches served, to all purposes, as supporting arches, flying buttresses, embedded columns. Patches of ice glistened in what little remained of the light, adding the only sparks of color to what was otherwise a stew of shadowed blacks and rocky grays.

Death scrambled down the cliffs, allowing himself to drop a great deal of the way, then bolted for the tower's entrance—a gaping maw of a cave in the rock face—at a dead sprint. The few constructs that stood in his way were clustered together within the hollow, drifting slowly forward, focused on guarding against attacks from before, not behind. Death swept through them without slowing, Harvester cutting them down or hurling them from the edges, and not one managed a single stroke in return.

Just inside the cave mouth, a great sculpture of a crow stared impassively at them all from its perch half embedded in the stone. Beyond *that* lay only shadow and frost.

And still no small trek. Death briefly cursed the Crowfather's paranoia and egotism both, and continued.

Through frigid corridors so high that he could scarcely see

the ceiling, through barren chambers in which the shapes of things long dead were only just visible within the ancient ice, and finally through a cavern so vast it generated its own currents and winds, the Horseman traveled. In that last, he picked his way between jutting rocks and fierce stalagmites, sliding across great sheets of slick frost. Feathers formed a sporadic carpeting, and the entire cavern smelled of guano and—despite the eternal cold—growing things from deep within the earth that no sentient beings of any world had ever seen.

He ignored them all, walking until the great pillar at the cavern's center—a column of calcification and ice as thick as a hill—had come and gone. Until finally, *finally*, Death came to an open cave mouth at the grotto's end, passed through to the stairs beyond, and began once more to climb.

CHAPTER SEVEN

I T WOULD HAVE PROVED SIMPLEST AND MOST EFFICIENT, OF course, if War could simply cross over into the White City directly beside his objective. Unfortunately, the angels—like the Charred Council, and several of the other great powers of Creation—were paranoid of their many enemies infiltrating through precisely such methods. They couldn't *prevent* him from doing so, not as the Charred Council did, but the White City boasted sufficient wards and safeguards that the entire population would be alerted to his presence if he were to so materialize. And not only aware; they'd almost certainly assume, due to his means of arrival, that his intentions were unfriendly.

Whereas, if he arrived formally, they'd only *suspect* that his intentions were unfriendly.

So he appeared from the void between realms atop the great bridge and moved openly toward the gates of the White City. Nor, this time, was he alone.

The Rider sat atop a horse of phenomenal size, bulging with an almost overdeveloped musculature beneath hair of such rough gray it appeared to be granite. Indeed, perhaps it *was* granite, in places—for the horse's lower legs and hooves were cracked like the plains of the Charred Council's abode, showing the glow of a molten core within. Gouges in the flesh along the neck and flank, shaped into runes of ancient mien, shared that fiery radiance, as did the beast's eyes and nostrils. The saddle on which War sat was as much steel as leather; the bridle, like Death's, was a chain, though this one was thick and free of blemish or rust.

Patches of bridge blackened beneath the beast's hooves. It gave a guttural snort, as though in satisfaction.

"Easy, Ruin." For his mount, War's voice turned as gentle as it ever got—which wasn't very. "No enemies here."

Ruin's low whinny sounded disappointed. War almost chuckled.

"Have no fear. There should be plenty of chaos and blood for the both of us soon enough."

The span on which they trod was a gleaming gold, near enough to blind anyone who spent too long gazing down. Sweeping arches provided the bridge its support, while spouts with no natural source provided scintillating waterfalls between each arch. They flowed from the bridge itself, plummeting into depths unseen. It was musical, in its way, that constant rush.

Rocky outcroppings stood beside the bridge, boasting an array of knotted trees and thriving brush. Great statues of warrior angels, the stone worn and pitted by the flow of centuries, towered three or four times War's own height from a few of those crags. They made, so far as the Horseman was concerned, unimpressive guardians. Grand in design, perhaps, but he would have expected a martial community to have *live* sentinels upon the bridge.

His first sight of the city itself was not the wall, but the highest of the flying isles. These small parcels of earth floated freely overhead, not merely ignoring but actively mocking a great many natural laws. They were jagged at the base, rather like mountains flipped upside down, and housed various fortresses and towers atop them. From this distance, War could make out few details, either of those structures or anything else. The faint shape of wings, flapping around the islands, might have been either angels or great birds for all he could tell.

Nor did his attention remain on those for long, for it was only moments later that the ramparts themselves hove into view.

The lines and angles—windows and cannon ports, embossed emblems, and of course the gate itself—gleamed in the light, though not so brightly as the bridge. These looked more brass than gold, due to that contrast, but War knew well that they were far sturdier than either metal. The walls themselves were of some pale stone; not quite like marble but, at least in War's personal experience, even less like anything else. These, too, were carved and inlaid into sharp panels and inset layers, so that the entire bastion was a work of art. The ramparts were too high for War to see if any guards stood atop the wall, just as the cannon ports were too narrow to expose anyone within, but he felt certain they were present. The angels might leave the bridge unwatched, but never the gate itself.

The light, War could not help but notice, was purely ambient, radiating from all directions at once. Although the world was noon-bright around him, he saw no sun in the sky, nor any shadows falling across the luminous roadway. It was almost uncomfortable, in a way. The wall stood several dozen paces in height, the ornately sculpted barbican more than twice that. The approach *should* have been cloaked in deepest shade, yet there was none.

The portcullis was raised, presenting a long and seemingly empty corridor that cut straight through the impossibly thick

wall. As Ruin approached, however, hooves ringing metalli-
cally on the bridge, War heard the blast of a great trumpet.
Almost instantly his path was blocked by a small phalanx of
angels, all heavily armored and clutching the race's infamous
halberds. Wings flapped above, as other soldiers appeared from
over the wall, and though he couldn't see them War could
somehow *feel* the barrels of a multitude of cannons gaping his
way.

That's more like it, then.

The guardpost's commander—War knew him to be the
commander, as he was the only angel whose face and platinum
hair were unconstrained by any helm, and who carried a great
axe rather than a halberd—marched ahead of the others. He
planted himself directly in Ruin's way, and War couldn't quite
restrain a nod of respect. Not only did the angel handle his
bardiche easily, never mind that the weapon was twice his
height with a blade broader across than the warhorse's girth,
but he showed no qualms about standing before a potential
adversary whom he *knew* was far deadlier than he.

The portcullis remained up, but War knew well that it
could be dropped in the blink of an eye, if necessary.

"Horseman," the angel greeted him with a cold courtesy.

"Commander."

"What business has a Rider of the Charred Council in the
White City?"

"I'm to deliver a message."

Silence, then. Clearly, the answer didn't strike the angel as
a likely one, not with War, yet he had no formal standing that
would allow him to question the Horseman's word.

"To whom?" he finally asked.

"Not your concern."

Again, a moment of silence. The angel seemed at a loss.
Heaven and the Council were not at war. The Rider had of-

fered a legitimate purpose, and he wasn't legally *required* to tell the gate guards who the recipient might be. So, no formal cause existed to deny him entrance. On the other hand, the presence of a Horseman rarely, if ever, boded well for either the inhabitants or even the property unfortunate enough to find themselves in his vicinity.

In the end, however, angels were creatures of law, and the law was clear. With an obvious reluctance that bordered on the offensive, he stepped aside and waved for his warriors to do the same.

"Welcome to the White City, then, Horseman. May your sojourn be fruitful and blessedly free of any unnecessary delay."

War didn't even need to flick the reins, as Ruin clearly recognized the meaning in the corridor that abruptly sprouted between the armored figures. Mount and Rider passed beneath the portcullis, heads held high, and it would have been difficult to say which of the two more effectively conveyed the impression that far more magnificent sights than these had, in the past, failed utterly to dazzle them.

It was, for all that, an act, performed for the sake of the watching angels. Not even War could gaze upon the White City and not find himself a *little* bit awed.

The city was constructed in layers, as high as the clouds and deeper than the eye could see. Some of those layers consisted of the floating isles War had noted on his approach. Others were wholly artificial: entire neighborhoods, structures and roadways, built atop ornate pillars and graceful arches. Bridges and winding stairs connected one to another, though a few had crumbled from disuse, leaving several of the older isles and buildings isolated from the rest.

Courtyards, paved in geometric patterns, were surrounded by statues as tall as those on the bridge outside. The buildings . . . By Oblivion, the buildings! Towers that stabbed the sky, great cathedrals as broad and as tall as small mountains. All were made up of sharp angles or elegant archways, and all were of the same stone-and-gold construction as the outer wall. Only trees sprouting in the courtyards and the stained glass of the many windows provided any real color to the tableau.

Or rather, those—and the outfits of the angels who did *not* wander the White City in full armor.

Most of these were clad in flowing robes of deep reds and violets, though a handful wore green and a great many wore white—these last failing to stand out from the background as much as the others. Gold belts and ostentatious headdresses were common, as were slightly more subtle circlets.

War found it peculiar, contemplating non-warrior angels. Angel craftsmen? Angel couriers? Angel merchants? It was difficult to picture—but then, the race had the same needs as any other, did they not? The Horseman briefly found himself wondering what they used as currency, before deciding he didn't care enough to give it any real attention.

Even the *sounds* of the city were magnificent. Where the amalgamation of labors and voices in most communities formed an ugly, cacophonic drone, the conversations of the angels and the blare of distant trumpets produced an almost orchestral tenor.

Ruin marched along at a stately pace, War taking it all in, though he was careful never to be caught staring. The same could not be said of the angels. All those who passed him by, on foot or on the wing, stared until it seemed their eyes must burst. Most either took a couple of steps away or made a deliberate show of *not* doing so, but few showed any inclination toward approaching him.

Few, save the flight of five circling high above, who had been with him since the gate. Guards, doubtless, watching to be sure he started no trouble. Well, let them watch!

It occurred to War that he must be passing all manner of establishments: workshops and warehouses, shops and homes. Yet he could see no way of telling one from another. Every structure was grand and imposing, more magnificent than temples or palaces in most other worlds. Some boasted sigils in angelic script above or near the doors, and War assumed that these were sufficient to tell the angels what they needed to know. Other than those, he could find no pattern, nor any hint of what purpose any given building served.

And he had plenty of time to examine them, for his route could generously be called circuitous. Even though he'd chosen the most efficient and straightforward path to the structure that the Council's agents had dubbed his objective, he would be long in reaching his objective—because the most efficient that *he* could manage was still not efficient at all.

The angels had to transport goods and building materials, and they often played host to Makers or other Old Ones, so the vast majority of their structures were indeed accessible by bridge and by road. For their own part, however, the angels were creatures of the air as much as the ground, and the most direct path between this building and that, this district and that, was often open sky. War and Ruin, bound as they were by gravity, had to wend their way around entire neighborhoods, up and down multiple levels, for hours on end, to reach a destination that, for an angel, was only a few moments away.

Finally, just as War was growing truly irritated, and the wonders of Heaven had ceased to hold any appeal, he recognized the landmark for which he'd been searching. Recessed into a niche in the side of a great cathedral-like hall stood a particular statue. It, like nearly all the others, was the effigy of an angel, nearly three times War's height. Where most either crouched, as though kneeling to some higher power, or stood rigid in an attitude of endless vigilance, this one leaned forward as though just beginning to swing the massive sword it clutched in both hands.

Once he'd spotted that statue, he was to continue on, past the next intersecting bridge, to the first building on the right. There, if the Charred Council's informants had not deceived them, he would find Abaddon's hidden arsenal.

If the spies *had* deceived them . . . Well, War had no idea who the informants were, or what influence the Council held over them to command their assistance, but if he'd been lied to, the Horseman was quite prepared to spend decades tracking them down.

War was now several levels deeper than the gate. The web-work of bridges and platforms above were sure to give his "escorts" some difficulty in keeping an eye on him, though he knew they were still above, trying their best. He was certain, as well, that many of the passersby on the roadway were actually guards, watching over the covert installation. So, although he'd much have preferred an open and comprehensive reconnaissance of his target, he settled for halting Ruin in the midst of the intersection, glancing about as though trying to remember his way. From here, he could at least study his objective from the corner of his eye. Several angels grumbled as they were forced to detour around the massive beast, but none seemed inclined to challenge him directly.

It was unimpressive, so far as White City architecture was concerned. It was less than two hundred paces across; the sweeping walls and minarets were "only" the height of a great castle. It was, for an angelic structure, downright humble.

Its walls were of that same white stone, however, and the shuttered windows far too narrow to allow entrance.

The Horseman dismissed the gold-edged front door the instant he spotted it. Abaddon might not rely much on el-dritch defenses, according to the spies—a high concentration of magic would be too easily detected by rival White City factions—but he'd be an utter fool if the main entrance wasn't warded by *something*. It could be as simple as an alarm, or a trap of flame or cannon-fire; or as complex as a teleportation portal designed to transport visitors somewhere other than the building's interior. Those who had proper business doubtless had some means of deactivating the wards, or some hidden entrance elsewhere on the property. War didn't know, and hardly had the time to go searching.

So if the door wasn't an option . . .

The Rider twisted in the saddle to look back at the way he had come, and his teeth gleamed in a vicious grin.

CHAPTER EIGHT

At the terminus of the twisted stair, beyond a smattering of additional chambers, Death finally found what he sought.

A hazy cavern of equal parts ice and stone sprawled out before him, itself large enough to hold a small village. The wall gaped open at the far end, revealing an endless vista of snow-capped peaks. Rune-carved rings and crescents of metal, many of them hundreds of paces across, glowed with an inner light and rumbled with the grinding of metal on stone as they slowly rotated in and around each other across that gap. Some sort of orrery or timepiece, Death assumed, though any hint of its ultimate purpose escaped him.

From atop an array of columns, tiny against the creaking mechanism but still massive enough, more crow sculptures loomed, glaring down with eyes of gleaming scarlet.

And what they gazed upon was utter chaos. The ice-coated chamber swarmed with figures of brass and stone. Scores of them pressed forward, advancing on a single goal. Death couldn't see their objective, not from where he stood, but he knew full well who it must be.

Death hit the back of the formation, a veritable cyclone of blades. Harvester spun, metal parted, limbs and torsos and spindles fell. He moved constantly, dancing through gaps in the line through which he should never have fit. Each time one of the constructs spun to strike back at whoever had just obliterated the soldier next to it, their enemy was already gone, turning someone else into so much scrap.

The sheer press of numbers, however, meant Death could only push so far before he was hemmed in. When a formidable contingent of the automatons spun on their bases, turning to focus on the new danger from behind, he had no choice but to fall back several steps and reassess.

"Go away, Horseman!" The words were as rough and pitted as the stone of the walls, carried on an ancient and ill-used voice, yet they crossed the great chamber clearly. "I neither desire nor require your assistance!"

"You're welcome!" Death shouted back. The resulting grumble, though audible, *was* impossible to interpret.

Death warily surveyed the ranks of the enemy, drawing almost experimentally upon the necromancies at his beck and call. Three skeletal hands rose from the floor, which rippled like water around them rather than cracking like ice, and grabbed viciously at the constructs. The whirling spindles, however, proved too much for them; powdered bone flew, accompanied by a high-pitched whine, and then the hands exploded into fragments.

Summon the ghouls once more? The shambling corpses might occupy a few of the brass soldiers, but they'd be far too hemmed in to provide more than a mild distraction, and far too slow to compete with the flashing blades.

And while he had plenty of other magics on which to draw, he found himself reluctant to call upon them here. He wasn't entirely certain that they wouldn't harm the Crowfather himself, or at least do substantial damage to his abode, and if they should fail to end the battle, he might find himself too exhausted to continue.

So, no necromancy. He had to cross the battlefield. Death knew the sorts of powers the Crowfather could bring to bear, here in his own home. The pair of them standing side by side could easily repulse an army thrice this size.

He scowled behind the mask as he casually parried the first attack to come his way, ignoring the sparks that rained over him as brass blades skittered over Harvester. Yes, they could repulse the attack with relative ease, but only if he could get over there! Fighting isolated, as they were now . . . Well, the Rider had the utmost faith in his abilities, but it did him no good if the Crowfather fell before he reached the Old One's side. Such a thing *probably* wouldn't happen, but Death disliked even taking the chance. So, how . . . ?

Ah.

Death backpedaled, drawing the back rank of construct soldiers after him in loose formation. They weren't utterly mindless, these things; they approached slowly, carefully, wary of some trap or trick.

Harvester rippled in his hands, becoming a thin spear more than twice Death's own height. He took a few sharp jabs at the advancing enemy, as though determined to keep them at length.

And then he flipped the spear to an underhand grip, hefted it, and hurled the massive projectile as if it were the lightest of javelins.

Up and out it flew, arcing over half the assembled constructs, until it plunged straight down. It struck none of the enemy—its parabolic flight allowed more than sufficient opportunity for the speedy automatons to dodge aside, even on the crowded platform—and sank its tip deep into the floor, not merely through ice but through rock. It quivered briefly before it settled, jutting upward like some wayward sapling.

Even before that quivering had fully ceased, Death was sprinting straight at the nearest construct. His first bound carried him over the thrusting blades to the thing's shoulders, where the head ought to have been. From there he kicked off again, with more than enough force to send it staggering.

Like his weapon before him, Death soared over the enemy, beyond their reach. The Horseman knew, before he began his leap, that even his prodigious strength and dexterity weren't sufficient to carry him across the entire cavern; that if he tried, he'd come down smack in the middle of the enemy, and find himself more hemmed in than he'd been before.

But then, he wasn't *trying* to cross the entire platform. Not in a single bound, anyway.

Had it been any weapon less mystical, less potent, than Harvester, it could never have pierced the stone deeply enough to remain stable. Had it been any creature less agile than Death, he could never have targeted so minuscule a surface.

The Horseman's bound carried him perfectly into the center of the chamber, directly atop the waiting weapon. With his left foot only, he kicked off the end of the shaft, setting it once more to wobbling violently, tucking into a forward roll as he jumped. It wasn't nearly as high or as graceful an arc as the first—couldn't have been, what with the precarious launching point—but it was more than enough to carry him the rest of the way.

He landed awkwardly, slightly off balance, his feet at two different levels on what looked to be yet another staircase, but he recovered well before the startled constructs could even begin to react. An outstretched hand, a mental call, and Harvester jumped free of the stone and hurtled back to its master. It was once more a scythe by the time Death's fingers closed.

"Well, now that you're here," the Crowfather grumbled, "I suppose you might as well do something useful."

"Your gratitude and geniality make it all worthwhile," Death said, taking just an instant to absorb the new situation.

The Crowfather, perhaps the most ancient of the Old Ones and Creation's most notorious recluse, seemed unchanged from the last time Death had seen him, nearly five centuries gone by. The same wrinkled, bearded face he'd seen in his earlier vision peered out from a thick mantle of onyx-black feathers. He was clad, otherwise, in a drab robe, its hue so faded that it fell somewhere in the gritty overlap between brown and gray. The wrists of his spindly, age-spotted arms were chafed raw without apparent cause.

In one hand, he clutched a twisted walking stick that apparently served double duty as a cudgel. The other was raised toward the enemy, gnarled fingers and ragged nails curled into veritable talons. As he moved, Death could see that he wore *something* on a chain around his neck, but the robe and the mantle of feathers prevented closer examination.

He stood upon a raised dais in the shadow of the orrery. Behind him rose a great throne, carved from the living rock and adorned with uncountable effigies of . . .

"I see you're still going with crows," Death observed aloud. "Bold choice."

"Your sarcasm is unwelcome here, Horseman," the Crowfather rasped at him.

"Pity. It seems determined to follow me everywhere."

The old hermit opened his colorless lips, but whatever comment he might have made would have to wait. The animated soldiers surged forward once more.

They were clever enough not to advance in a single mass, where the sheer press of numbers would hinder their movements. They came, instead, in small squads of three or four, each group approaching the dais, and its defenders, from different angles. The bulk of the constructs waited at the base of the dais's steps, ready to plug the gap should any of their brethren fall. They came at Death and the Crowfather from every direction but directly behind, attacking on multiple fronts at once, their every strike orchestrated to leave their enemies open to a blow from some other quarter.

Against any normal foe, they'd likely have succeeded.

The Crowfather lashed out at the oncoming soldiers, and the world lashed out with him. A stab of a finger brought an icy gale from on high. It froze a trio of constructs solid, shredded a handful of others with razor-edged hail. Static, building in the swirling particles, gleefully arced from construct to construct, attracted to their metallic carapaces, searing holes through brass and blackening stone. A vicious slash was matched by the talons of a thousand crows; the clench of a fist summoned the permafrost and stones to wrap around a target and squeeze it into a shapeless lump. Every so often, one of the constructs drew uncomfortably near, having made it up the steps largely unscathed. At such times, the Old One swung his gnarled cudgel, striking with a force more than sufficient to crush metal and end their artificial lives.

He grumbled and groused under his breath throughout it all, as though engaged in some onerous but largely mundane chore that he'd much rather have shirked.

Given the constructs' speed and inhuman tenacity, it seemed just conceivable—not likely, but *possible*—that, had the Crowfather been alone, a few might have slipped past his defenses, both mystical and martial, to pose a true threat to his life.

Each time one of them so much as drew near, however, Death was there to block its path. Harvester spun in short, vicious arcs, blurring back and forth between one weapon and two. So violently did some of the constructs burst apart beneath the Horseman's assault that several other automatons were destroyed, not by any direct action of Death himself, but by the flying shrapnel that had once been their compatriots.

It was laborious, time-consuming work. It was painful, as even the Rider's astounding prowess couldn't shield him from *every* attack. Here and there, an edge sliced his skin, revealing only pale and mottled tissue below, without so much as a dribble of blood.

They never so much as slowed him down, and the outcome could never have been in doubt.

A final gust of chilling wind from above, a final cut of Harvester's ever-sharp blade, and the last of the brass legion lay scattered across the platform. The crows, screeching and fluttering, rose in a thick mass toward the vast temple ceiling. There they continued to circle, but the sounds of their passage were less cacophonic, less deafening.

The Crowfather shuffled to his throne and sank into it with a contented sigh. Death studied his every move, and only as the hermit settled did his guest spot the heavy chains bracketed to the floor just behind the throne, and the blocky manacles fastened at their other end. He turned his head, pointedly staring first at those, and then at the Crowfather's abraded wrists.

"None of your concern," the Old One snapped at him.

The Horseman nodded. The orange gleam of his eyes flickered briefly, passing from the Crowfather's wrists to the small bulge where he wore *something* on a chain beneath his robes. "I suppose you're entitled to your secrets."

"Oh, how *generous* of you. What are you doing here, Horseman? If I'd wanted guests, I would have—well, actually, I *never* want guests."

"*You* called me here, old man. Or at least, your little servant did."

"I? I've not the vaguest idea what you're—"

Death raised his arm and whistled. The sound pierced the crying of the crows, seeming to shatter their own screeching like a rock through stained glass. A moment, a flurry of feathers, and one particular bird swooped from the others to land on the outstretched wrist.

Dust squawked once, clearly adamant about making some point or other, and then began idly pecking at the loose flaps of skin around Death's nearest open wound.

"Ah," the Crowfather said.

Death took the few intervening steps at a methodical, inexorable pace, until he loomed over the Old One in his throne.

"When I came to you," the Horseman said, his voice dangerously soft, "and offered you the prize you so desired . . ." Again his eyes flickered toward whatever it was the hermit wore beside his heart. ". . . you told me that, to break its link to me and take it upon yourself, you would have to create a new bond, a symbolic tie between my soul and your own. Hence . . ." He raised Dust to eye level. The bird squawked again, dancing sideways to maintain his balance.

"Yes, I recall," the Crowfather said blandly. "I was there at the time."

"Apparently, you neglected to tell me that Dust also *remained* bound to *you*! I do not like being spied on, Crowfather. I'm inclined to take it personally."

"Oh, do get over yourself, Death. I've not been spying on you."

"No? How do I—?"

"Of course Dust remains bound to me." The hermit's lip curled as he spoke the name. He seemed unimpressed, ill amused with Death's choice—or even that the Horseman had felt the need to bestow a moniker upon the bird at all. "He's a crow. I am the Crowfather. Thus we are linked, until the one or the other of us is dead. I can observe the world through his eyes, feel what he feels, know what he knows. Such is the natural order.

"But," he continued as Death seemed about to speak, "I have not, and will not, take advantage of that link. Not with Dust."

"And I'm to believe this why, exactly?" Death's tone remained faint, but Harvester actually creaked beneath the pressure of his tightening fist.

"Because you are here, Horseman."

Silence, for a moment—or at least, silence between the two of them. The symphony of crows above sang as stridently as ever.

At last, the Crowfather coughed angrily, dragged his overlong nails on the arm of his throne with a high-pitched grating, and spoke once more. "Have you even the faintest glimmer of a suspicion that I desired your presence here, Death?"

"You made it fairly clear that you didn't."

"And yet, here you are. The only way you could have known something was amiss is through Dust."

The Horseman nodded brusquely.

"I did not make contact with him deliberately. He must have sensed, through our lingering bond, that I was engaged in most violent pursuits, that his brethren in my domain were afraid. And due to your link with him, you became aware of the situation soon after.

"Do you truly suppose, then, that you would not be equally aware if I were to make *deliberate* contact with Dust? The bond he shares with you is far stronger than that he and I still possess. I could not use him to spy on you without your knowledge. And as you would most assuredly never again leave me alone, I have not the slightest interest in making an enemy of you."

For long moments, Death studied the Old One, eyes blazing through the slits in his mask. And then, eventually, he gave a third and final nod.

"Very well, Crowfather. I'll accept that—for now, anyway."

"I'm *so* very delighted. Now, regarding that *leaving me alone* concept—"

"Not so fast." Death strode to the edge of the dais, then knelt to examine one of the deceased constructs. "We share an enemy, old man. I need to know what you know of them."

"I know that they are composed of stone and metal, and are very irritating."

Death turned back to his host. "You really want to be left alone? Your best way to accomplish that is for me to find out who's sending these soldiers, and cut them in half. To say nothing of the fact that you really don't want *me* to have reason to keep pestering you, do you?"

"Hrmp. Fine." The Old One drew himself up in his chair. "I truly do not yet know who sent them, Horseman, or how they even knew where to find my home! One of them told me—"

"They *spoke* to you?"

"Oh, yes. The first of them came as emissaries, not invaders. They wished to consult me on lore that nobody else had proved able to share with them."

Death felt a chill, colder even than his own dark soul, flutter like one of the hermit's crowfeathers against the back of his neck.

"I, of course, instructed them to depart immediately," the Crowfather continued. "With results that you have just witnessed for yourself. I imagine they intended to force me to speak, or to abscond with what information they could once I was dead. How little they knew me . . ."

"I've never before known these things to communicate," Death mused. "Could they have had a leader present? A sentient creature or a more advanced construct, giving orders? Speaking through them?"

"It's . . . possible." The Crowfather shifted, his robes and his mantle of feathers rustling. Had Death not known better, he'd almost have thought the Old One *embarrassed.* "I have not yet assimilated all the details of the intrusion. I see and know all that my crows do, and they observed far more of the battlefield than I. But they are many, and they are unaccustomed to violence of this magnitude. It may take me some time and concentration to sift through all their memories and impressions before I have all the facts in hand."

"And here I thought you were supposed to be all-seeing and all-knowing," Death taunted.

The Crowfather's face folded in a scowl so fierce that his eyes and lips utterly vanished among the wrinkly crags of his face. "Why don't *you* attempt omniscience for a while and see how easy it is for you to readily recall all the little details?"

Death wasn't entirely certain if he was being ridiculed, or if the Crowfather actually meant it—and he decided that this probably wasn't the best time to push the issue.

"You'll let me know if you learn anything?" he asked instead.

"Of course," the Crowfather said with a mocking bow. "I'll send a message through Dust. I would hate for you to feel any pressing need to return. Ever."

"And we were getting along so well." The Horseman gazed almost wistfully over the broken carapaces. "Hundreds of the dead, and not a damn one I can speak with."

"Oh?" For the first time, the hermit actually sounded interested. "They may be artificial, but they *are* living beings. Or they used to be, at any rate."

"But these are lesser constructs; *tools* of a Maker, rather than *children* of one. They've no soul. Nothing for me to call back from the dark. My necromancies might return a temporary false life to one of them, for a few moments, but it would make no difference. With no mind or soul, it wouldn't be able to do anything beyond lie there as though it *were* dead."

Again the Crowfather began tapping his nails—this time on his crooked front teeth. "I am perhaps the eldest of my kind," he said finally. "You know only a fraction of my power—and here, in my domain, that power is absolute."

"Not even you can just cook up a soul," Death protested. "Plants and animals, perhaps, but nothing sentient."

"Correct. *But...*" The Crowfather rose from his throne with surprising energy. Death almost thought the old hermit looked *excited*. "I can create my children." Here he waggled his twisted fingers at the crows overhead. "I customarily allow them to breed in the natural fashion, but I crafted them once, and I can do so again. To do *that*, to create not merely life but awareness, however animalistic, I must be able to manipulate the stuff of their own living spirit. Not souls, no, but perhaps near enough for our purposes.

"And as we were just discussing, my bond is such that I can commune with them *despite* their lack of sentience. So ... We need one of those."

Although still more than a little unclear on what the Crowfather intended, Death waded through the detritus until he located a construct that remained at least mostly intact. Heaving the massive weight over his shoulder with barely a grunt, he trudged across the chamber once more and let it fall at the Old One's feet.

"Excellent. Now, Horseman ... Observe, and become wise. Or wiser, at any rate."

The Crowfather closed his eyes, his lips moving in an inaudible mumble. At first, the only sounds in the great chamber were the grind and click of the orrery, and the occasional crack as dead constructs settled and split beneath their own weight. Until, eventually, a crow—initially indistinguishable from the thousands more who flocked above—dropped to land atop the hermit's walking stick. It sat, head cocked to stare at its master with a single gleaming eye, while he continued to murmur.

As Death watched, his curiosity enflamed, he gradually noticed that this was *not* precisely like any other crow after all. Its feathers were ragged, many missing entirely. Its beak was scratched and worn, and one eye—the one it had turned away from the Crowfather—was partly hidden behind a milky sheen.

This crow was old, not long for the world. And Death finally began to understand what the Old One had in mind.

It had, to his knowledge, never before been tried—probably *could not* be tried anywhere but here, in the core of the Crowfather's power. And certainly, Death reluctantly had to admit, it would never have occurred to him to make the attempt.

The bird bobbed its head once, in what the Horseman could have sworn was a deliberate nod. The Crowfather held up a hand, into which the crow hopped, and then cupped it tight in his other. His eyes squeezed more tightly still, until it seemed the lids must fuse, and then snapped wide open. A few feathers, all that could be seen of the bird he clutched, trembled once and lay still.

"Haste is essential now," the Crowfather announced. "I can only hold the crow's spirit a few moments before it must dissipate as any animal's would. Weave your necromancies, Rider of the Charred Council. Summon life, however temporary, however meaningless, however *mindless,* to this artificial creature. And *I* will provide the necessary essence."

Death had never practiced his magics on a soulless construct before. He'd never had cause; as he'd explained, without a spirit or a mind, there was precious little difference between dead metal or living metal. Still, the Crowfather was wise—if also eccentric, standoffish, rude, and overbearing—so it seemed sensible to give him the benefit of the doubt.

Besides, it wasn't as though Death had any better ideas.

The magics coursed through him as they normally did—if anything about breaching the barriers between life and death could be called "normal." He experienced the same sensations of cold and heat, fear and fury, that invariably accompanied his necromantic spells. It *felt* like it was working. He saw no reason it should not be working.

But he had no way to tell. Constructs did not breathe, did not bleed. Without a mind to tell it to act, it lay there precisely as it had when it was dead.

As Death neared the end of his incantation, the Crowfather knelt beside the construct, laying the little avian corpse on the ground behind him, and pressed a hand to the brass-coated rock of its chest. Death staggered as an unfamiliar magic intruded on his own, a second energy intertwining with the stuff of unlife.

"Keep your questions straightforward, Horseman. I may be able to commune with it, but it's still the mind of a crow. It may have difficulty with complex notions, or interpreting the memories of the construct."

"I have only a few. Who sent you here?"

The Crowfather once more closed his eyes, willing the essence of the bird within the carapace of the automaton to understand. For some time, nothing happened, and Death had begun to believe their process, innovative as it was, had failed, when . . .

"Our creator," the Crowfather intoned softly. "He says 'our creator' sent us."

"And who is your creator?"

Another pause, as the spirit grappled with understanding. Then the Crowfather actually reached out and poked the body with a finger. "No, not *me*. The creator of the metal creature! Its memories still reside within; sense them, know them . . . Yes . . .

"Belisatra. Their creator is Belisatra."

"I'm not familiar with that name," Death said.

"She's a Maker. A worker in stone and metal." The scorn through which his words struggled and swam left little doubt how he felt about such "lesser" Old Ones.

"Yes, I know what a Maker is, thank you."

"Well, how am I to know the limits of your ignorance? I've heard of her, but I've never felt any pressing need to study her."

"At least the name's a place to start. I—"

Death and the Crowfather shuddered as one at the sudden tug on their souls. "The spells are failing," the Old One whispered.

"Noticed that, did you?"

"Ask your questions! Quickly, while there's still time!"

"What was your purpose here? What did you seek from the Crowfather?"

It took so long for the avian spirit to wrap its mind around the concepts that Death was certain they must lose it before it could answer. Eventually, however, the Crowfather spoke again. "Some of the most ancient of lore. The means of awakening the relics of the Slaughtered Ones."

Even had the magics not been failing already, they would have ended at that moment, for the Horseman's concentration shattered like crystal on an anvil. It wasn't a term he'd heard before, but given the crow's limited vocabulary, he knew that the "Slaughtered Ones" could only mean his own people. The Nephilim.

I was right. Damn them all to Oblivion, I was right!

Death spun with an abrupt cry, hefting the construct— once again an empty, lifeless shell—and hurling it across the chamber. It crashed into one of the standing pillars, marring several of the ancient carvings.

The Crowfather's teeth clenched so that his beard began

to quiver. "The enemy hasn't inflicted enough damage on my home? You feel the need to assist them?"

The Horseman stood, shoulders heaving. The need to lash out burned in his soul; Harvester was in his hand, and he couldn't even recall summoning the weapon. Slowly, deliberately, he forced himself to calm.

Later. Plenty of time for anger later . . .

"What is it?" the Old One asked once Death had visibly composed himself.

"The Abomination Vault." His voice was barely a whisper, as soft as the Crowfather had ever heard it. "They're after the Abomination Vault."

CHAPTER NINE

I T HAPPENED SO FAST THAT NEITHER THE ANGELIC SENTInels circling above, nor the soldiers on the street, could do more than gape in utter astonishment.

A fearsome cracking, not unlike the shattering of some great peak, echoed from down the street, followed by shocked and fearful cries. Angels scattered in all directions, on foot and on the wing, hurling themselves clear of some sudden danger. Many were already recovering their wits, reaching for weapons, but to little avail.

Before the echoes of that crack had faded away from between the massive walls nearby, it was replaced and overwhelmed by what seemed, at first, to be the dull rumble of rolling thunder. The roadway shook, so that dust and bits of detritus sifted out over the edges—along with the occasional angel who hadn't yet taken to the air.

From the chaos charged War and his terrible mount. The flaming hooves of the beast seared their mark into the paving stones, and it was those swift, inexorable strides that shook the street beneath. Ruin galloped unrestrained, for the Horseman had no hand upon the reins. He held both high above his head, and with them he supported an inconceivable weight. The effigy of the lunging angel, larger than horse and Rider combined, carved of solid stone, would have required two or three of the White City's mightiest to lift it off the ground—yet it seemed scarcely even to *slow* the fearsome pair who carried it now.

The first shots began to rain down as the angels circling above took aim with their halberds. Between Ruin's speed and the intervening obstacles, however, only a few got through, and those accomplished little more than to dig chips from the statue. Only one or two of the guards on the street had shaken off their astonishment enough to open fire, and these had no success in penetrating either War's armor or his mount's toughened hide.

The building loomed before him, growing ever closer. War rose, standing in the stirrups. With a deep grunt he snapped his body forward, hurling the sculpture with all his unnatural strength. The massive projectile soared ahead of them to slam with devastating force, not against the door, but against the stone wall some few paces to the right of the entryway. The statue shattered into heavy chunks that bounced and skittered along the roadway. The wall itself was shot through with a cobweb of deep cracks and fissures, but it had proved thick enough to stand against the bombardment.

War didn't so much as slow. Hooves pounded against the road, the wall was almost upon them . . .

And Ruin leapt.

Twin trails of smoke marked his passage, sketching an impossible arc through the open air. The Horseman, still standing, whipped Chaoseater from his back. He spun it once, twice, and then leaned out over Ruin's head, the great black blade jutting forward like a lance.

At the apex of Ruin's flight, the split-tongued tip of Chaoseater seemed, almost gently, to kiss the already compromised wall.

Stone exploded inward in a billowing cloud of dust and jagged shrapnel. Angels, alerted by the sounds from outside and standing ready in the center of a great lobby, recoiled with a chorus of cries as they were briefly blinded, their exposed flesh slashed and bruised. A few fell under larger slabs of wall, crushed by enough weight that they would not rise again soon, if ever.

A couple of others were flattened by Ruin himself as he finally came down in the midst of the open chamber. Instantly he reared, hooves lashing out to crush cuirasses and helms, ribs and skulls. War laid about him to either side, wielding the massive Chaoseater as though it were a toy. Limbs, blood, wings, and feathers clattered and splashed across the walls.

Several of the angels opened up with their energy-spitting halberds, but between the clouds of dust and Ruin's constant rearing and prancing, few came anywhere near the target. Those that did were once again deflected by War's great armor. On occasion he would raise his left arm to shield his face from a particularly lucky shot, but otherwise he focused on killing.

A second fusillade nearly clipped him from behind, as the soldiers outside finally converged on the gaping hole in the building. At that same moment, from a balcony across the chamber, an angel took flight. This one carried not the small firearms War had faced so far, but one of the Redemption cannons for which the White City's artillery divisions were so infamous.

War snapped an order, and Ruin again broke into a charge across the lengthy hall. The first blast of the cannon slammed into the floor where they had stood just an instant earlier, leaving a smoking crater.

Again Chaoseater spun, once, twice—and War hurled the blade like a javelin. It should never have flown straight, not shaped and weighted as it was, but by now none of the Horseman's foes should have expected natural behavior from that awful blade. It sank through the angel's chest, spraying blood from front and back. With a cry that swiftly devolved into a wet, bubbling gurgle, the soldier plummeted.

Carried by his galloping mount, the Horseman passed beneath him as he fell. War rose up, snatching Chaoseater from the wound and the Redemption cannon from the angel's fists, and was gone before the body hit the floor.

"Stairs!" he barked, and Ruin obediently made for the broad and sweeping staircase against the far wall.

War slung Chaoseater across his back once more and slapped the butt end of the cannon to his shoulder. Left hand on the pommel of the saddle, he slipped his right foot from the stirrups and spun. He hung, now, off Ruin's side, held fast by left foot and left hand, facing back the way they'd come. The Redemption cannon roared, again and again, and those angels who'd been entering through the shattered wall crumpled in smoking heaps.

With a satisfied nod, War threw his leg back over the saddle, returning to his proper position and transferring the cannon to its intended—and far less awkward—two-handed grip.

The steps, sturdy but never intended to withstand this sort of physical and mystical abuse, splintered beneath Ruin's hooves. Horse and Rider swept up and around, following the curve of the staircase. War pumped shot after shot from the cannon either into the chamber below or toward the balcony above, wherever an enemy might appear. He wasn't killing *all* of them, certainly, but those he missed were apparently wise enough to take cover rather than try shooting back.

The balcony opened up into a hallway with multiple rooms to either side. The Rider knew, from the proximity of the doors to one another, that the chambers to either side were small— almost certainly *not* the laboratory itself, or the home of the sacrament bomb. He put multiple cannon shots through each door as Ruin bolted past, just to be sure, but never once slowed the horse's headlong flight.

It was not particularly defensible, this building. Large open rooms, straight corridors with no good choke points . . . Clearly, Abaddon had repurposed an existing structure, rather than building his own. And equally clearly, he'd been relying on secrecy and the laws of the White City as his primary defenses. Perhaps that made sense, given how determined he'd been to keep the entire project covert, but . . .

War sneered in contempt. The great general wouldn't be making *that* error again!

As he neared the end of the passageway, he spotted a door at the far end, larger and—at least by appearance—sturdier than the others.

And the angels very clearly did not want him passing through.

Several soldiers leaned abruptly out of the last two doorways on either side of the hall, sending a barrage of halberd- and cannon-fire in War's direction. The Horseman threw himself to the left, his grip on the reins and the saddle sufficient to topple Ruin along with him. The deadly bombardment whisked overhead, near enough to singe. War allowed the fall to throw him clear of the saddle and into the nearest of the empty rooms. He reached out and literally dragged his mount after him, barely wincing as the wall and floor around him shuddered with new impacts.

Once inside the room, Ruin clambered to his feet and snorted indignantly.

"I'll just permit them to shoot you next time, then, shall I?"

The horse tilted his muzzle away, the very image of wounded dignity.

"I thought not."

A quick glance was enough to tell War that the room in

which he'd sheltered was bare of anything even remotely useful. It had apparently been a study of some sort. The shots he'd pumped through the door as he passed had pretty well obliterated the desk, but the legs were still recognizable at the edges of a smoking hole in the floor.

If he stepped out into the line of fire, his armor and his own innate resilience would probably allow him to survive whatever the angels threw his way, at least long enough to reach them—but he couldn't be certain that he'd be strong enough to continue the mission afterward.

"I'd been hoping," he grumbled to Ruin, "to hold this in reserve for later, but . . ."

Carefully, he laid the cannon on the floor and drew his sword. He inhaled deeply, once, twice; his skin began to tingle and burn with power.

It was appropriately named, was Chaoseater. The havoc and carnage of battle *fed* the weapon, and what strength it gained, it passed to its wielder. War allowed that strength to settle in him, suffuse him—and then he called upon the magics that were his by right, as Nephilim and as a Rider of the Apocalypse.

Crouched low, War bolted into the hall. He moved fast, incredibly so, his hair and cloak streaming out behind him, twin banners of war. Again the enemy opened fire, but for a few precious seconds the Horseman was swift enough to weave through the fusillade.

He dived forward into a roll, coming up in a crouch directly between the four occupied doorways. The angels within hesitated, holding their fire lest they overshoot their target and wind up striking one of their fellows instead. And that moment of hesitation was all War required.

With a fearsome cry, he drove Chaoseater point-first into the floor, channeling a surge of magics through the blade. The hallway *rippled* for an instant, and then a forest of blades—

each similar to Chaoseater itself—burst from the floor in all directions. The steel thicket occupied several paces around the Horseman, more than enough to catch the angels gathered in the nearby doorways.

Only one died instantly, but the others suffered wounds grievous enough that they could do nothing but cry out as War approached. They did not suffer long.

This close to the corridor's end, War could make out further details of the larger room before him. The door seemed sturdy enough, but nothing he and Ruin couldn't manage. A window near that door had been largely bricked over, but it was still sufficient for him to judge the thickness of the wall—far less than the building's exterior, but sturdier than any other internal wall he'd seen thus far.

As fiercely as the angels had fought to keep him from this room, War couldn't imagine it would be unguarded within. So . . .

"Ready to go again?" he asked Ruin as he returned to fetch his mount and retrieve the Redemption cannon. He could have sworn that the horse actually glared at him. He chuckled and leapt into the saddle.

As soon as they were back in the hallway, War pointed at the far door. "Hit it low," he whispered. Ruin tossed his mane in acknowledgment.

Again the great beast charged, and again War rose. Without the first hint of difficulty or imbalance, he slid his right foot from the stirrup and placed it upon the saddle, so that he rode in a one-legged crouch. Then, as the wall drew near, he jumped.

Ruin dropped his front legs as he hit the door, smashing it open with his head rather than his hooves. As for War, a single blast of the cannon opened the wall *above* the door. The momentum of his leap carried him through as though he had an angel's wings himself.

The guards within were, of course, ready and waiting for the intruder to come bursting through the door. When Ruin came in beneath their anticipated line of fire, however, and War above it, it took them an instant to reorient themselves.

War's stolen cannon, and Ruin's thrashing hooves, denied them that instant. Half the guards were dead before the Horseman's feet had touched the floor.

A storm of vicious cuts with the fearsome black blade, a few blows that glanced harmlessly from War's armor, and the other half followed. War stepped over the fallen bodies, the rent armor, the limp wings, to study his prize.

He found nothing.

No superweapon of any sort, nor even any obvious components thereof. A few scratch-covered anvils and steel worktables encircled a central forge, but it looked as though few of them had been employed in recent memory. Only a single table showed any sign of use, and it held nothing but ammunition clips for Redemption cannons and small arms.

It would have been too easy, War supposed, to have found the main workshop in the first hallway of the second floor; the structure boasted scores of levels and literally miles of corridor. But then why had the angels been so determined to keep him out of . . . ?

Ah.

"I'm a fool," he said gruffly, laying a hand on Ruin's neck. "We'll need to rethink our—"

Horseman and horse cocked their heads as one, listening intently to the faint clatter of running footsteps and heavy equipment moving about on the floor above. Clearly, they were going to have to fight hard for every step they advanced above this level, and with so much of the building remaining to search, the odds of success—even survival—appeared abysmally low.

Despite his prior self-assessment, however, War was not

such a fool as to fall for the same trick twice. The angels had fought so hard to keep him from this room precisely *because* it contained nothing of value, and the same was almost certainly true of the many floors above. They *wanted* him wasting time and effort battling impossible odds in a game he could never win.

Time, then, to change the game.

His entire face seeming to burn with a sudden inner light, War scooped up the ammunition clips and jammed them into his belt. He hefted the Redemption cannon inelegantly with one arm, then knelt beside each of the fallen angels collecting yet more of the clips. Ordering Ruin to follow behind, he strode out into the hallway, listening carefully until he felt he'd located the largest concentration of guards on the floor above. The cannon alone wasn't powerful enough for what he had in mind, but then, he wasn't *using* the cannon alone.

Standing some few paces back, he tossed one of the clips in a gentle arc and, just as it hung in the air directly beneath the enemy, opened fire.

FROM THAT POINT ON, it was more a massacre than a battle.

On each floor, War blasted through the ceiling above, taking the enemy by surprise and, as often as not, killing a great many in the initial explosion. On occasion, the thick stone prevented him from hearing the footsteps on the next level, but Ruin's more sensitive ears never failed him.

The building did not boast all *that* many guards. Still, had every angel in the building converged on him at once, they might have stood a chance. Most were determined to stand fast at their posts, however, so that was where they died.

By the time War found what he sought, roughly two-thirds of the way through the building's many floors, the structure's outer walls contained as much debris as they did intact rooms and halls. War stalked down a wobbling corridor, stepping over chunks of stone and chunks of angel, his armor scratched and smoking from those few shots he hadn't managed to avoid. Acrid smoke swirled in his wake, leaving trails of soot where it passed.

The door, when he finally reached it, didn't stand out at all from any of the others. Indeed, the Horseman very nearly passed it by, until he noticed one tiny discrepancy. All the other doors were scarred and singed from the explosion that had obliterated whole swaths of the hallway. This one, other than a few ash-blacked blotches, was undamaged.

A blast from the Redemption cannon confirmed his initial assessment: The portal was *definitely* reinforced, perhaps mystically bolstered, to withstand attack. So much so, in fact, that it took three distinct blows from Chaoseater before it split down the middle. War stepped through the jagged gap, cannon held (albeit awkwardly) in one fist, sword in the other.

A peculiar hum, irritating as a mosquito trapped in the ear canal, permeated the room. War had no doubt that it came from the device that dominated the back half of the chamber.

It was a sphere of brass, so large that it would have required a score of angels, stretched fingertip-to-fingertip, to surround the thing. It was not, however, of a single piece; rather, the apparatus consisted of thousands upon thousands of tiny hexagons. These were not in any way sealed together, but simply hovered in their spherical configuration. At seemingly random intervals, a number of the hexagons would flip suddenly on one of their three axes. In that brief instant of rotation, War could catch the swiftest glimpse of the sphere's interior. It seemed full of an amorphous whiteness, less than a mist, more than a dream; similar, but not quite identical, to the void-stuff between realms.

This, then, was the sacrament bomb.

Standing between him and the weapon was a single angel,

her face a mask of determination. She held a blade nearly the size of Chaoseater in both hands, and her armor gleamed in the light.

She was also the youngest angel War had ever seen, barely out of adolescence.

"Does Abaddon employ children as sentinels now?" the Horseman asked.

Her features, if anything, grew harsher still. "I am *not* a child. I am Ghauniel's finest student!"

"And Ghauniel is . . . ?"

"Guarding the corridor." Her voice shook, despite her obvious efforts against it.

"Ah. And he never expected you to actually see battle on this assignment, did he? That's why he stuck you here, in the safest room."

"Maybe, but I know my duty. And you will not pass while I live."

War found himself smiling, though he struggled to hide it—for the sake of the young angel's pride, more than anything else. "What's your name?" he asked her.

"Uriel."

"Well, Uriel, I've no interest in killing children, and you have to know you've no chance. Stand down, and let me do what I must. Nobody will blame you."

"I know my duty," she repeated stubbornly.

"So be it."

Uriel hurled herself across the room with a fearsome cry, wings propelling her like a living missile.

War knocked her sword aside with Chaoseater, then blasted it from her hand with a point-blank shot across the blade from the Redemption cannon. Uriel staggered, half blinded and buffeted by the detonation. She was completely open, and War was never one to let an opportunity pass him by.

Yet, at the last instant, he turned Chaoseater on edge, so

that it was the flat of the blade that cracked across Uriel's temple. She dropped in a heap, but she breathed still. War could almost hear the weapon wailing its disappointment.

"You have spirit, girl. Given a few centuries of experience, I'd be honored to face you in *real* combat."

As for his purpose in coming here, disposing of a weapon that harmed only demons, while it sat in the middle of the White City, was simplicity itself. A few moments of study, and War located the hidden controls: a sequence of those spinning hexagons of slightly darker hue, each sporting a faint angelic glyph.

No expert in the language of Heaven, even War knew the numbers well enough. A bit of fiddling and poking, and finally they began flipping, one after the other, in a very specific order.

The flash, when it came, was blinding, clearly visible across the breadth of the White City. It was all the more disturbing for its utter silence, and for only the faintest rush of air, barely even felt.

The sacrament bomb was gone, and so, too, were War and Ruin, having stepped once more through the membrane between worlds. The Horseman's last thoughts, before he once more found himself in the void, were that he would do well to avoid Heaven for some time . . .

And that this, hopefully, was the last time one of Creation's major factions would devote its attention to any sort of doomsday weapon.

CHAPTER TEN

THE ABOMINATION VAULT," DEATH SAID AS HE FINALLY concluded his recounting of recent events, "is one of the greatest surviving secrets of the Nephilim. And also one of the most vile." His voice was oddly distant, almost unfocused. "I'd hoped never to hear or speak of it ever again."

He stood, back straight and head unbowed despite his obvious discomfort with the topic, before the triple-idols of the Charred Council. His normally cadaverous skin glowed ruddy in the flickering, infernal light.

Although he faced the great visages of fire and stone, his voice was pitched so that everyone present, even those behind him, might hear. And a good thing they did, for they each, with various expressions of fascination or simmering resentment, hung on his every word.

War stood farthest from him, near the stairs that led back to the cracked earth below, arms crossed over his chest. The same illumination that granted a false vitality to Death's pale flesh also reddened War's white hair until it blended with his enveloping hood. He had grumbled, initially, at being summoned back so soon after completing his prior mission—a task whose details Death had not yet heard, and wasn't certain he cared about—but his eldest brother's tale had swiftly captured his full attentions.

Between those two, her eldest brother and her youngest, Fury stood with left hand on hip. Her eyes, gleaming bright but framed in black tattooing, were narrowed in contemplation. Skin of near ivory white, paler even than Death's but also far healthier, stood in sharp contrast with hair almost the color of wine, and to high-collared leather armor and a slit kilt of a violet darker still. Beyond these, the only other hues to stand out were the gold trim and piping along her armor's edges, and the sharp, almost blinding crackle of the whip—made, apparently, of something that could only be described as a distant and unloved cousin of the lightning family—hanging coiled at her waist.

And speaking of black sheep, the last of the quartet leaned almost indolently against the ring of jagged rocks marking the edge of the Council's platform. Armor of formfitting, gleaming steel encased him entirely, its sleek lines broken only by the heavy cloak that came very near to matching his sister's hair. His own hair, black and haphazardly shorn, framed a cold-eyed face that seemed capable of few expressions that were not some variant of a sneer. He wore a pair of pistols, and under his left arm he carried a grim helm, its full-face visor sinister, predatory, almost insectile in aspect if not in detail. True to his name, Strife appeared irritated by all Death had said, though whether this was a genuine reaction or merely his typical contemptuous demeanor remained unclear.

Above them, his presence condoned and even insisted upon by the Council despite Death's strenuous objections, Panoptos flitted side to side like a child listening to an exciting campfire tale.

"Funny that *we've* never heard of it," Strife said. "Can't have been all *that* important, can it?"

"Just the opposite, brother," Death retorted. "You've never heard of it because we kept its existence hidden even from most of our own. Only the Firstborn generation of the Nephilim were aware."

Three frowns greeted that pronouncement. "And after the Nephilim fell?" Fury asked him. "Why not tell us then?"

"Because there was no need. The Vault was hidden away, and I wanted it to remain that way."

"But why would—"

"**Enough!**" The flames roared high, as though to emphasize the demands of the Council—or at least, its leftmost visage. "**You waste time bickering over the unimportant! Speak, Death.**"

The eldest of the Horsemen nodded. "It was at the beginning, brothers. The early years of the Nephilim's ride across Creation, in search of a realm to call our own, long before the four of us split from our people to serve the Council. It started, in fact, on the very first of the worlds we destroyed.

"I doubt you recall much of it. To most of us, it held little importance or meaning, save that it *was* the first. What the Firstborn never told you is that we chose that particular realm as our opening gambit for a reason."

Death, normally so impassive, so unshakable, began to pace.

"They were called the Ravaiim, that people. Never a numerous race, they were some of the eldest of the Old Ones. Related to Makers, but they were *not* Makers. They were . . . something different. Something more primal."

"Dramatic," Strife muttered.

"The Ravaiim," Death continued, undaunted, "hailed from an epoch so early in Creation that life itself was more fluid than it is today. The lines between craftsman and craft were blurry. The Ravaiim didn't create tools the way the Makers do;

they *sculpted* them of their own flesh and bone. It was a process of months, even years, but with proper training and focus, one of the Ravaiim could remold a hand into an osseous blade, or weave a sculpture from shed strips of his own sinew and skin.

"Perhaps because of their, shall we say, *personal* bond with their creations, the Ravaiim weren't just powerful, but *imaginative*. Many Makers had shaped portions of their realms around them, creating life and sculpting geography to their whim. But the Ravaiim were the first to attempt to shape an entire *world* for themselves. The first to develop a true society beyond a few small villages. Eons before the Makers' Realm became what it is, before the White City, in a very real sense they birthed the concept of civilization."

"How very scintillating," Strife muttered behind his hand, through a deliberate yawn. "I can't begin to tell you how much I—"

"Assuming you don't want your tongue used for raw materials the next time I have to resole one of my boots," Death said cheerfully, "I suggest you stop moving it."

Strife's face went cold at first, then red at Fury's snicker and the curl of War's lip, but he did, indeed, shut his mouth.

"Continue."

"Of course. The point I was coming to is that the Ravaiim had great power—but more than that, great *potential*. And we . . . harnessed it."

His pacing ceased but he remained at one edge of the court, staring out across the fiery landscape.

"We knew the Ravaiim could never stand against us. They would prove an easy first victory, but an important one. A powerful symbol, to the Nephilim and to all those other realms and worlds that we would eventually trample into the dust. But we would also make them a *tool* of that conquest. We knew, even then, that many would rise against us, and some might succeed in matching our own power. We needed every advantage we could acquire.

"And so, when the Ravaiim were no more, a few select Firstborn gathered all that they had left behind, and used it all for . . . parts. Raw materials," he added, with a brief glance back toward Strife.

"What resulted were the Grand Abominations. Tools of slaughter, of genocide. World-killers. The most powerful, most terrible weapons you can conceive."

War started briefly, as though disturbed by a sudden thought or memory, but Death chose to ignore the reaction.

"Lamentation," he named them. "Anathema. Black Mercy and White Anguish. Gravesire. Bleak Tranquility. And several dozen more, the weakest of which made any of our prior efforts—Harvester," he said, with a vague gesture toward the scythe, "Affliction, all of those—look like the first student fumblings of Maker children."

"I'm not certain I follow," Fury admitted. "If the Ravaiim had technology to make such devices, why not build them for use against us? I know some of the Firstborn Nephilim were skilled crafters in their own right, but I doubt seriously they could build anything out of the same resources that a society of Makers could not."

Death nodded. "You're right. They couldn't. But they didn't build the Grand Abominations out of Ravaiim technology alone. That made up only a minor portion of their resources.

"The Nephilim constructed the Grand Abominations from *the remains of the Ravaiim themselves.*"

Fury looked vaguely sick; War bordering on outrage. Only Strife seemed relatively unperturbed by the announcement.

And Panoptos might actually have giggled, though Death could not be certain above the crackling fires.

"How else do you think we could create relics so potent?

We are not Makers—normally our own crafting skills would never have been sufficient—but the peculiar nature of the Ravaiim made the process *so* much easier . . . Flesh, bones, organs, all of it went into the forging of those weapons. And with it, an element of the race's essence. All the magic and strength that they devoted to Making, all the vicissitudes of their own bodies. More than that, even, the strength of purpose and the *potential* of the Ravaiim—all the power and glory and magnificence that they *would* have created, had they lived—were funneled into the Abominations. They're not just organic; in a very real sense, they're *alive.*

"Not sentient. They don't think in any way we recognize. They don't communicate with their wielders, save through emotion and impression. But they're capable of a base level of judgment—and more than that, they *hate.* Oh, they hate, as even the demons of the foulest Hell can only imagine! For everything that was done to them, everything that was denied them, everything they should have been, they find solace in murder, and nothing else."

"And the Vault?" Strife asked. He sounded far more polite, now, cowed either by Death's threat or by the enormity of the tale.

"Ah. Right, yes. Even the most bloodthirsty of our brethren knew that such weapons could not be set free in Creation without safeguards. It's why we never even told the rest of you about them, though I'm sure some of you must have heard rumors of at least a few of the weapons, given how often some of the Firstborn used them."

War grunted in affirmation, even as Fury nodded. "We suspected some secret," she said. "Some object or rite of power, but nothing like *this* . . ."

"My brothers who created the Abominations included a fail-safe," Death continued. "Some very specific means without which even the Nephilim themselves could not fully awaken the weapons. Some were completely nonfunctional, some could only be partly roused and a fraction of their power unleashed, but without the proper knowledge, their full potential was utterly inaccessible.

"And even that, we decided, was insufficient. So some of the same Firstborn who forged the weapons set out to create the Abomination Vault—a depository that nobody but us could possibly access. The Vault occupies its own separate dimension; a 'hollow realm,' if you will, utterly unconnected to anywhere else save for one single entrance. We moved that entrance over time, as the Nephilim advanced through Creation, so that we had access, but only the Firstborn ever knew where it was, or how to enter.

"And now, only *I* know."

"Then it remains only for you to tell us where it stands. From that point, we can ensure—"

"No."

Never had the flames within the great stone idols burned so hot or so high. The Horsemen each took an involuntary step back, flinching from the raw power—each of them, save Death.

"Remember how many of your gifts are ours, to give—or to *reclaim*—as we choose! We do *not* take disobedience lightly, Horseman!"

"I do not disobey lightly. But I will not reveal the location of the Vault, or how to bypass the weapons' safeguards, not even to you. So long as only I know, I can be sure the secret remains safe. Punish me if you will; sap my strength, strip away my powers. Strike me down if you must. You only ensure my silence all the more."

The fires roared until Death's hair and clothes literally smoldered, and the others couldn't look directly at the visages of the Council. Three godly voices boomed as one, promising the most vile of fates. Yet even the threat of Oblivion itself would not sway Death's resolve.

The Charred Council finally fell silent, perhaps deliberating the proper penalty for such open defiance. Death, too, said nothing, allowing his masters to come to whatever decision they would.

But not everyone remained so calm.

"Tell them, brother!" Fury appeared beside him, a pale white hand on his arm. The rustle of crimson and the clatter of armor announced War's arrival on Death's other side a moment later. "You've been gone half a millennium. We'd rather not lose you again."

"I appreciate that, sister. But if the Charred Council decides that all my potential use to them is not worth the right to keep one secret to myself, then they must act as they see fit."

"What I fail to understand," War said, in what was blatantly an attempt to shift the conversation, "is what threat the Grand Abominations could pose. If the Vault remains hidden, and all the Abominations are locked within—"

"That's just the problem," Death interrupted. "They *aren't* all locked within."

The eyes of the triple idols filled once more with flame. **"Explain!"**

"I thought that might get your attention. The *bulk* of the weapons are indeed within the Vault. Over the many eons of the Nephilim rampage, however, some were lost. Abandoned on scattered battlefields, or perhaps taken by a truly fortunate foe who never knew what he had. We *believed* that most of those lost had been destroyed, but of course we could never be positive.

"Now I'm fairly certain that our enemy, whoever they are, already have possession of at least one, if not more. Two were lost on the fields of Kothysos, and the pieces that remain there now are insufficient to entirely account for them. And I cannot imagine that our foe would be so foolish as to tip his hand by attempting to breach Eden—in order, one assumes, to search our fallen brethren for more of the Abominations—if they didn't already know *precisely* what trail they were on."

"Do you think they've learned how to awaken the ones they have?" Strife asked from behind the gathered trio.

"I've seen no evidence of that level of power," Death answered. "I have to assume not. But they're most certainly making every effort."

"So be it." It was from the leftmost head that the pronouncement boomed. **"You are correct, Horseman. Your usefulness does, for now, outweigh your insolence. Your punishment shall wait for a more opportune time."**

"Thank you *so* much."

"For the nonce, you will locate this Maker, Belisatra, and anyone else at the heart of this cabal. You will eradicate them, and any threat they pose. Above all, you will *ensure* that none outside the purview of the Charred Council locate the Abomination Vault, or obtain the weapons."

Death offered a shallow bow, only marginally sardonic. "As I'd intended. It will be done. Do you, perchance, know anything about Belisatra? I have nothing but her name to go on."

"We do not. Whatever her activities, she has never involved herself in anything to threaten the Balance, or otherwise attract our attention, until now. No doubt you'll come up with something."

"No doubt," he muttered as he began to turn away.

"Make use of your brethren in this."

The eldest of the Horsemen froze. "I'm not certain that—"

"The Grand Abominations might tip the balance

throughout Creation in favor of any faction to gain control of them—and you may rest assured that, the longer this takes, the greater the number of factions that will take an interest. You can afford neither to fail, nor to dally.

"Leave one of the Riders available to deal with any other disasters that may arise. Take the others.

"Panoptos!"

Instantly the many-eyed creature swooped down from above. "Yes, my lords?"

"Escort the Horsemen from the court. See to it that they have access to any resources they require."

"But of course."

"All of you, then. Go!"

They departed, all five. Death stood rigid, his shoulders tensing further with every step.

"Well," Strife said, idly spinning his helm in one hand. "This ought to be fun, don't you think?"

The haft of Harvester creaked in Death's grip.

He stepped off the stairway, his boots immediately kicking up soot and cinders from the blasted earth. He broke into a long-legged, distance-eating stride, seemingly with no destination in mind. The others, after an exchange of puzzled looks, moved to keep pace.

Columns of fire roared between the motley group and the horizon. Smoke swirled about their heads and feet, stalagmites snapped off at the base as Death refused to veer from his chosen path. Until, when the court of the Charred Council itself was just another distant bulge in the terrain, he halted.

"Panoptos, go away."

"So sorry to disappoint you, Death, but I have my orders. You heard them yourself. You must have heard them; I'm almost positive you were standing *right there,* unless it was some other grim, glowering—"

"Then go over *there*," Death growled, gesturing with the scythe. Even through the mask, it was clear enough that he spoke through clenched teeth. "The four of us need a moment to talk."

Apparently well aware that he'd pushed about as far as he dared, Panoptos flitted off to one side.

Death stared at him. "Farther."

Muttering something unintelligible under his breath—a clever trick, for a creature that seemingly had no orifices through which to breathe—Panoptos darted beyond earshot.

The other three Riders waited as Death froze a moment in obvious concentration. A small patch of smoke, rising through the blazing cracks in the earth, abruptly turned a sickly green. The cloud expanded, rolling outward from some unseen center, and Despair appeared in their midst. Dust—who had his beak tucked under a wing and would have appeared to be asleep, had he not been furtively watching them with a half-lidded eye—was perched atop the saddle horn.

"So," Fury said, once it became clear that Death was not prepared to start the conversation. "Who goes, and who stays?"

"I go," Death told them. "The rest of you stay."

That pronouncement ignited a veritable eruption of protest.

"If you believe for one instant—!"

"Who the hell do you think you—?"

"I'm not sure that—"

"This is not a discussion!"

War, Fury, and Strife fell silent at Death's bellow, though each wore an expression suggesting that the argument was not, in fact, settled.

"In the absence of Council orders to the contrary," he said, his voice again calm now that he'd regained their attention, "I still command. And I've made my decision. If I require your help, rest assured I'll call for you. Until then, I need you to remain where I know I can find you."

"Wasting our time?" Strife demanded. "Accomplishing nothing?"

"Death," Fury said, "surely we can be more useful out there assisting you than we can waiting for—"

"Traveling in a group would slow me down, and attract far more attention than I will alone. It's far more efficient for me to track down the enemy on my own, *then* bring you in. Besides, if Belisatra *has* managed to awaken one of the Grand Abominations, I'm far more likely to survive contact with it than any of you."

"Oh, I see," Fury said scornfully. "This is to *protect* us, is it?"

"Among other things, yes."

"I've never heard such gall!" Strife was leaning forward, as though it was all he could do not to lunge at his brother. "What are you hiding from us?"

"I've told you the plan," Death said, turning toward his mount. "Accept it."

"And if we don't care for your plan?"

"Then please, by all means, consider yourself more than welcome to grumble about it while you *follow it anyway.*"

Death had reached Despair and placed one hand on the saddle horn, dislodging an irate Dust in the process, when the dull metallic *click* sounded from behind him. He froze, then slowly craned his neck to look back over his shoulder.

Strife still held his helm in his left hand. In his right, he clutched a dreadful pistol, its quadruple barrels gaping wide, the hammer cocked back and almost quivering in readiness. War and Fury stood rigid, waiting to see if their interference was required—and, perhaps, deciding which of the pair they would support.

"'In the absence of the Council, I command!'" Strife parroted. "Says who? A lot's changed in the five centuries you've been away, Death! What makes you think you can just stroll back in after all this time and take over?"

Death's hand slipped from the horn as he turned. Leaving Harvester to lie across the saddle, he carefully, methodically, crossed the distance separating him from Strife. Each footstep seemed impossibly clear, despite the muffling of the crumbled dirt and the roaring of the distant fires. He halted scarcely an arm's length from the four gleaming barrels, and when he spoke, his voice was preternaturally calm, almost flat.

"What makes you think," he asked his brother, "that I *can't*?"

Strife's eyes and his pistol slowly turned downward, weighted down by the weight of Death's scrutiny, aimed almost meekly at the earth.

Fury unleashed a hiss of breath, not so much in any recognizable emotion as it was the simple release of building pressure. War grunted something deep in his hood. Their elder brother had already turned away, presenting his back to them—Strife included—without apparent concern.

"Did anyone else care to add anything?" he asked as he returned to his horse's side.

Oddly enough, nobody did.

"Good." Death climbed atop Despair, then held himself still just long enough for Dust to settle upon his shoulder. "Unless the Council assigns you otherwise, I'll expect to find you either here, or in your homes, if I need call on you."

Despair broke into a fearsome gallop, pulling swiftly away from the others. They whipped past a startled Panoptos without pause, heralded by Death's shouted "Keep up if you can, lackey!"

Muttering again, with rather more vehemence than earlier, Panoptos soared after him, wings flapping madly as he struggled to match pace with the rotted horse.

Strife and Fury watched the horizon long after Death had

gone, various conflicting emotions warring for control of their expressions. But War, who had remained abnormally silent during the entire affair, gazed instead in an entirely separate direction. His face remained hidden from his companions by the blood-red hood, and his thoughts, whatever they might have been, remained his own.

CHAPTER ELEVEN

A ND WHERE, PRECISELY, ARE WE GOING?"
Panoptos's voice lacked its typical mocking lilt, primarily because the creature had to shout to be certain that Death heard him over the cannonade of Despair's hooves and the ubiquitous crackle of the flames. For all that effort, if the Horseman *did* hear, he gave no indication of any intent to answer. The monolithic stalagmites and bulging columns drifted gradually past, the only real indication that they were covering any distance at all.

"We're not just taking the horse out for a run, I trust?" Panoptos tried again, a bit later. "Because I don't think the Charred Council would consider that to be a profitable use of time. And honestly? The beast can't really afford to lose any more weight. Already skin and bones, that one . . ."

Without either slowing or looking back at his fluttering tagalong, Death said, "I'm going to see the Keeper."

Four of Panoptos's eyes blinked at once, while the other five swirled around his face in crossing orbits. "What? *Why?*"

"Because I didn't think he'd come see me."

"Ooh, I wish the Council had killed you!"

"Stick around. Anything might happen."

Death reined Despair to a halt in a mixed cloud of dust and rolling green mists, before a gaping hollow in the rock. This far from the platform where the Council held court, the hellish realm had taken on a slightly more civilized aspect. It was still a pit of blasted badlands, flaming crevices, lava flows, and jagged crags half mountain, half stalagmite. But here, portions of the stone had been worked by the hands and tools of living creatures. Great humanoid figures, their specific features long since worn away by the harsh environs, half emerged from the sides of columns and hills; ancient sentinels, their vigils long ended, left to slowly return to the rock whence they came.

The cave where Death had halted was flanked by two of these vague figures. The floor here was worn smooth by the passage of many feet—or, more accurately, a few feet at a time over the course of centuries. The opening itself gave some sign of having been worked, for it was just a bit too symmetrical, a bit too smooth.

The light gleaming from deep within, a steady yellow-white glow rather than the reddish flicker of fire, might have provided something of a clue, as well.

"So, why are we here?" Panoptos asked again.

"*I'm* here to speak with the Keeper. Alone."

"Oh, Death, Death . . . Haven't we already had this conversation? I'm supposed to escort you while you're here—"

"And provide me whatever resources I require, as I recall it."

Something in the creature's face suggested a smile, despite the lack of anything even resembling lips. "I fear 'privacy' doesn't qualify as a resource."

"No, but information does." Death slid from the saddle, landing with a soft *whump*. "Just because Belisatra has never come to the Council's attention doesn't mean one of their *agents* hasn't run across her a time or two. It just means the context wasn't vital enough to report. Flutter on down to visit the archivists, will you? See if you can dig up anything on her, then find me and report back."

"I . . . you . . . *We passed the archive on the way here!* Why didn't you say something *then?*"

"Oh, did we?" The death's-head mask did absolutely nothing to conceal his broad grin. "I must have forgotten. *So* sorry to inconvenience you. Haven't you left yet?"

Spitting curses nearly venomous enough to imprint themselves into the nearby rock, Panoptos shot away into the distance. The petulant snapping of his wings was, Death assumed, the closest he could come in this environment to slamming a door. Snickering, the Horseman entered the passageway, leaving Despair behind. Dust soared in beside him and settled once more atop Harvester's blade.

"You're going to cut yourself one of these days."

A derisive caw was his only answer.

"All right, then. Don't come squawking to me when you're desperately hunting for your missing tailfeathers."

The corridor took on an ever-more-artificial aspect as Death progressed. The floor grew smoother, the walls more symmetrical. When the stone abruptly ended and the steel began, it wasn't jarring at all; it just felt like a natural stage of progression. The steady illumination Death had seen from outside had no clear origin, but seemed to emanate from points upon that steel, as though it were reflecting a light source otherwise invisible.

At random intervals, small sigils had been etched into the otherwise seamless metal. The Horseman ignored them. They weren't keyed to trigger in his presence—and besides, they were mostly focused to prevent creatures *leaving*, rather than entering.

The barred gate ahead, formed of that same steel, was also so intended. Opening it from this side was a simple matter of pulling a winch recessed into the wall. From the other side? An intricate combination of levers had to be positioned just so before the many latches would slide from their sockets.

In this particular instance, however, Death needed to do neither. The gate hung open, as some creature or other of the Charred Council's was currently coming the other way. And the eldest Horseman, who believed he had seen just about everything Creation had to show him, was struck practically dumb in shock. Even Dust spread his wings and hissed through opened beak.

"*Panoptos?* What are you . . . ? How did . . . ?"

Except it *wasn't* Panoptos, though it took Death several long instants to realize it.

It looked almost exactly like him: the same freakishly long arms and fingers, the same dark and glossy skin, the same twitching wings. It even trailed off into rags and mists where its legs should be.

In one respect, and one only, did it differ. Only six eyes, rather than Panoptos's nine, gleamed emerald from the otherwise featureless face. These, rather than shifting and swirling, were fixed in twin columns of three.

Death was just raising Harvester before him, half convinced he'd discovered some attempted impersonation and infiltration, when a *second* creature, identical to the first, appeared from beyond the gate.

The two creatures giggled and snickered, and the voices certainly held Panoptos's accustomed derision. They placed their hands together and bowed in unison. "Hello, Horseman," said the first.

"*So* pleased to meet you," said the second. They both snickered once more.

"You don't know about us!" the first realized. Their laughter grew louder.

"No," Death said coldly. "But I'm betting your corpses would be a lot less aggravating to talk to."

That, at least, put a stop to the laughing.

"We're not enemies," said the first.

"We could hardly be coming from the Keeper's sanctum if we were," said the second.

"We're servants."

"We're messengers."

"And we've delivered our message."

"So we'll be going."

"Unless you plan to kill us."

"But the Council might take that amiss."

They swooped past him, one to each side, and Death—for lack of any better option—let them go. Bemused, he continued on his way, bypassing several side corridors until he reached a massive door of black iron.

If the corridors had boasted walls with the occasional rune, this door was essentially a mass of runes with iron ridges between them. He could feel the magic radiating from it, a physical atmosphere through which he had to push, and he knew that this was nothing to what lay beyond. He hammered at it four or five times with the heel of his left fist.

He heard nothing. The portal seemed to absorb the impact without the slightest sound. Yet *someone* was aware of his presence, for he heard the bar sliding aside. The door drifted open on massive hinges, still utterly silent.

"I welcome you, Horseman."

The figure in the open doorway, his face downcast in a gesture of nervous respect, was that of a young Maker. His hair and beard were gold—not blond, but quite literally golden—and his eyes just as purely silver. He wore vest and trousers of thick brown leather, which clashed rather fiercely with his ruddy, almost *rusty* complexion. That leather was scored with all manner of small slits and burns, suggesting that the apprentice had been hard at work.

"Hello, Berrarris. Is your master in?"

"Oh, most certainly—though he might wish otherwise. It's been quite the day for visitors."

"I just met two of them. Since when does Panoptos have siblings?"

"I'm told they are called Watchers, Sir Horseman. I know only that they serve the Charred Council, much as Panoptos himself does. You'd have to ask the master for details. Oh!" Berrarris flushed—though it was barely visible, given his natural coloring—and stepped aside. "Please, enter."

Death stepped past him with a muttered "Thank you," choosing to ignore the fact that the young man was trembling.

I'm not that frightening, am I?

Well, maybe . . .

"I'd like to speak to him," Death continued.

"Of course. I believe he's with yet another guest at the moment, but I've no doubt that he'll make time for you. If you'd follow . . . ?" He led the way, still unwilling to look up and risk meeting the Horseman's gaze.

The rooms through which they now passed displayed shelves and podiums of wonders. Weapons, armor, peculiar mechanical devices with functions that Death couldn't begin to guess . . . But all were, in some way or another, crude. Just a little imperfect in shape, or a tad awkward in construction.

These, Death knew, were Berrarris's creations—the many projects on which he worked as he studied his art beneath his master's tutelage. Of his master's own works, however, there was no sign.

Not until the final chamber.

"Would you permit me just one moment, Sir Horseman?" the apprentice asked before scurrying on ahead. Death heard a few muffled voices—including one he failed to recognize—and then Berrarris returned. "He'll see you. Please call if you require anything."

He hurried off in one direction as Death headed the other. Just as he moved to enter the chamber, he felt a faint surge of eldritch forces and caught the faintest foul odor.

"Well. My home appears to be a popular place today." The voice was deceptively soft, humble, even gentle.

The man to whom it belonged was not.

He was clad in similar leathers—trousers, boots, and vest—to those worn by his apprentice. Where Berrarris boasted the muscular stature of a worker at forge and anvil, however, this figure, though tall and broad of shoulder, was gaunt to the point of emaciation. Paler than Death, he truly appeared to be one missed meal away from the grave.

Yet there was nothing of decrepitude or weakness in his movements, his stance, or his presence. He gave, in fact, the impression of boundless strength, held in reserve until the precise moment it might be needed.

It could not have come from his expression, such an impression—because he, like Death, was never seen by living eyes without a mask. His own, however, was an angular slab of iron, featureless save for the narrow eye slits, and for the trails of corrosion that ran down from those hollows to create an image of eternal weeping.

The Horseman nodded his greetings to perhaps the only servant of the Charred Council who was feared as widely as he himself. If Death was the highest enforcer of the Council's will in their defense of Balance, then this was their magistrate, their jailor, their executioner. This was the creature who held the worst of all possible fates in his hand.

The Keeper of Oblivion.

"I encountered some of your guests," Death told him. "Watchers, Berrarris called them?"

"Ah, yes. The Council's latest errand-runners. Designed and bred to serve. Seems our dear friend Panoptos was something of a prototype, Death. A template. Now that he's proven both his efficacy and his loyalty . . ."

"A slave race, then?" The distaste so thick, it practically stained the surface of Death's own mask.

"Can you ever imagine the Council trusting—*truly* trusting—anything else?"

Death *almost* replied with *Other than us?* Ultimately, however, he couldn't even pretend to fool himself that much.

Instead, he grunted and wandered across the chamber. The walls sported the ubiquitous glyphs, as well as several doors, but the room was otherwise bare of adornment save for a single bench of stone . . .

And the portal.

Broad and tall enough to have admitted all four Horsemen, while mounted, it was a circle of glass contained within a ring of intertwined iron- and gold-forged serpents. It might almost have appeared to be a giant mirror, save that the glass reflected absolutely nothing. Neither was it remotely transparent. It was just . . . there.

Few beyond the Keeper himself—perhaps *none*—knew the proper rites to open that portal; a fact for which most in Creation had reason to be grateful. Beyond that thin dimensional membrane lay nothing. Nothing at all.

Oblivion.

Some scholars theorized that this was the void beyond Creation, an emptiness outside the Trees of Life and Death. Others that it stood as a pocket of the Abyss, well below even those metaphysical pits whose fearsome gravities slowly drew reality's dead and dying realms into the depths.

Ultimately, the truth of its location—if concepts such as *location* even applied at all—was unimportant, compared with what it *was*.

Nonexistence, not as an absence but a *presence*. An emptiness that exerted its own nature. Anti-light, not darkness; anti-sound, not silence.

Anti-life.

For beings that were so very nearly immortal—for creatures who knew as fact that, after death, the soul returned to the source of being, so that *some* manner of existence continued—it was, bar none, the most dreadful of fates. Consignment to Oblivion made even the most fearless entities tremble, formed the basis of horror tales told throughout Creation.

It was the most fearsome sentence the Charred Council could levy, reserved for only the vilest of enemies and the greatest threats to the Balance. And, quite possibly, Death's own fate should the Council ever decide that his defiance had crossed the line; it was a thought even he could not face without apprehension.

And it was all in the hands of the Keeper. Death wondered, not for the first time, what sort of mind and soul lay beneath that iron mask, and how it possibly kept itself from going utterly mad.

"And your other guest?" Death asked, staring into the portal just as intently as if there had been something to see. "Consorting with demons now, are you?"

"What makes you think—?"

"Come on, Keeper. I felt the teleportation just before I entered, and there's still a touch of brimstone in the air."

A chuckle echoed, distorted, from behind the iron. "I deal with all sorts in my position, you know that. Unpleasant, but occasionally necessary. And yes, the Council is aware."

"Of course they are."

Silence, then, interrupted only by the faintest reverberations of a few particularly deafening eruptions from outside.

"Come, my friend," the Keeper said a moment later. "This

is your third visit since your return to the Council's embrace. I'm flattered, but I doubt very much that you came to discuss my taste in houseguests."

Death turned to find his host now seated upon the bench, leaning back against the wall in an attitude of repose quite at odds with his normal energies.

"You, more than anyone besides my brothers," the Horseman said, "know much about the atrocities I have committed in my time. A few of those I told you, even the other Riders don't know. But I've not told you *all* of them."

"Nor would I expect you to. Just as I'm sure you know that, in all our talks, you've barely dipped beneath the surface of *my* deeds. We do what we must, when we—"

"Spare me the platitudes!" Death interrupted. "For all our talks of responsibility, even of guilt, have you ever once known me to question my actions?"

The Keeper raised a calming hand. "My apologies. It sounded to me as though—"

Again the Rider cut him off, though this time with little heat in his voice. "No, I can't blame you for misinterpreting. I'm still working out precisely why I wanted to speak to you. I've long thought that only you hold a position that would allow you to understand my own past, but now . . ."

Death turned his head for a moment to meet Dust's eyes, perhaps struggling to read in them what he could not yet extract from his own thoughts.

"As I just said," he continued thoughtfully, "for all I've done, all the terror and carnage I've wreaked, I've never once questioned or doubted my choices. All of it, every last action, was necessary in the greater cause. I've regretted the *necessity* of my duties on several occasions, but never the *performance* of them."

"Then what's disturbing you now?" the Keeper asked him.

"Have you ever learned, after condemning someone to

Oblivion, that the Council was wrong? That the convicted wasn't deserving of that fate?"

"Never. Of course, I don't *investigate* such things, either. I have to trust the Charred Council's judgment, Death. I *have* to. It's the only way I can perform my duties without losing whatever remains of my sanity."

Death nodded. "As I've always trusted that the cause I serve justifies any action I take in its name. But," he admitted, "the 'greater cause' I've served has changed over the millennia. Some of my earlier sins—my actions when I rode at the forefront of the Nephilim horde, before my brothers and I realized the extent of our transgressions and broke away—were committed in the name of beliefs and agendas to which I no longer subscribe."

"In other words, there were atrocities that you *can't* justify to yourself any longer. Something you don't merely regret, but actually feel guilt over."

The Horseman nodded. "It's not a feeling I'm accustomed to. And it's more than a little unpleasant."

"And this comes up now because . . . ?"

"My current assignment. Not even the other Horsemen, or the Charred Council, know the *full* story. Nobody living does, except me. I was hoping it would stay that way. Now . . . Now, for the first time in a *very* long life, I'm faced with the repercussions of my 'unjustifiable crimes.' I can readily accept the consequences of any act that I still approve of, that I would commit again, but . . ."

"Are you seeking advice?" the Keeper asked.

"Not especially." Death abruptly straightened, and whatever doubt had crept into his voice vanished. "That is, I'll happily tell you what's happened . . ." *Well, most of it.* ". . . and consider any council you care to offer. But that wasn't my primary purpose. I think, before I do what I must to make things right, I just wanted to unburden myself to someone who might understand."

"Fair enough. I appreciate your trust, Death."

"Who said anything about trust? You're just the only person I know who's potentially as vile as I am."

The Keeper offered a soft laugh, though it may have been out of courtesy rather than genuine amusement. "So what lies ahead?"

"Hmm. I have Panoptos searching the archives for any knowledge of our enemy that the Council's agents may have picked up over time, but I don't have high hopes. Odds are, if there was anything important written there, the Council would know of it.

"I think my best option is the Library of the Argent Spire. You know what sort of sticklers the angels are for record keeping. They're mostly devoted to writing about their own kind, but they should still have quite a bit about Makers in . . . Something funny, Keeper?"

"Only," the other said, once he was able to catch his breath, "that you might want to tread lightly in the White City. I fear they may take a dim view of a Horseman's presence just now."

Death actually sighed. "Which one this time?"

"War. It was official Council business, if that helps at all."

"Oddly, it doesn't. Why in the name of the Abyss can't anything ever be—"

As he had done on the fields of Kothysos, Dust went berserk. It wasn't nearly so extreme this time, consisting primarily of an array of loud screeches, a violent fluttering of the wings that resembled some sort of fit, and a clenching of the talons. On the other hand, last time he hadn't been sitting on Death's shoulder when it happened.

The Horseman, wincing in discomfort, reached out to remove the bird's claws from his flesh. Holding Dust in his cupped palms, he lifted the beast to eye level.

The mental link forged itself almost instantly, the voice of the Crowfather cracking through his skull. *"Death!"*

"More accurately, 'Deaf,' if you keep shouting like that."

"Oh, be silent and pay attention! I've discovered something in my children's memories that you need to know."

Images buffeted Death's vision, though not nearly as chaotically as they had before.

Soaring over the mesa and the surrounding lands of the Crowfather's domain . . .

Fields overrun with strange creatures, shining rather than fleshy, utterly beyond the ken of avian minds . . .

Blood and pain and feathers as the flock fell upon the enemy, every instinct overridden by the need to defend the Father . . .

There! At the very edge of the gleaming stampede, a spread of snowy wings cocooned in light . . .

Death blinked as the contact was severed. He glanced down at Dust, who peered around nervously before beginning to preen the underside of his left wing.

"Well," Death said to the Keeper, "apparently it's a good thing I've already worked the White City into my itinerary."

"Oh? And why might that be?"

"Because the man who led the attack on the Crowfather's realm," the Horseman said, scooping up Harvester from where it leaned against the wall, "and who is presumably Belisatra's partner in all of this . . .

"Is an angel."

"Perhaps," the Keeper said softly, "you had best start at the beginning . . ."

CHAPTER TWELVE

As War had done earlier, Death decided on a diplomatic and formal approach to the White City, rather than simply materializing in the midst of the ivory towers and gleaming architecture. And so Despair, as Ruin had done earlier, trod the nearly blinding expanse of the angels' golden bridge.

The hooves of this unnatural creature echoed hollowly with every step, in a manner that even Ruin's had not. The glow emanating upward from the span was warped and muted by the ugly vapors clouding those hooves, until it appeared that the light itself had grown vaguely nauseated.

Horseman and horse ignored it, as they ignored the magnificent falls, the imposing outcroppings of ancient stone, the sculpted sentries who watched their progress with eyes made partly blind by the erosion of ages. Dust circled overhead, alert for any danger, but Death himself had eyes only for the gate, which rose slowly, ever higher, as the horizon drew near.

When the crow swooped low to screech a warning, and certainly when the Rider drew near enough to the wall to observe the abnormally large contingent of guards—all of whom were pointing halberds, Redemption cannons, and other weapons his way—Death finally allowed his attentions to be drawn from that gate itself.

A second phalanx circled above, just as heavily armed. Death reined Despair to a halt some dozen paces before the gate, and spoke.

Briefly. "Hello."

"How *dare* you?" The phalanx commander, carrying a naked blade taller than he was, and just as broad, took a single step forward. "How dare you show your face here, Horseman?"

"I am not my brother. I bear no responsibility for whatever occurred during his visit."

"Visit? *Rampage* would be a more accurate term!"

"Perhaps. He was going about the business of the Charred Council. As am I." Then, as an afterthought, "I'm also working on the same problem as Azrael. In the interests of etiquette, I'd be happy to wait here long enough for one of you to check with him."

The commander seemed disinclined to follow that particular suggestion. "You can turn around, is what you can do, Rider! While we still remember ourselves well enough to let you live at all!"

"Would Heaven declare war on the Charred Council, then?"

Several of the soldiers muttered and whispered behind their leader's back. "The Council did that when they sent your brother to attack us!" he shouted, but even he didn't sound quite as certain as he had.

"Did we? Odd that we've heard nothing from the leaders and generals of the White City. I wasn't aware that your laws granted every solider in your army the discretion to declare acts of war." Death waited for no answer, but set Despair to moving ahead at a slow, inexorable walk.

"You can admit me," the Horseman told them as he approached, "because you have no legal or wartime standing to stop me. Or you can admit me because I am allied with Azrael in my current endeavor. Or you can admit me because you're all dead, and therefore unable to prevent it.

"I leave the choice entirely in your hands, but I do suggest you make it quickly."

The untempered rage and simmering resentment of the angels were very nearly a palpable force. It actually felt as though Despair was struggling to wade through a clinging mire of Creation's fiercest emotions. Fists tightened on weapons, jaws clenched with force enough to bruise the bone beneath, fingers twitched on triggers almost of their own accord. The loathing these angels felt for him now might have given even one of the Grand Abominations a contest in hatred.

But each of them stepped aside, however grudgingly. They knew, as Death knew, that the laws they held so sacred would allow nothing else.

He did draw Despair to a halt once more, only briefly, just before passing beneath the barbican. Ignoring the fuming angels around him, he directed his attention instead to those hovering above.

"If even one of you takes so much as a single shot at that crow," he told them, his tone matter-of-fact, "then after you are dead, I will summon your spirits to provide me with the names of your siblings, your parents, and your children. And I will animate your corpses to murder them with your own cold hands."

The eyes that watched the horse and Rider as they passed beneath the gate remained impossibly wide, but it was no longer rage alone that shone within.

* * *

DEATH EMERGED ONTO THE STREETS of the White City, the artificial valleys that wound between the equally artificial bluffs of angelic architecture. The glowers that swirled around him in a tempest of hostility, coming from every angel in every direction, were ample evidence that the city's anger was not limited to the guardians of the wall.

He raised an arm, along with a mental call. Dust landed hard upon his wrist an instant later.

"I'm thinking," Death said to the crow, "that perhaps I should have questioned War on the details of his little sojourn here before I left the Council's realm."

Dust croaked at him and hopped over to the saddle horn.

"Pride," he said in answer to the bird's unasked question. "I'd already dismissed them, told them I was leaving them behind. To go back after that and ask his counsel . . ." Death shrugged, then stood briefly in the saddle so that he might get his bearings. Satisfied, he directed Despair to the next intersection and began up a shallowly inclined road to the city's higher layers.

His gradual ascent had carried him through three levels of the White City, with roughly four or five more to go, when he found his progress hindered.

An angel, not markedly different from any of the hundreds of others Death had seen, dropped from above to land, kneeling, in Despair's path. His armor, though massive and imposing, was perhaps a bit plainer than the norm for his people. It lacked most of the ornate edges and fluting, though what adornment it *did* have glinted as brightly as any other. He carried a Redemption cannon—the weight distributed between his right hand and a heavy strap looped over his shoulder—and the hilt of a sword jutted from behind his back.

"Welcome, Lord Death." He bowed his head so low, his snowy hair nearly brushed the roadway.

"Um . . . thank you. And you would be?"

"I am called Semyaza, Lord."

"Don't call me that. And stand up!"

The angel obeyed, finally meeting the Horseman's gaze. He appeared . . . Well, he appeared pretty much like most of the other angels currently fluttering about. "Of course. I was merely being respectful."

"That would make you the first," Death noted.

Semyaza smiled shallowly. "Yes, I'll beg your pardon for the others' behavior. War brought down an entire building while he was here, to say nothing of killing a few score of us."

Behind the mask, Death blinked. *What in the name of Oblivion were you* doing *here, brother?*

Aloud, he said, "I see. And why, then, have you chosen to play gracious host, Semyaza?"

"Azrael sent me. He felt that an escort would help ensure that none of our more short-tempered brethren cause you any difficulty. Not that he was in any particular fear for *you*, you understand, but he wished to avoid the shedding of any further angelic blood."

"I see," Death said again. The stirrups creaked as he shifted his weight. "And I know that you're not leading me into an ambush how, exactly?"

The angel's smile grew wider. "I'd have thought ill of you if you *weren't* suspicious. But I'm not 'leading' you anywhere. My duty is to accompany you. There are several routes from here to the Argent Spire, where Azrael awaits. You're welcome to choose whichever you wish, and to stay as near or far from the more populated streets as you prefer."

"All right. This way, then. And Semyaza?"

"Yes?"

"Stay where I can see you. Slip behind me, even for an instant, and I might get the wrong idea."

So they went, Despair keeping his pace moderate, less for the sake of their new companion than because of the angelic traffic around them. Semyaza walked several paces to the left and a few in front. Death watched him as carefully as he watched their surroundings, and the angel clearly *knew* Death watched him.

So long as we understand each other, the Horseman mused.

Up they marched, and over, and up some more, following the rising roads and suspended bridges that brought them ever nearer their goal. Angels swooped overhead in numbers at least as great as those who chose the roads, the steady beat of their wings creating a constant downdraft between the monolithic structures. Death regretted the White City's ambient light— or, more accurately, the resulting lack of shade. The appearance of a sudden shadow would have made it easier to spot any potential attack from above.

Still, the Horseman's attention never wavered, and both Dust and Despair were equally alert. Any enemy who could catch them unawares now, whether in league with Semyaza or not, would be an impressive foe, indeed!

As they approached the center of a lengthy bridge, where traffic was moderately more condensed because of a passing cart, Semyaza pointed up and ahead. "There. The Argent Spire."

Death's eyes were drawn, for only the briefest flicker, in the direction the angel had indicated. And in that moment Semyaza proved that he was, indeed, an impressive foe.

Not all the Horseman's wary suspicions, his caution, his supernatural reflexes, were sufficient protection. When Semyaza had lifted his arm, the gesture had also, however unobtrusively, raised the Redemption cannon very near to firing position.

The blast was enough to topple Despair, shrieking his pain

and his fury, to the roadway. Death, staggered by the detonation, still managed to land unsteadily on his feet . . .

Only to be bowled over by the angel, who had taken to the air the instant he squeezed the trigger. He succeeded in shoving the Horseman back only a few more steps, but Semyaza had chosen his moment well, and a few steps was all he needed.

The two combatants, angel and Nephilim, tumbled from the bridge.

Harvester soared to Death's fist at his call, but by then they'd already fallen too far for him to repeat his stunt from the Crowfather's domain. Nor could he lash out at his attacker, for Semyaza had once more spread his wings, gliding in circles as Death plunged straight down.

No bridges or protrusions near enough for Death to reach. Nothing he could do but ride it out until he reached the closest level of ground, some five or six full layers down. Oh, yes, Semyaza had chosen his spot *very* well.

No way around it; this was going to hurt.

But Semyaza would hurt a lot worse afterward. If only briefly.

Earth shattered at the impact. A column of dirt and debris roared upward, slowly mushrooming out as wind and gravity reached for the particles that had so briefly escaped their grasp. The stained-glass windows in several nearby walls blew out, scattering the courtyard with glittering shards.

Death crouched in the midst of it all, kneeling in a massive crater, one hand on the ground, the other wrapped around Harvester in a clutch that not even the end of Creation could loosen.

He displayed no *visible* injury, other than a few bloodless lacerations that were almost invisible against his cadaverous skin. From a fall like that, however, not even the eldest Horseman could walk away entirely unscathed. He began, unsteadily, to rise to his feet, trying to focus past the pain and the deep ringing in his head. He heard the swoop of air behind him, saw the ambient dust swirling—yet his disorientation rendered him just a hair too slow.

Agony ripped through his back, his innards, and it was all Death could do to bite back a scream as the tip of Semyaza's sword punched through his chest amid a garden of ashen scraps of flesh.

Death was no stranger to pain or injury. The eldest surviving Nephilim had been dealt ostensibly fatal blows from weapons nearly as potent as Harvester or Chaoseater, and scarcely even slowed down. But this . . . This was something new. This was a torment he'd never known, and it was only the Horseman's pride and adamant will that kept him silent.

His vision blurred, as though the entire world were an old tattoo that had begun to bleed and fade. Harvester shook with the tremors in his arms, and only by leaning on the haft of that weapon did Death manage to stay on his feet. It felt *wrong*, that wound. Burning, feverish, corrupt, as if it had been left to fester in filth for weeks. He could consciously feel his supernatural essence attempting to knit the injury shut, and some external power that fought his body's efforts.

Once more he peered down at the weapon protruding obscenely from his flesh, and now he recognized what he saw. The narrow blade, the serpentine filigree that formed a blood groove up the center . . .

Affliction.

"This . . ." Death gasped, "has nothing to do with my brother, does it?" He took a lurching step forward, then a second, slowly pulling himself off the blade. "It was you who attacked the Crowfather's temple!"

The soft, mocking laughter was all the answer he needed.

As soon as Death felt the last of the eldritch steel slide from his flesh, he allowed himself to topple forward, flopping bonelessly toward the paving stones of the courtyard. The angel behind was already lunging forward, Affliction raised for another strike.

He found, however, that Death—no matter his injuries—was no helpless victim.

The Horseman's "stumble" turned into a forward roll, so that he abruptly stood some paces away, beyond Semyaza's immediate reach. The tumble across the stones only widened the wound in his back, but Death's posture was steady, and the scythe equally so. Already he felt the first twinges of relief now that the weapon was no longer corrupting his innards. In a relatively short while, the Rider should have recovered fully from the weapon that had permanently maimed even the mighty Abaddon.

Assuming he lived long enough. Injured, pained, in an open arena against a flying foe armed with both a Redemption cannon and Affliction, it wasn't a sure bet that he would.

Whether Death could, indeed, have found the strength to defeat Semyaza in his current state would, however, have to remain a mystery. Just as the airborne angel spread his wings to the fullest, prepared either to fire or dive down upon his foe, his attention was diverted by a fearsome battle cry from above. He had just enough time to look up and see what was coming before a living, crimson-clad meteor crushed him to earth.

Again the courtyard shook and the golden stones split. Semyaza lay amid a cobweb of cracks and a small puddle of blood, groaning as he forced himself up. And standing before him, great black blade to hand, cloak still billowing with the momentum of the fall . . .

"*War?*"

"Well met, Death. With you in just a mo—"

The last of War's greeting was lost in the roar of the Redemption cannon. The younger Horseman gritted his teeth and stood firm, allowing his armor to absorb the bulk of the blast. By the time he could see clearly once more, Semyaza had again taken to the skies—skies otherwise empty, as any nearby angel had wisely abandoned the vicinity once the Horsemen drew arms. He never even looked back as he soared up and out of sight, presumably unwilling to take on two of the Riders at once.

"Coward," War spat, slinging Chaoseater once more across his back. "So, Death, how—"

And again the younger Horseman was cut off, this time by a fearsome two-handed shove to the chest powerful enough to hurl him into the nearest wall. Death was practically on top of him before the building finished shuddering.

"What in the name of the Abyss do you think you're doing here?" he demanded.

"Saving your worthless hide," War retorted, brushing broken stone and dust from his shoulders.

"I didn't need your help!"

"Not how it looked to me from two levels up, Death."

"Then your sight's as feeble as your hearing. I gave you very specific orders, War! You were to stay behind until and unless I called for you!"

"I chose not to obey them. And neither," he added at Death's hissing inhalation, "do I choose to return now."

"Don't you?" The tip of Harvester's blade slowly intruded itself between the two faces, one hooded, one masked. "We both know that I have the power to *make* you obey, brother!"

"Perhaps," War said. "But you'd likely not come through the attempt *entirely* unscathed. Do you really think that's best for your mission?"

Death spat several syllables of a language so ancient, even War didn't recognize it—but then, he hardly needed fluency to tell that the words weren't polite.

"What of the others?" he asked finally, retreating a step to allow War breathing room. "Have they disobeyed, too?"

"No, only me. Fury almost accompanied me, but she ultimately decided that your wishes should be respected—for now, anyway. Strife claimed the same motivation, but I think he's mostly sulking at how you shamed him."

"And you, War? You're neither respectful nor sulking?"

"Not at all. I'm simply quite sure that this undertaking is too important to let your pride get in the way."

"*My* pride?" Again the space between them vanished, so that Death's mask was practically pressing against War's own face. "You arrogant—!"

"Yes, damn you! *Yours!* There's more to this than you've told us. You've decided only *you* need to know the entirety of what's happening around your precious Vault. That mask may hide your face, brother, but it does damn-all to hide your intentions. Not from us. Five centuries may change much, but never *that.*"

"You bastard . . ." Once more Death fell back, quaking with suppressed fury. "You have *no idea* of 'what's happening'! You're thrusting yourself into affairs that do not—"

"Horsemen! Hold where you stand!"

"Damn," War muttered into his hood. "I thought I'd lost them."

Death growled something utterly unintelligible into his mask, and the pair of them craned their heads toward the sound.

Where Semyaza had disappeared into the upper layers of the White City, a circle of roughly two dozen angels now descended. One was a young woman, barely out of adolescence, whom Death had never seen before, but the others were clearly strong and seasoned warriors. All were heavily armored and armed, but it was their leader who instantly arrested Death's attention. The thick white beard and the gleaming eye patch, sculpted of lustrous new gold, were more than enough to identify him from any distance.

"Do *not* mention the angel who just attacked me!" Death hissed. Then, ignoring War's bewilderment, he said more loudly, "Hello again, Abaddon. You're looking better."

"Begone, Death!" The general landed firmly on solid ground, his brethren following only an eyeblink behind. The swords and pikes they carried practically shone with an enchantment far greater than was typical for angelic blades. "We've no dispute with you, unless you interfere. Our business is with your brother."

"And what business would that be?" They might as well have been discussing menus or fashion, so casual was his tone.

"Justice!" Abaddon bellowed. "War attacked us! He murdered scores of us! He destroyed irreplaceable military secrets that—"

"That you knew you weren't supposed to have!" War interjected. "That could have ignited—"

"*Silence!*" Abaddon's blade rose, as did those of his soldiers.

Death instantly stepped between the general and his youngest brother. "I'd rather like to hear the specifics, actually."

"Go ask your precious Council!" Abaddon said. "I haven't the time or the patience!"

"Oh, good!" The smile hidden by the mask on Death's face was more than blatant in his tone. "So you acknowledge that my brother's actions were sanctioned by the Charred Council. That should make this much easier."

Abaddon's mouth opened briefly, then clamped tightly shut as a slow flush spread across his cheeks.

Death turned slowly, surveying each of the surrounding angels—and then, in a single leap, impossibly swift, he stood directly before the general. He held Harvester casually, in no obvious pose to strike, but the presence of the blade's tip a dagger length from Abaddon's remaining eye sent an unmistakable message.

Every other weapon in the courtyard, Chaoseater included, was now drawn and held in hands that all but shook with eagerness, but the two elders, Horseman and angel, were as still as any of Heaven's statues.

"An attack on my brothers is an attack on me," Death told him. "An attack on any of us in retaliation for a sanctioned operation is an attack on the Council. Are you prepared to shatter the pacts, General? To plunge Heaven into war with the Charred Council—and, most likely, with Hell, once the treaties are no longer binding? Make no mistake, that *will* be the result of any further violence here. I explained this to your guards at the gate; I shouldn't have to explain it to you.

"And even if it's a war that the White City could win, you won't be around to see it. Because I assure you, you and your contingent here are *not* enough to defeat two of us side by side, and I will make it my mission, above even survival, to ensure that you are among the first to fall."

Death took a step back and shrugged. "Besides," he continued more lightly, "you still need my assistance. Or have you already forgotten that Azrael and I are cooperating against an enemy far more harmful than anything War might have done?"

Abaddon was almost literally seething. His shoulders heaved; his breath came in short squalls from between the slats in a fence of clenched teeth. The Horseman wondered if he'd made one assumption too many, if he'd actually have to carry through on his threat. Unlike those simple sentinels at the White City's walls, General Abaddon just *might* have the authority to personally declare such a war. That would certainly make Death's efforts at tracking down this Belisatra—to say nothing of her angelic ally—a lot harder.

Harvester, Chaoseater, and twenty angelic blades all waited, ready, eager . . .

But Abaddon, for all his pride, knew his duty.

"Go!" he snapped. "Go quickly, before I change my mind!" Then, as the brothers walked past, even though it had been he who exhorted them to hurry, he called out again. "War!"

"General?"

"My hands may be tied now. But I will *not* forget your crimes!"

War nodded and spun on his heel, following his elder brother from the courtyard and into the winding streets beyond.

CHAPTER THIRTEEN

"HOW DID YOU FIND ME, ANYWAY?"

Death still sounded sour about the whole thing, but he'd clearly given up on trying to convince—or order—War to depart. They were now some four levels above the courtyard, traveling at an almost leisurely pace. Although they had recovered Ruin from the spot where War had leapt from the precipice, the younger Horseman still walked, his mount's bridle in one hand, in deference to his brother. Death, in turn, had chosen not to summon Despair to him, but to remain on foot until he'd returned physically to the horse's side. He knew his mount's injuries wouldn't last much longer than his own, but still he felt reluctant to stress the creature unnecessarily.

Dust, once the Horsemen had left the angels behind and it became clear that no further violence was in the offing, had fluttered down to Death's shoulder without waiting for a summons.

"Great help you were," Death had accused him. The crow seemed about as properly chastised as ever.

They were still surrounded by streets full of angels, as well as the occasional Old One or other visitor to Heaven, but word of them had clearly spread. While Death and War each received their fair share of hostile frowns—the latter receiving rather more than the former—nobody seemed at all interested in harassing them any further.

"It wasn't difficult," War explained, grimacing as his shoulder collided with an armored angel who hadn't stepped far enough aside. "You *did* report to the Charred Council again before you left. You told them the Argent Spire was your next destination."

"Yes, but *you* weren't there. I'm quite sure I'd have seen you. You tend to stand out from the scenery."

War ignored the jibe. "I wasn't there. But the Council had no cause not to tell me when I asked."

Death halted in the middle of the roadway, if only briefly. "You went before the Council without being summoned first? *You?* Have things changed so much while I've been away?"

"It was necessary, brother."

"Oh, of course. That sound I hear is the weeping of your pride, then."

"Don't push me!"

Death felt his own temper flare once more, then forced it down. *Nothing to be gained in bickering* . . . "All right," he said. "So you knew I was heading for the library."

"Right. I thought, as you'd had a reasonable head start, that you were likely almost there. So I stepped through the realms to appear at the Spire itself, rather than taking the long way around. I'd hoped that, by the time anyone hostile to my presence had responded to the triggering of the wards, we'd already be inside and, with luck, speaking with Azrael."

"I suppose there's good reason you chose the epithet War and not Tact."

Again War's lip twisted, but otherwise he didn't react. "When it became clear that you hadn't yet arrived," he said, determined not to be sidetracked, "I decided to come looking for you. Given how near you were, it wasn't hard to detect the commotion when that angel threw you over the ledge. You pretty well know what happened after that."

"I remember it as though it had just happened."

Ruin snorted something, to which War nodded in apparent agreement. "I didn't see your attacker among Abaddon's retinue," he said in a blatant change of topic. "Why did you want me to avoid mentioning him? Even if the general had tried to cover for him, I don't see that it would have made our position any worse."

Death took a moment to trade glares with a passing pedestrian, one who came across as a bit too openly antagonistic for his liking. Only when the angel, cowed by the Horseman's implacable stare, had scurried away with as much dignity as scurrying could actually permit did Death return to the companion walking beside him.

"That little ambush," he said, "had nothing whatsoever to do with your prior antics, War. That wasn't retribution for dead angels. That was our enemy in the . . . other matter we're dealing with."

War's head snapped around quickly enough to dislodge his hood, which fell in several folds to lie back with the rest of the crimson cloak. "What? How do you know? Did you recognize him from the Crowfather's vision?"

"The Council really did tell you everything, didn't they? No, I couldn't make out any features in that vision. I was seeing a thirdhand image, taken from the memories of a crow who only caught a glimpse of the angel in the midst of battle. I think it's understandable that his recollections were a bit lacking in detail."

"How, then?"

Death touched a finger to his chest, beside the puckered

wound that had still only partly closed. "Affliction" was his only answer.

"Ah." And then, "I had wondered why being run through only a single time had slowed you down so. I've seen you shrug off far worse. Makes me wonder . . ."

"Hmm?"

"How you'd do against Chaoseater."

Even without the shadows of the hood, War's expression was so flat, so bland, that even Death couldn't tell if this was a jest, some idle musing, or something more.

"I suggest," he said, "that you make an effort never to find out. I can't imagine either of us being happy with the outcome."

"No, probably not. Well, rest assured that if I ever run you through, it won't be from the back."

"I feel better already. Thank you so much."

Another hundred paces passed without conversation.

"So if your attacker wasn't one of Abaddon's," War eventually asked, "then why did you care if I mentioned him?"

"I don't know who he is. I've never heard the name Semyaza—if that's even his true name. I've no idea what influence he holds, or what allies he might have in the White City. Probably none of any consequence, given that he's partnered himself with a Maker and relies on her constructs for his army. But until I'm *certain,* I'd rather not risk saying the wrong thing to someone who might be more knowledgeable, and less trustworthy, than we believe."

"And our search? We have to trust *someone* here, brother."

"Azrael can be trusted, at least where our interests overlap. And I'm prepared to rely on anyone *he* trusts—to an extent. Otherwise, it's mouth shut and eyes open."

"What if we should—?"

But Death had broken into a rapid, long-legged walk that

swiftly carried him farther ahead than War and Ruin. "Mouth shut starting *now*," he called over his shoulder.

Had War not already seen what had attracted his brother's attention, being addressed in such a manner might well have soured any chance of the pair working together. But *this* was something that any of the Riders would understand. War absently placed a hand on Ruin's neck.

Despair stood before them, and it was to his side that Death had rushed. The partially decayed creature had planted himself only a few strides from where he'd fallen, blocking a good half of the bridge in the process, and had refused to budge despite everything the irritated angels could do. He didn't *seem* particularly worse the wear from the assault, but then Despair's flesh gaped open, showing muscle and bone, when the beast was *healthy*. Not even Death, tightly as they were bound to each other, could be entirely certain of his mount's condition.

Still, Despair had at least recovered sufficiently to greet his master with a sepulchral whinny, and to travel without sign of hitch or discomfort. That, for now, would do.

The Horsemen mounted, letting the animals proceed at a lackadaisical pace in deference to Despair's potential injuries, but drawing inexorably nearer their goal. Behind them, a throng of bewildered, resentful angels, and twin trails of hoofprints—one seared into the roadway, the other marked by fading wisps of bilious green vapor—and before them, visible on the horizon long before they'd come anywhere close, the imposing steeple of the Argent Spire.

Even for angelic architecture, the place was colossal; the other great cathedral-like structures of the White City were as humble shanties by any comparison. Hundreds of levels of gradually sloping walls, etched columns, and stained-glass windows in deep alcoves rose majestically from one of the city's floating islands. A handful of winding stairways linked the

Spire's foundation to the "mainland," as well as to several smaller isles drifting nearby.

Other than the Spire itself, the only notable feature of the island it occupied was a copse of trees. The leaves were the brilliant reds and golds of an eternal autumn; the great boles appeared little more than a flower garden against the grand structure's walls.

The surrounding airspace was surprisingly free of angels. The Argent Spire might well be renowned as one of the wonders and most vital installations of the White City, but that didn't make it popular. The majority of that warrior race, for all that their laws required meticulous records, looked down upon sages and archivists as their inferiors.

Without any overt signal, Ruin and Despair broke into a gallop as they neared the edges of the terrain. Great leaps carried them, surely and steadily, up the curved stairs—and with startling rapidity the Library of the Argent Spire drew ever nearer.

He hurled Affliction across the chamber, howling his disdain. The weapon sparked and screeched off walls of raw, pitted ore before finally clattering sullenly to the floor. He'd hoped, prayed, that separating himself from the touch of that diseased blade might mitigate at least *some* of what he felt.

It did not, and he'd known it wouldn't. It wasn't Affliction that harrowed him in mind, body, and soul. It was, in part, frustrated rage at the interference of the second Horseman, the loss of opportunity that would likely never come around again.

In part. The rest . . .

The angel hugged himself tight with arms and wings, as though he might physically hold himself from flying apart. Feverish. Sickened. Somehow impure, unclean, as though a thousand slime-encrusted parasites squirmed between his muscle and bone, wrapped themselves about his organs, insinuated themselves in every thought. His memories were fire; his ambitions goads of leather and barbs. The last iota of his self-control, he devoted to preventing every word from becoming a scream; every gesture from becoming a blow.

He never forgot his true purpose, never swayed from his course. But oh, how he wanted to! Most of the emotional drive was gone, and all he felt now was a roiling, swelling urge to kill.

No—*almost* all he felt. Still, in the depths of his soul, clinging to the reins that kept his newfound mania in check, there remained his love. For *her*. For her, he would check these urges. For her, he would tolerate the spiritual worms eating slowly through his core.

For her, he could stand firm against even the pernicious influence of the ancient horrors he would unleash upon creation; against the endless, implacable loathing of the Grand Abominations. For her, he would shed only what blood need be shed, and no more.

No more . . .

For now.

CHAPTER FOURTEEN

I T'S JUST ... AN ANGEL? ARE YOU *CERTAIN?*"

"Just as certain as I was the last time you asked, Azrael,"
Death said. "And the time before that. I don't see the answer changing anytime soon, either."

The trio of speakers—the grim Riders and the learned
angel, in his traditional robes of verdant greens and blinding
golds—stood gathered on a walkway not terribly far below the
absolute peak of the Argent Spire. Everything was dyed in dis-
cordant blots of color, cast by the ambient light of the White
City streaming through the panes of stained glass across walls
of polished silver. It was oddly disorienting, on initial exposure,
but more than sufficient to find one's way around.

Or to read.

Beyond the platinum guardrail by which the Horsemen
stood, the entire center of the spire dropped hollowly away, so
that the uppermost third of the edifice formed a single extended chamber. All throughout that chamber, awash in pre-
servative and defensive magics, stood the treasures of the
library itself.

Everything from scrolls to bound books to graven tablets
could be found upon those shelves, numbering not in the
thousands but the *hundreds* of thousands. Cases that were ef-

fectively freestanding walls spiraled their way up, stretching floor to ceiling. They seemed almost winding columns of smoke, or intertwining serpents, petrified and put to practical use.

Numbering in their dozens, but still few and far between against the sheer length and height of shelves, the librarians and scribes of the Argent Spire went about their endless tasks. Some spent decades on end without ever leaving this chamber, cataloging, recording, altering, transcribing, protecting, repairing—and always studying, studying, studying.

Most simply flew to whatever section of shelving they required, but for the occasional guest, or for the rare angel who preferred to walk, the library offered a system of balconies and suspended walkways. These corkscrewed alongside the shelves, offering a path both twisted and awkward. For even the most clever outsider, the question was not *if* one would get lost trying to traverse these walkways, but *when* and *how badly*. Neither Death nor War believed the fairy tales of researchers who became so disoriented centuries ago that they walked the library still, desperately seeking a way out—but now that they'd seen the place, they could, at least, understand why such stories had spread.

That the library had some rigid, meticulous system to catalog and properly place every text, Death knew the nature of angels too well to doubt. So, too, did he know them well enough to know that only those who had been educated their entire life in that system would ever prove able to master it.

Thankfully, he'd been correct in assuming that Azrael would be here, attempting to discern the identity of Eden's attackers. If he hadn't been, the Horseman would have been utterly helpless to glean anything useful from the archives of millennia.

And this, according to what Azrael had proudly told them

when they'd first arrived, was not even the angels' greatest archive. "It's tiny," he'd said, "compared with its new sister installation. In one of our most distant outposts, where we watch over Creation from beyond the gates of the White City, we're currently constructing another library—the Ivory Citadel—even more magnificent. My own *personal* collection will reside there eventually!"

The angel's mood, however, had swiftly soured while the Horsemen spoke. "I'm sorry," Azrael told them softly. "I have a difficult time imagining any angel willing to slaughter so many of his own, no matter what prize he thought Eden might offer. Is there *no* possibility that this was one of Abaddon's faithful, seeking vengeance for War's actions?"

"With the weapon that took Abaddon's eye at Eden?" Death scoffed.

"Wait a moment," War interjected, dragging his attention from the seemingly bottomless drop and back to the conversation. "Abaddon was constructing a weapon for use against Hell. It's not beyond belief that he'd be interested in the Abomination Vault. Could he have faked the attack on Eden as part of a greater scheme?"

"No." Azrael's tone left no room for argument. "Abaddon can be devious, when necessary. It's *just* possible that he might even be willing to permanently maim himself in pursuit of a greater goal. But he would *not* be responsible for the deaths of so many under his command in a ruse. If we truly number an angel among the allies of this . . ."

He glanced at Death. "Belisatra," the Horseman reminded him.

"Yes, this Belisatra, then I can assure you that whatever else he may be, he is *not* Abaddon's agent."

"Then we're back to figuring out who he *is*," War grumbled.

Azrael nodded thoughtfully. "You said he called himself Semyaza?"

"I did," Death said. "But if that's his real name, I'll eat Harvester. I can't imagine he'd be that foolish."

"Still, better to be sure." Azrael spread his wings and drifted upward until he hovered directly over the meandering shelves. *"Ecanos!"* he shouted.

Instantly one of the angels—identical, so far as Death could tell, to any of the others, save for his golden robe and thin white beard—swooped up from below. "How can I serve you, my lord?"

"This is Ecanos," Azrael said, floating back toward the Horsemen. "He's one of our scribes, tasked with recording, in the minutest detail, the lives and deeds of our people. Ecanos, I trust you do not need me to identify our guests for you?"

"No, my lord." If the scribe felt any hostility toward War for his earlier visit, he showed no sign. Of course, it was entirely possible that he'd been in the Argent Spire this entire time and had heard no word of it.

"Good. Do you know of Semyaza?"

Ecanos's eyes glazed as he peered at something in the unknowable distance. "Yes," he said after a moment's thought. "Second lieutenant to Mebahiam, commander of the Winged Lightning phalanx. There was also, of course, the *first* Semyaza, in whose honor the second lieutenant is named, who was slain at the battle of—"

"Only the living concern us right now. Do you happen to know where Semyaza is at this moment?"

"Unless he's abandoned his duties—something that would, I should stress, be very out of character—he's with the Winged Lightning as we speak. They are currently stationed at the shores of the Empty Sea, watching for any further Abyssal incursion from that region."

"Hmm. Be so kind as to send a message to Mebahiam, confirming Semyaza's presence."

"Very good, my lord."

Ecanos had just flexed his wings to dive when Death raised a hand. "See, also, if you can come up with anyone with a connection to Semyaza, who might have reason to use his name as an alias." He shrugged, then, at the three pairs of eyes that turned his way. "It's not probable," he admitted. "Odds are, our friend chose the name randomly from among those angels he knew to be elsewhere. But as you said, better to be sure."

Azrael nodded to Ecanos, who in turn nodded to Death, and then dropped from sight. "This will take some time," Azrael said. "In the interim, I will assign some of the librarians to unearthing anything they can find of this Maker, Belisatra. With any luck, what we need can be found here, and you won't be forced to travel to our new outpost.

"And *you*," he continued, landing with a thump on the floor beside Death, "will fulfill your promise to keep me apprised of ongoing events. Starting with this Abomination Vault you mentioned. Creation contains very little that I haven't at least *heard* of, yet the term is foreign to me."

The elder brother turned briefly toward the younger, and only one who knew Death as well as War did could tell, despite the mask, what it was Death silently demanded of him.

I'm telling this my way. Do not *interject!*

So they walked, meandering along footways between the spiraling shelves, and War remained mute while Death spoke. He told Azrael no lies, but neither was he particularly forthcoming with the details. At the conclusion of his recital, the angel still knew nothing of the Ravaiim, or the precise nature of the Grand Abominations. He knew that they were ancient Nephilim weapons of war, alive in their own peculiar way, capable of cracking worlds. That they were hidden away in a minuscule realm of their own. And that the enemy *probably* didn't know the means of awakening them.

That, really, was more than enough.

"Your people," Azrael growled when the Horseman finished, "have much to answer for."

"They've answered," Death said flatly. Then, when the angel drew breath as if to ask something further, "Change the subject. Now."

Azrael, perhaps the wisest of the angels, was *certainly* wise enough to obey.

"This 'hollow realm,'" he asked instead. "Are you certain it's secure?"

"It's utterly outside Creation, save for a single anchored portal. Yes, it's secure. And no, I will not tell you where that portal lies."

"I wouldn't expect you to." Azrael frowned thoughtfully. "I wonder if a realm—I mean a full-sized one, a community, a nation, maybe even a world—could be locked away in a similar manner. Something to think about . . ."

He did just that, remaining silent until the peculiar trio came upon the first of the librarians and Azrael began issuing instructions.

"What about the Well?" Death asked at one point, when it became clear that Azrael wasn't merely delegating, but planned to do much of the research himself. "Can you be away this long?"

"My duty," the angel replied, "is to guard the Well of Souls from outside interference. It functions perfectly well without me, and until we've ended the threat of these Abominations of yours, the wards I've left behind will have to prove sufficient protection."

The angels, Azrael included, remained at their hunt for a good long while. Death stood utterly still, as if he'd simply stepped out of his body, or even out of time, until the task was complete. War paced, first before this one section of shelving, then ranging farther and farther out into the library. Even his footsteps somehow managed to sound impatient.

"If you get lost," Death called—the first words he'd spoken in hours if not days—"you're on your own."

War grumbled something and went back to pacing within sight of the shelf.

Ecanos returned with confirmation that yes, the true Semyaza was still with his phalanx; and no, the scribe could not come up with anyone who might have a particular reason for choosing that name to steal.

And still the angels searched.

It was finally Azrael himself—after a prolonged discussion with the other scribes, conducted while hunched over a tableful of heaped scrolls—who brought the Horsemen their answers. He glided over, bearing both a fretful grimace and a tattered parchment. Brittle, yellowed, it looked as though the slightest touch, or even a moderate breath, would set it to crumbling, yet it held up under the angel's fingers without so much as shedding dust.

"We have something," he announced, utterly unnecessarily, as he set down once more upon the walkway.

"And well past time!" War said.

"Absolutely," Death concurred, casually turning to face the new arrival. "Much more pacing and I believe War would actually have worn himself shorter than he used to be."

"Yes, I do apologize for taking so long," Azrael said. "It turns out there's very little written about her, and then only as a few passing references in the history of others . . ." He trailed off, shook his head. "Well . . .

"Belisatra, or so we have it written, was the apprentice of a Maker called Gulbannan."

"I've heard that name," the younger Horseman muttered. His brother nodded in agreement.

"I'm unsurprised. Gulbannan was one of the truly ancient Old Ones. He was a master of many crafts, many magics. Some even say that he combined the arts of the Forge Makers with those who focus on the genesis and shaping of the living."

It was the elder brother who next interjected. "I cannot help but notice," he said, "your consistent use of the word *was*."

"Um, quite." It was Azrael, now, who began to pace. War and Death exchanged worried looks at the normally imperturbable angel's agitation. "Gulbannan was murdered, some ages gone. As best our records show, Belisatra was never again seen in the Makers' Realm, nor ever heard from, after her master's death. Which, the other Makers presumed at the time, made her either another victim, or . . ."

"Or the killer," Death finished for him.

"The Makers never hunted her down?" War asked. "It seems that if he was ancient and a respected member of the race as you say, *someone* ought to have been seeking justice. Or at least vengeance."

"Had it happened a few centuries earlier, they doubtless would have. At the time of his demise, however, Gulbannan was thoroughly estranged from the community and the company of his fellow Old Ones."

Death lashed out with an arm, snagging Azrael by the shoulder and tugging his pacing to an abrupt halt. "All right, Azrael. This *drag it out of me line by line* routine isn't like you. You're avoiding something."

The angel smiled, though he sighed through it. "You never were one for the gentle approach, were you?"

"I prefer to stockpile my patience rather than spend it frivolously."

"All right." Azrael shrugged the hand from his shoulder. "Gulbannan had taken up with a lover, until shortly before his death. The other Makers disapproved, vehemently, of his chosen paramour."

"Who?" War demanded. But Death had already turned away, once again cursing in that language so ancient, even his fellow Horseman could not comprehend it.

"It would seem that your brother has already guessed."

War turned, then, to Death, who was again absently picking at the wraps on his wrists.

"Lilith," Death hissed at him. He didn't bother even to note Azrael's nod of confirmation. "The poor, deluded fool took up with Lilith."

"And if anyone has any further answers to give you regarding Belisatra," the angel said, "it would be the Mother of Demons herself. I fear very much, my friends, that if you're to continue on this little endeavor of yours, you've little choice but to go to Hell."

CHAPTER FIFTEEN

MOUNTS AND RIDERS EMERGED FROM THE NEUTRAL emptiness of the barren paths between the worlds, and into a furnace.

One might have thought, at first glance, that it was similar to the realm of the Charred Council. The earth was a cracked and blasted badland, lit only by the glow of distant columns of flame, and the air was choked with soot.

Yet the differences, though perhaps more subtle than the similarities, were simultaneously more dramatic to those who knew what they were seeing. The sky, though veiled and clouded, was indeed open, lacking the hanging stalactites or the impression of a lowering ceiling. No lava flowed from the fissures in the broken earth; they seemed dried, empty, as though the world itself had somehow mummified in its desiccation. The miasma here was harsher, redolent of brimstone and roasting flesh rather than the cleaner aroma of purer smoke. The pillars of fire were more distant, yet far larger, than those in the Council's realm. Faint shapes of towers and ramparts, barely visible as silhouettes of deeper darkness, rose from the horizon, suggesting a large and varied population in this world that was utterly lacking in the other realm.

None of these, however, held a candle to the most predominant distinction, utterly immeasurable by physical senses but nearly overwhelming on a spiritual level. The heat here, though no more severe than that of the Council's domain, was *unhealthy*. It was thick, somehow oily. It left a sticky sheen on the skin that was most assuredly not sweat, and a memory of discomfort in the deepest recesses of the mind. It was the heat of dream-fire. Soul-fire.

Hellfire.

War shifted in Ruin's saddle, glowering around him, apparently trying to keep watch in every direction at once. "This is a vile place."

"This is the least of what Hell offers," Death told him. "This is nothing. *That* is a vile place." He held Harvester before him, pointing, and even War could scarcely repress a shudder at what he saw.

He'd taken it, initially, to be nothing but a hill in the landscape, an uneven but otherwise mundane fold in the contours of this hellish plain.

No. A moment's scrutiny revealed that to be an illusion, created by the layers of soot and dust that had, for centuries, coated that bulge.

It was, in fact, a mound of *flesh*, protruding obscenely from the fractured rock. Had it been more uniform, more—*squishy*—it might have seemed almost a blister against the skin of Hell. As it was, the irregular shape, to say nothing of the folds and creases of skin that marred its surface, contradicted that particular impression.

Even as War stared, the entire mound quivered, as though growing excited. Almost aroused.

"That's . . . repulsive," War said finally.

"No less so on the inside, I'd imagine," Death answered.

"No guards?"

"I rather doubt Lilith feels the need. Probably a few within, hidden away or even a part of the architecture, but nothing more."

War turned, briefly, back toward the horizon. "Seems a foolish oversight for one who lives in Hell. Even this far from the cities proper."

"Lilith's always been confident. Shall we?"

Together the two brothers dismounted and strode toward the bulbous hillock. Dust fluttered from Despair's saddle to his accustomed spot atop Harvester's outer curve.

"Ruin and Despair?" the younger asked.

Death shook his head. "They'd be too constrained to be any use, I expect. And I imagine they'd both be more comfortable out here."

"I imagine *we* would, too."

"Yes." Death shrugged. "But it seems they're smarter than we are."

As War felt there was little he could say in response to that, he strode forward and, with only a faint scowl of repulsion, pushed aside the folds of flesh so that he and his brother might enter.

TOGETHER THEY WALKED those cramped and twisted corridors of fevered skin, their feet sliding in slick secretions, occasionally tilted one way or the other by the faint pulsating of the flesh. They passed through the pools of sickly light, and alongside the towering candles—and their prisoners—from which that grotesque illumination shone. They saw, throughout, no sign of inhabitants, let alone guards, yet they both knew full well that they were watched at every step.

"I cannot help but notice," War said, trying to avoid the worst of the aromas by breathing only through his mouth, "that this is an *interesting* location for us to be visiting in our hunt for . . ." He paused, perhaps wondering how much it was safe to say. ". . . objects that are also of a partially organic nature," he concluded. "I find it hard to credit that entirely to coincidence."

Then, when his brother gave no indication of having heard, "Death?"

"The arts of Making weren't as completely delineated in the earliest ages as they are now. You heard Azrael tell us that Gulbannan was said to have combined the two, and if Lilith spent much time with him . . ."

"And our own objective?" War pressed, clearly unwilling to let it lie.

The face behind the mask twitched. "It's possible that some of Lilith's works inspired their own creation. I don't recall, assuming I ever knew."

"I don't recall the Nephilim having much to do with the Queen of Demons," the other growled. "Not after the very beginning, anyway."

"We had some contact beyond those earliest days. The Firstborn engaged in much that the rest of you never heard about."

"So I'm noticing. When do you plan on telling us about all this?"

"No sooner than I absolutely have to," Death said. "If even then." He refused, despite War's continued efforts, to be drawn out any further on the subject.

What he did say, when he finally deigned to speak again, was, "We're here."

Here was another door—if by *door* one meant two masses of skin pressed together in a lipless kiss.

"I'll go alone from here," Death said. "I want you watching to make sure we're not hemmed in or attacked from behind."

"Do you truly think me that stupid, brother?" War demanded.

"No. No, I suppose not. I know Lilith of old, War. I know things of her that you, Fury, and Strife do not. Things that would horrify even you, that render me somewhat less than susceptible to her charms. You will wait in the corridor."

"You think me too weak to resist her wiles?"

"If I do, there's no shame in that. Just about *everyone* is too weak to resist Lilith's wiles."

"I'm walking in there with you, and if you think you can—"

Death spun, and War found himself with his back pinned against the slimy, oozing wall. "I relented," Death said coldly, "against my better judgment, in allowing you to come with me thus far. You've been useful, and may be so again, so I *continue* to allow it.

"But let me be absolutely clear, brother. You are not going in there. If I have to feed your legs to Harvester and leave you outside as a crippled wreck, *you are not going in there*. You are no good to me, or to anyone, as a besotted slave of that demonic harlot."

War's chest was heaving, his teeth grating audibly, and had he not been pressed tightly against the grotesque surface, he might already have drawn Chaoseater and damn the consequences!

Another moment, however, was enough to calm him—not fully, no, but enough. He nodded. Death stepped away without another word, then pushed through that last disturbing portal and then the diaphanous curtains beyond.

"My goodness." The voice was thick, sultry—a sweet cream just on the cusp of going bad. "I was beginning to think you were going to stand in that hallway arguing *forever!*"

The Horseman crossed the vast chamber, climbing the stairs of the dais until he was only a few steps from the top.

The gasping, undulating demons strewn about the base of the throne hissed and growled briefly before once more turning their full attentions to their mistress.

"Lilith."

The violet-skinned creature presented a broad smile, made jaundiced by the ugly lights. She ran a slender hand through her hair and across her array of horns, as though primping for her unexpected visitor. The other hand continued to idly stroke the writhing demons. Occasionally she squirmed where she sat in the skin-and-hair-cushioned throne. "Oh, my, Death, if I'd known you were coming I'd have prepared a more suitable welcome. It's been such a long time since—"

"Save it, demon." Whatever effect Lilith's presence might be having on the Horseman, it didn't seep into his voice, and the mask prevented it from showing on his face. "I have no interest in *acknowledging* our past history, let alone discussing it."

"Why, Death! Is that any way to speak to your—"

"I said *stop!*"

Lilith's laughter was soft, almost dainty, yet weighted down with the promise of pleasure and pain in equal measure. "You're such a sensitive boy . . ." Then, when some of her amusement had passed, "I rather doubt that this is a social call. What do you want?"

"I need your help." Death sounded as though he'd sooner have borrowed Chaoseater to clean out his ears than to utter those words.

"Really? I'd *never* have guessed it." The Mother of Demons leaned forward, partly in emphasis, partly reveling in Death's peculiar discomfort at the quantity of skin thus exposed. "You're being awfully rude for someone who claims to want my assistance."

"I think I've been the very picture of courtesy," he said,

with an idle twirl of Harvester on its base. "But if you want to see rude, I'll be happy to demonstrate."

For the first time, Lilith's smile slipped. "You should have more care whom you threaten, Horseman. Someday you'll find someone who doesn't take kindly to it."

"I'll be sure to think of you if and when that day comes. Tell me about Belisatra."

A trio of rapid blinks was her only sign of surprise, but it was enough to tell Death that, whatever she'd expected, that wasn't it. "Why should I?" she asked, leaning back again.

"Well, that's already more than I expected. I assumed you'd start by denying you knew her."

"What would be the point? It's far more satisfying to let you *know* I could help you, but choose not to." Again, that peculiar laugh.

"I might consider putting in a good word with the Charred Council," Death said. "Try to convince them to return some of your abilities."

"Now I truly *don't* know what you're talking about, Death," she said, but the corner of her lips had crinkled.

"Of course you do. You and I both know that you cannot create the sorts of—let's say, *entities*—you once did. The Council stripped that knowledge from you, so that the sorts of nightmares you unleashed on Creation could never be duplicated. And of course, most of those you *did* create are dead now."

"Keep down this road, and you may join them!" she snapped. Then, more thoughtfully, "Assuming I hadn't long since moved on in my plans, and was even interested in such a proposition, do you really believe there's the slightest chance the Council would agree?"

"I think there's absolutely no chance of that. I think, though I've never heard the Charred Council laugh, that they'd laugh at me for even asking. But still, I would try."

Lilith idly reached down and twisted, ripping a small strip of skin from one of her pets. The pathetic little demon cried out in ecstasy at the wound, while the others around him licked at the exposed blood while it still, perhaps, held the echoes of Lilith's touch. "I find your argument just a bit lacking, Death. If that's all you brought, I believe this audience is at an end."

Death put one foot on a higher step, then leaned an elbow on the raised knee. "Oh, but it's not. That was just the appetizer. I don't think you'll find the main course nearly as palatable."

"If you're through with the dramatic metaphors . . . ?"

"Very well, then. Belisatra seeks the Grand Abominations."

Some peculiar crossbreed of a hiss and a sigh escaped from between Lilith's lips.

"I thought you might remember that term," Death continued. "She's working with an unnamed co-conspirator, and they've already acquired at least one or two of the devices."

"Troubling," the Demon Queen admitted, having recovered her poise. "But I'm still unclear as to why *I* should—"

"We do not know the specifics of your relationship with the Maker, but we know that you have one. Indeed, yours is the most recent connection we can find between Belisatra and anyone still living.

"The Charred Council, therefore, has no alternative but to assume that the pair of you are still colluding, and that Belisatra is serving your interests. As such, in the interests of maintaining the Balance, you'll have to be declared an enemy of the Council. We are now at war."

Lilith's eyes grew wide, and perhaps just a bit wild. "Wait just a moment—!"

"You've no friends in Heaven, Lilith. Precious few among the Makers, or even, at present, in Hell. It seems to me that you can't really afford the Council's enmity just now. *If,* however, you were to offer us incontrovertible proof that Belisatra is *not,* in fact, your servant any longer . . . Well, then, the Council would have no need for open hostilities against you."

"Proof such as what, precisely?"

"Oh, I imagine that a heartfelt, concerted effort to aid us in *stopping* Belisatra would make the point unmistakably and undeniably."

Her fingernails dug long, shallow furrows in the stone arms of the throne and the scalp of her nearest pet—and then, with an abruptness that startled even Death, she laughed. No gentle, seductive sound, this, but ugly guffaws that left her bent nearly double where she sat. Long and loud they echoed through the vast chamber, until the curtains seemed to rustle with their passage, and all the creatures at her feet had ceased their undulations to stare in confusion at their mistress.

"Oh, Death," she said when she could manage a breath, wiping a tear from her eye, "you should have been a demon. You played that *magnificently.*"

"Your approbation means everything to me."

"I'm sure." Another few laughs, and then Lilith swiftly sobered. "I do not fear the Charred Council, Horseman. But you're correct that their attentions would be, ah, *inconvenient* just at the moment. So . . . Belisatra . . ."

She paused a moment, lost in thought, then made a short, sharp sound that could only be described as a bark. Instantly the demons gathered about her throne turned and made their way—walking, crawling, slithering, flopping—down the side of the dais. There they vanished into a narrow cavity in the back wall, largely hidden from view. It was a moment more before their weeping and sobbing faded with them.

"Relationships such as ours deserve some privacy, don't you think?"

"Belisatra," Death prompted again with a faint tinge of revulsion.

Lilith smiled. "Of course. I made Belisatra's acquaintance some millennia gone by. I was struggling to learn and master those gifts of creation to which you earlier alluded, and as those are Makers' arts, I had determined that I required a Maker to teach me."

"Gulbannan," the Horseman interjected.

"My, you *have* been studying, haven't you?"

"I'd heard of your dalliance with him, yes. And we both know that you never offer yourself to anyone unless there's something to be gained."

"Oh, not true, Death. Sometimes it's just *fun*. But yes, I was seeking Gulbannan's secrets of Making. And in the process, I also spent quite a bit of time with his apprentice.

"A fascinating specimen, Belisatra. In some ways, I think, the *purest* Maker I've ever encountered."

"I'd hazard a guess that you and I have very different definitions of that word, Lilith."

"Do you want to hear this or not, Horseman? I have plenty else I could be doing."

Death sketched an exaggerated bow. The motion caused Harvester to lean, nearly dislodging an irately squawking crow. "My humblest apologies, oh Queen."

"Hmph. My point was this: Belisatra possesses a burning intellectual curiosity without much in the way of emotion to cloud it. She's focused, fascinated, and utterly unburdened by anything resembling conscience or loyalty. She wants to know everything, and she thinks nothing of shedding blood to learn the tiniest morsel. It's not even that she enjoys violence; it simply means nothing to her one way or the other. I've no idea what she told her partner to justify her interest in the Grand Abominations, but I can tell you her *true* reason: She's curious about them, how they were created, and how they function. And if seeing that function requires the obliteration of a few realms, well, such is the price of enlightenment."

Little in Creation truly had the power to disturb the Rider called Death any longer, but he felt the slightest urge to shudder run its fingers down his back. Bad enough to destroy worlds, consign whole races to extinction—he knew, for he'd done both—but to do so without any *cause* . . .

And abruptly, Death picked up the *other* implication of Lilith's words. "It wasn't you who slew Gulbannan when you were done with him, was it?"

"Such a clever mind you have! No, I had only just learned that my dear love had finally realized that he'd taught me, told me, far more than he should; that he was planning to reveal the full extent of his indiscretion to the other Makers, in hopes of making amends. I honestly hadn't decided whether to take steps against him or simply to leave when Belisatra took the matter out of my hands.

"I found her holding one of her master's prized weapons, coated in a fine spray of his own blood, yet calm as a drugged statue. She told me that she had done this so that nobody would interfere with my own plans for creation and Making, and that she would be fascinated to see the results. She's been one of my more useful and reliable servants ever since. Until recently."

"Let me guess. Her interest waned when the Charred Council scoured that knowledge from your mind."

"You needn't sound quite so gleeful every time you reference that, Death."

The Horseman shrugged. "I find the image to be a soothing one."

Lilith's face pulled in three different directions at once, until she apparently decided it wasn't worth taking any further offense. "And yes, you're correct. Belisatra was more frustrated by my loss of ability than I. Oh, I fumed for a time, I won't deny it. But I've moved on.

"She has not. Long after I told her to abandon it and focus her energies elsewhere, she's continuously searched for ways to restore my creative powers to me. Or perhaps to earn them for herself; it wouldn't surprise me."

"And you allowed such overt disobedience? Why, Lilith, are you growing soft in your old age?"

"You are *truly* straining the last of my patience, damn you!"

Death gently shook his head, so that a few locks of black hair drifted across his mask. "I don't believe that."

"You don't believe that you're straining my patience?"

"I don't believe that you *have* any."

Again the demon's lovely face twisted in a very *un*lovely scowl. And again, just as quickly, she burst out laughing.

"You truly enjoy having the better of me in this little discussion, don't you, Death? Very well, I can be a good sport." Her mirth vanished as surely as if the Dark Prince himself had appeared to claim her soul. "So long as you understand that this is a hand you only get to play once. Try to coerce me in this fashion again, and I'll destroy you and everything the Charred Council can throw at me, even if I die myself in the effort."

"Understood."

"Good. Well. There's little more to tell, actually. Yes, I tolerated Belisatra's obsession with the matter, because she still proved useful in creating all sorts of goodies for my soldiers and me throughout the centuries. And because, of course, if she *did* find a means of undoing the Council's edict, I certainly wanted to know of it.

"All this finally came to a head a short while ago, when that peculiar angel arrived."

For all his efforts, Death couldn't quite keep the sudden blaze from his eyes. "Angel?"

"Oh, yes. He thought I wouldn't be able to tell, just because he had his wings strapped down and hidden beneath a voluminous robe. Ha! I can identify any creature alive by the way it moves, speaks, even stands."

"Or the smell of its musk," Death added helpfully.

"He'd hoped to enlist *me* as an ally in his little quest," she continued, ignoring him. "Naturally, I had no interest, and told him as much. But that was the last day I saw Belisatra."

Death began to pick idly at the traveler's dirt lodged under his nails—mostly because the width of the stairs wouldn't allow him to pace. "Then you were not surprised when I told you. You *knew* what Belisatra was doing."

"I suspected. Given the timing, how could I not? But no, I didn't know for certain—and I didn't know that *you* knew.

"Nor do I know precisely why Belisatra would be interested in the Grand Abominations, aside from her insatiable intellectual curiosity, but I can offer a supposition or two. She may believe they have sufficient power to force the Charred Council to do as she asks. That was the leverage *I* was promised, after all. But as I said, I think she's mostly just fascinated. Doomsday weapons, built from the remnants and the potential of a dead race? I've no doubt she'd kill all of us just for a *chance* of learning how they work. I've no idea if her partner actually plans to *use* the devices or simply to wield them as leverage, but I can promise you that *she* wants to see them used."

"Then it's in all our interests to find her before that happens. You've known her better than anyone else. Where would she go?"

Lilith pondered for long moments, one hand on her chin; the other gently caressed the soft material of her gown, as though, even unconsciously, she couldn't long pause her efforts at overt, vulgar seduction.

"Gulbannan's realm has long since been claimed and parceled out by other Makers," she answered eventually, "so she cannot return there. She'd want a workshop, somewhere she can study the Abominations and tinker with any other crafts or constructs they require. She'd settle for one of angelic construction if forced, but she'd prefer . . . Ah!

"I had my own laboratory, hidden in the wilds just beyond Gulbannan's domain. It was there that I practiced and perfected the arts I won from him. I hosted her there a time or two, after she murdered her master. I took everything of value with me when I abandoned it, but the laboratory itself may remain. *That*, my dear Rider, is most probably where you'll find her. Even if she is no longer present, I would wager a great deal that she *was*."

"The Makers' Realm is a large place, Lilith. How—?"

"Oh, don't be tiresome! Of course I've thought of that. Have your little pet flap up here. I'll implant the location in his mind, and you can then draw it from his. You'll be able to travel right to it."

Death and Dust somehow mirrored each other, studying her with the precise same tilt of their heads.

Lilith allowed herself a lusty sigh, one that anyone but Death might well have found fascinating in its own right. "I'm not going to harm the revolting little creature. I just want this done with so you can go away."

"If you do," the Horseman told her, "you'll be dead before any of your guardians or any of your magics can save you."

And Lilith, for all she strove to hide it, flinched. Had his voice boomed or lowered, had he shouted or threatened, she might have found him easier to dismiss. It was the calm, almost *explanatory* tone that chilled even the Mother of Monsters.

Dust was obviously less than happy with the idea; he sidled across the outer curve of Harvester, wings and beak spread, screeching an almost painful protest. In the end, of course, he went anyway, as Death wanted.

He appeared even less happy when he returned, and he had a wild, almost feral look about him, but he was indeed unharmed.

"Now, Death, kindly be somewhere else. I've grown irritated at humoring you."

The Horseman merely nodded and began back down the steps, toward the distant hallway of flesh. *Need to report to the Council first; Lilith's involvement, peripheral as it is, is something they need to know. Then maybe we can end this . . .*

Lost in thought, Death paused only once, as though having just remembered some token left behind.

"Lilith? The angel who came to you . . . Did he happen to give his name?"

"Hadrimon," she called back after another moment's thought. "His name was Hadrimon."

CHAPTER SIXTEEN

DEATH AND WAR, DESPAIR AND RUIN, HAD APPEARED from the paths and the mists between worlds onto a grassy plain baked golden brown by a summer-bright sun. Sporadic trees, too few to qualify as woodland, cast pennants of shade across the landscape; sporadic hills, too few to qualify as a range, provided that landscape with contours of its own. A few of those hills, mounds of rock rather than hummocks of earth and soil, were barren save for the occasional bit of scrub. Their slopes offered no shelter; their rocky carapace was too brittle and flaking to be worked. In other words, nothing about them could conceivably interest any of the Makers who occupied the sundry regions and communities of this realm.

Which, of course, was the point.

Dust, having shaken off the worst of his discomfort but still behaving in a vague, almost fugue-like manner, had swooped from Despair's saddle as soon as they arrived. Without once stopping to get his bearings, he'd made a rapid flight toward one of those austere outcroppings and begun to circle.

Even with Dust's guidance—Lilith's guidance—it took Death and War long hours of searching to locate the entrance, so cunningly was it concealed. It blended perfectly into the rock, with layers of illusion stacked atop even its mundane camouflage. Without the crow's vehemence, even the highly attuned senses of the Horsemen would have been fooled into thinking this was nothing but a normal hillock.

That the mechanism for opening that door was equally well hidden, doubtless fiendishly complex, and possibly even trapped, War and Death had found themselves in complete agreement.

So they would not *use* the mechanism.

Death had dropped from Despair and knelt, hands held just above the sun-dried earth, whispering words that were not words at all. The temperature dropped, and even War felt a chill across the back of his neck.

Bones burst from the soil at the Horseman's bidding, but these were not the skeletal hands he had attempted to wield against Belisatra's constructs. They danced in a veritable cyclone, a sandstorm of jagged edges and heavy knobs. The noise as they whirled across the stone, blasting away layer after layer, was terrible; the lust-spawned bastard of the earthquake and the tempest.

The Riders could only hope that the thick stone itself would, at least for a time, prevent those within from detecting their arrival.

The bone storm, however, exhausted Death's energies as few of his other necromancies did, and normally served to rend flesh rather than rock. After only a few moments, when the osseous deluge had blasted only partway through, the elder brother rose to his feet and dropped his arms to his sides. Instantly the cloud scattered, leaving few traces of itself behind.

He stepped forward, placed an ear to the roughened stone, and rapped with a knuckle. "Still fairly solid. If anyone was just on the other side, I'm sure they heard us coming, but should they be farther within, we could still have the advantage of surprise." The scowl, unseen on Death's face, was obvious in his voice. "If I try much more of that, though, I may not be all that useful within. I'm not sure how—"

"Step aside, brother," War said, "and allow me to offer you a small sample of just what had the angels so furious at me."

So Death had done, remounting Despair, calling to Dust, and waiting to see what his younger brother had in mind.

It was impressive, to say the least.

As in the White City, War wheeled his horse about and broke into a furious charge. He stood in the saddle, Chaoseater thrust forward to become a devastating prow. The summer-dry grass ignited beneath Ruin's hooves, leaving twin tails of flame in his wake.

Ruin leapt. War bellowed. Chaoseater met weakened stone, and the stone kindly got out of their way.

Anyone within must have been shocked almost unto paralysis by the unheralded explosion of rock into their midst, and the fearsome emergence of the crimson-cloaked War and his smoldering steed from the dust cloud.

I suppose War's brute-force approach does *have its merits.* Though Death would never admit that to his brother aloud, of course.

Several of the six-limbed stone constructs Death had battled on the fields of Kothysos lay crushed by the explosion of the hillside. A few twitched feebly, but none would ever again prove a threat. Whether they had come to investigate something they'd heard from farther away, or whether they'd been positioned by the door and had simply proved too stupid to recognize the threat when they heard it, the Horsemen neither knew nor cared. They rode over them, trampling the few that had survived, and shot along the passageway revealed by War's violent arrival. Ruin in the lead, Despair only paces behind, they filled the corridor with the fusillade of hooves.

It wasn't long, that tunnel. It led not only onward but

slightly down, suggesting that the hollow hill served only as the uppermost portion of Lilith's hidden laboratory. Between the length of the hall and the speed of their supernatural steeds, Death and War had reached their destination before the rubble at the entrance had finished settling.

In a small way, the laboratory was similar to the Argent Spire. Not remotely in size or magnificence, but simply in that it consisted largely of a single chamber, far greater in height than in width. Roughly fifteen paces across, it was more than three times that in depth. Balconies, bridges, and retractable gantries protruded from the walls at seemingly random heights, presumably so that whoever was working here could examine and manipulate their creations from every possible angle. Open archways led from those protrusions into the rocky walls, allowing access to whatever small rooms and passages made up the remainder of the facility.

The Horsemen reined in their mounts—Ruin and Despair could not possibly navigate those narrow halls and multileveled balconies, at least not with any alacrity. For a dramatic instant, pregnant with all manner of possibilities, they stared down into the farthest reaches of that chamber.

And from below, their horrified foes returned those stares.

The angel was familiar enough, for they both had seen him in Heaven not long ago, attempting to strike Death down. The dusky-skinned, heavily armored giant who loomed a head taller than the angel they had *not* seen before, but neither had any doubt as to who she must be.

As synchronized as if they'd practiced the maneuver, Death and War heaved themselves from the saddles and plummeted into the abyss.

Hadrimon and Belisatra, shaken from their astonishment, dived in opposite directions—the angel taking to the air, hands reaching for the weapons at either hip, while the Maker lunged for something that lay atop a slab of stone in the enclosure's center. A worktable, most likely, especially judging by the fire pit and anvil both positioned nearby, but neither Horseman chose to waste the time contemplating it.

Harvester had split in two, a scythe for each hand, and Death sent both razor-edged missiles hurtling downward before his own fall had covered even half the chamber's height.

The first slashed across Belisatra's arm even as she reached for her prize. Metal screamed, sparks flew, and though the armor held—truly she must be a skilled Maker indeed, to craft protections that could stand against Harvester!—it was enough to force her back, recoiling from the attack and abandoning whatever she'd meant to grab.

Death's second blade proved even less effective. Hadrimon, encumbered only by the weaker but far lighter angelic armor, reacted faster than his companion. Affliction swept from its scabbard to parry its sister weapon. That scythe, too, rebounded from enchanted steel, and then both swept back through open air. They arrived in the Horseman's waiting hands at the same instant his boots touched stone—the stone of the worktable, rather than the ground.

The chamber shook, and War stood some way to his left, cracks radiating through the floor around him.

Belisatra took one more step back, just beyond reach of the twinned scythes, and crossed her arms. Great chains, their heavy links bristling with barbs and blades, slid from the underside of the vambraces that covered her forearms. Longer than Ruin from nose to tail, almost as thick around as Belisatra's own arms, they could not possibly have fit concealed within her armor—but then, such was the wonder of the Maker's art. The chains rose and coiled of their own accord, as though Belisatra had as much control over them as over the arms from which they sprouted.

Above, the wide-winged angel hovered. Hadrimon held Affliction in his right hand. In his left, a triple-barreled pistol of iron, flesh, and bone. Death, of course, knew the weapon at once, and his rage at those who would stir up the memories and sins of a dead race flared hotter than the fires of Hell.

Black Mercy had not yet awoken; that much he could feel from clear across the chamber. Still, even at a fraction of its potential power, a shot from that profane gun wasn't something he could afford to take lightly. He hefted Harvester, which was once again a single scythe, and readied himself.

Chaoseater seemed almost to hum with impatience. The chains swayed like angry cobras. The bone-whittled hammers on Black Mercy clicked back, ready to fall.

And that was when everything *really* went to Hell.

Or, rather, the other way around.

CHAPTER SEVENTEEN

THEY ALL FELT IT. To DEATH, AT LEAST, IT BEGAN AS A peculiar prickling on the skin, almost like immersion in a fluid just slightly caustic. Frost formed in the surrounding corridors, only a few feet from the main chamber—yet the temperature *in* that chamber spiked, rising until shimmers of heat visibly rose from the stone slab on which Death stood.

The air grew thick, heavy, not as though it were choked with some sort of fume, but rather with a growing pressure. Something loomed from a direction that had nothing at all to do with north or south, east or west, depth or breadth or height. Something pressed against the walls through which the Horsemen so easily stepped, and it, too, wanted *in*.

Something ripped in the air above them—no, it was the *air itself* that tore!—revealing a ragged hole, black as matricide, reeking of brimstone. It fell away, a tunnel of nothing that led to a pit of liquid fire.

Hell, it seemed, had followed the Council's Riders, and now it disgorged a fine selection of the horrors it had to offer.

Squawking, shrieking, shouting, gibbering; running, flying, slithering, flopping; they tumbled into the laboratory. On and on, until it seemed even the huge chamber could not contain them all. Those that could clung to the walls, skulking overheard, while others mounted the balconies and gantries. Blades and guns of a blackened, twisted nature, formed from the desiccated secretions that were the heart of demonic craftsmanship, protruded from the occasional fist or tendril. Most of the hellish beasts seemed more than content, however, with tooth and talon.

For the length of several breaths they held, pausing in their cries and howls. The tableau grew silent, save for the skittering of limbs, the occasional splatter of dangling drool . . .

And Death's muttered, "Well, *that* was unexpected."

A single demon roared a command—Death could not, in the crowd, tell which it had been, but the voice was wet, burbling, like someone speaking through the scum congealed atop an old stew—and the horde fell upon them.

Hadrimon soared, twisting between flying horrors. Affliction licked out at any who dared come too near, and Black Mercy spoke in rapid bursts. Demons howled in pain as the teeth launched by the ancient weapon ripped through flesh and spirit alike.

The jagged chains stretched even farther from Belisatra's wrists, then shot up and around, shredding flesh from every demon they passed. They wrapped around some targets—a limb if it was all they could catch, a torso or head when possible—and either crushed the creature within to pulp or unwound so fast they sawed the thing in half.

War stamped and thrust, spitting demon after demon on Chaoseater's black edge. He had little room to maneuver, trapped in the center of the workshop, surrounded by more foes than any of the others—and that was fine by him. Claws and blades screeched harmlessly off his armor, his blade fed on the chaos and carnage, and the grin on his face was almost, itself, demonic.

Behind his mask, Death smiled—and leapt.

He could have reached any of the lower bridges or balconies with that leap, so high did it carry him, but that would have meant coming up in the midst of a demon cluster. He'd be delivering himself into their hands before he could bring his own weapon to bear.

So instead, he leapt toward the wall *opposite* his goal.

The Horseman swung his legs forward so that they struck the stone first. His knees folded, absorbing the impact, and thrust out again in a second jump straight from the wall itself. Once more across the chamber, and he plummeted down onto his target from above. The startled demons thrashed about on the balcony, moving to reorient themselves to face the unexpected attack, and succeeded mostly in getting in one another's way.

Stupid move. You thought to intimidate us, and all you did was crowd yourself so badly your numbers scarcely matter.

Death tucked his legs tightly under him as he fell, so that they would not present the demons with potential targets before he could strike back with Harvester. The weapon now boasted two blades, one on each end of the haft. It was already whirling with impossible speed, nothing but a razored blur. Death's wrists passed over and around each other, and he himself was spinning when his feet finally struck stone.

Blood and various ichors spattered in a series of short, swift geysers, followed by limbs and larger gobbets. And just that swiftly, the small balcony was empty of any living being but Death himself. Harvester's twin blades had proved long enough to reach to all edges of the platform, and the tightly packed demons had left themselves no room to run.

A trio of duskwings—bat-like, venomous horrors of frightening speed—swooped down on the blood-slick balcony from above, their high voices screeching in fury. Leather wings battered the air, casting the stench of clinging, caustic guano before them. They descended in a simple but effective formation, the two on each side a bit lower and farther back to ensure their target couldn't dive aside from the central duskwing's strike.

Death let them come, and then dived *forward* into a tight roll.

Harvester split before he was back on his feet, becoming a pair of long, narrow javelins. The Horseman rose and stabbed. The lead bat-demon was behind him now, still trying to recover from the dive he'd avoided. The other two flopped, screaming, on Harvester's twin points.

But not for long.

The surviving member of the trio swung back around, but Death was already in the air. Harvester, again a single scythe, he held in one hand. The other snagged the creature by the throat, leaving them both dangling high above the floor.

The duskwing, not strong enough to maintain flight for long with a passenger, began to descend in a broad spiral. It lashed its barbed tail at Death, hellish poisons glistening in the light. It was the obvious move, however, and a simple flick of Harvester removed the threat. The demon shrieked once more as its severed tail tumbled into the massed demons below.

"War! Clear me some room to work!"

Below, Death's younger brother was almost laughing, his entire body quivering with the energies Chaoseater absorbed from the battle. The creatures around him were humanoid, bursting with obscenely oversized muscles. Stunted wings, vestigial and useless, dangled morosely from their back. Their heads were horned, their mouths fanged; they were, in purpose and nature, not even individuals but weapons, no less so than the axes they carried.

These were the Phantom Guard, the core of almost every hellish army, feared throughout Creation.

But not by War.

The first sweep of Chaoseater shattered one axe and knocked three others aside. The second gutted all four of the Phantom Guard demons who had held them. Then, his blade and his soul equally empowered, War knelt and drove Chaoseater into the stone.

As in the White City, blades similar to Chaoseater itself burst upward in a thicket of deadly steel. Demons fell or retreated, screaming obscenities. The blades vanished as swiftly as they'd appeared, and Death had the space he'd requested.

Death snapped the duskwing's neck and dropped down beside his brother. And he, too, began to draw on the power he'd drawn from the defeated foe.

Unlike War, the elder Horseman did not require any specific weapon to feed on the strength of the fallen. It came to him naturally, bits of energy sloughing from the departing souls and dispersing essence. But that meant that, for him, the chaos that fed War was insufficient. It was the deaths themselves that mattered.

Against the automatons on the fields of Kothysos or in the Crowfather's domain, he hadn't bothered. Though technically living, such lesser constructs, being soulless, granted him only a fraction of the power he could gain from other creatures.

Demons, though? Demons were vile engines of destruction, utterly irredeemable—but they were *alive*.

And Death grew strong as they fell.

He raised his arms, and a cloud of bone fragments sprang from the floor, precisely as they'd done outside. Again they whirled, a semi-solid cyclone with Death and War at the center.

This time, however, it was not several feet of solid stone at which the Horseman threw them.

Demons disintegrated into flapping fronds of shredded

meat. So loud was the whirlwind, the Horsemen couldn't even hear the enemies' screams. When Death allowed the bone storm to disperse, more than two-thirds of the demons in the chamber were dead or dying.

Of course, the downside to this was that the survivors consisted almost entirely of those demons tough enough to withstand such an assault.

Again the horde's leader barked his orders, and this time Death could see who—or rather what—that leader might be.

After a good long look, he still wasn't sure.

The creature was enormous; not the largest demon Death had ever seen, by any means, but certainly one of the largest *humanoids* he'd encountered. Better than twice War's height, it was . . . fat.

Not as a descriptor; this was no humanoid creature that happened to be obese. It literally *was* fat. Ripples, rolls, bulges, and slabs of fat formed something vaguely the shape of a torso, with smaller columns or protrusions that might be arms and legs. It seemed to have no structure, no bones; it bent where it needed to bend, compressed where it needed to compress. The demon walked with a horrid, lurching gait, pointed with thick, gummy fingers.

And the head . . . Nearly as broad as the creature's shoulders, it sat on a short stump of a neck, and it, too, was fat. No hair, no features, just more folds, stacked and rumpling where the face should have been. Only when the thing screamed its orders could Death see that one of those folds concealed a mouth. Ringed with jagged teeth—the only visible part of the demon with any rigidity—it proved nearly as wide as the head itself.

Death knew a great deal about demon taxonomy, but this monstrosity was new to him. He was about to ask his brother if *he'd* seen such a creature before, when War asked, "Do you suppose that thing has internal organs?"

I'd guess that means he doesn't know any more about it than I.

"Let's find out, shall we?"

The Horsemen moved, and the remaining demons—as well as fresh reinforcements, dashing through the hanging portal and flinging themselves to the walls and balconies— roared as one.

"You go high this time." Death's burning eyes flickered meaningfully across the demons massing on the floor, then upward. War followed that gaze, nodded, and jumped for the nearest balcony.

Death waded into the horde, Harvester split, one scythe in each hand. Primarily more Phantom Guards, these, but accompanied by squat, powerful beasts whose stone claws crackled and smoked with undying flame. Even from halfway across the room, he could feel the heat on his skin. *Those,* the Horseman decided, *I think I'll handle at a distance.*

A wise tactic, perhaps, but insufficient. Death was in the midst of a veritable ring of Phantom Guards when one of the flame-clawed demons dug its talons into the wall, ripped loose a chunk of stone twice its own size, and hurled it.

It was an attack he'd never anticipated, and for all his agility, the press of Phantom Guards meant that the Horseman couldn't evade its flight.

Neither could at least three of the demons surrounding him, but that would prove little consolation in the moments to come.

The slab of rock—which seemed, impossibly, to have ignited beneath the demon's flaming claws—slammed Death to the unyielding floor. Several of his attackers were pulped or incinerated, and it was only the Horseman's greater resilience and swift reflexes that *partially* saved him. He lay pinned, his left side in flaring agony, fire licking at his arm, his shoulder, his neck. He could actually hear the sizzling as some of his hair, and bits of his skin, boiled away.

He did not scream—that would be a satisfaction Death would *never* offer any foe—but it was a near thing.

The remaining Phantom Guards clustered around him, striking with their brutal axes, and though the stone itself limited their angle of attack, it also prevented Death from dodging or rolling aside. Steel cut through flesh, severed muscles, cracked bones. Nothing he couldn't recover from, and swiftly, but only if he had the *time*.

Death lashed out once with the scythe in his free hand, just enough to make the demons jump back, and then threw all his focus into a single instant's concentration.

Harvester flowed, becoming a single weapon once more. The scythe in Death's free hand disappeared; the weapon in his left, pinned beneath the rock, became an ugly, thick-bladed knife.

The demons closed in once more, axes raised high. Straining every muscle, ignoring the searing pain shooting through those already torn and bleeding, the Horseman turned his wrist so that the blade pointed more or less upright, taking a small fraction of the stone's weight.

Then, at Death's silent command, Harvester again resumed its natural shape.

The scythe expanded instantly upward and outward, flinging the flaming rock aside. Death rolled, smothering the worst of the flames that had caught across his body, and then, he, too, was upright once more. The Phantom Guards howling on his heels, he bounded forward, limping but still swift. Above, his brother seemed to be faring somewhat better; Death caught War's eye, tilted his head, and then dashed in the direction he'd just indicated. He ran until he stood in the shadow of one of the lower balconies, his back to a wall of stone.

They could not come at him from behind, and the overhang prevented the squat beast with the flaming claws from chucking more rocks his way. Tactically sound, but it also meant he was backed into a corner. Once the demons had surrounded him on all three open sides—which, indeed, they did almost instantly—Death had no room to maneuver.

The Phantom Guards and their clawed leader advanced, grinning and growling until their lips and teeth glistened with unshed drool. Death retreated a step farther, his back now pressed tight against the wall . . .

And shouted, "*Now!*"

Above, War broke away from his own foes and leapt off the side of the gantry on which he'd been fighting. He plummeted, swiftly but surely, to land on the balcony directly above his brother. He spun, putting his own back to the wall, bellowed a fearsome cry, and slammed Chaoseater point-first into the stone by his feet.

Again. And again.

Stone splintered, cracks shooting swiftly across the balcony as though literally fleeing the black blade. Dust flew, and gravity reached greedily for a prize long denied.

The entire balcony—save for a nub about a pace across, on which War stood—collapsed.

It passed only an arm's length before Death's face, a blinding cloud and deafening clamor, but the Horseman didn't flinch. He might not always trust his brother's judgment, but of War's accuracy he harbored no doubt at all.

His wounds already beginning to close, Death broke into a run before the dust had settled. Most of the demons he'd lured beneath the balcony had been well and truly macerated, or at least pinned, but those at the very edges might yet have strength to haul themselves free.

Harvester flying, Death raced around all four sides of the fallen slab, trimming whatever demonic parts and limbs still jutted from beneath as though removing the crust from a trencher of bread. Blood and oozes spurted, screams rose and fell, and the balcony settled more firmly into place as those who had still struggled beneath it ceased their efforts.

Only a few Phantom Guards remained on the ground, a smattering of bat-like duskwings hovered uneasily in the air. It shouldn't prove difficult to—

A low shout echoed from above. Death beheld the demons' leader, that creature of fat and fang, dangling from a gantry. Its mouth had stretched open, unhinging wider than its own body, to clamp down on War from above. The younger Horseman now hung from that loathsome maw, his entire left arm and shoulder having disappeared into the demon's gullet. The high squeal of rending metal suggested that those teeth hadn't yet punctured War's armor, but it was only a matter of seconds.

Death slapped a bare hand against the stone wall and whispered his necromantic rites. Skeletal hands erupted, not from the floor around him but from the gantry above. The Horseman had no doubt that they could do little to the flabby demon, but then, he wasn't trying to hold or injure the thing.

Instead, at Death's orchestration, the entire swarm of bony digits *shoved*.

Demon and Rider toppled from the gantry and struck the floor with a loud clang and a sodden splat. The impact threw War free and he scrambled upright, Chaoseater raised, jaw trembling in anger.

The demon, too, seemed no worse for wear as it rolled and bubbled and flopped to its feet. This close, the creature reeked of sweat and mildew and gangrenous sores.

Ebony sword and jagged scythe swept in and out; flesh and fat split, spilling gouts of blubbery, mustard-hued tallow. But no matter how broad or how deep, the wounds seemed to cause the demon no great inconvenience. It never slowed, never staggered. If it did, indeed, have organs, as War had wondered, they were buried too deep for even the Horsemen's potent weapons to easily reach; and each time they tried, they brought themselves uncomfortably near that impossibly wide, impossibly flexible jaw.

Until, finally, War and Death had both grown heartily sick of the whole thing. A quick whispered exchange and they darted forward, approaching the demon from either side.

The maw stretched wide once more, the entire head flopping to and fro as the beast decided which of them to bite. Death lashed out with an empty hand and grabbed the thing's upper jaw, his fingers slotted in between the razor-edged teeth. War did the same, snagging the lower.

And then both, with a strenuous heave, yanked the gaping, unhinged mouth down past the demon's shoulders, literally turning it partway inside out.

Blubber folded, viscous fat fountained up in an oily geyser, and a sound that might or might not have been something akin to a scream burst from the newly exposed and glistening mass. The demon spasmed once, twice, and collapsed to leak slowly away across the floor.

CHAPTER EIGHTEEN

OST OF THE SURVIVING DEMONS FLED SCREAMING
back through the portal, which slipped shut behind
them with an almost obscene slurping. The few
who remained—either too stupid, too arrogant, or simply too
slow to escape with the others—fell swiftly and without much
difficulty to Harvester and Chaoseater.

Spattered with gore, their boots squelching wetly with
every step, the Horsemen examined the carnage. Neither could
help but notice, almost immediately, which particular bodies
were *not* present.

"Belisatra?" War asked. "Hadrimon?"

"Lost track of them in the battle," Death admitted dis-
gustedly. "You?"

"The same. I imagine they ran as soon as our backs were
turned."

Death proceeded slowly to the chamber's center and leaned
heavily over the worktable, his weight resting on his knuckles.
Had any enemies still been present, they'd have died swiftly,
painfully, bloodily in that moment. There were none, however,
and smashing the furniture, though perhaps satisfying, wasn't
his style.

"All right," he said finally, drawing a ragged breath. "They've escaped us. We've wasted an opportunity, but it won't be our last."

War grunted something noncommittal, then said, "Hadrimon and Belisatra seemed just as surprised by the demons as we were. It would appear that word of the Abomination Vault is starting to spread."

The older brother ran his hand through a bit of the gore that had sprayed across the table, examined it between his forefinger and thumb. "It was inevitable, I suppose. And there'll just be more of them, the longer this takes us." He shook the goo from his hand with a flick of the wrist. "So which lord of Hell did they serve? I'd have thought that Samael was the most likely to figure out what we were doing, but this was awfully overt for one of his—"

"Don't assume," War interrupted, "that our new enemy is necessarily a demon."

"Oh, of course. How foolish of me. What evidence could I *possibly* have based that on?"

War's smile was utterly lacking in mirth. "You've been gone a long time, Death."

"So everyone keeps reminding me. What of it?"

"So a few things have changed in those centuries. One of which was, people took notice of the fact that the Nephilim's greatest defeat—before Eden, of course—was at Kothysos."

Death began to speak, paused, began once more. "The demons only agreed to fight for the Old Ones at Kothysos because they believed that we were a common enemy."

"Since then, a number of Hell's smaller factions have hired themselves out to anyone who can offer them sufficient payment—in weapons, souls, slaves, what have you."

"Demonic mercenaries? Who's foolish enough to trust *demons*?"

War shrugged. "I don't imagine anyone really trusts them, but when all they need are soldiers . . ."

"In essence, then, you're suggesting that these demons could be working for anyone or anything." Death shook his head. "And here I'd just been thinking that this whole affair had been far too simple and straightforward up until now."

"Can you question any of them, brother?"

Death nodded slowly. "Not immediately. I need some time to gather my strength and to heal. Soon, though. In the interim, a bit of searching wouldn't be wasted time, I think. We might just turn up some hint of where Hadrimon and Belisatra have gone. And by the way . . ." He'd raised his voice, clearly no longer addressing his brother. ". . . you can come out now."

Dust plunged from the highest passageway to alight upon Harvester, feathers puffed proudly erect and head held high, as though he himself had repulsed the demon horde.

War chuckled softly. "Don't encourage him," Death demanded.

Their first discovery was interesting, though not immediately helpful. Various deep gouges on the floor and the walls— older and of a very different texture from those caused by Death's storm of bones—suggested that something of truly prodigious size had recently occupied the workshop. In fact, considering the marks on all sides of the room and on gantries and bridges of various heights, it might actually have taken up almost the *entirety* of the workshop.

"One of the Grand Abominations?" War asked.

"I certainly hope not. I remember a few of the devices that were that big, and I dislike the idea of Belisatra and Hadrimon having access to *any* of them. Either way, we can be sure of one thing."

"Hmm?"

"Belisatra has the means to create some truly gargantuan

portals." Death waved vaguely at the various passageways. "There's no door here large enough for something that size to pass through."

Then, after briefly tapping a finger against a blank expanse of mask, he continued, "We need to speed this up. You keep searching here. I'm going to take a look at the side chambers."

Death's examinations carried him through myriad winding corridors. All were carved through the living rock; a few had been further reinforced with iron bands and bracings. The rooms to which they led varied in size, though none was nearly so large as the central laboratory. Some were simple storerooms, containing tools or raw materials: mostly stone and brass. Mostly, but not all. Some held, instead, the remains of bodies—strips of flesh, cords of muscle, ropes of sinew, piles of bone. All were notched, torn, or misshapen, as though someone had been attempting to construct something out of them. Most, to judge by the damage and the patterns of stained blood, had been removed while their prior owners were still alive.

A couple of the other rooms were austere sleeping chambers, boasting only bedrolls and a few simple amenities. One—the largest of these side chambers—contained a machine of dark steel with dozens of rotating gears, sliding shelves, pistons, and tubes. Death couldn't begin to guess at its purpose, until he finally found a few scraps of brass lying atop a conveyer belt. He theorized, then, that this was a device designed to accelerate Belisatra's work, enabling her to create her constructs far more rapidly than she might with only hand tools and a forge.

If so, it explained how she'd created such vast armies of artificial soldiers, but it still didn't bring Death any nearer to determining where they might have gone.

He was struggling ever more fiercely to keep his frustration in check as he grudgingly made his way back toward the central chamber. If War hadn't found something, *anything*, their search might just have come to an abrupt dead end after all.

He needn't have worried. Entering the laboratory, Death saw something lying atop the worktable, something coated in blood and gore, something that most assuredly had *not* been there when he'd departed.

"I found it under one of the dead Phantom Guards," War said without preamble. "I believe it's the object Belisatra was studying when we arrived. It must have gotten knocked off when the battle started. She either didn't see where it had fallen, or lacked the time to recover it." He flashed another humorless grin. "I picked it up with the tip of Chaoseater. If it's what I suspect it is, I'm not foolish enough to touch it until I know more about it."

His frustration slowly eroding away beneath a growing current of curiosity, Death approached the table. It couldn't be one of *them*—he'd have felt its presence from the moment he entered, just as he had that of Black Mercy—and yet . . .

Beneath the caked ooze, he saw what appeared to be a small buckler shield with an integrated gauntlet. He brushed his hand across it several times, scarcely touching it, until he'd wiped away some of the grime. It consisted primarily of old, discolored bone, though the joints on the fingers were a mesh of chain steel. The buckler itself appeared to be made up of an elongated *face*. The jaw, which gaped open just above the wrist of the gauntlet, sported an array of fearsome teeth, while the remainder of the shield was rimmed in ragged horns. A single, enormous eye protruded just above that yawning mouth.

"Mortis," he whispered.

"It's one of them, then?" War asked. Then, when Death nodded, "I sensed something in the air, just before Hadrimon pulled that pistol—"

"Black Mercy," Death told him.

"All right. But I don't feel that here."

Death leaned in until his face was nearly touching the vile thing, almost as though he were sniffing at it. "I think," he said slowly, "it may be dead."

"Dead?"

"I told you: The Grand Abominations are living things, albeit in a way we can barely recognize. It's that awareness, that *malevolence,* that we feel in their presence, at least as much as it is their raw power. But here . . ." Again he ran his fingertips over the gauntlet, never *quite* touching it. "There's *some* energy left, but it's minuscule. Mortis might still function, at the slightest fraction of its former strength, but I'm not detecting anything of life."

War, too, leaned over the peculiar object, though not so close as Death. "I hadn't realized that any of the Abominations were defensive in nature."

"It's not, really. Yes, it's a shield, but its purpose was never to protect the wearer—at least, not directly."

"Then . . . ?"

Death straightened, his eyes focused on the far wall rather than anywhere near his brother. "When awakened and at full strength," he said, his voice grim, "Mortis reacted to any attack on the wearer by sending out a concentrated burst of profane energies. It was incredibly swift, capable of traversing an entire world in a matter of heartbeats."

"And its target?" War asked when his brother seemed disinclined to continue.

"A random friend, family member, or other loved one plucked from the strongest memories and emotions of the attacker."

Now he *did* turn toward his younger brother, who glared at him through a mask of horrified revulsion. "Even at the height of our depredations," Death told him, "most of you knew barely half of what we of the Firstborn were doing."

"So I'm starting to understand."

"It's who we were at the time. It's unfortunate, but I make no excuses." Death lifted Mortis from the tabletop. "I doubt Belisatra can do much with it, but leaving it here would just be asking for trouble. I'll hold on to it until we can—"

Had Death been mistaken? Was there a sliver of awareness remaining in Mortis, so flimsy and buried so deeply that he'd failed to sense it? Or was it, perhaps, some residual instinct, a hyper-sophisticated version of an insect's continued running and twitching after being crushed?

The Horseman had no way of knowing, nor did it particularly matter. He felt a surge from deep within Mortis; a white, searing agony that crackled across every nerve, finger to arm to shoulder to mind. A rigid, iron will that might well have kept the alien semi-sentience at bay if it had been even remotely prepared was instead swept aside by the tide of psychic fire. Emotions and defenses burned and scattered. A brilliant illumination rippled across his soul, casting the dark shadow of memories upon the walls of his mind.

Death stumbled, almost collapsing to his knees, as Mortis began to *know* . . .

WORLDS AWAY, in a realm where day and night were measured in centuries, and the seasons in eons, a thousand clanks and clatters echoed from the depths of a glacial cave. What had only ever been intended to serve as a temporary staging area, an isolated grotto large enough for the gathering of hundreds or even thousands of soldiers—as well as several devices far, far larger—was now the primary headquarters of a desperate angel and his seemingly soulless ally.

Uninterested in whatever mechanical adjustments and improvements Belisatra might be making to her countless constructs or the moribund Abominations, Hadrimon paced the cramped confines of a small side cavern. No, *paced* was insufficient; he marched, stomped, each stride a separate expression of impatient wrath. Permafrost cracked beneath his heels, slivers of icicle fell at every step. Wings furled and stretched in irregular twitches; wrists and fingers spasmed as though wrapped tight about some hated throat. The glistening whites and gritty grays of the cave were tinged with crimson, and the angel was too overwrought to tell that this was no mere illusion cast by the hatred enshrouding his brain. His vision truly was obscured, for Hadrimon was weeping blood.

How had the Council's hounds *found* them? Nobody, *nobody* should have known of Lilith's abandoned laboratory! Had Belisatra deceived him? Had she told someone of their sanctum? Planned this? Betrayed him? Perhaps he should . . .

It wasn't until he actually heard the hollow *click* of tensing hammers and rotating chambers that Hadrimon realized he'd drawn Black Mercy, was cradling it almost sensuously in his palm as he stalked toward the cave mouth.

No. His arm trembled as he forced the pistol back into the holster at his side. *Belisatra's not the enemy. Remember the enemy. Remember the plan. Remember* her, *if nothing else.* He needed to maintain control, to—

Hadrimon screamed, tumbling to his hands and knees, wings flailing in uncoordinated sweeps, as his mind abruptly burned. A white-hot lance, a chewing parasite, a nightmare with claws and doubts with fangs . . . All these burrowed through his thoughts and seared his soul.

But they carried with them the thoughts of another, the deepest knowledge, the answer to everything he sought.

Through his agony, through the bloody tears that smeared

his cheeks and dribbled across his lips, Hadrimon began to laugh.

BELISATRA WAS NOT, in fact, working on her mechanized warriors at just that moment. Instead she, too, occupied one of the caverns branching from the primary grotto. Unlike the relatively diminutive cave in which Hadrimon paced, however, this one was only moderately smaller than the vast chamber in which the brass-and-stone army awaited her command.

She was not alone in this cave, not entirely—not yet. Hanging in chains from the pitted walls, almost two dozen figures decorated the periphery of the chamber. Some were angels, some Old Ones, a couple demons. Most were dead; the others wished they were, if they remained sentient enough to wish for anything at all. None retained more than a third of their skin or half their muscles, for these had proved raw materials for Belisatra's so-far-unsuccessful experiments in awakening the Abominations.

No screams, whimpers, or cries emerged from these broken, pitiful bodies. Tongues and vocal chords had been the first pieces removed, lest they disturb the Maker's concentration.

The only source of light was a crystal sphere glowing with a pure white radiance. It hung in the air above her, supported by absolutely nothing at all, shedding a column of illumination that allowed Belisatra to see what she was doing while keeping the remainder of the cave in cloaking shadow.

And something waited within those shadows, something enormous, something she could sense looming over her even in the darkness.

In her hands, Belisatra cradled what might, at first glance, have been a rifle. It consisted primarily of a perfect tube, carved from the femur of some lumbering giant. Both the handle, near the rear of the weapon, and the secondary grip farther up the barrel, were made of humanoid hands. The first was joined with the bone along the top, where the thumb should have been, so that the wielder's fingers would interlace with the handle's own. The second had its fingers wrapped about the barrel, providing a simple bit of cushioning and texture for the wielder's off hand. A faceted lens of blackest obsidian filled the tip of the barrel, and an impossibly long rope of braided hair trailed from the rear of the weapon, linking it to whatever it was that lurked unseen in the depths of the cave.

The Maker had spent less time in contact with any of the Grand Abominations than had Hadrimon, and she certainly had a much tighter grasp on her emotions. Thus far, then, she'd experienced only the faintest inklings of the seething hatred and endless bloodlust that had begun to consume her companion.

And thus, when the surge came, it struck her with a much weaker intensity.

Belisatra rocked on her heels, shoved with an almost physical force by the unexpected pain. It was fearsome, piercing, yet it was *nothing* compared with the understanding that came with it.

The corner of her broad, unfinished lips quirked in a shallow smile as she dropped the weapon and strode from the cave, searching for Hadrimon, as rapidly as dignity would permit.

WITH A CRY of frustration and fury, Death hurled Mortis from him as though it had begun to bite. It smacked into the far wall, where it sent a cascade of stone chips and dried blood floorward before it followed them to land with a hollow clatter.

"Damn it!" The skin of the Horseman's palms split and tore beneath his fingers, so tightly were they clenched; had he any blood to shed, it would have poured in torrents. "Damn it, damn it, *damn it!*"

"Brother . . ." War took a single tentative step, almost but not quite reaching out. "What—?"

"I should have anticipated that!" Death—normally so unflappable, at least on the surface—was as distraught as War had ever seen him. "How could I be that *stupid!*"

"What—?" the younger Rider tried again.

"We have to go."

"I thought you planned to question—"

"We have to go *now!* The Council must be informed, and we have preparations to make. With any luck, it should at least take them some time before they can move. If we—"

War's gauntleted hands closed on the other's shoulders, physically spinning him around. *"What's happened, damn you?"*

Death froze in the midst of raising his own hands to knock his brother's away, then allowed himself, however slightly, to slump. "They know, War. Something, some vestige of Mortis's mind, still lingered, still communed with the others, and I didn't prepare myself for it. The Abominations tore the knowledge from me, and I've no doubt that Hadrimon and Belisatra now have it as well."

"What knowledge?" War asked the question, but they both knew full well how Death would answer.

"All of it. The history of the devices, the location of the Abomination Vault . . .

"And the means to fully awaken the damn things."

CHAPTER NINETEEN

WHEN MOST INHABITANTS OF THE MANY WORLDS, the myriad examples of sentience that had arisen across a thousand domains, spoke of "Creation," they thought primarily of the Empyrean, the metaphorical Tree of Life. Thriving realms of light and life, uncountable in even an immortal's lifetime, sported angels, Old Ones, and animals in infinite variety.

Broad enough, varied enough, for any race and every purpose, was the Tree of Life. Yet it was *not* the full extent of Creation, for all that many of its inhabitants might wish it were.

Beyond the Divide lay wholly half of existence, a dark and twisted mirror of the Empyrean and all its wonders. The Underworld. The Tree of Death.

For every Heaven, a Hell. For the vibrant Forge Lands, the Kingdom of the Dead, vestibule to the Well of Souls, dominion of the Lord of Bones. For Eden, the peculiar—almost nightmarish—semi-reality of Purgatory.

And for the many worlds of the Old Ones, in the deepest metaphysical bowels of the Underworld, among the very roots of the Tree of Death, below even the darkest pits of Hell . . .

The Abyss.

If Oblivion was nothingness made manifest, the Abyss was darkness incarnate. Shadow, not as an absence of light, but a black radiance of its own; death, not as an absence of life, but a cold and ravenous presence. It was from the depths of the Abyss that the rampaging Nephilim had gained much of their power, and they fed the Abyss in exchange.

They fed it whole realms.

The Abyss had few, if any, to call its own. It was, rather, the Graveyard of Worlds; the final resting place of any realm well and truly murdered. Such dead worlds gradually but inevitably drifted from their cradles in the Tree of Life and fell, here, to nourish the gnarled tendrils of the Tree of Death.

Yet the Abyss was not without *some* native life. Like any cemetery, it attracted vermin, scavengers, and predators: things that fed and thrived on the decay of worlds. Some dwelled in the void; most made their homes in the dead and desiccated realms that made the Abyss their final place of rest. And because the Abyss had few rules of its own, and corrupted those of the worlds it claimed, each of those realms, and each of those creatures, obeyed vastly different laws of nature from any other.

Some were merely grotesque and violent, like the demons or the topography of Hell writ large. Others were . . . worse.

This particular world was worse.

The air, already hazy with an unidentifiable noxious fume, roiled and thickened before finally parting, almost sullenly, for the Horsemen's magic. Ruin and Despair gradually appeared, a process far less comfortable for mount or for Rider than it ever was in worlds beyond the Abyss. Death and War sat rigid in their saddles, leaning slightly forward as though confronting a fearsome headwind. Of Dust, oddly, there was no sign at all.

"This . . . this is . . ." War was clearly taken aback. Death, who had thought himself prepared, found himself nearly as disconcerted.

He had seen dead worlds in his time, that eldest of the Horsemen; had, in fact, helped make more than a few of them. He had seen worlds burned to cinders and scoured of life, such as the one on which he made his current home; worlds blasted and blackened, barren echoes of the Charred Council's fiery domain; worlds of glistening ice and worlds of sterile stone.

Never before had he seen a world . . . *infected.*

A gritty, almost scabby crust cracked and shifted beneath the horses' hooves, exuding a clear, vaguely sour fluid with each step. Scattered pits were literal gaping sores in the landscape, radiating a feverish warmth, wreathed in rot. The hills, of which several were visible before the cloudy air obscured the distance, were fleshy, bulbous—tumorous rather than geological, growing and shrinking in starts even as the Horsemen watched.

The wind, though placid and weak, moaned with the voice of an old man dying, and Death had finally identified the tang of the putrid air.

Gangrene, bile, and the eye-watering breath of a mouth full of rotting teeth.

"Welcome back to the home of the Ravaiim," Death muttered bitterly.

"I don't understand," his brother said. "Even at our worst, the Nephilim never did *this.*"

"But we did." Death slid from Despair's saddle and knelt to examine the sickly earth—not so much because he expected to learn anything as because he felt he *should.* "We didn't just slaughter all life on this world, we *corrupted* it. We murdered the Ravaiim, yes, and then we compounded our sin by warping them into something they were never meant to be, something Creation was never meant to contain. We planted the seeds of all this, brother—or first cultivated the pestilence, if you prefer that metaphor. It was here, waiting, and when the world slid into the depths, the Abyss itself helped it to bloom.

"We did this. Perhaps the return of the Grand Abominations is no more than we deserve."

"All right, enough of this!" War dropped from Ruin, ignoring the faint trickle of puss oozing up from where his boots cracked the surface, and halted less than a pace from Death. "You've always had a morose streak running beneath your bitter sarcasm, but that only goes so far. Yes, this is horrific. Yes, perhaps we, and the other Nephilim, were responsible. But you're taking this personally, brother, and it's time you told me why."

"It doesn't matter. We—"

"No! You've been keeping your precious secrets since we started this, and I've permitted it, but it ends now!"

Death rose, smoothly, lithely, from his crouch, so that the two Riders stood face-to-face. "You've *permitted* it, War?"

If the younger Horseman felt any trepidation at that tone, he managed to keep it from his expression. "Yes. But no more. I need to know whatever it is you've kept from me."

"No, you don't. Now step back."

"No, Death."

"Step. Back."

"No."

Death's uppercut did not merely lift War off his feet, it sent him hurtling up and back with enough force to shatter the ground where he finally fell. A pink-frothed puss puddled in the shallow crater, soiling the ornate armor and the crimson cloak.

By the time he'd struggled to his feet, his jaw already coming over a mottled purple, Death had closed the distance between them.

"Am I clear?" he demanded.

War's hand clenched of its own accord, his entire body trembled with rage, but he refused either to lash out or draw Chaoseater. "No."

A second blow, this one to the chest, threw him back farther still. Again he split the crust of the world with the impact, and again he staggered upright.

This time, when Death approached, he held Harvester in both hands. "And now?" he asked. "Consider, before you answer, that I'm done with my fists."

"So be it," War said, then paused to spit a mouthful of blood. "Cripple me. Kill me. Discard your greatest ally in this, to keep your precious secret. Because that's the only way you will."

Harvester quivered. Death's eyes blazed bright enough to reflect in his brother's armor . . . And then he began trudging back toward the horses.

A moment's delay, and War was on his heels.

"You reminded me of me, just then," Death said softly.

"Well, of course." War managed a faint grin with his split lips. "Since you were behaving more like *me*, someone had to be you."

Death's chuckle was one of courtesy, not amusement, but at least he managed it. "I do appreciate you keeping Ruin out of it."

"It was everything I could do. I'd not turn my back on him for a while, were I you."

"Understood." He lay Harvester over Despair's saddle, then gazed over the leather toward the clouded horizon. "War . . . *I* did this."

"It wasn't you alone, Death. You told us that the First-born—"

"I was one of their primary crafters. We certainly could not turn to the Makers for aid with this, so all of us with any skill were involved. You already knew, did you not, that it was I who imbued the power of the Nephilim into Harvester and Affliction, as well as some of our other ancient weapons? I was the nearest thing to a crafter—a 'maker'—that we had. So of course I was involved in the birth of the Abominations."

"Even so, that hardly makes it your—"

"It was *my idea!*"

War, who had held fast against Death's earlier assault, fell back before the power of that declaration.

"All of it," he continued more softly. "Using the Ravaiim themselves as a basis for the weapons; feeding not only on the magics and creations they'd achieved, but all the potential they *should* have achieved, had we not exterminated them . . . My idea. Oh, I only helped craft a few of the Abominations personally, but that they exist at all is my responsibility.

"I rarely feel guilt for any of the countless lives I've taken, brother. I'm not certain I'm even capable of it any longer. But for *this* obscenity . . ."

He turned, finally, away from Despair to face his younger brother. "So, yes, I take this personally, War. Because it *is* personal. And *private.* I have just trusted you, however reluctantly, with secrets that nobody else knows—not Strife, not Fury, not the Council. I don't believe even Samael or the Crowfather can possibly have discovered this. And I am asking you, without threat or demand, to keep it that way."

"And is this everything, then?"

"Everything you do not know about me? Not even a fraction. Everything you did not know about my involvement with the Grand Abominations? Yes."

War, his features screwed tight in an expression of disgust, still managed to force through the faintest vestige of what might, under other circumstances, have been a smile. "Then I see no reason I should ever need to speak of it, brother."

Death clapped a hand on his companion's cloak-covered shoulder, then hauled himself back into Despair's saddle. "Come on, then. We've a way to go yet."

The decayed beast set off at a brisk trot, War and Ruin swiftly pulling alongside.

For a time they rode in silence, each lost in his own thoughts. Eventually, however, when one of the nearby dunes split to reveal a weeping, bloodshot eye that stared at them as they passed, War spoke once more.

"What you've not yet explained," he said, very deliberately not meeting that gruesome gaze, "is why we need ride overland at all. Why did we not just step into this world nearer our destination?"

"You felt that abnormal pressure building around us as we crossed the veil?" Death asked.

"I did."

"Anywhere other than where we appeared, and a few other specific spots, the resistance is even stronger. The Firstborn warded this world, back when we were first creating the Grand Abominations. We left only a few entry points accessible. It's possible that this world's time in the Abyss has weakened some of those barriers—but then, it's equally possible that it's made them dangerous and unpredictable. Not a chance I'd care to take."

"Understandable."

"I thought you'd find it so."

Long they rode, ignoring, as best they could, the bizarre horrors of this corrupt realm: the cracked and oozing terrain, smoldering beneath Ruin's hooves; the ever-present stench of putrefaction; the shifting of the landscape, as veins bulged from beneath the dead soil and boils the size of hills shriveled as they drained.

On occasion, the shifting of the terrain suggested the presence of something else, some separate and distinct creature burrowing through the ground, but whatever it was seemed disinclined to emerge.

Finally, the pair reined in their mounts in unison.

"We're here," Death said.

"I'd rather assumed," his brother replied.

It almost appeared as though the world simply ended. A rough precipice dropped away until it was lost to the ubiquitous haze. It wasn't precisely jagged so much as *torn;* it looked less like the edge of an escarpment than the edge of a wound. Indeed, rubble accumulated along the rift revealed itself to be, not rock, but dried and crusted secretions bubbling up from pockets within the cliff face itself.

"On the plains below," Death said, "the Ravaiim once made their homes. Mostly, though not exclusively, within the shadow of the ridgeline. They mined it for raw materials back when anyone would actually want something dug from this world.

"This region we're looking over now is where the greatest number of them died. But some of them fell all throughout their territory, and we're going to have to scour every bit of it for signs of Belisatra's minions."

"You're certain they'll come?"

"Absolutely. Thanks to my carelessness, they know, now, that they require the blood of the Ravaiim to awaken the Grand Abominations. This is the only sizable source left in Creation."

War reached down, absently patting Ruin's neck. "But if they died here *eons* ago . . ."

"I have means of drawing the essence from the earth, no matter how long or how widely dispersed, and reconstituting it. We have to assume the enemy can come up with their own methods."

"Hmm." War dismounted and stepped to the very edge,

struggling and failing to see any sign of the ground so far below. "If the enemy arrives before our own reinforcements do, we may be hard-pressed to locate them in this muck."

"If your tactical concerns are our biggest problem, War, I'll be well pleased." Then, at his brother's furrowed brow, "*My* concern is that Hadrimon or Belisatra might have enough historical knowledge to realize that while this is the only *substantial* source of Ravaiim blood, there are a few others, small but viable. Anywhere the Ravaiim fell in significant numbers—and you may recall that the Nephilim did indeed battle some of them in other realms, before we closed in on their own.

"It would only be enough to awaken a few of them, and only for a short while. Nevertheless, we need to prepare for the possibility that our enemies may arrive with one or more of the Grand Abominations *fully empowered.*"

War began walking the edge of the escarpment, looking for the best spot to climb down. He said nothing in response to that warning, and Death could hardly blame him.

There was, really, precious little to say.

CHAPTER TWENTY

W HY THE BLOOD?"
The Riders now stood on a thick lip of what might have been stone, or might have been desiccated, rigid flesh, protruding from the face of the cliff. It was part of a large network of ledges and tunnels they had just scouted, and which might as well have been carved specifically for their purposes: defensible, low enough to see the plains below even through the murk, and with as broad a view as one could possibly hope for. They could not have asked for a better base camp from which to launch their wider efforts.

It was also hideously unpleasant, as the rough contours, leathery surfaces, foul air, and occasional unexplained gusts all combined to suggest that they'd taken shelter in something's bronchial system, or perhaps its sinuses, but one couldn't have everything.

"Hmm?" Death tore his attention from the sheer wall, where he'd been contemplating the notion of a ramp that the horses could climb. "What?"

"It would seem to me that you and the other Firstborn could have chosen any manner of safeguards for the Abominations, including constructing them so they'd only work for you and nobody else. Why design the safeguards around Ravaiim blood?"

"Not that simple." Death resumed his examination of the escarpment. "Building in recognition of who was Firstborn Nephilim and who was not would have proved difficult, at best. And then, what if the time came when we wanted some of the following generations to wield these weapons against our enemies? You wouldn't be able to, if the weapons only functioned for the Firstborn, but if the weapons functioned for *all* Nephilim, we'd lose our mastery over them. No, it had to be a resource that we could control, but could be disseminated when we wished.

"Once we'd decided that much, Ravaiim blood was the obvious choice. We'd slain most of the race; we knew where their remains were and had total control over the realm. And since the Grand Abominations themselves were constructed from Ravaiim remains, the use of their blood both was easier to incorporate and enhanced their innate power."

"I see. Makes sense, I suppose."

"Is there anything else I can enlighten you on, as long as we're standing around failing to accomplish anything?"

War either missed the irritated sarcasm in the question or—more likely—had become so inured that ignoring it was now second nature. "Actually, yes, since you're in such a forthcoming mood. Why hasn't the world on which you're building your new home slid into the Abyss? I've heard it's just as dead as any other we left in our wake."

"It's anchored," Death said curtly, and refused to elaborate any further.

War might well have continued his barrage of questions, much to Death's mounting exasperation, had the conversation not been interrupted by the sudden flutter of feathers. Dust appeared from the cloaking fog with a series of sharp squawks and settled on the elder Horseman's outstretched arm.

"Well, you certainly took your time. Enjoyed our little journey, did we?"

Squawk!

"So you've said." Then, more loudly, "War, I believe our reinforcements have arrived."

Precisely on cue, the light—already gray and diffuse—turned black as night. High above but swiftly descending, something blotted the sun from the sky. Dirt and flakes of what might almost have been dried skin swirled around their ankles, dancing in the sudden downdraft, and the world was all but flooded with the sound of wings. Great wings, far larger than Dust's, numbering a hundred if not more.

For the first time in living memory, angels had come to the realm of the Ravaiim.

Armor of rich silvers and golds, incandescent even in the near darkness, descended on all sides. Some of the White City's warriors landed on the ledges and trails around the two Horsemen; others descended to the earth below, setting up a perimeter guard before their feet had so much as disturbed the dust. Redemption cannons and halberds—some placed in rotating racks that allowed a single angel to fire six or eight in rapid succession—abruptly sprouted, almost fungus-like, from the corrupt soil.

And from the center of the great winged phalanx, wearing a simple silver breastplate over his traditional robes of green, appeared Azrael.

"Death," he greeted them as he settled upon the lip of stone. "War."

"Azrael," Death returned. Then, after a puzzled look shared with his brother, "Don't take this amiss, but—"

"What am I doing here?" the angel concluded for him.

The featureless mask dipped in a nod. "I sent Dust to the domain of the Council. I was expecting my brother and sister."

"Apparently, the Charred Council has decided Fury and Strife are required elsewhere. Word of the Abomination Vault has begun to spread, Death. More than a few factions throughout Creation are preparing to move."

"We've met some of them," War said blandly.

"Funny, that," said Death. "Considering that it wasn't long ago they were telling me that all four of us were assigned to this endeavor."

"Hell's interests could be more widespread than we've seen," the younger Horseman suggested.

"It could. Or . . ."

"Or?"

"Or the Council has decided, now that there's a real risk of Hadrimon and Belisatra awakening the Abominations, that they want to keep Strife and Fury in reserve to protect them in case we fail." Death shrugged. "I suppose I can't blame them, really."

"I'm sorry," Azrael interjected, "but did you say *Hadrimon*? I—"

"In a moment. One issue at a time." Death leaned over the edge, watching the angels settling in below. "So the Council sent you instead?"

"The Council doesn't *send* us anywhere," Azrael bristled. "They sent Dust to us, along with a message *requesting* our assistance. Since we're already allies in this, and none of us wants these weapons awakened, I agreed."

"Why you?" War asked. "You're a scholar, not a soldier."

"I'd be offended if you thought otherwise," the angel replied. Then, more seriously, "I may not have devoted my life to warfare, but I've still seen more of it than most of my people. And my powers are not entirely without use on the battlefield."

Death snickered. "I imagine not."

"I felt it to be, um, less than politically expedient to ask Abaddon to lead this particular force."

It was now War's turn to laugh softly.

"I could not," the angel continued, "simply reassign one of the other generals without a long discussion. And I felt that sending a phalanx to serve under your command *without* a ranking leader might prove equally problematic—again, given recent, shall we say, misunderstandings between the Horsemen and the White City. So that left me. You're certain the enemy is coming *here?*"

"They need—something in the earth, here, to awaken the Abominations," Death said. "Or at least, to awaken them for any great duration. I'll tell you the rest later, if necessary."

"I see." Azrael didn't sound especially thrilled with the arrangement. "Tell me, can your steeds make the leap to the ground from this high up?"

The Riders both started briefly at the sudden non sequitur. "Um, yes," War said. "I wouldn't want to risk it from much higher, but yes. The trouble was getting them down to the ledge and the tunnels in the first place."

Azrael nodded. "The same wards that prevent us from entering this realm, save at specific points, prevent you from dismissing them and summoning them as you normally would."

"Precisely."

"I'll have some of my angels construct a harness and fly them down. It won't be the most dignified position—for anyone involved—but we'll get them there. Just make sure you tell them to cooperate."

War scowled; Death just snorted once.

"I think," he said to War, "that we ought to keep our feet out of reach of their hooves for a few hours after this. Thank you, Azrael. We appreciate the assistance."

"You're most welcome. Now, if you please, I dislike having to ask multiple times . . . You said *Hadrimon*?"

"According to Lilith," Death told him, "that's the true name of the angel we're facing. Apparently he sought her assistance before joining forces with Belisatra."

"Hadrimon . . . I can't believe it . . ." Now it was Azrael whose attentions seemed focused solely on the activities below.

"You know him." It was clearly not a question.

Azrael sighed deeply. "Yes." Then, at the expectant pause, "It's not a tale I enjoy telling, Death. It doesn't exactly paint the angels of the White City in our finest light."

"As opposed to *my* people exterminating whole worlds and creating the obscenities that have gotten us into this whole debacle in the first place?"

"Ah. Yes, I suppose when you put it that way, shame is a relative thing."

"Then let's hear it, while we have the time."

The angel permitted himself a second, lighter sigh, and spoke.

THIS BEGAN, you must understand, quite some centuries ago. It was in the early days of the Charred Council's reign—that is, the Council had made themselves known to us as guardians of the Balance, but they had not yet succeeded in, ah, let's say *convincing* Heaven and Hell to abide by their proffered pacts and treaties. As such, we were in the midst of one of the most brutal warring periods between the forces of the Blessed and the Damned. The bloodshed, the devastation . . . The worst of it was just as horrible as the devastated worlds that your own people left in their wake, and in *our* case we weren't even trying to destroy the realms, just the enemies who had conquered them. A terrible, violent time.

I emphasize this, you understand, because it is the only justification for what came next. Not *sufficient* justification, I think, but all I have to offer in our defense.

You know of the *Codex Bellum*? The angels of Heaven have lived by that register of laws, codes, and customs for eons, now. Only those of us who were involved in its creation, or who were born under its aegis, can hope to fully grasp its intricacies. No outsider, however wise, has managed to do so. It is that layered, that complex, that precise.

That restrictive. Too restrictive, I sometimes think.

It includes, among so much else, the rigid conventions of interaction between angels of differing positions, different social castes, different military ranks. What behavior is appropriate, and when—and what behavior is *never* appropriate. For the most part, we have little difficulty in following those strictures; we angels are, by and large, creatures of thought, not emotion. Still, we have our drives, our desires, our needs, the same as anyone else; and like anyone else, sometimes what we desire and what we *should* desire fall out of alignment.

You already see, perhaps, where this is going? It was not the first time that two angels of widely disparate ranks fell in love. It will certainly not be the last. But it is, in all the history of the White City, the most infamous.

Hadrimon was, at the time, a . . . Well, I think there are no equivalents in any military structure with which you're familiar. The ranks of the angelic militias are varied, and the differences remarkably subtle. Let's say that he was a field officer of some authority, in command of multiple flights of underlings, and that should suffice.

Her name—you knew there would be a "her," of course— was Raciel. She was the field leader for one of the squadrons that fell under Hadrimon's command. Had she been nearer his equal in rank and position, they might have found some legal means of legitimizing the love they felt for each other. Had they been more widely separate, then at least the conflict of interest would not have been as great, and perhaps our leaders at the time would have felt less of a need to . . . To . . .

Ah, what use speculating? What was, was.

Their love could never be, and they both knew it. Again, they were hardly the first among angels to find themselves in such straits. The Library of the Argent Spire has multiple shelves devoted solely to the mythic poetry inspired by such hopeless romances, whether unrequited or shared. For other races, other cultures, the triumph of such a tale might involve the illicit lovers finding some means of thwarting convention, of allowing their passions to flower.

But we are angels. We are warriors. Mind, law, *discipline* . . . these are our heroic ideals. For us, a soldier worthy of respect tends to his or her duties, obeys the strictures of the *Codex*. Emotion, satisfaction of one's desires—these must come second.

Throughout our history, they always had. Not this time.

Most angels know this story; it's one of our most popular cautionary tales. The general belief in the White City is that Raciel was weak, somehow lesser than those who faced such temptations before. Me? I'm not so certain; sometimes, I wonder if she might not have been among the strongest of us, to knowingly risk so very much . . .

Either way, it scarcely matters.

Raciel acknowledged her feelings to Hadrimon—and in the face of her admission, he could no longer deny his own. They arranged a later meeting, in which they might discuss their possible futures, any options that might allow them to be together. That their love might also, at that time, be consummated went unspoken, but I doubt that the thought had failed to occur to either of them.

Once the immediate encounter had passed, however, Hadrimon began to reconsider. Either, depending on whom you ask, he rediscovered the courage of his convictions, or his courage *failed*. However one looks at it, Hadrimon pondered all the possibilities, everything that could go wrong, all that he would have to give up, whether he was prepared to violate the *Codex Bellum* for love.

I'm uncertain precisely how he phrased his report, but when Raciel arrived at their prearranged meeting place, she found a squad of soldiers waiting to detain her, to hold her until she could stand before a military tribunal for such gross violation of legal proprieties. Of Hadrimon, she found no trace. To my knowledge, the two of them never faced each other again.

Had it ended here, with Raciel suffering demotions in rank, reassignment to unpleasant duties, social stigma, then this tale would be a sad one still, but ultimately of little importance. Unfortunately, what happened was . . . not nearly so rational.

I remind you, again, that we were at the height of our war against Hell. Further, the Charred Council had only recently emerged as a power in the struggles across the Tree of Life, and the White City did not yet know whether or not they would prove to be an enemy. As such, military discipline—always of paramount importance among my people—was at its most fevered pitch. This was absolutely the worst possible time for any sort of breakdown in the chain of command or the social order, and the generals of Heaven determined to take advantage of the opportunity presented them.

They would make an example of Raciel, a chilling precedent that would be remembered through the millennia.

Standard disciplinary action would not suffice. Long-term imprisonment or physical mutilation would resonate, but it would also make her a burden on resources that could be better used elsewhere. Death? That might do, save that dying for a cause in which one believes is the highest possible honor to many of my people. It might make her a rallying cry for others who harbored secret desires to challenge the stringent laws of the *Codex Bellum*. And besides, death was a threat with which every angel lived. The notion of losing oneself, of returning to the Well of Souls, was unpleasant but hardly terrifying.

I understand they even approached the Charred Council, to request that Raciel be banished to Oblivion, but the White City's envoy was rebuffed. Raciel had committed no crime against the Balance or the Council itself, and they were unwilling—rightfully so, I should think—to serve as a tool of vengeance for others.

All of which, alas, left one option remaining. First, Raciel was stripped of some of her memories—not many, only those that involved the defenses and military tactics of the White City, so that her knowledge could not be used against us. So, too, was she robbed of the magics and powers that would otherwise have allowed her to locate or manipulate the passageways between worlds.

Then, with great ritual, in a ceremony observed by thousands, Raciel was exiled to Hell.

I know. Her crime hardly seems worthy of such a fate, does it? Yet that, I am forced to confess, was her sentence. A great portal was opened and Raciel was allowed to fall, fall until the very notions of distance and depth became meaningless. And there, in Hell, she would suffer whatever torments and tortures the demons chose to inflict, to say nothing of whatever vile transmutations the Pit itself might wreak upon her, until the day the infernal creatures finally tired of the game and killed her. A day, her judges knew, that would not come for a very, very long time.

Hadrimon abandoned his duties not long afterward and disappeared. I would like to think that if he had any notion of what would be done to her, he would never have reported Raciel's lapse in propriety. His later behavior certainly suggests a guilty conscience. Several times since then, he has briefly re-appeared, engaged in some half-planned scheme directed against the leadership of Heaven, Hell, or both. At times, he has attempted to reignite the war between Above and Below—staging an attack of one upon the other with the aid of merce-nary soldiers, committing sabotage and leaving evidence to implicate the enemy, that sort of thing. At other times, he's made abortive efforts at raising a force of soldiers powerful enough to invade Hell itself. He's never said as much—or if he has, I never heard about it—but I can't imagine he thinks of it as anything else than a rescue mission.

The sad truth is, he's something of a joke in the White City. His efforts are desperate, feeble, easily detected and thwarted. They're almost the workings of a child, as though his regret and sorrow have overridden whatever strategic acumen he once possessed. As such, and because some of us still felt sorry for him, no concerted effort at locating and capturing him has ever been undertaken. We all assumed that he would eventually wear himself out and disappear, or would attempt something so foolish that he would be caught in the act—by Heaven if he were lucky, otherwise by Hell. Not an angel alive would ever have believed that he might become a real danger, especially after all this time.

And I imagine he never would have, had he not come across one of your profane devices. I don't know where he found it, or how; and again, I don't imagine that it matters. All I know now is that, for the first time, Hadrimon may have the power necessary to wreak whatever vengeance he still feels is his due. And now that he has the influence of the Grand Abominations stoking the hatreds in his soul beyond all com-prehension or sanity, I shudder to think of just how appalling that vengeance may be.

CHAPTER TWENTY-ONE

I T REALLY DIDN'T TAKE THEM ALL THAT LONG.

Even with three score angels on the wing—operating in organized flights from a central base camp, working in an ever-expanding spiral—it could potentially have been quite some time before they discovered anything of note. The territories occupied by the last of the Ravaiim, though certainly limited when compared with an entire realm, still covered a vast expanse. As such, their blood had spilled across and infused the earth over a broad swath of terrain, all of which had to be thoroughly searched. Further, much of what had appeared from above to be featureless plain had now revealed itself to be festooned with jagged crevices and narrow ravines, the entire region cracked and rough as an old callus. With these, the thick fumes that seemed to be the final lingering breaths of this dying world conspired to make any sort of search, however methodical, a dubious proposition at best.

Yet it was only a couple of days between the angels' arrival and the first report of contact with the enemy, found scattered over a wide plain festooned with mushroom-like polyps of glistening, clot-speckled meat.

Now, following the directions of the scouting party—who had themselves returned to keep an eye on Belisatra's forces—

the Horsemen and their allies silently closed on their targets. Death and War traveled on foot; the steeds of the Council's Riders possessed many strengths, but stealth was not high on that list. Around and above them were forty of the White City's soldiers; all that could be spared without leaving the base camp undefended or recalling the most distant scouting parties. And in the center of the slowly advancing forces, Azrael, his lips and fingers moving in eldritch incantations. They were simple spells—one to cloak the company in an illusory mist, making them all but invisible in the drifting haze; another to enhance their vision so that they might see just a bit farther through that haze than otherwise—but extending them over so many at once, while on the move, was proving tricky even for the ancient mystic.

Despite their difficulties, they drew ever nearer, step by soft and careful step. Until Death, peering intently through the fog and scattered particulates in the air, finally managed his first glimpse of what lay ahead.

He'd known the enemy forces were numerous—the scouts' report had been explicit on that point—but it still came as something of a jolt to see them scurrying over the encrusted flatlands. Without taking the time to actually count, he estimated more than two hundred of the multi-legged stone workers, and almost half that many of the brass myrmidons, their spinning shafts kicking up clouds of dust.

He saw something else as well, something new. Several iron cauldrons, complete with articulated legs without and rotating gears within, crept slowly through the midst of the other automatons. At irregular but frequent intervals, the stone servitors would dump loads of earth into those peculiar receptacles, which would then, via the grinding of the gears and various magics that the observing Horseman could sense but not see, be compressed into so much pulp.

A pulp that left behind it trickles and stains of a deep crimson extract.

Death would have liked a closer look, purely out of curiosity, but it wasn't necessary. He knew precisely what those devices were doing, even if the principles and methods remained unclear.

This was how Belisatra was extracting the long-lost residue of the Ravaiim blood from the flesh of the world.

"Still no word from the other scouts?" Death called softly.

Azrael shook his head, his voice still devoted to maintaining his spells.

"War? Thoughts?"

"Until we know otherwise," the other replied, "we should operate under the assumption that this is *not* the only enemy force in the region. Avoid a prolonged engagement if possible, and devote a portion of our forces to perimeter guard if we *are* drawn into one."

"I thought much the same."

"We should hit them from all sides," War continued. "Keep them from setting up any defensive lines, or organizing to protect the workstations."

"Agreed. Four squads of ten angels each. Azrael, you, and I will each lead one. Azrael? Whom do you trust to serve as a fourth?"

The elder angel pointed, indicating an angel with a halberd over her shoulder, a warhammer with a beak nearly as long as her wingspan slung at her back, and a perpetual squint.

"All right. You!"

"Ezgati, Horseman."

"Fine. Ezgati, you command the fourth division." Death stepped aside, allowing War to indicate which unit should approach from which direction.

"The scouting party?" Ezgati asked. "We don't know precisely where they're stationed."

"Keep an eye out," War answered. "Hold off on any cannonades until you've located them—*unless* one of the other units requires immediate assistance. In that case, the scouts will have to take their chances."

Ezgati grumbled under her breath, and Azrael scowled, but neither voiced any objection.

"Remember that your primary targets are the cauldrons. We—"

"Look there!"

Both Horsemen turned at the interruption. One of the angels held his halberd before him, pointing toward a clear spot where the eddies and currents of the breeze had temporarily opened a window through the fog. There, roughly a third of the way around the edge of the enemy operation, the aforementioned scouts had taken shelter behind an encrusted, necrotic dune. Their position should have kept them out of sight of the constructs, yet a small squad of the brass-and-stone soldiers were advancing on them, gradually, silently, from behind.

"Damn it!"

Several of the angels were already moving, weapons out and wings spread, but War raised a hand to stop them. "If we engage, the others will know we're coming!"

"We are *not* just going to leave them out there to be cut down from behind!" Ezgati retorted.

"We need to—"

"Both of you *shut up!*" Death hissed. No, they couldn't launch an overt attack without giving away their presence—but he might just have another option.

The elder Horseman dropped to one knee and plunged his fingers into the rotten, flaky soil, already whispering. Doing this at such a distance was taxing, but not impossible. If he could just . . .

There!

Just ahead of the advancing myrmidons, skeletal hands bristled from the ground, already grabbing at the enemy. Death knew from experience that the rapid spindles would grind those bones to powder, but perhaps if he focused them *all* on a single construct, they might slow it for at least an instant—and, more important, ought to make sufficient noise to warn the scouts of the approaching attackers.

At the Horseman's command, nearly a dozen of those hands converged on the construct in the center of the advancing line, reaching over and around one another so that they might all grab the rotating stalk at once.

Bone snapped, dust flew . . . And then the necromantic strength of so many hands dragged the spindle to a sudden halt.

The upper half of the construct instantly began whirling uncontrollably in the opposite direction, metal screeching under the sudden stress. Like the mad project of some drunken toymaker, part child's top and part marionette, it wobbled as it spun. Its arms flailed wildly, and with them the killing blades into which the construct had already formed its hands. The two myrmidons to either side, as well as one standing a bit too close behind, were instantly hurled aside to land in heaps of shredded metal. Faster and faster the runaway automaton spun, leaning ever farther as it began to topple, until finally one of those arms dug deep into the earth and ripped itself free of the rotating torso in a spray of metal filings, dust, and something that might have been a mix of blood and groundwater. At that point the construct, now completely unbalanced, crashed to the dirt where it flipped a few times, denting itself grotesquely out of shape, before finally going still.

War, Ezgati, and Azrael stared, their jaws comically slack—first at the wreckage, then at Death.

Who, in response, could offer up little more than a half-hearted, "Huh."

Still, while the attempt might not have gone precisely (or at all) as Death had expected, it worked. The small scouting party, alerted by the sensational cacophony, took to the air and vanished into the swirling haze long before the surviving members of that ill-fated ambush could reach them. And while the larger force of constructs clearly knew, now, that something was amiss—they couldn't possibly have missed the clamor, either—they could only respond by converging on the fallen myrmidon, given that the attack lacked any more obvious origin.

Death shrugged, allowed the hands to fade back into the earth, and gestured for War to order the attack.

Things could, perhaps, have gone a bit more smoothly— the four separate divisions had to rush into position, now that the enemy was on guard—but ultimately, it made no difference. Two of the Riders of the Apocalypse and forty angels laid siege to an army of constructs that outnumbered them nearly eight to one, and the constructs never stood a chance.

Sacred energies and tearing shrapnel detonated across Belisatra's forces as a dozen circling angels opened fire with Redemption cannons. Around the edges, those artificial creatures that sought safety away from the enclosed ranks of their comrades instead found themselves peppered into chunks by volley after volley from the ranks of halberdiers. Unable to fire back—none of them was equipped with gun or cannon of its own—the constructs sought shelter within the shallow ravines that crisscrossed the plain, gathered in bunches to shield the "distilling" cauldrons, or darted forward in crooked paths, trying to close on their attackers.

Which was, of course, when the angelic blades came into play.

Swords of impossible width sliced stone and brass as readily as parchment. Ezgati's warhammer whirled in murderous arcs, detonating anything unfortunate enough to meet with the blunt head it boasted on one side, often piercing two or even three constructs at a time with the bill on the other. Azrael and two handpicked soldiers meandered casually through the melee, cloaked in illusions to resemble a trio of the gleaming myrmidons. The scholar focused on maintaining both the phantom image and a second incantation, one to allow the other angels to sense their true natures—didn't want their *allies* to mistake them for constructs, did they?—while his companions lashed out and obliterated enemies who never knew they were threatened at all.

The Horsemen, frankly, were almost superfluous—not that either of them gave any thought to hanging back. War treated the affair more as exercise than battle; he waded through the thickest of the enemy, letting stone claws and brass blades rebound impotently from his armor. Chaoseater rose and fell with an almost monotonous precision, leaving only rubble in its wake.

And Death . . . Death amused himself by clearing those ravines of constructs that had managed to survive everything else hurled their way. In leaps and bounds he passed into and out of crevices faster than the things inside could respond, and each time he left fewer of the living behind. Harvester flashed, singly and in pairs, as scythe or knife or spear as befit the width of any particular cleft. Eventually he borrowed a cannon from one of the angels and began clearing out huge swaths of each fissure at once—not because he needed to, but simply because he was growing a tad bored with it all.

This couldn't *possibly* be the full extent of Hadrimon's and

Belisatra's efforts; he'd faced more than this at the Crowfather's temple, as had the angels at the gates of Eden. Either they had multiple bands working on the Ravaiim homeworld at once, or the bulk of their forces hadn't yet arrived.

Neither was an option that Death particularly enjoyed contemplating. Time to wrap this up and figure out what was going on.

He leapt up from the last crevice, casually tossing the cannon back to its rightful owner, and examined the field. Only a score or so of the constructs remained, and they had been backed into a couple of awkward pockets, easy pickings for the surrounding angels. None of the cauldron-like machines survived; Death reminded himself to check the wreckage, to make sure the enemy couldn't salvage even a drop of Ravaiim blood.

The angels themselves had lost only three of their number. It was an impressive showing, given the numbers they'd faced—even considering how utterly they overpowered the foe on an individual level.

Impressive . . . and easy. Death's unease grew stronger.

It was an unease that his brother clearly shared. War appeared at his shoulder and, without preamble, said, "It can't be a trap. They'd have sprung it by now. Are they truly foolish enough to spread their forces out so thin?"

"I haven't seen a great deal of tactical acumen in their previous efforts, but no, I do not believe they're *that* careless. Either this was a test meant to gauge our strength, or the bulk of their army is occupied elsewhere, or—"

Whatever he'd intended to suggest, Death's *or* effectively became *or we can worry about it later*. Because it was at that moment that the Horsemen and their angelic allies learned that the armies of Belisatra and Hadrimon were not their only competition for the blood of the Ravaiim.

Once more the forces of Hell had found them.

CHAPTER TWENTY-TWO

THEIR FIRST WARNING CAME AS A LOW UNDULATION IN the earth. Not the simple vibrations of marching or running footsteps, this, but a tensing and flexing of the crust as though it cringed from some loathsome contact. The Horsemen, and all the angels not currently in flight, swayed with the unnatural palpitations. Even the surviving constructs, despite their utter lack of facial features or even recognizable heads, managed to convey a vague sense of unease as they braced themselves, skittering about to peer in all directions.

Next was the sound: a terrible, endless din, high and low, shrieking and roaring. A choir of lunatics, chanting hymns as they slowly drowned beneath the crashing waves, might have produced a similar blend of tones.

And then the ground *was* shaking and shuddering with the tromp of an approaching horde, utterly obliterating any trace of the earlier, more subtle fluctuations. Along with that new, more violent tremor, a stench began to permeate the air around them, somehow carried not on, but *ahead of,* the desultory breeze. A stench, or rather a combination of stenches: the thick, coppery tang of blood; an animal aroma of musk and shit; the acrid fetor of sweat . . .

And brimstone. Underlying it, intertwined with all else like a writhing lover, the overwhelming reek of brimstone.

"How?" The steel of War's gauntlets actually began to warp between his ever-tightening grip and Chaoseater's indestructible hilt. "How could they have known to find us *here*?"

"It could be worse," Death said softly. "On any other world, they could have appeared right on top of us."

War might have offered a response to that, had the other not at that moment reached back to unclip something from his belt. The fist on Chaoseater clenched harder yet. "I'm still not convinced it was wise to bring that, brother."

Death slipped his left hand into the gauntlet, which fastened about his forearm with an ominous *click*. The fanged maw and single eye both quivered once, all but unnoticeably, before falling still once more. "We've been through this. It caught me unprepared last time, that's all. Now that I know to be on my guard, it's simplicity itself for me to ward my mind against any further probing. And while Mortis may be almost dead, it retains *some* power. We'll need every advantage we can muster."

Again, War would almost certainly have argued further. Conversation swiftly became impossible, however, washed away beneath a torrent of shouted orders from Azrael and Ezgati, and equally loud acknowledgments from the other angels. The Redemption cannons were swiftly positioned along the tops of the various crevices, angels crouched behind them waiting for the enemy to step into range. Over half the soldiers had taken to the air and spread themselves wide, presenting only small, scattered targets while covering multiple angles of fire with their halberds.

Those angels armed only with—or with a strong preference for—more intimate weapons moved out in groups of three, again positioning themselves so that no single blast or barrage could easily target more than one trio at a time. There were no roads to guard, and the plains were too flat and expansive to provide convenient bottlenecks. Still, the soldiers posted themselves as strategically as they could, hoping at least to encourage the coming foe to charge into the cannoneers' line of fire.

And Azrael, of course, raised his magics, once again cloaking his forces in an image of thickened, swirling fumes. It wouldn't fool the demons for long, but it should at least buy the angels an opening salvo or two.

Belisatra's surviving constructs fled, and the angels allowed them to go. So long as they posed no immediate threat, the soldiers of the White City couldn't afford the time or manpower it would take to hunt them down and finish them.

It was, all told, an impressive display of battlefield discipline; the angels had regrouped and deployed a makeshift defensive line in mere moments.

A good thing, that, since moments were all they had. The haze grew dark, thickened by an array of half-obscured shapes, and the demons were upon them.

The Knights of Perdition appeared first, having pulled ahead of their allies atop their gruesome steeds. Inhuman crusaders encased head-to-toe in scored and rusted armor, Hell's answer to the Horsemen themselves, wielded mighty falchions broad enough to cleave their own mounts in a single blow. Those steeds stamped and snorted, shedding blue flame from hooves and nostrils, their flesh as torn and ragged as Despair's. Where the wounds on Death's steed seemed old and desiccated, however, these bled freely, dribbling strands of crimson to sizzle and smoke in the fires below.

They paused, mounts rearing, thrown for only an instant by Azrael's illusion and the apparent vacancy of the plains. And in that instant, the angels opened fire.

The halberds failed, for the most part, to penetrate the infernal armor, delivering bruises and abrasions at best. The Redemption cannons, however, proved rather more productive; several of the riders were hurled back in smoking heaps of rent flesh and twisted metal, and a handful of the horses literally fell apart beneath the barrage. How much of the earsplitting keening was rider, how much was horse, and how much the crumpling steel, none could say with any certainty.

Even before the first casualties had finished twitching, the demonic Knights responded in kind. Azure fire swirled about them, crackling and snapping across their swords, their arms. Then in the blink of an eye those forces shot downward, melding with the blue flames of the horses' hooves, and raced across the earth in a fearsome torrent. Most of the angels sheltering within the ravines, crouched behind Redemption cannons, were able to hurl themselves aside and evade the worst of the profane energies. Most—not all. Roughly a quarter of the White City cannoneers were blasted from their posts, armor melted to flesh and flesh cooked from bone by the blazing Hellfire.

The soldiers above redoubled their assault, but again only a few of the halberd shots came near to penetrating the Knights' corroded armor. The demon crusaders might be unable to strike back against their flying foes—their unholy blasts seemed capable only of traveling across the earth—but the angels above proved almost as ineffective.

The fumes flowed and shifted yet again; the Knights of Perdition were no longer alone, and the angels no longer owned the skies. Duskwings soared on leather membranes, envenomed tails whipping about with maniacal fury. Alongside them, writhing and slithering through the air in defiance of all natural law, came four-armed demons half humanoid and half serpent. Great tusked maws gaped in silent laughter, horns and matted hair swept from monstrous skulls, and in their taloned hands they crafted globules of bile-green flame. These they hurled with horrific speed, and though their hellish missiles lacked the power of the Knights' own magics, there seemed no end to the constant barrage.

Even more demons surged over the rough terrain, spreading out around and behind the riders. Humanoid, serpentine, quadruped, and others, they marched, ran, skittered, and loped toward the heavenly host. The Knights of Perdition spurred their mounts, leading the charge—and the angels, careful to leave corridors of fire open for their cannon-armed comrades, charged to meet them.

War was with them every step of the way, Chaoseater raised, cloak streaming behind him as though inspired by the wings of his allies. Death, however . . . hesitated.

Not from fear, nor uncertainty. No, the Horseman peered intently into the airborne flakes and haze, struggling for a second glimpse of something he *thought* he'd seen . . .

And there it was, almost obscured by the gritty atmosphere, lurking in the rearmost ranks of the demonic throng. Something tall, horrifically bulky, possessed of wings as magnificent as the angels' own but far uglier—almost as bat-like as those of the duskwings, despite the tattered ivory feathers that adorned their expanse in ragged patches. A tail, cruelly barbed, twitched behind the creature, as idly as a cat's. From here, Death could not see the heavy, twisted horns protruding from a pallid, waxen face, but he knew they would be there, just as he knew precisely what sort of demon led this motley horde of Hell's terrors.

Such creatures were among the most potent soldiers of the Pit, and certainly the most poignant—for it was this form into which angels almost invariably twisted, mutated, should they plummet from Heaven's graces, succumb too long to the temptations of Hell's most vile perversities.

All this Death saw, and seeing, he could only wonder.

It couldn't be her. *Out of all the Lost Angels, of all the many demons making themselves as available as soldiers beyond the borders of Hell, it* couldn't *be* her!

Could it? The odds against such a coincidence were surely astronomical.

Unless it was no coincidence at all.

The profaned angel—whoever it might once have been—drifted backward on outstretched wings, until even the Horseman's potent senses could no longer detect it within the heavy fumes. Brow furrowed in thought behind his immobile mask, Death hefted his own weapon and darted ahead to join the others in battle.

FROM HIGH ABOVE, out of immediate danger but near enough to keep track of all that occurred, Azrael watched the exchange of fire and the abrupt collision of opposing forces. Most angelic commanders would be down there, shoulder-to-shoulder and wingtip-to-wingtip with their soldiers, wielding blade or gun against the foe. Even the lifelong scholar's blood pounded at the thought, his militant heritage surging within his soul.

Brutally, he forced it down. He had his own strengths, his own contributions to make, and none of them involved getting in the way of warriors with far more acumen than he. Instead, Azrael raised his hands high and began to call upon the magics that only he, among all the scions of Heaven, possessed.

"Be ready." He barely spoke, yet the soldiers with whom he'd orchestrated this maneuver heard him clearly, his words carried to them on eldritch currents. "We begin . . . *Now!*"

At Azrael's command, the skies burned. Columns of roaring flame, white and blinding, infused with the sacred essence of Heaven itself, twisted down to strike at the various masses of demons. Three, four, five of them touched the earth, crackling, howling—and the demons scattered, howling in turn.

By the time the slowest of Hell's soldiers, those unable to avoid the blazing pillars, could realize that they were unharmed—that the entire firestorm was nothing but another of the scholar's illusions—their swifter companions had already broken formation and put themselves at the mercy of the White City's gunners.

Redemption cannons spoke, over and over, blasting the more potent demons, leaders and elite soldiers, who would otherwise have proved difficult to reach through the ranks of lesser minions. Halberds barked from above, cutting down those weaker creatures whose defenses were not so impenetrable as the Knights'. Many demons fell, then and there, to the carefully aimed weapons of a relatively small band of angels.

The Knights of Perdition and other commanders instantly called their soldiers back, gathering them once more into tight formation—or at least, as tight as the generally unpredictable and undisciplined creatures of Hell could manage. Once again they surged forward, closing on the outnumbered angelic line.

Again Azrael summoned fire from on high. This time, the demons knew better than to scatter and expose themselves in the face of an illusory attack.

This time, of course, the sacred flame was real.

Demons burned by the score, charred to ash and less than ash, and Azrael could only smile at his soldiers' cheers.

WAR STOOD AT THE FOREFRONT, where the converging forces would meet, all but daring the enemy to attack him. His cloak swirled, tossed about in a breeze created mainly by the rapidly passing bodies, and Chaoseater gleamed darkly beside him. He didn't even bother striking at the lesser demons that dashed or flitted past him, choosing to leave them for the angels, and they, in turn, knew better than to draw his attentions. War was the greatest threat on the field of battle—well, one of the two—and certainly the most overt. He waited, his pulse quickening, for the forces of Hell to respond in kind.

And respond they did. From out of the dust clouds came the thunder of hooves, presaging the arrival of the Knights of Perdition.

Among the most fearsome of the warriors present, these champions of the Pit had been crafted by the rulers of Hell when the Horsemen first arose, and while they were not so potent as the Riders of the Apocalypse, neither were they to be underestimated. War allowed himself a moment to wish that Ruin stood with him, rather than pacing the ledges back at the base camp; if they'd only been less concerned with stealth, had known what they'd be facing . . .

Well, so be it. This could not have been foreseen, and War needed no ally, even his most trusted and valued, to deal with the likes of these.

They burst into view, rust-armored shapes on their rotting mounts, massive blades poised to strike, the earth around them crackling with cerulean fire. Three of them, indistinguishable from one another save for the precise shape and location of the horses' wounds, scrutinized the Horseman through visors thick with shadow. The beasts all but pranced in place, snorting and howling, angry and eager. They fanned out, as War had known they must, and came at him from multiple angles at once.

He would not be escaping this confrontation unscathed, of that he had no doubt. He crouched, placing the fingertips of his left hand on the corrupted ground. As before, he drew upon the might stored within Chaoseater, absorbed from the surrounding carnage.

Rather than blades bursting from below, however, this time it was the Horseman himself who changed. A dull cast spread swiftly over him, beginning with his outstretched hand as though drawn from the earth itself, traveling up and out, until he appeared to have been coated in soot—or, perhaps, a dusting of rock.

The initial pass was scarcely more than a test, and they conducted it well. Their approach, the careful intervals between one strike and the next, meant that their target must always have his back to at least one of them, could never be certain that all three blades would converge at once, or in what order. Even in this first, almost gentle exchange, War found himself hard-pressed to avoid them all. He parried one blade with Chaoseater, ducked beneath a second that might otherwise have claimed his head, but he could do nothing for the third save to take the force against the back of his armor. The blow staggered him, dropping him—if only briefly—to one knee; but thanks to the unnatural rigidity of his temporarily rocky skin, it drew no blood. His arm and his face burned at the touch of Hellfire lingering in the hoofprints, but not nearly so severely as they otherwise might.

He was standing once more as the riders circled, and still he waited.

Again they turned and charged, faster this time, standing in their stirrups to add just that much more strength to the coming strikes. *Still* he waited, one hand on the great black blade that stood, tip-down, beside him, as they pounded closer, closer . . .

War thrust against Chaoseater with impossible strength, burying a good portion of the blade in the dirt, but also propelling himself forward at the same time. Feetfirst, he slid swiftly *between* the front hooves of the nearest beast. Again his arms and his chest burned at the touch of the unholy fire, but he wouldn't have to endure it long.

Before either horse or rider could begin to respond to the sudden maneuver, War tensed both knees and straightened once more to his feet. With the flat of both hands, he lifted and *threw* rider and steed together. Propelled by both the Horseman's unnatural might and their own forward momentum, they tumbled and flailed across the battlefield, fully airborne, until colliding with a deafening, bone-rending crash against the second of the three Knights of Perdition.

War ducked into a roll back the way he'd come, passing easily beneath the blade of the last of the trio, and shot upright into a fearsome leap. His skin had resumed the color and texture of flesh, and Chaoseater was again clutched in hand. He landed hard beside the entangled riders, blade readied in a two-fisted grip. Metal, demons, and mounts screamed in unison as it punched through armor, through flesh, through bone, until the tip once more rested in the sickly soil.

From his crouch, War gazed calmly up at the remaining rider, some few dozen paces distant—and though the demon's face remained hidden behind shadow and steel, the Horseman had no difficulty reading his enemy's fear.

The Knight's mount reared, the bale-fire crackled, and another burst of unholy force shot across the earth. War, his ears pounding as the pain of his injuries and the surging flame of bloodlust clashed and roiled in his soul, yanked Chaoseater from the heaped corpses. He offered the champion of Hell his broadest smile as he waited for it to come.

THE SERPENTINE DEMONS WOVE complex knots in the sky as they swerved and dodged every attack the angels could hurl at them. Death had once overheard this sort of demon called a "shadowcaster," and had initially wondered why—until he realized the damn things were blind as mushrooms. Their forked and flickering tongues tasted vibrations on the earth and in the air, and their unnatural flight made them far more maneuverable than the angels. The shadowcasters' ability to avoid even the best-aimed halberd fire was matched only by their own unnatural precision with those balls of green flame. Against the ground-based forces or the large and ponderous duskwings, the angelic halberdiers were devastating; against the shadowcasters, more than a dozen had already fallen, crashing in heaps of singed meat and blazing feathers.

Death, however, needed no wings, and was not so readily burned.

He soared over the battlefield, standing tall on the back of an abnormally massive duskwing, almost half again as large as the one that his weight had brought down in Lilith's laboratory. The bat-demon shrieked and gibbered, its world awash in viscous pain. Harvester, split now into two scythes, served as reins: Each tip sat snug within the bloody, mangled flesh of one of the creature's shoulders, and the Horseman needed only the slightest tug to inform the duskwing in which way it had better turn.

After a few desperate attempts at shaking its Rider, including a maddened upside-down flutter that still hadn't been enough to dislodge either the scythes or their wielder, it had given up the struggle and meekly obeyed.

Despite the immediacy of the carnage and bloodshed, Death couldn't help but spend a moment circling, staring with unabashed astonishment at the wake of devastation slicing through the figures below. War, as far as his older brother could determine, had lost himself fully to the havoc of battle. Not merely the initial trio of Knights of Perdition, but two more of those hellish warriors—as well as several *dozen* lesser demons of various and sundry types—littered the battlefield.

Literally littered the battlefield, as not a single one of them lay in any fewer than three pieces.

Chaoseater moved so swiftly it seemed to form a solid arc. War's cloak streamed behind him in tatters; his armor, scored and blackened, smoked visibly in the somewhat lighter haze; blood streamed from a veritable legion of wounds scattered across his body. The younger Horseman didn't appear to care, or even to have *noticed*. A dull reverberation echoed from the whirling figure, and Death was stunned to realize that what he heard was nothing less than a continuous, breathless battle cry.

It was, the airborne Rider realized with a faint twinge in his gut, a damn good thing that they weren't counting on any meticulous plans or tactics for the remainder of the struggle. War didn't seem *sentient* enough anymore to follow them; and in any effort to halt him in his tracks, Death wasn't certain that even *he* would come out the victor.

With a quick shake, he dragged his attentions back to his own circumstances and left War to his efforts. The massive demonic bat wouldn't remain aloft much longer—with each flap of the wings, each jolt of the body, Harvester sawed deeper into muscles and tendons—but that was fine by Death. The creature had gotten him where he needed to be.

He hauled left until the screeching thing began to circle. He watched the airborne battles beneath him, meticulously tracking the undulations of the shadowcasters. Only when he was certain he could anticipate them, despite their erratic paths, did he act.

Death jerked both scythes free, dragging one deep across the duskwing's spine to ensure it would not survive the coming plunge, and dropped from its back.

Even his calculations, his reflexes, weren't *quite* on target, not given the preternatural awareness and constant winding of the demonic serpents. His target sensed him coming and whipped itself aside, leaving the Horseman with nothing between himself and the corrupted earth far below.

Just as he plummeted past the snickering demon, Death lashed out. Neither of the two scythes he'd carried was long enough to bridge the gap—but then, Harvester was no longer two scythes, but one of far longer haft. The shadowcaster howled, partly in bewilderment but mostly in agony, as the blade sliced across its body. Using the weapon as a hook, much as he had on the mountain spur in the Crowfather's realm, Death swung under the creature, transforming his momentum into a backward flip so he now stood *atop* the snaking coils.

Not precisely the most stable footing—especially since the shadowcaster was currently in the process of splitting almost in half—but enough for the Rider's needs. He tensed and leapt, landing on the second shadowcaster almost as he would a horse, legs clamped tight to either side. Harvester, now a pair of heavy knives, rose to strike . . .

When two more of the demons swooped in from the side and launched Hellfire directly at him.

Death's left arm tensed, swinging Mortis into the path of the oncoming missiles. Searing heat licked around the edges of the shield, and the tips of his hair crisped and sizzled, but nothing more.

An instant later, Mortis howled.

Shimmering waves, something between a heat mirage and a fever dream, billowed from the Grand Abomination's single eye. With deceptive speed, it bridged the distance between Death and yet another of the shadowcasters—the fifth and final member of this particular group.

Mortis's howl ceased, and the demon's began. An enormous chunk of flesh simply vanished from its body, letting blood and viscera pour, steaming, into the open air. Death couldn't help note, as the shadowcaster fell from sight, that the size and shape of the wound perfectly matched the fanged maw of the device he wore.

And it's nearly dead, at only a fraction of its former strength . . .

Death shook off his astonishment; time for that later. Instead he drove both blades home, then hurled himself from the spasming body toward the next nearest shadowcaster, still half frozen in bewilderment at its failed attack.

It had been a near thing, this demonic assault, something

for which he and the angels had been woefully unprepared. Still, it looked, after a few questionable moments, as though they would once again come out on top.

Assuming nothing *else* unexpected happened, of course.

WHERE THE HELL—so to speak—had the demons come from this *time?*

Not that it actually mattered, not really. In fact, their timing couldn't have been better. He and Belisatra hadn't expected the Horsemen to find their constructs so swiftly; nor had they anticipated that the brothers would bring angels with them. They'd assumed their enemy would conduct the search by ground, not by air. And as such, they hadn't been ready, hadn't been in position to launch their ambush once the constructs came under attack.

Then, almost as though they were a gift from Fate or the Creator, the demons had appeared to delay the Horsemen and the angels. And that had provided all the time they needed.

Belisatra wanted to wait; wanted to learn more about the demonic forces, figure out how they fit into ongoing events, what their presence meant for the larger plan. But no; there would be no waiting! Fire burned in his soul, hatred churned through his thoughts. He would have the blood of the Ravaiim. He would have the corpses of the Horsemen, and the first of so many angels to come. And he would have them now!

Hadrimon drew Black Mercy from the holster at his side and took, screaming, to the skies. He didn't even look to see if the others were following; he knew they would, knew they must. It was time.

He would have them *now*!

CHAPTER TWENTY-THREE

O F COURSE," HE MUTTERED TO HIMSELF. DEATH HAD just landed with a resounding *whump,* surrounded by a cloud of dust and various lengths of plummeting shadowcasters, when the first of the brass myrmidons came spinning through the ubiquitous murk. He'd heard their unique high-pitched whirring an instant earlier, had known what he'd see before the first even appeared. "This was absolutely the worst time for them to appear, so naturally it would be now. Most common substance in Creation is dramatic irony."

Still, as he hefted Harvester and wearily surveyed the situation—or what he could see of it—he decided it might not be *that* bad. The constructs had moved in across their flank. That meant they were hitting the demons at the same moment as the angels, and the demons were already hitting back, taking some of the pressure off Death's allies. And while the angels were verging on exhausted, their earlier encounter proved that they were more than a match for this particular enemy. So long as the constructs didn't appear in numbers several times their prior efforts, they—

The Horseman shuddered, a chill such as he hadn't felt in ages running across his normally unfeeling skin. Something cast a deep shadow over his mind, over his soul, until even the *memory* of warmth had faded away.

"Is that—?"

He didn't know when War had appeared at his side, but wasn't at all surprised to find him there. The spiritual taint of the Abomination had apparently shocked him back to his senses. The younger Horseman's armor was scored and singed, small splotches of blood were drying on his gauntlets and his left cheek, but Death was certain that the faint uncertainty in his voice was caused by something more than the pain of his injuries.

"Yes," Death told him. "One of them, at least, is awake."

A single shot rang out. It was no louder than any other gun, and certainly quieter than the Redemption cannons. Yet everyone *felt* the report in a way unlike any other; it was a roiling in the gut, an involuntary flinch, a quick skip of the heart.

One of Azrael's angels fell dead through the fumes, landing almost at Death's feet. His flesh was shrunken, his skin maggot white, as though he'd been dead for some hours. His body bore no visible wounds, save for a single graze along the left wing.

"Black Mercy," Death said. "Any wound it delivers, *every* wound it delivers, kills, no matter how minor."

"Even us, brother?"

"We're more than we were when we rode with the Nephilim, but enough to stand against *that*? I couldn't begin to guess, and I'd as soon not learn the hard way."

"Makes sense." Another shot rang out, another angel fell, and War scowled into the fog. "He's keeping too high. I can't even see where he is!"

Death abruptly sprinted across the field, hurtling fallen bodies and narrow crevices without pause. War, startled and somewhat encumbered by his armor, could scarcely keep up, but the elder Horseman seemed not to notice.

"Azrael!"

The scholar, his hair limp and his eyes drooping with fatigue, spun at Death's call.

"Need you to do something about this fog."

"It won't be for long," the angel warned. "I can't maintain the magic over an area this large. That's why I—"

"Fine! Briefly is fine, just do it!"

Though his entire visage curled in distaste at being so addressed, Azrael raised his hands and began to chant.

The fumes swirled, drifting apart in a widening sphere. The flatlands around them were crawling with constructs; their numbers were, if not overwhelming, then at least somewhat daunting. Above, so high he was barely a speck even to Death's keen vision, circled an angel who could only have been Hadrimon. Distant though they were, the Horsemen—and the angels, albeit to a lesser degree—could sense the presence of the Grand Abomination he wielded; a tumor in Creation.

Except . . . Hadrimon was maintaining his height, not diving. So why was the sensation growing *stronger* . . . ?

Again Death broke into a run, and this time War and Azrael, as well as several other winged soldiers, remained at his side. The Horseman scrambled to the edge of a small rise—not much of a dune, but all that these open plains had to offer other than the various ravines—and watched the fog rapidly retreat before Azrael's magics.

Belisatra stood revealed, clad in blocky armor, surrounded by more than a hundred of her artificial soldiers. She held before her what appeared to be a rifle made of bone, linked by a cord of hair to . . . *something*. Something that loomed, dark and heavy, even before the vapors had faded.

"Oh, no . . ." Death's shoulders slumped. *It was destroyed! We were so* sure *that one was destroyed!*

"What is it?" War asked, more alarmed by his brother's reaction than by anything he'd yet seen on the battlefield.

The response, when it came, was barely a whisper. "Earth Reaver . . ."

What emerged from the fog, following the tug of that hair like a hound on a leash, was a mobile platform the height of a four-story building. It crept, slow but inexorable, on four quivering crab-like legs, constructed of linked femurs and other long bones. Its upper body—if *body* was even an applicable word for this monstrosity—consisted of nine separate tentacles the color of rotting flesh. In fact, they *were* rotting flesh, for each tentacle was formed of dozens of handless arms, connected one to the next, wrist-to-shoulder. And at the end of each of these nine limbs, a shrunken, lipless mouth, constructed from jawbones and skin, blackened gums and jagged teeth.

In the center of those tentacles, looming above the rest of the grotesque device, rose an enormous obsidian mirror.

"Tell your people to fall back," Death ordered Azrael. The words were ashes and bile in his mouth.

War spun. *"What?"*

"We are the greatest of the White City," the angel proclaimed, holding himself almost rigid. "We do not—"

Death's fist closed on the fabric of Azrael's robe, just above the edge of his breastplate, and lifted the angel clear off his feet. "If you want any of the White City's greatest to be alive this time tomorrow," he spat, shaking Azrael like a child, "then *run!"*

His grip opened and Azrael landed with an awkward stumble. The angel's face had gone red with fury, but War stepped between them before one or the other could act further. "I've never seen my brother like this," he said. "Perhaps we should—"

A symphony of hisses, clatters, and squeals sounded from the thing Death had called Earth Reaver. The four legs halted and dug into the soil, followed by the awful tendrils. The wet sounds of *chewing* drifted across the plains as all nine mouths literally ate their way down into the dirt.

When Death stopped arguing and ran for cover, War and Azrael were wise enough to do the same. What they did not know, what troubled Death even as he pounded across the brittle earth, was that "cover" would do them precious little good.

Behind them, the Maker aimed her rifle at the mass of combatants still battling in the center of everything, apparently unconcerned that she was targeting more than a few of her own constructs in addition to many angels and demons. The great obsidian mirror rotated and angled itself with a low grinding, tracking the smaller lens of obsidian in the barrel of the gun, so that each was always aimed at the same spot as the other.

Belisatra squeezed the trigger.

A blur passed through the ground, so fast as to be almost invisible, between the platform and the target. And when it struck, the ground exploded.

Not just any detonation, this. Not a column of fire. Not a geyser. Where the Grand Abomination spoke, there burst a full-fledged, world-shaking volcanic eruption.

Earth Reaver. The Nephilim had christened it well.

The initial blast launched enough debris to plug the sky: dust; shattered stone; the dried skin and sludgy humors of this infected realm; and tiny bits of what had once been angels, demons, and constructs—all became a cloudy film that cast the plains into early midnight. Cooked and diseased meat wafted on the air, thick enough to *taste*, let alone smell. Jagged rock and blazing cinders rained in vicious squalls, shattering and burning whatever they struck. The ground rippled and split, forming a whole new array of crevices and slow-moving rivers of pink-veined puss.

All of which, really, was just a precursor for what was to come.

If the initial cloud had briefly cast the region into artificial night, the spout of lava that followed was a bloody, hellish dawn. It surged from the newly made pit, engulfing everything it could catch. Most of the demons, and more than a handful of constructs, vanished into the roiling torrent. Only a few angels were caught within, but of those who managed to fly up and over the lava flow, almost half died anyway, either struck by falling debris or plummeting once their wings ignited in the rising heat.

Behind the stunted dune—poor protection indeed, but better than none at all—a heap of debris shifted, jolted from within. Dirt and sludge sluiced away, revealing the Horsemen, Azrael, and a handful of angels. In addition to the smeared filth coating them head-to-toe, most had suffered various degrees of singeing and burning, though Death had an almost comical clean spot across his face and chest roughly the size and shape of Mortis.

"*Now* can we call a retreat?" Death asked.

Azrael waved a hand at one of the angels accompanying him. She, in turn, produced what appeared to be a small golden trumpet and raised it to her lips. The sound, when it came, reverberated from all directions, in the mind as much as the ears. The surviving angels reacted instantly, assembling from all corners. They were a sorrowful lot, battered and filthy, but their backs and wings remained straight, their heads unbowed.

"What good is a withdrawal against *that*?" The question came from Ezgati, who had come in response to the summons. Her left arm dangled uselessly, bone and blackened meat strapped to her side by what appeared to be the reins off a Knight of Perdition's mount, but her right—and the warhammer clutched in that hand—appeared as steady as ever.

"They'll have to move Earth Reaver to a new location before firing again," Death said, shouting to be heard over the ongoing, frighteningly close eruption. "It can't affect the same area twice; all the region's faults and magma have already been channeled into the first volcano. And it's slow. If we regroup at the cliff, we ought to have at least a short while to strategize."

"Squads of five!" Azrael barked. "Keep moving, but maintain some distance between each group. Each flight is responsible for covering the one behind. Move!"

They moved. Death and War watched as the angels gathered, guided by either instinct or prior training into organized groups. "They'll need to stay low," War pointed out. "With everything in the air, it would be too easy to get lost, disoriented."

"That works in our favor." Death stepped out from behind cover, leading his brother toward a nearby ravine with several dead angels sprawled within. Kneeling at the edge of the crevice, he scooped up two of the fallen Redemption cannons, heaving one over to War. "It means Hadrimon can't easily pick us off with Black Mercy."

War snapped the heavy clip from the front of the weapon, checked the ammunition, and shoved it back into place. "Be easier on horseback . . ."

Death merely grunted, and then they were running, keeping some few score paces behind the last of the angels.

Unseen things crunched, slid, burst, and squelched beneath their feet; they hurtled narrow but seemingly bottomless gaps, through rising curtains of steam and other, fouler vapors. Despite its difficulties, Death welcomed the terrain. Between the generally flat plains and the thick fog—volcanic and otherwise—it was all that provided them any sense of travel, no matter how fast they moved.

Belisatra's soldiers appeared sporadically through the fog, as did the occasional lingering demon, but none posed much of a threat. Among Harvester, Chaoseater, and the pair of cannons, the Horsemen faced precisely no difficulty whatsoever in covering the angels' retreat.

Not, at least, until they neared the escarpment. In the final crevice before the flatland leading up to the cliff face—a crevice far enough from the nascent volcano that it was not yet filling with boiling fluids—Azrael and several angelic squadrons had taken shelter. More angels crouched nearby, or circled low in the air above.

And several lay sprawled in the dust farther ahead, strewn across the plains like flowers after a storm.

"Hadrimon is somewhere overhead," Azrael told them as they neared. "With all the fumes, I doubt he can make out more than vague shapes and movement, but with that weapon at hand, that appears to be all he needs. He's picking us off as we attempt to cross over to the cliffs. I thought you said that the enemy needed to take this realm before they could awaken the Abominations." From anyone else, it would have been accusing, almost sullen. From Azrael, it just sounded curious.

The time for dissembling and half-truths had clearly passed. "Awakening the Grand Abominations requires the blood of an extinct race called the Ravaiim," Death said. "Most of them died here, making this the only *reliable* source. But some fell in battle on other worlds, and if Hadrimon or Belisatra learned where, they could have distilled a small amount of blood from the earth there. Not much, but enough to awaken Black Mercy and Earth Reaver for a short while."

"Not short enough, I fear. If you've any further plan in mind, now would be an auspicious time to share."

It was War, not Death, who answered. "We don't actually have to *defeat* the enemy here. If we just keep them from acquiring what they need, we can wipe them out later."

"Easier said than done," one of the nearby soldiers pointed out.

"True. But it does, if nothing else, alter our strategy."

Death was already nodding. "I do have a thought, but we need shelter and we need time. A lot more time than . . . Azrael, Ezgati? Have you much in the way of explosives? Preferably large ones?"

"No," Ezgati called from farther down the line. "Firearms only."

"I've had some luck using the ammunition clips from Redemption cannons as explosives," War said blandly. Through masks of filth and soot, several nearby angels glared at him.

"Good enough." Death gestured at the nearest soldier. "Go up and down the line, gather one clip from everyone who has spares."

"But we might—"

"You appear to have mistaken me for someone who's *asking*."

A beseeching glance at Azrael, a subtle nod from the scholar, and the angel was off to do as he had been . . . "asked."

"I'll draw Hadrimon off," the Horseman continued, "and slow Earth Reaver a bit as well. Once that's done, Azrael, I may have a way to end this, but I'll require your assistance."

"Of course."

"Brother, I'll need you and the cannoneers to cover me. Once I'm away, get everyone into the caves and establish the best perimeter you can. I'll trust you to—"

"I should go."

"—come up with . . . What?"

War squared his shoulders. "Tell me what you have in mind, and I'll go. You must survive to enact your plan with Azrael, whatever it may be. And," he added, his voice dropping, "I'm not certain our current allies would be all that pleased working beside me alone. Seems they hold a grudge."

"They'll get over it. I'm going."

"But—"

"No. You've a better grasp of tactics than I; you'll be more useful in planning the defenses."

"The angels are more than capable—"

"And I'm faster than you are. And I'm done arguing."

War was far too disciplined—and certainly too proud—to protest or complain further, but his expression and his posture were more than loud enough to convey everything he wouldn't say.

But then, Death hadn't said everything, either. *If Black Mercy does shoot one of us,* he hadn't told War, *I'm more likely to survive it than you are.*

A little.

"You need to move the injured," he said, returning to Azrael. "Get them as far to the other end of the crevice as you can."

"If I may ask . . . ?"

"The plan is for Hadrimon to follow me. He may come in low, in order to see me through the fumes, and that could bring him within range."

"Range of what?"

"Black Mercy doesn't need to fire in order to kill. Any wound it delivers is fatal, yes—but so is any wound *at all* if it's suffered by an enemy of the wielder, and if it's still bleeding in the Abomination's proximity. This weapon has slaughtered entire *armies*, Azrael."

The angel recoiled, ashen. "And how far does this power extend?"

"Depends on how many it's killed since it awoke. I'll lead him past as far from the wounded as I can, but I make no promises."

"Every time I think I've finally begun to understand how depraved the Nephilim actually were . . ."

"Trust me, angel. If you live until the last star burns out, until the Creator Himself has died and putrefied away to nothing, you still won't even *begin* to understand how depraved we were.

"Be grateful."

DEATH VAULTED FROM THE CREVICE and broke into a dust-churning run across the open expanse. He swerved randomly, never quite breaking his course for the escarpment, but doing what he could to avoid making himself an easy target. From behind, War and the White City's surviving cannoneers opened fire, saturating the sky in a blanket of detonations—less concerned with actually hitting anything than with ensuring Hadrimon himself never had a moment to aim.

Still it was close. Black Mercy's teeth tore into the ground uncomfortably near the sprinting figure. Bits of rock and soil flew, some rotting away before they could fall back to earth. At one point, Death sensed a line of impacts stitching its way toward him and could only crouch, Mortis held high. His entire arm went numb as the bullet plunged into the shield, and he could swear he heard a faint moan from the bestial maw. Again he saw the wavering and shifting as Mortis lashed out against one of Hadrimon's allies—likely a random construct closing in from the plains beyond the angels—but he couldn't even begin to see the results.

One of the cannons blasted the air directly above him, showering him with flaming bits of debris. Death winced, but rose and ran once more. The near miss, uncomfortable as it was, had probably also forced Hadrimon out of position.

Probably War. If anyone was going to fire the shot that would both shelter and sting Death at once, it would have been War.

He was close, now, close enough to see the ledges and the caves through the haze. The shots from above had ceased; Hadrimon was probably waiting for Death to begin climbing, where the angel could pick him off at leisure. Not even the Horseman was fast enough to make such an ascent without providing a tempting target.

Except that Death had no *intention* of climbing the cliff face.

Drawing deep within, Death put on a burst of speed, sprinting faster than he ever had—and at the same moment, he uttered a piercing mental cry.

The mists swirling about one of the cave mouths suddenly thickened, taking on a soggy olive hue. Despair bolted from the shelter in answer to its master's call, charging at speed despite the precarious footing.

Death took a final few steps, tensing as his foot came down. At the precise instant Despair hit the edge of the shelf, they both leapt.

Despair arced downward, a grotesque comet trailing a toxic tail of fumes. Death soared up, carried by a bound that few entities in Creation could have rivaled.

A dismayed shout sounded from behind and Black Mercy began to cough once more, but the lethal barrage passed clear beneath the Horseman's feet.

Almost halfway between the protruding lip of stone and the rocky, scaly earth, their paths crossed.

Death lashed out, snagged the saddle horn with his left hand, and swung himself bodily over and around. His boots slipped into the stirrups almost with a mind of their own. A massive jolt and they were down, Rider and steed reunited once more.

The horse uttered a single, sepulchral cry that might, just might, have rung with exultation, and *ran*.

In mere heartbeats they had once again crossed the expanse, drawing a thick line of flying soil and ocher fumes across the face of the realm. An easy jump, almost casual, carried them over the ravine in which the angels had sheltered. Death heard, faintly, the constant fire of Black Mercy, the raving screams of the maddened Hadrimon, but none of them came anywhere near.

Give Despair his head and open ground, and not even an angel on the wing could hope to keep up.

He would try, though. Blinded by wounded pride and worry as to what Death had planned, Hadrimon would follow, allowing War and the others to reach the caves.

Crevices and slow rivers of viscous humors passed beneath Despair's hooves. The world grew darker, the air grittier and far, far hotter, as they again approached the scene of the hopeless battle and the roaring volcano.

Once, as he neared a cluster of angels and demons who had slaughtered one another early in the struggle, he slipped a foot free of the stirrups and leaned down from the horse's back, so that his fingers nearly dragged the ground. He snagged one of the demon corpses, hauling it with him as he righted himself. He casually ripped the head from its shoulders and tied it to his belt by the hair, letting the rest of the body fall away. He had a few questions to ask, once things had calmed down.

And finally, there it was: Earth Reaver. The construct army had been forced to scatter, to pass around the lava flows the Grand Abomination had unleashed, but not the weapon itself. On its massive legs of bone, it trudged through the roiling sludge, utterly untouched by the heat. Death couldn't see Belisatra, though he knew she had to be near. That leash of hair was lengthy—could, in fact, grow or shrink based on the needs of the wielder—but not indefinite.

No matter. She was not his target.

The weapon lumbered forward, splashing through the shallow pool, and Death realized he could not have asked for a better location. Just ahead, Earth Reaver would have to stretch its legs to step across one of the crevices, now flowing with lava. Not much, not at its size, but enough.

Death reined Despair to a halt; the horse reared, pawing at the air, eager to keep moving. "Easy," the Rider whispered. "Easy. Just for a moment . . ."

The Horseman still saw no sign of Hadrimon, but he knew the angel would be coming up fast from behind. If the damn thing would just *move!*

Slowly, with an almost mocking languor, the platform raised a leg, reached, began to set it down across the ravine in a step Death could almost have called *dainty.*

Just before the leg settled, when the platform's balance was at its worst, Death hefted the bag in which his angelic errand boy had gathered the Redemption ammunition. He whipped it around his head once, twice, and let it fly in a high arc.

Even before the sack had reached its target, Harvester had split into twin smaller scythes, and Death hurled one of them as well.

Just before the bag completed its fall, Harvester whipped past, slicing open not only the fabric but several of the clips within, exposing the warheads. Earth Reaver's leg came down on top of the bag, crushing it and driving it deep into the lava in a single step.

The resulting explosion wasn't enough to actually harm the Abomination, but it was more than sufficient to send it toppling. Scrambling in a comic dance, the platform teetered and fell, splashing a torrent of lava into the air. At least one of its legs dangled into the ravine, robbing it of vital leverage.

Death reached out, snatched the returning scythe from the

air, and wheeled Despair around. He'd take the long way, so as not to pass back through Hadrimon's field of fire.

He'd likely bought himself several additional hours, before Earth Reaver could right itself and reach the escarpment. Maybe, *maybe,* time enough.

CHAPTER TWENTY-FOUR

Y OU UNDERSTAND, DO YOU NOT, THAT WHILE I HAVE mastered multiple styles of magic, I know very little in the way of necromancy? I have no truck with the dead."

The peculiar pair, the angel and the Horseman, currently occupied the deepest cavern in that cliff-face network of tunnels. The only illumination came from a small fire against the far wall and the blazing intensity of the Rider's eyes. Across the floor of the cave—dirt, soil, and that peculiar skin-like crust— Death had sketched an array of glyphs and sigils. They were spidery, squiggly little things, almost dizzying to look at, from a time before writing itself had fully decided how it should work, or what it ought to be.

Between Death and the fire sat a small cylinder of gold and crystal, one of several containers he'd borrowed from the angels' supplies. Dust perched atop it, head cocked as he studied the dancing flame. When the Horseman had returned from the battle and his mad ride, the crow had peered up at him with a look that seemed almost to scream, *Oh, were you gone? I hadn't noticed.* He'd then fluttered to Death's shoulder, where he'd remained until a few moments ago.

Other than the crackling fire and the occasional scrape of

Azrael's wings against a low-hanging stalactite, the only sounds in the cave were occasional hints of War and the angels in the passageways beyond, making preparations for the assault to come.

"I'm aware," Death said finally, his answer to Azrael so long in coming that the angel had been opening his mouth to repeat himself. "You won't need any necromantic acumen for this. I have another purpose in mind for you."

The Horseman plunged Harvester, tip-first, into one of the stone walls and left it hanging until he might need it. Over it he draped Mortis; the thing was *probably* too lifeless to react to what was coming, but why chance it? Then, with infinite care, so as not to disturb even one of the symbols in the dirt, he lowered himself to sit cross-legged before the fire.

"What I plan to do," he continued, "is simple enough in concept—only a minor manipulation of the essence of dead things. No more complicated than anything else I've done a thousand times before.

"The problem is the *magnitude*. I've never attempted necromancies on a realm-wide scale before."

"You require power," Azrael guessed.

"Precisely. I need you to gather your energies, as though to cast your greatest spells, and then channel them to me—or at least into my own incantations, if that's easier. Can you do it?"

The angel paused, his expression thoughtful. "I've never attempted anything exactly like it," he admitted, "but I have cooperated with other angels in the casting of a particularly difficult invocation. I imagine the mental effort should be similar enough. Death?"

"Hmm?"

"With all respect to you and what you do, I am not entirely comfortable with this—with necromancy in general. You're certain this is necessary?"

"Hadrimon and Belisatra—and Earth Reaver—will be here in a matter of hours. Have you any other ideas for keeping the blood of the Ravaiim away from them?"

"Let's begin, then," Azrael said with a sigh.

"I'll need to remain focused on the incantation once it's started," Death told him. "Dust will alert you when I need you to start channeling your reserves to me."

"I'm taking instruction from a crow now, am I?"

"Have no worries, Azrael. Dust is absolutely one of the smartest birds I know."

Death would have been hard-pressed to say which of his winged companions gave him the dirtier look. He straightened, placed both palms against the earth, and began.

The Horseman felt as though he were sinking through the dirt, submerged in the vile effluvium beneath the diseased crust. A wet, wretched heat beset him from all sides; he actually tasted the pestilence on his tongue.

Ignore it. Press on.

Deeper, following the beating of hearts long dead. Back, farther back, before the illness, before the rot, before the Abyss . . .

Before the genocide.

And he found it. A single weak voice in a deafening chorus; a single drop in the pounding surf. The essence of the Ravaiim.

From a great distance, he thought he heard the rough cry of a crow.

Power surged around him, through him. It didn't feel like an upwelling of strength, precisely, so much as a swelling of *motivation.* Willpower. The chance to perform miracles, not because he suddenly could, but because he suddenly knew he *would.*

He was back in his body, sitting stiffly on the cavern floor.

Before him, the flames burned low, snapping like some enraged hound. Dust shifted foot to foot atop the canister, struggling to look in all directions at once. Azrael appeared frozen, save for the beading perspiration on his forehead. An odd breeze, one that seemed to blow upward from the floor, through the scattered runes, ebbed and flowed without disturbing the dirt or the cinders thrown from the fire.

In the dirt, beneath his open palms, blood began to pool.

Thin at first, watery and black, almost more ink than blood, it seeped in fits and starts from the earth. Slowly, as the pools expanded, it coalesced further, growing thicker, the black fading to a rich crimson. From the soil into which it had soaked and evaporated thousands of years before, the dark magics and iron will of the Horseman summoned it back. Literally distilled from the essence of the world, the blood of the Ravaiim flowed once more.

Again Death reached out, mystically, spiritually, beyond his body, beyond the cave. Riding the flow of Azrael's magic as he would have ridden Despair, he spread his influence throughout the realm, stretching his necromancies, the call of the dead, farther than he ever had before. Farther than he ever *could*, without the angel's assistance.

An hour passed, then two. The twin puddles swelled, joined together, become a pool of blood that fully occupied the center of the chamber. Death sat in its center, soaked in crimson from the waist down. At the very edge of the fire, the creeping blood began to sizzle and spit.

The chant emerging endlessly from Death's throat shifted tone. The blood continued to pool, but now it also began to swirl, to fold in on itself in a way that liquid should never have moved. It thickened, darkened, as the Horseman condensed the true essence of the Ravaiim, keeping what he needed, allowing the extraneous compounds to seep back into the soil.

Finally, he ceased his incantation and rose unsteadily to his feet. The blood that had caked his legs, soaked into his clothing, was gone, absorbed back into the gelatinous mass. Azrael, almost shaking with exertion, staggered to Death's side.

"Are we through?" the angel asked.

"We are."

"That . . . doesn't appear to be enough."

"That's why I concentrated it, drawing forth only the purest components, the substances in the blood containing the Ravaiim's echoes. Otherwise, there wouldn't have been sufficient room in the cave, let alone any container we could carry. But I assure you, this is the entirety. All the blood of the Ravaiim, from this entire realm.

"And I thank you. This would not have been possible without your help."

Azrael offered a shallow bow in acknowledgment. "It still will not fit in that cylinder," he pointed out.

"No. After a brief rest, I'm going to condense it again. When I'm done, it'll scarcely qualify as a liquid, and it will be so concentrated that a single smear could awaken one of the Grand Abominations for years on end, but we'll be able to transport it."

The angel stretched, arms, neck, wings—the latter so wide that they nearly bridged the cave from wall to wall. "Very well. What do you need from me?"

"Nothing. Now that the blood's gathered, I can handle the rest on my own. Go, regain your strength. We may need your magics again before we're done."

Shoulders drooping, wings now practically dragging across the floor, Azrael shuffled from the cavern. The mere fact that he chose not to protest was sign enough of his exhaustion.

Death had been relying on that, actually.

As soon as his companion had departed, Death crossed the cave, his steps far more sure than they'd appeared only moments before. In one shadowed corner, near the mouth of the cave, lay several more of the crystal-and-gold cylinders. He and Azrael had brought several extras, as the Horseman had claimed he wasn't certain he could concentrate the blood sufficiently for just one.

It wasn't the only lie he would tell today, nor the worst.

For a long time he stood, turning the cylinder around and around in his hands. He still had time to turn back, to come up with some other plan . . .

No. Hadrimon and Belisatra were already nigh unstoppable, with only two of the Grand Abominations. They *must* be kept from obtaining the blood of the Ravaiim, no matter what it cost.

No matter *who* it cost.

Eyelids squinting in fatigue—or was it something else?— Death turned, squared his shoulders, and moved back toward the congealing blood on the floor.

THE VOLCANO BELLOWED STILL, though it had settled into a somewhat duller roar. Torrents of lava spilled over the earth, draining away, forming the slopes of what would become a brand-new mountain. No traces remained, here at the center, of the angels, demons, or constructs who were lost in the initial conflagration. Any parts of them that had not burned to nothing had been carried away and entombed in the liquid rock.

On the far edge of that molten lake, dozens of constructs hauled heavy chains through a makeshift system of pulleys hammered into the surrounding terrain. It had cost them hours, and more than a score of workers swallowed by the lava, but finally Earth Reaver had risen far enough to push itself up under its own power. Soon, very soon, they would finally be ready to march.

Circling above, Hadrimon observed the proceedings from

as high as the smoke and the cinders in the air would permit. He clutched Black Mercy close to his chest, almost as a child might cradle a favorite toy. His impatience seethed hotter than the lava, and it was all he could do not to shoot at those constructs moving too slow for his liking.

And there was something else as well, something more than the ravaged landscape and his tools of vengeance. Something picking at the edges of his soul, a nascent entity trying to hatch. Something familiar, something like the faintest echo of the Grand Abominations . . .

Something that felt just a bit like Death, and the last time the Nephilim had accidentally touched his mind through the conduit of the Abominations.

Hadrimon closed his eyes, allowed himself to glide on the warm updrafts of volcanic air, and waited.

CHAPTER TWENTY-FIVE

NOW IN ANOTHER OF THE CAVES, THIS ONE OPEN TO the ledge outside so they could see if the enemy approached, Death and Azrael had gathered along with War, Ezgati, and half a dozen other angels, representing all the ranking—and surviving—officers. They clustered around a crystal cylinder, now full of a tarry substance of red so dark it might as well, in all but the brightest light, have been black.

"The plan is this," Death was telling them. The others had to lean in to hear him, so softly was he speaking. His head drooped with obvious fatigue. Yet he seemed oblivious, both to his own apparent weakness and to the concern radiating from the others—particularly from War, who had never once seen, or even imagined, his brother in such a state.

"Azrael," he continued, "I've prepared a second canister, one filled with blood I drained from several summoned ghouls. Until and unless it's examined closely, it should appear very much like the real thing. You, and the bulk of your forces, will take the false blood and travel, as swiftly as you can, to the nearest hole in the realm's wards. With luck, it should appear to Belisatra and Hadrimon that you're attempting to flee this world with their prize. It puts you and your soldiers in harm's way, and I apologize for that, but less so than if we remained here and fought a hopeless holding action."

"None of us fears battle, Horseman," Azrael replied. "We'd not be here, otherwise."

"Of course. I, and a smaller contingent of angels, will remain here, holding the caves. It's a tricky proposition, but I intend to allow the enemy to detect us, while making it appear that we're trying to *avoid* detection."

The intertwining lines of puzzled looks between War and the various angels practically formed a latticework around Death, almost enough to hem him in.

"I'm not entirely certain—" Azrael began tentatively.

"The idea," the Horseman interrupted, "is that if the enemy does *not* pursue the larger angelic force—if they recognize it as a feint—they will instead waste their time attacking those of us who have dug in here."

"But you'll not have the Ravaiim blood, either!" War ventured in sudden understanding.

"Precisely, brother. It's a double feint. You, and a minuscule handful of angels, will have taken this cylinder—" Here he tapped the golden end cap of the vessel in front of him. "—and ridden for another hole in the wards, in a different direction from Azrael's contingent. Given the low visibility, I have hopes that so small a party can depart completely undetected. By the time Hadrimon and Belisatra realize that *neither* Azrael's group nor mine has the blood, you should have reached a point where you and Ruin can depart this world. You'll make the delivery to the Charred Council, then—"

"Wait just one damn moment!" War's face had flushed a deeper hue than his cloak. "This whole scheme is desperate at best—and I will *not* abandon the field of battle while you remain behind!"

"Besides which," Ezgati chimed in from beside Azrael,

"I'm not entirely sanguine about the notion of the Charred Council taking custody of this stuff. You already control access to the Abomination Vault itself. We ought to take the blood to the White City; that way, we can be certain that *nobody* can awaken the weapons!"

The other angels, Azrael included, were nodding their agreement.

"We're desperate, so of *course* the plan is desperate," Death retorted. "It's also all we have. War, *one* of us must be involved in the escaping party, in order to deliver the canister.

"And as for the rest of you . . . The blood *will* go to the Charred Council. It cannot be allowed to tip the Balance toward either side. If any of you feel strongly opposed to that, I hope you're prepared for us to kill each other until the enemy arrives to finish us both." Harvester flew from the corner in which it leaned to smack loudly into Death's palm, punctuating his proclamation with an unmistakable clarity.

"We've been allies in this thus far," the Horseman said. "We'd all be better off to remain so. But either way, decide now!"

Angels shifted and weapons quivered, but Azrael raised both hands, gesturing for calm. "We remain allies." Then, as Ezgati and several of the others drew breath to protest, "Hadrimon must not succeed. All else is secondary for the time being."

Death chose not to comment on that last little addendum.

"All well and good," said War. "*I'll* remain. You take the blood to the Charred Council."

"Brother—"

"You're *exhausted*! You can barely stand, after your magics; you'll do the defenders no good at all."

"But I can race headlong across the plains for hours on end? Be reasonable."

"It's far more believable that I would be the one responsible for maintaining the defenses. As you said earlier, I out-match you in tactical acumen. Besides which, everyone knows that I do not abandon the field."

"War . . ." Death actually reached out to grip his brother's shoulder. "If Hadrimon and Belisatra attack us here, I can survive them longer than you. We both know that. And the longer they delay here, the better the odds of everyone else getting out alive. I need you to do this."

The younger Horseman appeared to have no answer for that. Angrily, he shrugged away Death's hand and stalked across to the ledge where he could stare out into the rolling banks of smoke. But he uttered no further words of argument.

Death almost wished he had. War's acquiescence, however necessary, only made him feel worse. Head bowed once more, he disappeared into the darkness of the innermost caves.

HADRIMON'S HEAD JERKED upward as if he'd been punched, his entire body spasming so violently that he lost half his altitude before he could once again flap his wings. Through it all, scenes and images flashed through his mind, cutting across his own thoughts in a rushing torrent. It even, however briefly, cooled the fires of hatred and bloodthirst that were now as integral a part of him as his own heart.

It was all he could do not to laugh aloud, and only the presence of the pistol in one hand prevented him from actually clapping.

He'd made his mistake! The vaunted Death, eldest of the Horseman, last surviving Firstborn of the Nephilim, had made his mistake.

He thought he was so clever, absconding with the blood drained from the realm itself. And it *was* creative; Hadrimon certainly hadn't seen that coming.

But he'd also exhausted himself. He was on edge, careless.

Too much so to keep his guard up against Mortis. The angel had, indeed, sensed the half-dead Abomination pressing at the borders of Death's mind earlier—and now, finally, it had broken through. The "double feint" was a clever move, but it could be countered easily enough.

The mad angel swooped from the clouds and went hunting for Belisatra. Now that he understood the entirety of Death's plan, they'd need to come up with their own.

"... DO NOT KNOW who might have engaged our services, or why. Can't begin to guess how they knew to send us here, either. We go where our mistress commands, kill whomever she commands; she doesn't tell us more than that. And a good thing, because it means you cannot make me tell you any more than that! Are we done?"

The head of the demon—Death had been careful to select one of the more intelligent varieties, rather than the mindless and ineloquent brutes who made up so great a portion of Hell's hordes—sat impaled on a stalagmite, looking very much like some nightmarish puppet. Death stood to one side, questioning the spirit he had called back from the void. Had anyone other than Dust accompanied him, they might have been surprised at just how swiftly the Horseman seemed to shed the fatigue he'd previously shown.

He hadn't expected an answer to that first question, not really; asking who sent the demons had been little more than a formality, just in case. The meat of this brief conversation was question two.

"No, we're not done. The name of this mistress of yours?"

The head muttered something that might have been described as "under its breath" if it still *had* any breath.

"Louder," Death ordered.

"Raciel," it all but spat.

Death flicked his fingers as though freeing them of cling-ing dust, dismissing the lingering spirit to resume its journey. The answer could hardly be called a surprise—the suspicion had simmered in the back of his mind since he'd first seen the demonic angel at the rear of the horde—yet he still needed a moment to wrap his mind around it.

"Not a coincidence," he said to Dust. "The odds that someone would *happen* to employ the one demon to whom Hadrimon is connected . . . No. This was deliberate."

The crow hopped from Harvester to sit atop the dead de-mon's head, and began idly gulping down scraps of putrid scalp.

"Tactical advantage against Hadrimon—to say nothing of emotional and psychological—would be the best reason to choose Raciel specifically." The Horseman continued his mus-ing; the bird continued his buffet. "That would mean, though, that whoever's employing these demons, whoever else is seek-ing the Abomination Vault, would have to know that Hadri-mon was involved. And they knew, somehow, to send the demons *here.*

"Raciel could be acting on her own, I suppose. Still, some-one would at least have had to provide the necessary intelli-gence.

"Either way," he concluded, kneeling to meet Dust's eyes, "someone out there—someone who is neither on our side nor Hadrimon's—knows far more about all this than I'm comfort-able with."

Dust blinked languidly, perhaps wondering what all of this could possibly have to do with his dinner.

"Horseman?"

Death didn't bother to turn toward the angel now standing in the cave mouth. "Yes?"

"Both contingents have departed, Azrael's and your broth-er's. Still no sign of the enemy."

"All right. I'll be along shortly."

The soldier's wings rustled against the stone as he departed.

With a surprisingly gentle touch, Death lifted Dust from the head, heedless of the tantrum that followed. "Hush. Now's not the time."

The crow quieted instantly and allowed itself to be placed on the Horseman's shoulder. For some time, they simply stood, Death idly examining the horrid, half-dead thing he wore on his left arm.

It had been difficult indeed, one of the fiercest mental efforts he had ever made. To keep his *true* thoughts shielded from Mortis and the other Abominations to which it was linked, while making them *think* he'd dropped his guard—feeding them only what he wanted them to know—had almost proved too much, even for him. That, and not the necromantic labors from which he'd swiftly recovered, had been the true cause of his earlier exhaustion.

Yet he'd pulled it off. He'd deceived the damn thing before shutting it out once more, and through Mortis, Hadrimon. The enemy truly believed that he'd sent the blood of the Ravaiim with War in a desperate race to escape this gangrenous world.

Just as War himself believed.

"It had to be done," he told the crow perched beside his face. "I *cannot* let the Abominations wake, no matter what."

Dust cocked his head and hissed, clearly unimpressed.

"War's not much of a liar," Death explained—to whom, he was no longer certain. An unfamiliar churning in his gut threatened to double him over. "I couldn't risk him doing anything to reveal the deception. He *had* to believe it, no less than Hadrimon did."

And so they did. War and Hadrimon and Azrael and the angels, all convinced that they knew where the prize truly lay.

His brother would likely die defending a worthless cylinder of corpse blood—and Death had orchestrated it.

"I'm sorry, brother . . ."

He wasn't even sure he'd spoken aloud, and he had no time left to regret his choices. Death crossed the cave, shoved a few rocks aside, and hefted a third canister—this one with the *true* Ravaiim blood—from a hollow in the floor. Then, silent as the dead with whom he occasionally spoke, he left the chamber to meet up with Despair.

They had to be long gone before anyone, enemy or ally, realized they'd been deceived.

CHAPTER TWENTY-SIX

THE HOLLOW ECHO OF DEATH'S BOOTS, FIRST ON STONE and then on steel, was as the beating of some subterranean, tectonic heart. In one hand he carried his infamous weapon; in the other, that damn cylinder of crystal, gold, and blood. He seemed oblivious to the sigils etched into the surrounding steel, the occasional gates and doorways through which he passed, even the four creatures flitting excitedly through the air around him. The Watchers, those uncanny echoes of Panoptos, shouted, commanded, wheedled, and begged. The Charred Council demanded Death attend them at once! The Council was waiting. The Council would not be patient. The Council must not be disobeyed. He must report to the Council immediately!

Their words had no impact at all, and they knew better than to attempt to *physically* accost the unwavering Horseman.

They knew, because when Death had first entered the winding corridors, carved deep in the blackened stone of the Council's domain, there had been *five* Watchers attempting to impede him.

Again he came to the rune-covered portal, again he pounded on it with an open hand. This time, however, when the golden-haired and brown-clad figure of Berrarris opened the door, Death gave him no opportunity for formal greetings.

"Take me to your master. Now. And *you* four . . . This is as far as you go. I'll be traveling the rest of the way alone."

"We're not certain we can allow that," said the first.

"You've ignored our summons," added a second.

"The Council wants to see you." That from the third.

And finally, the last, "They do not take disobedience lightly."

"No, they do not."

"You ignore us. You think us unimportant."

"You have already slain one of us."

"But we speak for the Council."

"The Council speaks *through us!*"

"And you will obey!"

"You will obey!"

"We will not leave your side until you do."

"You have no choice."

"And you leave us with none."

"Do you suppose they rehearse this?" Death asked nobody in particular. Dusk, perched as usual atop Harvester, fluttered his wings in what might almost have been a shrug. The young Maker kept his attentions on the floor, unwilling to intercede.

"We—" one of the Watchers began again.

"No," the Horseman interrupted. "You've had your say. My turn—and unlike some, I'll be brief.

"Any one of you to follow me across this threshold dies." Death took a single deliberate step through the doorway and turned back, idly tapping one finger of the fist gripping Harvester. "Care to test me?"

The doorway filled with flapping wings and swooping figures as the Watchers milled about the brink, and then they were gone, retreating down the hall.

"I thought not," Death said.

"Uh, Horseman," Berrarris began nervously, "I haven't yet checked with my master. I do not know if he's receiving—"

"Now, Berrarris."

"Ah, of course, sir Horseman."

They passed swiftly through the various chambers and between the shelves and podiums, displaying the various creations of master and apprentice, until they stood before the final door.

"No need to announce me," Death said.

"But I'm supposed to—"

"You do not need to hear any of this."

"But—"

"*Go.*"

Berrarris fled, and the Horseman pushed open the door.

"Was is truly needful for you to terrify my apprentice?" asked the iron-masked Keeper of Oblivion from across the room.

"I have no time for pleasantries today." Death slammed the portal behind him with force enough to shake the steel walls. Dust squawked and shuffled sideways atop the scythe.

"I have never treated you with any less than the utmost respect," the Keeper said. "I don't believe it unreasonable to expect the same of you—for myself and Berrarris, both."

"Perhaps." Death stepped to the room's center and placed the cylinder between them. "But when I say I have little time, I mean it. The Council may soon dispatch messengers less easily dissuaded than these new Watchers, so I need you to listen . . ."

Long Death spoke, and the Keeper did, indeed, listen, though his shoulders grew tense and his back stiff as he came to understand precisely what was being asked of him.

"You know I cannot do this," he said finally. "Do you understand the repercussions if I were to violate the strictures of the Council where my duties are concerned? What would happen if they had reason to fear they could no longer trust me with access to *that*?" He didn't point or gesture toward the glass portal behind him, ringed in gold and iron serpents. He didn't have to.

"Unless I'm mistaken," Death replied, "the laws prevent anyone but the Council from banishing any living entity to Oblivion. They say nothing about you opening the portal where no living thing is involved."

"Death—"

"You know what's at stake here! Nobody—not even the Council—can be trusted with the Abominations!"

"I know. I understand, I do. But what you ask—"

When Death interrupted this time, his voice was low, almost inaudible. "We've spent many hours, you and I, discussing the sorts of burdens that only we share. The weight and responsibility—the *guilt*—we've taken onto ourselves, whether in the name of the Charred Council and the Balance, or for other, less noble causes.

"This is one of my responsibilities, Keeper. One of the worst. And I have stained my soul darker still in hopes of preventing my old sins from causing further harm. Help me lay down this one burden. I cannot do it without you."

Two expressionless masks mirrored each other; blank, unmoving, but no more so than the men who wore them. Until, without another word, the Keeper rose and faced the looming portal.

He held his palms straight, almost touching the glass. An unpleasant keening—not quite music and not quite words; sometimes high-pitched, sometimes low, sometimes impossibly both at once—reverberated from his throat. On and on it went, a single fluctuating tone, without pause for breath.

The glass of the portal rippled, and everything before it became oddly vague, unclear. Death squinted, trying to make sense of what he saw. Somehow, the Keeper now had two hands pressed against the glass, two more against the serpentine frame, one on each side—despite the fact that he possessed only the two arms, and wasn't nearly broad enough to reach across the width of the portal. Examining it too closely made Death's head hurt; Dust had already fluttered over to Death's shoulder and buried his head in the Horseman's hair so he wouldn't have to see.

How long it took, Death could never say, but it stopped as abruptly as it had begun. The Keeper lowered his hands—only two of them, again—and stepped away. The iron-and-gold border appeared no different, but the glass was gone. In its place . . .

Nothing.

Literally nothing. Not a blank wall. Not an empty space. It was an absence so profound that the eyes absolutely could not focus on it. Any attempt to look into that portal ended with the observer staring intently at one side or the other of the serpentine frame.

"Do as you must," the Keeper said. He sounded hoarse, strained. "But do it swiftly."

Without hesitation or ceremony, Death hefted the canister and hurled it through the portal into Oblivion. Just like that, Creation's only substantial source of Ravaiim blood ceased to exist.

"Thank you, my friend."

"Go away, Horseman." In contrast with the prolonged process with which he'd opened the portal, the Keeper simply clenched his fist, and the wavering void was once again a plain sheet of glass. "Go—and pray to whoever you still trust that you can make the Charred Council understand your choices here today."

"The Council," Death told him as he moved toward the door, "stands fairly low on my list of concerns just now."

When he reached the exit and stepped out onto the blackened, flame-ravaged and lava-kissed badlands, however, Death discovered, without the slightest sliver of surprise, that the same could not be said in reverse.

"You," Panoptos told him, his eyes orbiting one another in agitated patterns, "are truly beginning to irritate us!" Behind him, roughly a dozen of his Watcher "children" bobbed and hovered in the baking air. Far in the distance, silhouetted against the ubiquitous orange glow, Death saw additional figures making a ponderous but inexorable approach. He could see little, as of yet, save that they were far larger than the Watchers and lacking wings, but he had no *need* to see more. He knew the Council's brutish shock troops, golems of petrified flame, far too well to mistake them now.

"Us?" Death asked mildly. "You number yourself among the Charred Council now, Panoptos? Seems a bit presumptuous."

"Don't toy with me, Horseman, not now! You've irritated *them,* and that irritates *me.* You are to come with me *immediately* and stand before them!"

"I cannot." Death curled a finger in summons, and Despair stepped from behind a nearby ridge, his own fumes blending hideously with those of the lava flowing nearby. "Not yet."

"You seem to have forgotten your place in the centuries you were away!" Panoptos's voice had risen into a painful screech. "The Council does not make requests, and you do not get to say *no!* They will see you *now!*"

"No." The Horseman slid a foot into the stirrups, threw his other leg over Despair's saddle. "Give them my apologies, tell them I will return soon, but I've something I *must* do first. If the price is their wrath afterward, so be it."

"I . . . you . . . !"

"And Panoptos? Don't bother to bring the golems next time. I'll be long gone before they reach us—and even if I were not, I hold no fear of them."

"Death! I order you to—"

Despair was already walking away. "Was there anything else?" Death asked. "Before I depart?"

The creature's long claws twitched. "You'll at least hand over the blood of the Ravaiim before you go. Oh, yes, Death, the Council told me all about your 'quest.' They're quite determined to ensure the safety of your prize before either Heaven or Hell can get hold of it."

Death twisted to face not only Panoptos, but the entrance to the Keeper's sanctum. His smile was so broad, it showed in the shape of his jaw beyond the edges of the mask. "What do you think I was doing *here*, Panoptos?"

"You didn't!" Each of his nine eyes bulged, threatening to spring from his head entirely, and he was actually wringing his hands. "You *didn't*!"

"Please tell the Council that the Grand Abominations should be safe, and that I'll be with them as soon as I'm able."

"Death! *Death!* Damn you, come back here! You can't do this! You—"

But the Horseman and his steed were already gone, vanished in a shimmer and a cloud of mist, long before Panoptos ceased his screaming.

THE WRETCHED MIASMA and stinging fog of the Ravaiim homeworld-turned-graveyard was almost familiar by now. Despair's hooves scattered dust and dead skin across the plains, leaving leagues and hours drifting like shed feathers in its wake.

Day after day, Death, Dust, and Despair had wandered this diseased realm, first retracing their earlier path back to the escarpment, then onward, following the route that War's diversionary party was supposed to have taken.

No tracks remained; the constant powder flaking from the

world's crust, along with the flaccid but constant breeze, ensured any such traces were long gone. Dust occasionally spiraled outward, searching from above, but again the constant fumes, to say nothing of the smoke still pouring from the newborn volcano, cut visibility to almost nothing. Each time, the crow was able to find its way back only due to the mental bond shared with the Horseman, and each time the result was the same. Dust found nothing, nothing at all.

Death summoned ghouls, one after another, a veritable army of ancient corpses came shambling from beneath the earth to spread out and search the vile dunes and sweeping plains. Most returned empty-handed. Some failed to return at all.

Until finally, when Death had all but lost the last clinging scrap of hope, Despair's head rose, nostrils flaring. Instantly he broke into a gallop, moving at an angle off the path they'd been following. Death gave him his head, allowing him to go where he would. The beast ran for a time then reared, pawing at the air, giving voice to a deep, ghostly call.

Deep in the fog, something answered.

Now they began passing fallen bodies, the shrunken flesh and disembodied feathers more than sufficient sign of what must have occurred.

Hadrimon. Black Mercy.

War, and the angels who accompanied him, never stood a chance. The plan really had worked flawlessly.

Damn it.

At the edge of it all, just beyond the scattered angelic corpses, they found Ruin. He stood silent, save for his initial response to Despair's cry, the rifts in his skin blazing scarlet. Beneath him, sheltered from the elements and almost from sight by the bulk of the great warhorse, slumped a vague shape wrapped in a crimson cloak.

Death vaulted from the saddle. With an almost exaggerated care—was he, perhaps, stalling? he wondered—he leaned Harvester against Despair's side, straight enough so Dust could remain perched on the blade. Then, as stiffly as if he waded through some clinging muck, he approached his fallen brother.

Ruin snorted angrily, one hoof scratching a furrow in the earth.

"Don't," Death said. "I appreciate the gesture, as I'm sure he would, but *don't.*"

One more snort, and then slowly, reluctantly, Ruin stepped aside.

The Horseman knelt beside his fallen brother. He scarcely needed even to look at the ragged hole in War's chest; he recognized the scent, the *feel,* of Black Mercy's wounds. But maybe . . . The Abominations had never been intended for use against the Nephilim themselves, and the four Horsemen were far more, now, than they had been, so maybe . . .

He held a hand over the body, seeking something, *anything.*

Nothing. No trace of life remained in the sprawling figure. War, youngest of the Four Horsemen, was dead.

Death rocked back on his heels, numb in body and soul, save for a caustic squirming beginning to build in his viscera. Call back his brother's soul? To what end? Not even his greatest necromancies could restore true life to the departed. He could summon War's spirit, grant his body temporary animation long enough to talk, but nothing more. Apologize, perhaps? What good might it do now? It seemed unnecessarily cruel—to both of them.

Again he reached out, this time futilely working to brush some of the gathered soot from his brother's body. He succeeded only in smearing the stuff in filthy swirls across the cloak and pitted armor. With a gentle exhalation that might, coming from anyone else, have been a sigh, Death cradled the corpse in both arms and lifted it from the dirt. Even if he could do nothing else, he certainly wasn't going to leave his brother here to—

The dull black of Chaoseater, not *entirely* buried by the dirt, shone as a dark spot against the gray of the earth.

Chaoseater. The blade that not only feasted on the carnage and havoc of battle, but fed that power directly to War himself. The sword that was, however marginally, bonded to its wielder's soul.

Death dropped his brother in an undignified heap and reached for the sword, focusing with every sense in his possession . . .

Yes!

It was almost nothing, the faintest ember of War's essence. Little more than a trace, it remained, slowly fading away, in the spiritual conduit between Horseman and blade—much as a narrow trickle of water might linger in the pipe between two interconnected basins that were otherwise dry.

No, Death could not restore life to the dead, but if a spark of life were to flare from somewhere *else* . . .

He knelt over the body, placing Chaoseater in War's fist and carefully closing the fingers around it. A chanted invocation, difficult and peculiar, followed by a long silence. Death felt an odd pull from a direction he could not name, unlike any of the spirits he'd ever summoned before. It felt . . . not as if the soul was fighting him, precisely. More that this, one of the strongest souls he'd ever felt, was simply uninterested in allowing any outside influence to alter its course.

"I have never yet encountered a spirit strong enough to refuse my call," Death hissed between chants. "I am damn well not going to let *you* be the first, brother!"

He redoubled his efforts, and then again. Two of Death's fingernails cracked, so tight was his fist; a trickle of black, glistening oil, the residue of his necromancies condensed and made manifest, bubbled up from behind his ivory mask.

The body twitched. Once only, so slightly that Death almost missed it, but it happened.

He had War's soul. He had the last fading ember of War's life. The first he could infuse into the body without difficulty, but the second? How to coax that last flare of power from the conduit linking his brother with . . . ?

Ah.

Ensuring that War's hand remained tightly wrapped about the hilt, Death leaned over, lifted Chaoseater by the blade, and rammed it deep into his own chest.

Agony bloomed through him, a flowering vine of poison and thorns. He grunted once but otherwise held himself still, refusing to let the pain overwhelm him.

Which, given how much worse Affliction had hurt him back in the White City, wasn't actually all that hard.

Chaoseater fed on the injury, the violence, albeit self-inflicted. Fed, and passed that strength on to its wielder, carrying the lingering embers of life along with it.

War's body rocked in a violent spasm. A worm-like plug of old clots wiggled obscenely from the open wound, followed by a brief spurt of fresh blood and jagged fragments of what might have been Black Mercy's projectile. He groaned, a deep and juddering sound, attempted to sit up, and collapsed back onto the dirt.

"Steady," Death said, sliding off Chaoseater and sitting next to his brother. "You were close enough to have studied your reflection in the Well of Souls. Go easy."

Again War struggled to sit up. This time, he managed it, though he appeared as though he'd keel over at any moment.

"Perhaps . . ." It came out as a feeble croak. He coughed once, spat a gobbet of clotted blood and dirt, and tried again. "Perhaps you should have left me dead."

Sorrow and despondency were not emotions to which any of the Horsemen were particularly susceptible, yet Death couldn't possibly fail to note that his brother seemed as miserable as he'd ever appeared—and not, Death was certain, from the pain of his wounds.

"Why would you—?"

War actually snarled. "Don't patronize me, brother! I failed. I failed you, the Council, everyone. Death was the least I deserve."

Protestations rose in Death's throat, clung to the base of his tongue, and froze into an unbreakable chunk of ice.

"They have the Ravaiim blood now," the younger continued morosely, "because I wasn't strong enough to keep them from taking it."

"War . . ." *Tell him.* "This is not your fault." *He deserves the truth.* "The plan—" *Tell him!* "—didn't go as we discussed. Against Hadrimon and Black Mercy, what more could you have done?"

Coward.

"Excuses don't change—"

"And Hadrimon *doesn't* have the Ravaiim blood."

For the first time, War looked up. "What?"

"I . . ." *The truth, now.* ". . . was able to get hold of the cylinder before Hadrimon could escape with it. It's gone. Permanently."

"I don't understand. *How* . . . ?"

"Later. For now, we have to move. Do you need any assistance mounting Ruin?"

War snarled again, though with less apparent anger. Using Chaoseater as a crutch, he struggled up and shuffled toward the horse. Death watched until he was certain his brother had the strength to climb into the saddle.

Ruin stared back at him the entire time, and though Death knew he must be imagining it, the beast's expression seemed accusing.

So, too, did the crooked glance that Dust directed his way as he hauled himself, favoring the fresh wound in his chest, atop Despair.

"I don't know." Death spoke in a whisper; perhaps to Dust, perhaps to himself, perhaps to a Creator in which the Horseman only partly believed. "I don't know why not. But I can't."

The guilt when he'd betrayed War, potentially to his death, had gnawed at him. This was almost worse; he had never, in all his eons, felt so craven. In the face of danger, of battles that drowned entire worlds in blood, the eldest Horseman had never known the touch of fear. Now, for the first time, it had seized him in a grip he could not break.

"He doesn't need to know," he said finally, glancing back to ensure War and Ruin had not fallen behind. "*I* know. I do not forget.

"And though it take until the Apocalypse itself, I will find a way to make it up to him."

It didn't feel like enough, not remotely, but for now it would have to do.

Still, at least he'd succeeded. The Charred Council doubtless had nothing pleasant in mind for him; he wasn't certain who had sent the demons after them, though a suspicion had begun to churn in the recesses of his mind; Hadrimon and Belisatra would have to be dealt with, and Black Mercy and Earth Reaver might yet remain active for a short time.

But if nothing else, he could rest assured that the greater threat posed by the Abomination Vault was finally over.

CHAPTER TWENTY-SEVEN

WHAT DO YOU MEAN," DEATH GROWLED, "*IT'S NOT over?*"

"Precisely what it sounds like, Horseman." Despite the import of his announcement, Panoptos sounded delighted, almost giggly, as he hovered in the baking air at the edge of the Council's domain.

Death and War traded suspicious glares, uncertain what the aggravating creature was up to. They'd taken it casually, the long ride from the plains of the Ravaiim homeworld to the nearest spot where they could step between realms. Casually enough that what should have required only the better part of a day had actually required three. The respite had done wonders for the both of them—as had their little side trip afterward, to hunt down a flock of minor demonic entities on the borders of Hell, during which they fed gleefully on the death and the chaos of battle.

Still . . .

"Panoptos," War said, "we're tired, and neither of us is in the mood for games. We already know that we're late in reporting to the Council. Your jibes are unnecessary and unwanted."

"Ah, you two." The messenger began shifting side to side, as though standing atop a rocking ship. "Always so certain of yourselves. Listen very carefully to what I'm saying. Pretend I have lips, and watch them.

"I did not say, *The Council expects your report.* I did not say, *They're angry enough to spit fire.* Though they are," he added with a sidelong glance at the elder Horseman.

"The Council *always* spits fire," Death retorted.

"Fair point. But *my* point, Death, is that it's *really* not over. Your act of disobedience, your little tantrum? It doesn't seem to have worked."

Death jolted upright in the saddle with enough force to send Despair staggering back a few steps. "That's not possible!"

"I suggest," Panoptos said, his tone so smug it was clearly slumming just being there, "that you get moving. The Council's not known for patience at the *best* of times."

Ruin and Despair both launched into a steady gallop, leaving the winged creature struggling to catch up.

They reached the steps, dropped from their saddles in unison, and raced upward, brushing past several Watchers in the process. They found themselves once more standing before the burbling pool of magma, the faint stream that trickled from its borders, and the trio of blazing stone effigies that supposedly represented Creation's last hope for Balance.

"**Death!**" It was, initially, the leftmost idol that spoke. "**We are *not* well pleased! Observe.**"

Lava erupted from the pool, raining down in a thin sheet of drops and particles, almost but not quite a mist. As the geyser roared, streaks of color began wending through the torrent, as though some pocket of gems and minerals had abruptly dissolved in the boiling flow.

When those dribbles of color reached the apex of the spout

and started to fall as part of the lighter mist, they also spread, reshaping themselves—streams into blots, blots into recognizable images. Another moment, and an entire vista spread before them, crisp and clear save for a bit of liquid wobbling around the edges.

What the Horsemen saw was less a battlefield than a killing field; a charnel ruin of heaped corpses and shattered structures. The tattered wings, mangled armor, and singed white hair of the dead was more than sufficient indicator as to who they'd once been. The cracked marble, shattered glass, and hollow, smoking spires was equally strong indication as to *where* this might have happened.

"You are looking at Silverwall." The voice came from behind; clearly, Panoptos had caught up with them at some point. "Or rather, what used to be Silverwall. You know it?"

"An outpost on the very borders of Heaven," War said. "Of relatively little importance since they've begun building their new one, though it remains the best vantage point for a few of the minor rifts between Above and Below."

"But this," said Death, "was no demonic offensive."

"No."

At that simple utterance by all three of the Charred Council, as if awaiting precisely that cue, figures appeared at the edges of the vista: four or five angels, as well as the pale-and-purple dervish that was his sister, Fury. A pocket of Belisatra's brass myrmidons retreated before them, steadily shredded to bits by halberds and Fury's devastating whips.

War's cloak folded and rippled as he shook his head, in puzzlement rather than denial. "There's no sense to this. They should have needed longer to regroup, to recover from their loss of the Ravaiim blood, before they could once again pose any real threat. We should have had time to hunt them down."

Death had taken a step nearer the wavering image, oblivious to the occasional splatter of magma sizzling across his skin. "Those toy soldiers didn't slaughter so many angels, certainly not in their own bastion." He faced the Council, waiting for an answer to the question he had not asked.

"Yes. Black Mercy."

"Fury confirmed it the moment she arrived," Panoptos added from above. "Angels slain by the dozens, showing signs of only the most minor injuries."

"Any sign of Earth Reaver?" War asked.

"None." This from the central column. **"This was a surprise assault. Perhaps the larger Abomination proved too ponderous for their needs."**

"I don't understand." Death continued watching the flickering images, apparently hoping to alter their meaning by sheer force of disbelief. "This shouldn't be possible."

"You *did* say," Panoptos offered, "that they might have access to other, smaller sources of the blood. Perhaps one of those . . . ?"

"No," from both Horsemen at once. War alone continued, "Silverwall holds no strategic value for anyone except a few small communities in Hell. Destroying it—especially openly, without hiding their responsibility—accomplishes nothing for Belisatra or Hadrimon. If they *are* relying on a limited source of Ravaiim blood to awaken the Grand Abominations, an attack like this is a foolish, even asinine waste of resources.

"Unless," War added thoughtfully, "the angels have kept something from us? Something hidden there, like Abaddon's sacrament bomb?"

"No. We have kept an eye on Silverwall since the assault began. The enemy has killed and destroyed indiscriminately. They looted nothing; they search nothing."

"Then I am at a loss to suggest any other—"

"It's a test."

It felt, to Death, as though all of them—not only War and Panoptos, but the Charred Council as well, despite the utter immobility of the effigies—were now fixated solely on him.

"Explain, Horseman."

"A small outpost, one that wouldn't be exceptionally difficult to overrun but where it also wouldn't matter if they failed . . . Hadrimon and Belisatra have found some *other* source, something none of us anticipated. This was a test, to ensure that it worked as planned—that it would, indeed, empower the Abominations."

"Then your failure and disobedience are compounded further still! Your destruction of the Ravaiim blood, in blatant disregard of our orders, has not even succeeded in depriving the enemy of the Abominations! It has only ensured that *we* now lack the weapons with which to face them!"

"It had to be done."

"And this is all you offer in your own defense?" the rightmost column demanded in a torrent of flame.

"It's all I require."

"You will turn the Abomination Vault over to us—or, if it cannot be moved, you will reveal to us its location and means of entry. You will provide Panoptos with the locations of every battlefield that might yet yield any useful quantity of Ravaiim blood. We must be prepared for—"

"No."

Even Panoptos gasped at that.

"Death . . ."

"I am as horrified as you—more so, in fact—that the Grand Abominations still pose a threat. I will do everything within my power to *end* that threat. But I will *not* do it by loosing yet more of the damn things on Creation!"

"This has gone far enough, Horseman! We overlooked your insolence once; it will not happen again. You *will* do as we command!"

"No. I will not."

The pain, when it hit him, was like nothing Death had ever known. Chaoseater, Affliction, the fires of Hell, every injury he'd suffered in the Nephilim's final battle, none of it could compare. It seared through him, utterly bypassing the well of strength and stoicism with which he held the agonies of reality at bay. Every iota of his body burned; his soul felt like it was being skinned by a dozen ragged blades.

He was on his knees, though he'd no memory of falling. The hand he'd thrown out to break his fall was submerged past the wrist in the stream of magma, and he'd never so much as noticed. He heard Dust fluttering around his head, squawking and screeching; heard Harvester clatter to the floor; heard War's steps on the stone.

Above it all, he heard the voice of the Charred Council.

"This can end immediately, Horseman. Or it can persist so long that it must seem eternal even to an immortal. The choice is yours!"

"You . . . you will not kill . . . kill me. Will not . . . keep me like . . . like this." Even his voice seemed to have ignited, for every word seared his throat as it passed. "You need . . . need me too much."

"We need only servants willing to *obey*! You are the eldest and most experienced of our Riders, Death, but there is little you can accomplish that the other three cannot match. They—"

"Two," War growled softly.

"What?"

"Two, not three. Kill Death over this, and you will have to do the same to me."

For just an instant, a new swell of shame swamped Death's mind so utterly that the pain actually lessened.

"A noble gesture, War," the middle effigy said, **"But unconvincing. You do not truly mean to die here today."**

"Try me."

The flames dancing in the eyes and mouths of the Charred Council abruptly went dark, showing only the faintest glow of fading cinders. Death sat up with a gasp he could not quite repress, yanking his hand from the searing magma and lifting Harvester with the other.

"Brother?" War asked.

"The pain is gone. Thank you. War, why . . . ?"

"You stood beside me as we faced not one but two of the Grand Abominations. You understand them better than the Council possibly can. If you say that we are better off keeping the others locked away, I trust your judgment."

Trust. The word was a blade in Death's stomach; he wondered, briefly, how much more pain he could endure.

"War, you—"

The fires within the idols roared anew, heralding the Council's return.

"We have decided," the center effigy told them. Was it Death's imagination, or did the rumbling voice sound vaguely sullen? **"Owing to your personal history with the Grand Abominations, we will excuse your continued lapse in propriety. *This time.* Do not try our patience again, Horseman!"**

"I understand." Death bowed his head as he spoke, but inside he exulted. *He'd faced down the Council; they could be made to yield.*

Good to know . . . for the future.

"Death . . . ," the totem continued as though reading his thoughts, **"you possess your greatest strengths at *our* sufferance. You walk the worlds at *our* whim. These gifts can be stripped from you. Not every consequence for disobedience is a matter of simple pain."**

All he could do was repeat himself. "I understand."

"You will not be further punished, but neither can we

trust you further with this endeavor. Your judgment is compromised, and you both remain weakened by your recent travails. Fury and Strife will hunt down these enemies. You will stand guard over the Abomination Vault itself, lest Hadrimon and Belisatra locate it before Strife and Fury locate *them*."

"It is, in fact, already defended," Death said. "Some additional precautions wouldn't hurt, though."

War frowned darkly at this lesser assignment, but said nothing.

"**Panoptos! Dispatch your Watchers. Contact Fury, locate Strife, and summon them both before us.**"

"Of course, my lords." The wispy creature circled twice, then swooped from the platform.

"**Horsemen . . . Begone.**"

Both brothers bowed their heads shallowly, Death stretched out an arm for Dust to perch on, and they departed as swiftly as dignity would permit. They'd remounted Despair and Ruin, and traveled some moments across the shattered earth, before Death spoke again. "You're grumbling."

War straightened in his saddle. "Sentry duty? All we've done, all we've endured, and the Council won't even let us see this all through!"

"Calm yourself, brother." The elder Rider gently shooed Dust off his shoulder so he could see War without a mass of feathers blocking half his view. "I can assure you, we'll absolutely be seeing this through."

War started, then groaned aloud. "You're not seriously considering disobeying the Council *again*!"

"No." He almost—*almost*—shuddered. "No, I've no urge to do that again anytime soon."

Hooves smacked on soot-caked rock. The angry roar of flames drifted from over the horizon. The mounts drifted apart from one another, passed to each side of a monolithic stalagmite, drew together once more. Then . . .

"So what *did* you mean, if not that you planned to go after Hadrimon and Belisatra yourself?"

"Where do you suppose they came up with their new supply of Ravaiim blood?" Death asked, apparently having missed—or chosen to ignore—War's own question.

"You . . . I haven't the first idea."

"I have."

Again the conversation lagged; Death appeared lost in thought, and War stubbornly refused to give in and again be the one to speak first.

"I wondered," the older brother finally said, "what sort of source would be plentiful enough for Hadrimon to waste the time and effort obliterating a minor outpost, yet questionable enough that they'd feel the need to test the blood and make certain it would function."

"And . . . ?" War prompted.

"And I do not believe that Earth Reaver's absence was due to its ponderous nature."

War sucked in a breath through gritted teeth. "You think they opened up one Abomination to feed the other!"

The mask bobbed in a shallow nod. "It makes sense. The Grand Abominations are constructed partly of Ravaiim remains. They're old, desiccated, preserved—but if you squeeze even the driest fruit hard enough . . ."

"They'd eventually destroy the entire lot of them that way."

"True. But not for some time, especially if they continually use the larger, such as Earth Reaver, to power the smaller."

"Such as Black Mercy."

A second nod. "They'll run through the Vault eventually, but not before they've done more than enough irreparable damage.

"And *that,* War, means that they'll be coming for the Vault itself, and the rest of the Grand Abominations, soon enough. Now that they know they can dismantle one to awaken others, it's their only viable move."

A grin of brilliant white split the shadows beneath the crimson hood. "You mean they'll be coming to *us.*"

"Precisely."

The grin faded. "Assuming they locate the Abomination Vault before Fury and Strife hunt them down."

"Oh, they know where the Vault is. I think I told you, they've known that since the moment they learned of the Ravaiim blood."

War's jaw moved, but whatever protest he'd formed died before passing through his lips. "And you knew they'd make for the Ravaiim homeworld first," he said instead, "because there was no point in facing your defenses and trying to break into the Vault if you got to the blood before they did."

"Very good, brother. I knew you'd get there. Of course, that was before they—or I—had thought about tearing apart Earth Reaver to get at the blood within. But I suppose one cannot expect *everything* to go as anticipated."

"So you'll finally be showing me where you've hidden your precious Vault?"

"Not quite yet. It'll have to be quick, since we've no idea when Hadrimon and Belisatra might move, but if we're going to end this for good and all, we have a few stops that we must make first."

THE ASHES SEEMED TO GO ON FOREVER.

A light carpeting of fine particles over a thicker, more cal-cified sludge; a constant swirling in the air, biting at eyes and nose and throat, tossed and teased by perpetual winds; and always, at the edge of hearing, the tolling of a forgotten bell. A dead world; a murdered world.

All just as Death remembered it, as he'd left it only . . . Oblivion and Abyss, had it been so recently? Even for an immortal, it felt a lot longer.

"Something . . ." War raised a hand, partially shielding his face, and tried to peer through the drifts of ash. "There's something naggingly familiar about this realm."

"You've been here before," Death confirmed. "It didn't look quite like this then, though we left it in an ugly enough state."

"We?"

"Well, the Nephilim." The Horsemen had turned aside from the others by that point, but as they spent much of their time trying to curtail the race's rampage, they'd traveled to most of the worlds the Nephilim attacked. "This was the last world they ravaged before . . ."

"Before Eden," War finished for him.

"Yes."

They trudged through the drifts of ash. Despair seemed able to stride atop most of it, but Ruin grew ever more irritated as the powdery stuff sucked at his hooves. Once again, had any observers been present—and had they been able to spot such a minor detail through the impeding soot—they might have noticed the conspicuous absence of a certain crow. Wherever the Horsemen had gone between the domain of the Charred Council and here, Dust had apparently not accompanied them all the way.

"This is not a good plan," War groused.

"So you've said. A lot."

"Then why do you insist on following it?"

"Because, brother, you have yet to offer up a better one." Then, at the continued chorus of somewhat less articulate grumbles, "Some faith, War. Everyone knows his part."

"If your timing is off by so much as—"

"Then our timing had best not be off."

More grumbling, which lasted until they drew near enough their destination to see that the low structure was formed of old bone. Dried blood mortared the gaps solid, and most of those bones appeared to have been sculpted and warped, rather than carved, into shape.

It could be the work of only one particular architect.

"This is your home!" It sounded almost accusatory.

"Be it ever so humble," Death said.

War gawped a moment, and laughed softly. "Only you would lay your bed beside something like the door of the Abomination Vault, brother."

"What better way to keep an eye on it?"

"And when you told me your home hadn't drifted off to the Abyss because it was anchored . . ."

"Precisely. The Vault again. Worked out for everyone."

"Until a crazed angel and his construct army invade your bedchamber in search of the damn thing."

"As I've said before, War, you can't have everything. Enough of this. Step inside, out of the soot, and make yourself comfortable. Unless my timing is, indeed, off, we shouldn't have terribly long to wait."

CHAPTER TWENTY-EIGHT

I NDEED, THEY DID NOT WAIT LONG AT ALL.

Their first warning was a dreadful keening, louder than the phantasmal bell, sharper than the constant winds. Death shot to his feet from the bare floor of the equally bare chamber. He slid Mortis over his left hand and made for the door, Harvester flying to his side. War followed only two steps behind, cloak billowing.

They stepped out into the swirling ash and, at Death's lead, scrambled to the top of the squat edifice. "We can see farther from up here," he explained as he climbed. "Albeit not much."

Both Ruin and Despair watched them ascend, snorting and pawing at the soot, ears tilted toward the ongoing shrieks.

"What *is* that sound?" War demanded, kneeling on the roof and squinting into the distance. "That's no construct I've ever heard."

"No. Those would be the phantoms bound to the perimeter. Enjoy the show while you can. We'll have to go on stage ourselves soon enough."

Death leaned back, bracing himself on Harvester, and dropped his head in concentration. The wind whistled around him, adding a second mask of stringy hair atop the one that normally concealed his features. He'd done this before, and easily enough—but never across such thick boundaries, separated by so many realms.

The bone surface below him rippled, faded to a roughly contoured black. Brilliant as a lightning strike, and equally as fleeting, he saw the craggy visage of the Crowfather, expression sagging in one of his traditional scowls.

"Honestly, the two of you need to learn to damn well do this yourselves. I've got better things to occupy my time than play courier whenever you get lonesome . . ."

And he was gone. A sinuous conduit of pure thought stretched through the non-space his image had occupied, linking two distant minds, one great, one feral.

As War leaned over the roof's edge, studying the first of the distant shapes emerging from the ashen flurries, Death's attentions were worlds away, delivering the simplest, yet the most urgent, of signals.

THE CHAMBER'S WALLS WERE CONSTRUCTED OF OLD, pockmarked bricks; less stone, to all appearances, than tightly compressed filth. Mold flourished between them, having not only covered but utterly consumed whatever mortar might once have been there. A sticky film of condensation coated it all, as if the room itself were sweating.

Given the sweltering, feverish warmth of Hell—the hot breath of a leprous loved one sifting across one's skin, one's soul—perhaps it was.

For its single inhabitant, however, the chamber held no discomfort. It wore only portions of its chipped and corroded armor—from the waist down, gauntlets, helm. The remainder lay in a heap in the corner, awaiting the demon's attention. The skin of its exposed torso was softly chitinous, like the under-side of a roach, and riddled with cracks like old parchment. Those fissures glowed a grotesque blue, occasionally emitting tiny fingers of what might or might not have been flames.

Before the Knight of Perdition, atop a "table" that was really little more than a flat-topped mound of hardened mucus, lay his sword. The hideous blade—jagged, serrated, rust-pitted, and barbed—was so thickly encrusted with dried blood as to render it almost a blunt instrument. With careful, even loving attention, the Knight was slowly sanding and polishing the blade with what appeared to be someone's severed tongue.

His meticulous and rather wet-sounding ministrations ceased abruptly, however, as one of the chamber's doors crashed open. Made of the same dried demonic excretions as the table, it actually chipped flakes from the brick as it struck the adjoining wall. Through the doorway, winding so as to practically tie itself in knots, came the four-armed serpentine form of a shadowcaster.

"The mistress!" it hissed. Its voice was the crinkle of discarded snakeskin, flowing around a forked and flickering tongue. "I must be permitted to address the mistress! At once!"

Slowly, the Knight of Perdition lay the tongue upon the table and hefted its sword in gauntleted fingers. Its own words, emerging from within the helm, were hollow echoes. "Mistress Raciel has not called. We do not suffer her to be disturbed by the likes of *you*."

"Even," the lesser demon cooed, "when *the likes of me* have knowledge she craves? You underestimate our magics, sir knight. *We have located the Abomination Vault!* Even now, the forces of the mad one move to claim its wonders!"

"Wait here." The half-armored rider strode from the chamber at a stiff-legged pace suggesting he very much wanted to run.

The supposedly blind shadowcaster craned its neck so that it could peer down at its own chest. Something seemed to be making the faintest rustling sound within its flesh.

"I do hope," said the demon that was not *truly* a demon, "that you really were giving me Death's signal. If you were just going on a sudden rant regarding the quality of the local carrion or whatnot, this is *not* going to turn out well."

Squawk! answered Dust.

THE FIRST LINE of Belisatra's myrmidons came spinning through the ash, slowed only slightly by the particulate, and died as rapidly as they appeared. Inky shadow spread over them, poured from some unseen well, and the life, artificial as it may have been, simply fled their bodies. Even inertia seemed sucked from them, for they ceased spinning instantly and toppled, some tripping the next rank following behind.

Cyclones of bone, not unlike the storms Death had earlier unleashed upon the demonic hordes, rose from the ash, chewing through metal that might just as well have been children's candy. Forks of black lightning seared the drifting soot, blasting holes through constructs and craters into the ground—and from those craters leapt slavering ghouls to fall upon the enemy with ripping fang and rending claw.

"I'm impressed," War admitted, admiration for the unfolding mayhem rolling off him in an almost visible aura.

"I should hope so," Death said. "You'd never believe how difficult and time consuming it was setting those wards in the first place. I'll be fortunate if I can even muster the patience to re-create them after all this."

"If you survive this at all."

"And here everyone says *I'm* the gloomy one."

On and on, Death's necromantic defenses raged; and on

and on, Belisatra's army of constructs advanced, a rising tide of brass and rock. The Horseman, for all his power, never had the slightest doubt which would fail first. His home had never been intended to stand up to a genuine siege.

The black lightning, the swirling bones, the inky pockets all slowed. Fewer constructs triggered the wards, and those wards they *did* trigger killed fewer constructs. And still the soldiers came, as if the ash itself gave birth to them.

"I wonder," Death mused idly, "where they found *that much* brass?"

The last of the pre-prepared necromancies flickered and died. On that cue, the Horsemen dropped from the roof to land in the waiting saddles. The mounts charged, powerful enough that the churning ash posed only a minimal impediment. Before they knew what had happened, the automatons were falling to the twin edges of Harvester and Chaoseater.

War plowed through the center of the army, letting blades careen harmlessly from his armor. He swung Chaoseater in broad strokes, rending myrmidons half a dozen or more at a time. Ruin reared, hooves crushing anything foolish enough to stand too close.

Death and Despair swept around the edges of the mass, occasionally darting in and out to prove that even those farther from the borders were not safe. Against them he wielded scythes, knives, hammers, spears—all of them Harvester, all of them lethal. Few of the myrmidons came anywhere near to hitting him, and those who got close found their most precise strikes parried. Only when he had no other choice did Death rely on Mortis to stop an incoming stroke; he could not be certain how much power, how much life, the half-dead Abomination might retain, and he wasn't about to waste its remaining utility on these creatures.

Not when the *true* enemies had yet to appear.

Even now, not quite fully recovered from their recent travails, the Horsemen had nothing to fear from the whirling myrmidons. Had it been only a question of attrition, with no concern for time, they could eventually have whittled down even so large an army as this.

Unfortunately, slaying the two Riders was not the foes' only course to victory.

The constructs began to disperse, streaming around the edges of the conflict and making for Death's abode. And here, out in the open, even the vaunted Horsemen could do nothing to restrain the tide.

"Fall back to the door!"

War wheeled at his brother's call and sent Ruin plunging back the way they'd come. Death and Despair appeared beside them, and the horses swiftly outpaced the myrmidons.

"You'll do us no good standing with us," Death told the steeds as he and War dismounted. "Despair!" He pointed off toward the left. "Harry the flank."

War matched the gesture, indicating right, and barked a similar command at Ruin. A pair of snorts, one brutish and one spectral, expressed the horses' dissatisfaction with the arrangement, but both obeyed. Death and War stood shoulder-to-shoulder, blocking the only door to the small structure.

And to the Abomination Vault.

Again Chaoseater and Harvester flew, again the constructs fell. On rare occasion, when the sheer press of numbers threatened to force the Horsemen through the doorway, Death unleashed a storm of bones or War called a copse of otherworldly blades from the ash, driving back all who approached. Heaps of shredded metal expanded into hedges, hedges into walls, until the myrmidons could hardly even approach without first digging through multiple layers of their own dead.

The first shot rang through the sky, piercing the chaos of

battle. Death cried out to his brother—his precise words lost in the tumult—and dived forward, Mortis raised high.

The impact was enough to stagger him, even through the ancient shield. Mortis howled, lashing out to obliterate one of the nearby constructs, but Death scarcely noticed.

Hadrimon had arrived, and Black Mercy with him.

The Grand Abomination spat, over and over, raining a hailstorm of teeth across the doorway. Several constructs fell to misaimed shots, but clearly the maddened angel couldn't have cared less. Perhaps he wasn't even aware. Other shots pinged off the solid bone of Death's abode, but they left deep gouges and spreading pockets of dry rot behind.

The angel was slowly getting his eye in, even through the ashen clouds, and Mortis was far too small a barrier to rely on. Still reluctant, for all he'd known the moment would come, the elder Horseman ordered the younger deeper into the structure.

"Still not comfortable with this," War huffed between heavy breaths. "Not a lot of room to maneuver in there."

"For them, either. Besides, I told you, I can get us out if I need to."

Within the walls, the building opened up into a single broad room, just as austere as it appeared from without. The ghouls that Death had left here so long ago had finished their work, but it amounted to precious little. On one wall hung a variety of scythes—weaker and less versatile predecessors to Harvester, built while Death was still mastering his talents. Opposite the door, a slab of bone—a primitive cot, essentially— jutted into the room.

And that was it. Death was clearly a homeowner of few needs. If the portal to the Abomination Vault was indeed here, it certainly wasn't making itself obvious.

"We ought to have a few moments," War said, taking a quick peek past the doorjamb and then jerking back as Black Mercy pumped several teeth through the opening. "Just dig-

ging through the sprawl of shredded metal we left behind
should take them at least—"

A rapid fusillade of muffled *thump*s, like a full battery of
Redemption cannons firing at once, reverberated through the
walls. The entire structure shook as a series of concussive blasts
ripped across the battlefield outside, shock waves hurling earth
and dead constructs this way and that, white-hot flame melt-
ing into slag anything those shock waves missed.

"Unless," the Horseman finished lamely, "Belisatra shows
up with some new toy."

"That would be my theory, yes," Death told him.

Dozens of myrmidons began spinning along the paths,
newly opened through the field of shrapnel, and then through
the door. The first few died instantly, but every time either of
the brothers spent too long standing in the doorway, Hadrimon took potshots at them from beyond. Slowly but surely, the
chamber began to fill with stone, brass, and blades.

"Scarcely matters how many we kill, brother," War shouted
over the chime and screech of rending metal, Chaoseater
whirling in vicious arcs. "If they fill the room with metal, we
won't be able to move. Hadrimon can pick us off at leisure."

Death, who had already come to much the same conclusion, was crouched behind a circular barrier made of Harvester,
spinning double-bladed in one fist. His other hand he held
toward the nearest wall, slowly curling his fingers into a twisted
claw.

The long bones followed suit, flexing apart like curtains.
Death ducked his head and darted through.

Even from here, toward the rear of the structure, he could
see a winding line, a veritable river of constructs moving toward
the door at the front. Far behind them, half hidden in the soot,
stood a stout armored figure that could only have been Belisatra.

The Maker might have been deprived of Earth Reaver, but

she'd clearly constructed something else to keep her occupied. Both hands were fixed on some sort of gargantuan cannon, consisting of no fewer than half a dozen barrels, any one of which was more than half the thickness of a Redemption cannon. A pair of mechanical legs supported the front end, providing an aiming bipod when she was still, walking along before her as she moved.

Not a Grand Abomination, no, not even close—but a brutal weapon of war for all that.

Of Hadrimon—and Black Mercy—Death saw no sign at all.

"War?" he called back.

"The damn angel's in here!" came the shouted reply. "He's out of reach, but if I can just get through the front ranks—"

"No!" If that idiot even *looked* like he might prove a threat, Hadrimon would kill him; and this time, Death doubted he'd have either the power or the opportunity to bring him back. "Follow the plan, damn you!"

War squeezed through the newly opened gap, a grumbling mass of crimson and steel. Behind, they could already hear the sounds of blades against bone. Hadrimon, no doubt, directing the constructs to dig through to the hidden portal. A few of the myrmidons also pushed through the hole in the wall, but War dispatched them swiftly enough.

So far, Belisatra and the bulk of the army still outside hadn't noticed the two figures emerging around the back— thanks, in part, to Ruin and Despair, who were still keeping their attention along the flanks—but it could only be a matter of time.

"How long are you prepared to leave Hadrimon in your home?" War demanded.

"I'm . . . not sure," Death admitted. "It should take awhile to penetrate the last layer of wards on the portal to the Vault, but I don't know *how* long. If we have to go back in there, we'll be easy targets, but—"

Something squawked in the sky above. Plunging from the clouds in a steep arc, Dust fluttered past the Horsemen just long enough to be certain they'd seen him, and then was off once more into the drifting ash.

"Oh, good," Death said, relief obvious in his voice. "The demons are here."

CHAPTER TWENTY-NINE

HADRIMON STRODE THROUGH THE HORSEMAN'S PA-
thetic little domicile, surrounded on all sides by
Belisatra's metal soldiers. Already they'd smashed
apart the far wall as he'd directed, revealing the portal he'd
worked so hard to claim.

A shame, really, that Death hadn't chosen to remain and
defend the Vault to—well, to the death. Hadrimon, even
through the haze of generalized wrath and loathing that now
formed the entirety of his waking world, held a special fury for
the last surviving Firstborn Nephilim. Death had robbed him
of the Ravaiim blood. Although he and Belisatra had swiftly
found a way around that loss, it had cost him one of the greatest of the Abominations; and would, as his campaign progressed, cost him more. For that, he would see Death
perish—in agony, if at all possible.

But not yet. Hadrimon leaned in to examine the prize his
minions had uncovered.

He knew he could open the portal. He had a strong mastery of such magics, and where his rituals proved lacking, the
Grand Abominations themselves could guide him. The problem would be *reaching* the portal itself, for he knew that Death
would never have left it accessible.

Indeed, what lay revealed amid the crumbling bone was some sort of shell. It glinted, reflecting peculiar colors at peculiar angles that seemed only tangentially related to the surrounding light. Combine sheets of flame with layers of shadow, compress them into solid crystal, and the result might be something resembling what the angel saw before him now.

"The direct approach," he growled, either to himself or to the uncaring constructs around him, "would seem the best." From only a few paces away, he aimed Black Mercy at the crystalline shell and fired.

This was not, perhaps, the use for which the horrid pistol had been intended. Nevertheless, a slender chip broke from the crystal; a spindly crack ran from the point of impact to the many-faceted edge.

Already, through that single tiny fault, he could feel the unearthly presence beyond—the vast emptiness and semireality of the Vault itself, and the roiling hatreds of the Grand Abominations. They'd teased and caressed his soul from the very beginning, but never, never had they felt so clear. He burned in a furnace of the spirit, and though he writhed internally, he knew it was only purging him of weakness and doubt.

It would take time to punch through that shell, even with Black Mercy, but time he now had. Even if Death and War had not fled far, with his constructs to all sides and Black Mercy to hand, Hadrimon knew he could easily repel them—probably even kill them—should they again interfere. He raised the triple-barreled weapon of meat and metal, fired again, and again, and again . . .

"*Hadrimon!*" It was Belisatra's voice, transmitted through several of the nearby myrmidons at once. "*You'd better get out here.*"

"Not *now*, damn you! Whatever it is, deal with it!"

"*You need to get out here* now*!*"

Spitting vile curses in languages both living and dead,

Hadrimon yanked Affliction from its scabbard and passed it to the closest construct. "Keep hacking at that!" he ordered as he turned away. No, Affliction wasn't one of the Grand Abominations, but maybe it was strong enough to do *some* of the job while he was solving whatever problem his partner was too incompetent to handle.

Wings pressed tight to his body, struggling to keep from shooting everything in his way, the angel pushed through the throng of myrmidons to the front door, stepped out into the gray light of the ash-smeared sun . . .

And froze, gawping.

Constructs swept across the plains, blades slashing and stabbing. Belisatra stood atop a small dune, lobbing shell after shell from her fearsome cannon. But it was not the Horsemen with whom they battled!

A horde of demons, nearly equal in size to the one they'd faced on the Ravaiim homeworld, ravaged his forces from all sides, struggling to reach the edifice of bone. Knights of Perdition on their hellish steeds rode through and over the myrmidons; shadowcasters hurled fire that melted any construct it touched; flaming stone claws and Phantom Guards' axes rent metal into scrap.

For the first time, Belisatra's forces were growing thin. Constructs fell, and no more appeared to take their place. The Maker's army had finally, *finally* reached its limit.

No matter. They'd done their job.

Hadrimon took aim from the shelter of the doorway and began to fire. Black Mercy bellowed, monsters fell. So long as the myrmidons held out long enough to keep the demons from swarming him, this was just another inconvenience, no threat at all.

The barrels drifted as he took in the field, seeking his targets—and there was the most perfect of all! A single demon standing near the rear, different from all the others, shouting commands to its grotesque soldiers. Take out the leader, perhaps the rest would . . .

It was a thing of nightmare, a demon in the truest sense. More than twice his own size and blue as suffocation, it was all obscene muscle and ravaging talons, sweeping tail and wings so twisted and broken they hung upside down from its back. Scattered across those wings like mange were rough patches of feathers, made all the more horrid by their pristine, ivory gleam. Curved horns swept from the back of its head to frame a waxy face that might once have been beautiful.

The demon turned that pallid visage his way, perhaps sensing his scrutiny—and Hadrimon dropped to his knees, howling like a child.

He knew her. No matter how her time in Hell, her resentment, her hatred had twisted her into something foul and profane, he knew her. He always would.

"Raciel . . . Oh, Creator . . ."

Raciel shot skyward, then landed in an eruption of ash before the kneeling angel. Bestial claws and twisted wings lashed out, shredding the nearby myrmidons. Though the battle raged on around them, for a moment they occupied their own bubble of relative calm.

"You recognize me. I'm truly touched." Her voice was, by far, the most awful thing about her—for it, alone of all her traits, remained as sweet, as pure, as when she'd been a lovestruck angel of Heaven.

"How could I not? However long we're apart, whatever they've done to you, I—"

"*They?*" A gnarled, chitinous hand snapped shut around the angel's neck; piercing talons of bone scissored open and shut before his face. "*They*, Hadrimon? *They* didn't do this to me alone, my *love*." The venom oozing from that last word could have stricken entire realms. "*They* aren't why I've suffered so . . ."

Hadrimon's entire body quaked. Tears coursed unashamedly down his cheeks, etching abstract designs through the ashen coat. "I did this for you, to save you, to punish all who—" He swallowed hard. "All *others* who did this to you."

"Oh, my angel." Raciel's grip loosened, cupping his chin rather than his throat, gently guiding him to his feet. "You still can. We can punish them together, Hadrimon. Heaven and Hell will burn before us. All I require . . ."

The demon's other hand unfolded, presenting an empty palm.

". . . is the Vault. Surely you can do that, Hadrimon? You can do that for me?"

"I . . ." Creation wavered before his eyes, the urges of the Grand Abominations grappling with desires long buried within his psyche. "I . . ."

Slowly, the fingers clutching Black Mercy began to slacken, the hand to rise toward Raciel's own.

CURSING UNDER HIS BREATH, struggling to maintain control over his boiling blood and surging anger, War redoubled his efforts. Chaoseater was a machine, a force of nature, never stopping, never slowing; Ruin, with whom he'd reunited, was a juggernaut of crushing hooves. Brass and flesh, bones and cogs, blood and oil all marked the path of devastation they'd carved through the ongoing melee. And still War had not yet reached the angel and the demon who loomed before his brother's threshold.

For an instant it had almost seemed that Raciel would do part of the job for them. But no, she had stayed her hand; Hadrimon lived.

Not that the idea of one of the Lost with Black Mercy was any more appealing than its current wielder.

Cursing Heaven, cursing Hell, cursing Death's plan, cursing Death himself for darting off on his own, the youngest Horsemen spurred his mount through demon and construct ranks, desperate to reach the true enemy before things fell apart any further . . .

"*KEEP AWAY FROM HER!*"

Belisatra's shout may or may not have been audible over the general bedlam, but the twin cannon blasts that detonated at the demon's feet, hurling the creature headlong across the battlefield and Hadrimon into the bone wall, conveyed the message clearly enough.

That besotted idiot was about to ruin everything!

She sprinted through falling debris, the mechanized legs that supported the sextuple barrels struggling to keep pace. Neither her speed, nor the occasional leap to carry her over craters in the ash, was remotely equal to those exhibited by either of the Horsemen—but given her heavy armor and stocky build, they remained impressive enough.

The Maker slammed to a halt beside the building just as a battered Hadrimon was hauling himself upright. "What the hell are you doing?" she screamed at him. "It's a damn *demon*! No matter what she used to be, or what you *think* she used to be, you can't believe a bloody word she—"

Hadrimon smacked the cannon from Belisatra's hands with an abrupt thrust of a wing; the bulky weapon spun an almost graceful pirouette on one leg before toppling. The Maker's jaw clacked shut almost hard enough to break the bone as Black Mercy's barrels slammed into her chin. She could feel the slick surface of the unblinking eye between those barrels, moist against her skin.

"You've no idea! You cannot *possibly* comprehend what we

had! What she was, what she's been through!" The angel's trigger finger literally quivered. "I can't . . . They're all in my head, I can't . . ."

"Hadrimon, she—"

"Say one more word against her!" A horrid wheeze drifted from the barrels, as though Black Mercy itself were panting with desire. "*One more!*"

Belisatra swallowed past the pain. "Do not think, then. Do not doubt, or worry, or wonder. Seize the Vault, Hadrimon, as you always meant to. Master the Grand Abominations, and you can make it all stop while you figure everything out. You can be in control."

"Yes . . ." Belisatra almost stumbled as the pressure of Black Mercy vanished from her jaw. "The Vault . . . Need to get into the Vault . . . Tell Raciel I'll be . . ." Hadrimon turned and stumbled back through Death's door. He mumbled and staggered, but the hand that held Black Mercy was now as straight and steady as the finest anvil.

He was losing it; she'd known it was happening, had even felt a bit of it herself when wielding Earth Reaver, but she'd had no idea how bad it was getting. It might be just about time to abandon the mad angel and claim the Abominations for her own.

After he brought down the barriers, of course.

Belisatra lifted the massive cannon from the ash and steadied it, fully prepared to obliterate anyone who so much as glanced her way.

Or so she thought, until she heard the fearsome grunting of an enraged warhorse, and saw the mounted, crimson-cloaked figure looming from the haze . . .

RACIEL HEAVED HERSELF FROM THE DIRT, shrieking her fury for the world to hear. Smoke poured from her chest, her left arm and wing; her left eye was gummed shut with humors that only vaguely resembled blood.

But already, the pain was starting to fade. It took more, *far* more, than the Maker's little toy to kill a Lost Angel. The bitch had unleashed hell—literally—and would suffer for it. And then Hadrimon; oh, she had plans for Hadrimon, entertainments that would spawn legends even amid the torments of the Pit . . .

Beyond the great demon, one of her soldiers rose from behind a dune of ash, where it had waited out much of the battle. A shadowcaster—the same, in fact, that had alerted one of Raciel's Knights of Perdition, and then Raciel herself, to the Abomination Vault's location—wound through the murky air, closing in on its mistress.

If she noted its presence at all, she ignored it. Why should she not? It was, after all, one of hers.

Even as the corrupted angel tensed, prepared to take to the sky once more, the shadowcaster lifted an arm—and a blade of gleaming silver that seemed to have appeared from nowhere at all. The demon began to ripple and flow, an illusory guise shifting from one false form to another, as the burning sword fell . . .

HADRIMON STOOD TALL in the center of Death's home, firing Black Mercy at the crystalline shell, again and again. The barrier had worn thin; the emanations from within flared, burning his eyes, his mind, his soul, until nothing else remained. If someone could torture the gibbering voices in a madman's head, the resultant agony and fury and hate might have felt much the same.

So intense was his focus, his determination, his lunacy, that it was several moments before a rational thought was able to worm its way through the carapace encasing his awareness.

Where are the myrmidons I left here?

Tearing himself from the agonizing, irresistible call of the Grand Abominations—so close, now, *so close!*—he glanced swiftly around the chamber.

Chunks of rock, slivers of brass, even the broken shards of Affliction. He'd stepped right over them in his delirium and never noticed. But then what—?

With a sudden scream, Hadrimon hurled himself up and into the low ceiling, wildly firing Black Mercy at nothing and everything, filling the chamber with projectiles. Harvester flashed through the space he'd just vacated, close enough to sever several feathers from the angel's wing.

DEATH FELL BACK WITH A GRUNT, Mortis barely catching three separate teeth that would otherwise have shredded flesh and bone. An icy shock ran through his arm and across his chest, staggering him, as flashes of Black Mercy's power penetrated the shield. Mortis quivered, and he felt the surge of power through the half-dead Abomination, but it appeared to have no effect. Either Black Mercy was somehow shielding Hadrimon from its retaliation, or the thing was finally reaching the end of its lingering power.

The Horseman found himself hunched amid the same pieces of wrecked constructs beneath which he'd been lying in wait. *Should have struck sooner, you fool!* But he'd wanted to be certain the angel was well and truly distracted by his task . . .

He straightened, scrambling for better footing. Harvester was now a pair of scythes, one in each hand, ready to strike or to hurl at need. Hadrimon hovered in the far corner, neck bent against the low ceiling, feet hanging almost to the floor. He had no room to maneuver, no sky in which to climb. Smiling grimly behind his mask, Death let the rightmost scythe fly.

With impossible speed, Black Mercy tracked the spinning

blade, guided by its unblinking eye, and shot Harvester from the air.

The scythe returned to Death's hand, as it was designed, but it wobbled in its flight, damaged—wounded?—by the Grand Abomination.

A second barrel fired; again Death felt the impact even through Mortis, and again Mortis's response was weak at best. Too many more of those, and the shield might well give way entirely.

Hell, too many more of those, and he probably wouldn't have the strength to *use* the shield.

"Feeble and foolish, Horseman!" Hadrimon's voice quavered and rasped like an old man's. "Nothing can stand between us! They—she—will be . . . We will . . ."

Death let Harvester fly once more, both scythes at once. The first, aimed at the erratic angel, rebounded almost instantly, accompanied by Black Mercy's percussive song. But the second . . .

The second had not been directed at Hadrimon at all. It struck, instead, the crystalline barrier to the Abomination Vault.

With an almost musical cascade of cracks, the window between worlds crumbled. In an instant the full force of the Grand Abominations' hatred and pain flowed through the gap, a spiritual poison spreading through the substance of this dead world.

Hadrimon had lived so long with the emotions of those ancient horrors blazing in his mind, he had surely forgotten what life was like without them. Yet always they had come to him in faint wisps, impeded by the barrier of the Vault itself. He was not—*could* not be—prepared for the unrestrained deluge.

It was a risk, but one Death was certain he could manage.

The surge might empower the Abomination itself, but it should overwhelm the angel's own mind long enough to finish this once and for all.

Mouth gaping in a silent scream, Hadrimon slumped to the floor, wings folded as if to shield him, his free hand clutched to his temple. And Death, Harvester once again in the form of a single scythe, staggered forward for the kill.

Augmented by the proximity of its brethren, enraged beyond anything the Nephilim had ever anticipated, Black Mercy itself raised Hadrimon's arm and fired.

Caught utterly by surprise, Death couldn't begin to interpose Mortis. Twisting as swiftly as he'd ever moved, he managed to take the shot on Harvester's haft, but much of the Abomination's life-draining essence surged through the weapon. The Horseman toppled to lie awkwardly atop the metal scraps; alive, conscious, but weak, far too weak.

The angel stood, limbs shuddering and eyes rolling. Death had no way of knowing who was actually in control as Black Mercy's triple barrels rose, gaping open before him like the Abyss itself . . .

"Hadrimon!"

Death breathed—though he'd have denied it to anyone who asked—a sigh of relief at the sound of that dulcet voice. *Took our time, did we?*

Angel and Abomination turned from the Horseman to watch a colossal figure, bloodied and mauled, squeeze in through the gap Death had earlier opened in the back wall. One massive hand hung loose, seemingly broken; the other sought to plug a sucking wound in the demon's gut.

"Raciel!" Hadrimon darted forward several steps, halted, shoulders quivering. His eyes flickered madly from the broken angel to the weapon in his hand that struggled, of its own accord, to rise and fire.

"Hadrimon, help me . . . Please, my love, don't let them . . ." She stumbled and coughed, a wet, tearing sound.

It appeared, to Death, a naked ploy, an obvious manipulation until she might once again regain the upper hand. But Hadrimon, in his madness, was far beyond such suspicions. Weeping openly, he advanced once more, his empty left hand held forth, reaching, reaching . . .

Death felt the surge of roiling malice from across the chamber as Black Mercy rose, dragging the angel's unwitting arm with it. The shot might well have been the death knell of a world, for it truly seemed that *everything* fell silent in its echo.

Raciel teetered, oh so briefly, then dropped in a limp, shriveling heap before the broken wall. Hadrimon was so perfectly frozen, gawping in horror at the *thing* in his fist, that he might as well have been painted on the air itself.

And Death . . . twitched. He could almost, *almost* begin to move . . .

For just an instant, it appeared as though he wouldn't have to. Mouth agape in a silent wail, the angel raised Black Mercy to his own temple and pulled the trigger.

The hammers refused to fall.

Weeping once more, Hadrimon went slack and began to fall—only to halt half slumped, held upright solely by his grip on a Grand Abomination that refused to fall with him. Black Mercy turned, barrels gaping, hammers shivering in an almost carnal anticipation. Limp, looking very much like an empty robe hanging from a single sleeve, his knees nearly dragging on the floor, Hadrimon rotated with it. His face was slack, his eyes glazed; Death could no longer doubt which of the two, angel or Abomination, held sway.

The Horsemen tensed, preparing to channel his all into a roll he knew could never save him . . .

"Stop!"

Even Death, who had seen so much, could scarcely accept what he saw before him now. Above the demonic corpse of Raciel hovered a second figure, drifting on outspread wings—wings of purest, gleaming white. She wore armor of resplendent silver, and her ivory hair framed a face that was the truest embodiment of beauty.

He knew her, for all that he had never met her before, for her voice was the same as the demon's own.

"Hadrimon, stop. Please."

"Raciel . . . ?" A flicker of life returned to Hadrimon's eyes. His feet scrabbled for purchase, taking some of his weight from his twisted shoulder and the horror that held him upright. "Raciel, how . . . ?"

"I forgive you, Hadrimon. I could not go; I had to tell you I forgive you."

The angel gave a sharp cry, his back straightening—and again, the hand clutching Black Mercy began to turn.

"No!" Hadrimon's entire body shook. Sweat and tears mingled in sticky pools across his cheeks. He leaned at a slant against nothing at all as he struggled to turn the traitorous weapon away. His left hand locked about his right wrist, and the sound of grating bone sawed through the chamber.

Still, though he'd slowed the rise of Black Mercy, it edged ever higher with each passing heartbeat, bringing its maws to bear once more on the breast of Hadrimon's beloved.

"Not again . . . Not again! Heaven help me, *no!*"

His struggles turned him halfway about, bringing him face-to-face with the slowly recovering Horseman. Death gazed deep into the angel's eyes, his tainted soul. And what he saw in them, here at the last, was a desperate pleading.

With a low groan of pained exertion, using the haft of Harvester as a crutch, the eldest Horseman rose. And just as

Black Mercy centered on its target, its raging hatred almost an audible scream, he swung.

On Death's blade—weeping tears of gratitude, now, his whole face lit with a radiant smile—the mad angel Hadrimon died.

CHAPTER THIRTY

I FORGIVE YOU,'" DEATH PARROTED, FORCING HIMSELF TO remain upright despite the weakness racking his body, "You really felt that was the best approach?"

"It worked, did it not?" The angelic Raciel shimmered, the illusion falling away to reveal the slumped shoulders and exhausted face of Azrael. "And I think it was a kindness, at the end."

"To one who didn't deserve it. What about *her*?" Death hardly needed to indicate of whom he spoke. "She was supposed to be dead, and you standing in her place, well before she ever got near the Vault. How is it she's lying on my floor?"

"I underestimated how difficult she would be to destroy," the angel admitted. "My surprise attack landed well enough, but she fled before I could finish her. Probably just as well, though. If I'd come through the wall first, I'd have taken the shot instead of her."

"There's that, yes. Hell, for a moment—until the body failed to revert to you after it died—I thought you *had*."

For a moment they gazed down at the limp body beside them, somehow far smaller in death than it had been in life. But only for a moment.

Death moved to the far wall and raised his hands, reestablishing one thin layer of the barrier over the Abomination Vault. A more comprehensive warding would have to wait until he was stronger. *Much* stronger.

"What were *you* thinking?" Azrael demanded then. "Destroying your own ward?"

"I'd planned to take Hadrimon while he was overwhelmed by the emotional flood. I had no idea the Grand Abominations could wield the wielder, as it were. They *couldn't,* way back when. I suppose, after all this time of nursing their hatreds . . ."

He shrugged, then leaned over and hefted Black Mercy from the floor. Instantly he felt the hatreds and agonies fluttering at the edges of his consciousness, but he waved them off as he would a buzzing fly. He knew the Grand Abominations too well.

And he had his own agonies to bear.

Azrael at his side, he wandered to the door and peered outward.

The battle had wound down to a single clump of chaos. Belisatra, her armor rent and smoking, crouched behind a line of myrmidons, her cannon firing constantly. Across the field, War and Ruin sheltered behind a heap of the dead, waiting for any lapse so they might charge in and finish the job.

"Belisatra!" Death called from the doorway, turning sideways so she could clearly see what it was he pointed at her. "Time to quit."

The Maker's face sagged as she recognized Black Mercy. Without a word she dropped the six-barreled cannon. The constructs, presumably at some unheard mental command, froze and toppled to the ash.

"I could have handled her," War groused as he dropped from Ruin and joined his brother.

"I've no doubt. But you must admit this was faster."

"Hmm."

Death crouched and stuck a hand in the ash. Instantly a trio of ghouls sprang from below, gripping Belisatra by the arms and ankles. She was much larger than they, but the strength of the dead was greater than their size. "That should do for now," he said.

"What do you plan for her?" Azrael asked.

"Hadrimon was mad." The Horseman spoke loud enough to be certain the Maker could hear. "She has no such excuse, and still she sought to loose the Grand Abominations on Creation. I imagine the Charred Council will want to introduce her to the Keeper."

"Keeper? The Keeper of what?" Belisatra's eyes went wide, and she began to struggle and pull futilely against the ghouls. "Death! The Keeper of *what?*"

But the two brothers and their angelic ally had already stepped back into Death's seared and battered home.

Dust was waiting for them within, perched atop one of the scythes on the wall.

"Resting after all your hard work?" Death asked. The crow screeched and began ostentatiously preening the feathers under one wing.

"He makes an interesting traveling companion," Azrael said. "Not much of a conversationalist, as you once told me, but he does provide the most intriguing scents."

"You want him? Make me an offer." He could have *sworn* the bird actually stuck its tongue out at him.

"It was not difficult infiltrating Raciel's hordes, once you told me of her involvement," the angel continued. "But I fear I never could learn who engaged her services in all of this. Apparently none of her underlings ever knew."

"I didn't expect they would," Death said with a shrug. "Besides, I've got my own ideas about that . . ."

War sat down loudly on the bone cot, his shadowed face

moody. Death looked his way, then back at Azrael, who also scowled darkly.

"You two do realize that we *won*?"

Azrael shook his head. "I dislike the deception you had me orchestrate. Masquerading as a demon is bad enough, but abetting the murder of an angel in the guise of his lost love? I feel . . . soiled. I understood the urgency when you came to me, but I wish I'd not agreed to this."

The younger Horseman nodded. "It may be a victory, brother, and a necessary one. But there is no honor in it."

"Foolishness." Death leaned Harvester against the wall, then lay Black Mercy and Mortis beside it. "It never matters *how* you win; only that you do."

"I cannot accept that," Azrael told him.

"Nor I," said War.

"No, I thought not," Death said. "And, of course, the reason we have the luxury to debate this is *because* we won. The next time, when your need for an 'honorable victory' results in the destruction of half of Creation, feel free to come back and argue the point *then*."

Azrael's lip twisted angrily. "We have been allies in this, Horseman. Fought side by side, and it was well that we did; we've ended a threat to the Charred Council and Heaven both. For that, you have my gratitude.

"But I strongly recommend that you wait a good, long while before ever again coming to the White City in search of aid."

The two brothers watched him step through the doorway and soar upward to disappear in the ashen flurries.

"Touchy," Death said.

"What do you plan to do with the Abominations?" War asked him.

"For now, I'll return Black Mercy to the Vault and then

restore the full wards. Eventually—once the Council's temper has cooled and they're not watching me so closely—I think I'll see them all pass through the Keeper's portal. Even without the Ravaiim blood, I think Creation would be better off."

"Probably so." A pause, then, "Even Mortis?"

"Well . . . Mortis is all but dead. It poses no threat. Perhaps I'll keep it around, just in case." Death turned, eyeing the crystalline barrier warily. "Give me a hand with this, War, would you? We have a prisoner to deliver and a rather lengthy report to make to the Charred Council, and I want this place secure before we leave."

Grudgingly, each aching more than he'd ever confess to the other, the two Horsemen studied the only window to the Abomination Vault.

"And I *do* expect your help with all this," Death added, waving at the wreckage strewn across the chamber.

"Hah! Heaven, Hell, and the Grand Abominations are one thing, brother. Cleaning up? You're on your own."

"Ingrate."

". . . AN INTERESTING PROPOSAL YOU BRING US, **Panoptos.**" The rightmost of the Council's effigies flickered in the hellish glow, the dancing shadows painting a change of expression across the face that the stone itself could not properly manage. **"But we question the necessity. We have the Horsemen under control."**

"Of course, my lords, of course." Panoptos flitted to and fro across the platform—not idly, not pacing, but so that he might address each of the three visages with equal attention. "But Death, at least, has proved his capacity for defiance. Should he do so again in your presence, you can punish him as he deserves, and all is well. Suppose, however, he should rise above himself *elsewhere*? While wandering on his own, or worse, on an assignment for you?" Phantom wings flapped silently, invisibly, in the wafting smoke.

"Should you grant my Watchers some power of their own over the Riders, as I've suggested, you'd need never worry about such things. We can ensure your servants' obedience at all times, in *all* worlds."

A low rumble, perhaps the contemplative grunt of tectonic plates, reverberated from all three idols at once, carrying with it a peculiar burst of intertwined smoke and flame. Then, **"You make a compelling argument, Panoptos. Go for now. We shall consider it."**

A quick bow—less a bob of the head than a forward rotation on the axis of his wings—and the creature was gone, soaring down beside the stairs and swooping over the broken, empty earth.

No . . . Not *quite* empty, at that.

"Well, well, well. Look who's come calling! We were *just* talking about you."

Death halted his march across the blackened, lava-spotted plains of the Charred Council's realm. "I'm flattered. Hello, Panoptos."

"Off to report to your masters then, Death?"

"Something like that."

"Wonderful! I fear I cannot be there to hear it firsthand, but I'm certain they'll pass along the gist. And if not, I'll get it from the other Watchers. Can't serve as their favored agent without full knowledge, can I?"

"No, I'm sure you can't."

The Horseman began to walk in one direction, the winged creature to flutter in the other. But again, Death halted.

"Panoptos?"

"Yes? What?"

"In all this, we never did discover precisely who sent the demon mercenaries after the Grand Abominations. Obviously, we tipped them off ourselves, there at the end, to ensure they'd be there at the same time as Hadrimon, but who involved them in the first place?"

"A fair question." Panoptos's shrug made use of his arms and wings both. "Plenty of factions would have wanted such weapons. Perhaps we'll never know who it was."

"Perhaps not." Death idly tapped a finger on the chin of his mask. "It's funny, though. You see, whoever it was knew enough to approach Raciel specifically, of all possible allies in Hell. He knew enough to send the demons after us wherever we were—first in Lilith's old laboratory, and then on the Ravaiim homeworld. Why, it's almost as though it was someone with access to every single report we made to the Charred Council along the way."

"Hmm." Eight of the nine glowing eyes narrowed to slits. "Yes, I can see how it might seem that way."

"It got me wondering, who could *possibly* have access to that sort of information? The Council themselves, of course, but the last thing they'd want is for the Abominations to fall into demonic hands. The other Horsemen? Fury is faithful to the Council. So is Strife, for all his posturing.

"But of course, the Council's most 'favored agent' would also have access, would he not? It's possible, I'd think, that such a creature might have grown resentful at his eons of servitude—slavery, really. And maybe, just maybe, such a creature might find a whole brand-new servitor race, based on him, to be the perfect soldiers for his own army. Why, if only he had weapons of sufficient power to arm them, even the Charred Council couldn't keep him under their thumb!"

A soft, undulant hiss emerged from the emptiness of Panoptos's face.

"It's a fascinating notion," he said finally. "But of course, even if such a ludicrous, far-fetched tale were true, you would be stuck with an appalling lack of evidence. You *could* go to the Council with nothing but theories spun of supposition and moonbeams, of course . . ."

"But the Council is not particularly well disposed toward me at the moment," Death finished for him. "I'm aware. And even if that weren't the case, I would never put something of this magnitude before them without proof."

"Well, then." Panoptos began to drift backward on outstretched wings. "It seems we have nothing more to say to each other."

"It seems not." Then, after a brief pause, "Panoptos?"

"*What?*"

"Creation is quite impressionable. *Everyone* leaves a trail of their actions. And everyone, however wise, however powerful, however immortal, makes mistakes.

"All it requires is the patience to wait for them. And you'll find no one, in all Creation, quite so patient as Death."

For the first time, uncertainty shone through the creature's green glow as the Horseman turned on his heel and continued on his way.

ABOUT THE AUTHOR

ARI MARMELL would love to tell you all about the various esoteric jobs he held and the wacky adventures he had on the way to becoming an author, since that's what other authors seem to do in these blurbs. Unfortunately, he doesn't actually have any, as the most exciting thing about his professional life, besides his novel writing, is the work he's done for Dungeons & Dragons and other role-playing games. His published fiction includes both *The Conqueror's Shadow* and *The Warlord's Legacy*, from Del Rey/Spectra, and a variety of novels with other publishers, including *The Goblin Corps, Agents of Artifice* (a Magic: The Gathering novel), and *Thief's Covenant: A Widdershins Adventure.*

Marmell currently lives in an apartment that's almost as cluttered as his subconscious, which he shares (the apartment, not the subconscious, though sometimes it seems like it) with his wife, George, and two cats who really need some form of volume control installed. You can find Marmell online at http://www.mouseferatu.com and http://twitter.com/mouseferatu.

DARKSIDERS II

PRIMA OFFICIAL GAME GUIDE

▸ **EXPLORE EVERYTHING** - DETAILED WALKTHROUGH COVERING DEATH'S JOURNEY THROUGH EVERY DUNGEON AND SIDEQUEST

▸ **SOLUTIONS** - SOLVE EVEN THE MOST DIFFICULT PUZZLES

▸ **FIND YOUR WAY** - LABELED MAPS SHOW THE LOCATION FOR EVERY HIDDEN ITEM AND OBJECTIVE

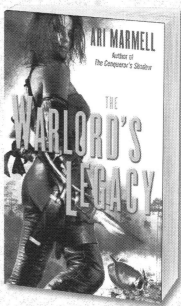